On Beyond Paris

Paris

A Geocaching Adventure Novel

by
Kelly Rysten

CCB Publishing
British Columbia, Canada

On Beyond Paris: A Geocaching Adventure Novel

Library and Archives Canada Cataloguing in Publication
Title: On beyond Paris : a geocaching adventure novel / by Kelly Rysten.
Names: Rysten, Kelly, 1960-, author
Identifiers: Canadiana (print) 20200332694 | Canadiana (ebook) 20200332732 |
ISBN 9781771434355 (softcover) | ISBN 9781771434362 (PDF)
Classification: LCC PS3618.Y78 O5 2020 | DDC 813/.6—dc23

Cover design and back cover artwork by: by Kelly Rysten: www.kellyrysten.com

Front cover artwork credit: Eiffel Tower © WDGPhoto, Hot Air Balloon © mblach |
CanStockPhoto.com

Author photo on back cover by Erica Stephens Photography:
https://www.ericastephensphoto.com

Publisher: CCB Publishing
               British Columbia, Canada
               www.ccbpublishing.com

This book is dedicated to all those geocache hiders and finders out there who lead us to quirky, interesting, and generally fun places to visit, who make us think and hunt and think some more before we finally spot the elusive container and go *aha*!

And to my husband Gary, known in the geocaching logs as TSPI, who drives the geomobile and finds roughly half the geocaches we search for. He also puts in long hours of work editing and advising me during the whole writing and publishing process.

Other books by Kelly Rysten

Kelly is the author of *Geogirl,* an action adventure romance novel that incorporates the hobby of geocaching. College student Gwendolyn Brody agrees to enter a geocaching contest to help her friend Tony win a trip to the Caribbean. Follow their hilarious cross country trip as they accidentally grow ever closer to each other.

Geogirl - Published 2014 – ISBN 978-1-77143-150-7

Kelly Rysten is also the author of the Cassidy Callahan Adventure Novels. Cassidy Callahan is a young woman who grew up on a quarter horse ranch. Given free run of the local hills she developed an eye for tracking, and with the help of Detective Rusty Michaels, she joined the local search and rescue team to track lost hikers. Unfortunately she is also a terrible trouble magnet, and her job brings her into contact with more trouble than the police can keep her out of. One adventure follows another as Cassidy tracks her way from one mishap to the next.

The books are:

Triple Trouble - Published 2009 – ISBN 978-1-926585-41-3

Car Trouble - Published 2010 – ISBN 978-1-926918-03-7

A Cache of Trouble - Published 2011 – ISBN 978-1-926918-87-7

A Double Dose of Trouble - Published 2012 – ISBN 978-1-77143-025-8

A Shot of Trouble - Published 2013 – ISBN 978-1-77143-107-1

Looking for Trouble - Published 2015 – ISBN 978-1-77143-249-8

Trouble in Hollywood - Published 2016 – ISBN 978-1-77143-294-8

A Little Trouble - Published 2017 – ISBN 978-1-77143-337-2

Trouble Grande - Published 2018 – ISBN 978-1-77143-366-2

Trouble's Last Call - Published 2020 – ISBN 978-1-77143-421-8

Chapter 1

I was a disadvantaged youth. Now, when a person says that, you automatically picture a waif on the streets, from a poor family, doing poorly in school, with very little chance at what society calls success. I am not, was not, that person. I think of myself as a silver spoon rebel. My father founded a successful company. My mother plays golf and bridge at the country club, volunteers her time to worthy causes, and drives a Mercedes. My childhood home is a two story in Hollywood Hills. I went to private school. My education was paid for, no matter what field I chose. So what did I do? I climbed Mount Everest. Then I spent two years on the streets seeing what the other side of the tracks looked like. I was the only "homeless person" I met who could walk into a car dealership and pay cash on the spot. I also learned that money was not the solution to the poverty that faces this country. But I didn't know what was. I could hand out hundred dollar bills to every homeless person I met, and most would have been grateful, but they would have fed themselves for a few days and brought out the sign again. So, no, I did not hand out hundred dollar bills. I offered, instead, friendship.

Homeless folks get around. They get kicked out of one part of town and so they pick up their backpack and bedroll and move on. And I happened to meet one of those men. His name was Darby. He had been a middle class worker until hard times hit and he got laid off. His job disappeared and his rent money disappeared, so eventually he disappeared. Into the land of the lost. Darby taught me about a hobby. He had a hard time maintaining it, since it required a GPS and GPS receivers require batteries. But he had some advantages, too, since he was on the streets anyway. Homeless people can basically do whatever they want and people try not to look at them. He found the hobby of geocaching to be an activity that put a little brightness into his day. If he was able to find a geocache before I met up with him he was always smiling and he'd talk to me in gibberish like, "I got an FTF on a LPC on Colorado Boulevard. I hate those LPCs but heck a smiley's a smiley."

And I would tell him that was nice, now speak English.

"Aw, man, you gotta try it sometime! You could even trade something. I can't. Can't log the find online either. No computer. But you could."

"I could what?" I asked.

"Find a geocache and log it online!"

"Why would I want to do that?"

"I'll show you," he said. He brought out the oldest GPS receiver I have ever seen. It was a simple little gadget. All it really did was give you an arrow. You followed the arrow until it said you had arrived. We followed the arrow down one block and then we turned and walked two more blocks. "Three hundred feet," he reported.

"How do you know?"

"There's a little number right here," he said.

As we got closer the number shrunk and the arrow turned. I was to learn later that his GPS was the type parents bought for their kids. It was the bottom of the barrel on GPS technology, but Darby valued that receiver as if his future depended on it.

"It's right around here somewhere," he stated.

"What is?"

"The geocache! Now look around. Look for anything odd or out of place."

"Darby, this is a street. A thousand cars will go by in the next ten minutes. I see a blank sidewalk, a telephone pole, a fire hydrant and a chain link fence. *There is nothing here.*"

"Yes there is!" he insisted. "It's here somewhere. Probably a nano."

"A nano."

"Yeah, itty bitty."

"How itty bitty?"

"Like... this big," he said as he held up his little finger. His thumb was positioned to indicate the geocache was as large as the tip of his finger. I didn't understand. Why would he be so intent on finding something as small as the tip of his finger on a blank section of sidewalk on an insanely busy section of road? But... he had the advantage of being invisible, or rather ignored, and the drivers sped by trying not to look at us so I began searching. I didn't even know what I was looking for. Something small, to be sure.

"No, no, no," he said when he saw my method of searching. "You got it all wrong. You got to look everywhere."

"I am."

"No, I mean *everywhere*! Look where... an ant would look."

"I can't do that. An ant could look between two blades of grass. It could fit between two wires of the chain link fence."

"Now you got the right idea," he said.

This had me even more puzzled. He looked in the oddest places: in the cable ties of the telephone pole, behind the reflective bands around the telephone pole, under the fire hydrant. When he stopped looking I was ready to move on.

"Give up?" I asked.

"Nope!" he said. "I'm just waiting for you to give up."

"Did you find it?"

"Sure did!"

"Okay, show me," I said, unconvinced.

"See, when you look for these things you have to think *why*. And you have to think *where* would I hide a cache. Now, this one here is a *why*. Why would the city put a reflector on a telephone pole and make it face the sidewalk?"

"I don't know. Why?"

"They didn't!"

"And I care about this… why?"

"Look," he said as if he was sharing a special secret. "I'm not supposed to show you, but I think I can trust you not to come back and take it."

"Uh, yeah, why would I do that?"

"You wouldn't. But… see?" he said as he snapped the reflector off the telephone pole. Behind the reflector was a plate and between the plate and the reflector was a single piece of paper. "Wallah!" he declared victoriously. He unfolded the paper and there was a list. Each name had a date by it. Some of the names were written by hand, some were made with an ink stamp and still others had printed their name on a sticker and stuck it on the paper. I thought about the layers of society that the paper represented. Darby was low man on the totem pole. He signed the paper *Not the Hat* and dated his entry.

"Millions of people pass by this spot and never know that there is a secret log there," Darby said. "But I know. Now. And there are thousands of these scattered all over the city just waiting for me to find them."

I was skeptical. I could see what he was trying to show me, but at the time I felt too self-conscious to allow people to stare at me while I searched for something that they would have no understanding of. So began, and ended, my geocaching hobby. I didn't see the point of it.

Chapter 2

Weeks went by. I went to dinner with my mother. She looked at me disapprovingly, but I didn't care. She was the one who chose a restaurant with crystal wine glasses and patrons in suits. I showed up looking better than usual in jeans, slip on boat shoes, and a collared shirt.

"What have you been up to?" she asked.

"Nothing."

"How can you do nothing? It would drive me crazy!"

Actually it did drive me crazy. But I didn't like the stiffness that comes with society. I thought Darby had a better life than I did. I had an apartment. I had a car. He had... freedom. Freedom to walk anywhere he pleased. I thought I should be better off, having the freedom to walk anywhere I pleased and enough money to walk as far as I chose without going hungry.

As I ate dinner with my mother I felt guilty eating filet mignon while Darby ate a ninety-nine cent sandwich that was lowering his life expectancy with each bite.

"What do you think I should be when I grow up?" I asked my mom.

"Earl, you've been grown up for a long time."

"Maybe. In years. I was thinking of doing some traveling. Where do you think I should go?"

"Paris," she said immediately. "Everybody should see Paris."

"I saw Paris when I was five," I reminded her.

"You need to see it as an adult. A five year old child cannot appreciate the fine arts, the wine, the culture."

The finery. That's what appealed to her.

Funny, I asked Darby the same question.

"What do you think I should be when I grow up?" The exact same question. You want to know what he said?

"A lion tamer."

"What!"

"I'm not kiddin' man. What's life without a little risk?"

"I've never even had a pet cat," I said.

He shrugged. "I hear McDonalds is hiring."

"Are you going to apply?"

"No."

"Why?"

"Because to get a job you have to fill in a form. To fill in a form you have to have an address."

"I'm sure there are addresses you can use."

"Yeah, general delivery, anyplace USA."

"You could use my address," I offered and then quickly regretted.

"No, thanks. I'd rather go door to door till I find a house that needs a gardener. If the grass is long I can make enough for the next meal or two. Hey, you want to look for another one of them geocache things?"

"No."

"Aw, why?"

"I don't appreciate the attention of strangers over a simple act of recreation."

"They aren't lookin' at you. They're trying to get where they're going. Admit it, you're paranoid."

"Self-conscious and paranoid are not the same thing."

"What if we found one that you don't have to worry about who sees you? What if there were hardly any people around?"

"This is LA. There is no spot that isn't full of people."

"I gotta show you something. Follow me."

He began walking away, heavy backpack and all. Even under a forty pound pack Darby could walk faster than me. When he walked he was trying to go someplace and he wanted to already be there.

"How far is this place?" I asked as I caught up.

He looked around to get his bearings. "Three quarters of a mile. Maybe?"

"Let's take my car."

You know you're a spoiled rich kid when you can go buy a used car just to blend in with the rest of your friends. I had a new car, but there was no way I was going to drive a bright red Jaguar to go visit a homeless man on the streets. I hated having two lives, but the truth was... I did have two lives. Even the ten year old Ford Escort was luxury to Darby. My neighbors considered it an eyesore. It was white and it had a little rust, but the engine ran well and it didn't ask for much in the way of gasoline. I didn't wash it and I never cleaned it out, just so Darby would feel at home in it.

"Hey," he said when we walked up to the car. "If I asked you to leave me in a different part of town, would you do it?"

"I don't know," I admitted. "If it was safe, I suppose."

"Okay, I'll let you know if I see a place. Saves a bit on bus fare."

"Now, where are we going?" I asked.

"The library."

It seemed a strange request. I'd seen Darby read a few times but he said the homeless shelter had a book shelf that you could either check out books from or trade for a new one to keep. Most of the books I saw him reading were very worn out paperbacks. They didn't come from the big city library.

"When we get there can I tell them I'm with you?" he asked.

"Of course. Why couldn't you? You are with me," I pointed out.

"I've been asked to leave a time or two."

Sometimes Darby's world seemed liberating and sometimes it saddened me.

It took me a couple of tries to find the library. I hadn't been there in years. Why go to a library when you can order any book you want? I actually only knew where it was because I had donated books to the big sale the library put on twice a year to raise money for more books. I didn't quite understand the concept of selling books to buy books, but I needed to make room on the shelf and I thought other people would enjoy them, too. Most of the books I bought were travel books. But then when I got the book home most of the places they highlighted in the book were places my parents would go. It was disappointing.

We still had to park two blocks away and like most of the streets in LA the parking was metered. I wished the meter was the old-fashioned coin operated one but this one I had to slide a card into and I hoped Darby didn't notice the card I used. It was gold and sparkly and… well, I bet he'd never seen one quite like it before. It seemed ridiculous to me to use a debit card for a dollar's worth of parking time. I grumbled silently while I paid the city for the privilege to park.

We walked past a security guard and Darby gave him a smug look, like, "whatcha going to do about it *this* time? Eh? Eh?" I wondered what he had done to get kicked out. I admit he looked a bit rough and it had been a few days since he had bathed but he was a guy. Guys could cope. Then it occurred to me that Darby was just barely coping.

"We get in line," he explained.

I was stunned that there was a waiting line in the library. I looked around and realized we were waiting to use a computer. In this day and age who went to the library to access the internet on desk top computers? Lots of people, I guess, because there were four people ahead of us in line and the people at the desks were in no hurry to leave. I noticed the person in front of us glancing at Darby uncomfortably and the person behind us had stepped back a couple of steps. It took half an hour to gain access to a computer. When Darby sat down at the keys his fingers flew. It was obvious that at one time he was very familiar with the workings of a computer. He brought up a website and navigated to a map.

"See all these icons on the map?" He asked.

"Yeah?" I said.

"This is just within five miles," he explained. "I zoom out and we got the LA basin. Zoom out again, we got a good sized chunk of southern California. Zoom out again…" he kept looking at larger and larger chunks of the country and finally the world and there were icons everywhere. Well, not everywhere. There was a warthog in Africa who didn't know what a geocache was.

"How many are there?" I asked.

"Last count? I don't know. The last big geocaching news about the count it was creeping up on two million."

I had a little more understanding than most people about how big a number a million was, but to think there were two million geocaches in the world stunned me.

"Like the one we found two weeks ago?" I asked.

"No! There's different kinds. Look. I'll show you some of them."

A few magical clicks of the mouse and he had brought up a semi random page about a single geocache in, I think, Europe. He began reading.

"Oops, my bad," he said. "I need one in English or German."

"You speak German?"

"Some. Enough to read a simple geocache page, but let's try… somewhere pictures would be taken a lot. How about the beaches of Australia?"

"Sounds good."

He clicked one of the icons on the coast of Australia and then he clicked on the gallery link. This particular cache only had four pictures. One showed a sunset over the ocean. The next showed a little toy sitting on a rock with odd looking trees in the background. The third was what Darby was looking for. It showed a plastic sandwich box with a GX symbol written on the top with magic marker. The lid was off and inside was a conglomeration of cheap trinkets. I thought I saw a shell, a coin, a charm and a ticket to some event. It was hard to tell what the paper thing was. I was just guessing it was a ticket.

"That is a geocache," Darby explained. "But it's just one example. I just want to show you that not all of them are as boring as the one we found. See these columns?" he said as he clicked back to a list of geocaches. This tells the size and these numbers tell how hard it is to find and how difficult it is to get to."

"And this whole list, that we see right now is…"

"The caches near that Australian beach. See, you can see how far away they are from our search point."

"They start out close and are listed nearest to farthest," I said as I figured out exactly what I was seeing.

"And that's just a small corner of Australia."

"You're telling me this is a worldwide… thing?"

"Hobby, obsession, sport… it's been called a lot of things."

"How did you learn about it if you need this map and this website?"

"It's something that can be done by anybody. You only need some kind of GPS receiver and a pen. I can upload the geocaches here at the library. I got the GPS at Goodwill. I don't know why they had one. I snapped this one up for twenty bucks. A buddy of mine had a better one, but I don't know where he got it. The screen was a lot better. It had more options. His was, like, the dream GPS to me, but I get along."

"How much are they usually?"

"I don't know. I've never been in a position to look."

"That was twenty bucks?"

"Yeah, though I don't know if that was high or low. I'd expect any electronic gadget to be more than twenty dollars."

"Yeah. Let's look."

The same website also sold geocaching gear so we were able to find several different models of GPS ranging in price from seventy to nearly five hundred dollars. To think a measly five hundred dollars could expand a man's world and bring him to places like that beach in Australia was humbling to me. I remembered the cache in the reflector. A dirty street corner in LA. It contrasted sharply with the trip to Paris that my mother was recommending.

"Do they have these in Paris?" I asked.

"Europe is really big into geocaching," he said. "There's probably thousands of them."

It was astounding to me to think that there might be a reflector on a post in Paris, hiding a little piece of paper just waiting for somebody to come by and sign it. I was used to signing things. Part of the drudgery of having a lot of money was delegating what happens to it and it seemed each financial decision came with a stack of paperwork which needed half a dozen signatures. I had an illegible signature which represented my being and standing in life. The more it got scattered around the more successful my parents thought I was. But my only real goal in life seemed to be managing my finances and I didn't go to school to learn how to manage my finances. I went to school to broaden my mind and it was beginning to feel very narrow. The computer screen before me felt… full of possibilities. All I needed was a GPS, a pen, and a little ambition. Given those three easily attainable things I could be out of here. I could fly to Paris and make my mother happy. She wouldn't have to know I was looking in little dusty corners of the city for geocaches.

"Do you have a passport?" I asked Darby.

"You're kidding, right?" he asked.

"No," I said trying not to act like everybody who was anybody had a passport.

"No, I don't. That's another one of those things you need an address to get."

"If you had one, would you use it?" I asked.

"No, because I can barely afford a bus trip across town. What makes you think I'd fly to a foreign country?"

Yeah, what did make me think that? And did I really want to travel with Darby? There were a lot of people who wanted to go to Paris. I could take a girl. The idea of travel and the pleasures of a woman was tempting. But what woman would want to delve into the lost corners of a city like Paris? No woman I knew. They would want to shop and go to museums and dine in elegant restaurants. That was precisely the life I was trying to get away from. But Darby... Darby could teach me the ins and outs of geocaching, eat regular meals, and sleep in a real bed. All I needed to have my own personal geocaching guide was to pay his way. I didn't mind the expense, but I did mind losing my place in his world. Even though I visited it and went home to a comfortable apartment at night I felt like they accepted me. If I revealed my other life I risked being outcast from them. I would be seen as a traitor. They shared. If another had a need and they could help in any little way, they shared. And I... I had failed in that regard. I would help them if I saw a need but often what they needed and what I could provide were not conducive to maintaining the image I was trying so hard to maintain. They would ask if anybody had anything for a headache and I would have a whole medicine cabinet back home full of remedies, but none on my person. They would need bus fare to go to the clinic and I only had fifty and hundred dollar bills. It was these things that stopped me from sharing with them. After the failed bus fare aid I made sure I had small bills on my person. I even made sure I didn't have to reveal the larger bills to give them the small ones. And I felt like such a loser for guarding my identity so closely. When I first walked into their camp I had no idea how much of a culture shock awaited me, but every day brought a new surprise, usually a surprise that showed me how far I lived from reality.

My parents would not understand my actions at all. If they asked what I was doing I described the state of my finances. I would tweak my stocks and report on their success or failure. If I told them that I drove down to the worst part of town and hung out with homeless people my mother would say, "Ewe, how can you stand it?" and my father would tell me it wasn't safe. But I'd found more cutthroats in the financial world than on the streets. Rich people need their riches. If their money is threatened they can turn on you. Darby, Henry, Reggie, and Wanda just wanted their next meal. The four seemed to have most of their other needs met. They each owned a sleeping bag. A few had pads they could lay on the ground for insulation and padding. They seemed to own several changes of clothes. Toiletries were a juggling act. They valued them, yet had no place to use them. When they got desperate they used gas station restrooms or walked to the homeless shelter. They preferred not going to the shelter because there they received more help than they really needed. They got a good meal, a shower, but they were expected to better themselves and their situation. They really didn't want to get off the streets. They wanted to cope on them. They scoffed at the idea of being a burden to society. They considered themselves to be a burden to society if they relied on the shelter, otherwise they were more like gypsies, without wagons and superstitions.

I spent a weekend once in Darby's camp, though we really didn't spend much time in camp. We wandered the streets. Darby talked the whole time, until he noticed a car with dirty windows. It seemed to work better if he noticed the car as it was parking, because that meant the owner might be away from their car long enough to get the windows washed. He was polite.

"Excuse me ma'am. I was wondering if I could wash the windows on your car while you are shopping. All I ask is a small handout. Coins. Anything."

He did a great job. I washed one side, while he washed the other and then he washed my side, too, saying I left streaks. The woman gave him thirty-five cents. Darby shrugged, pocketed the coins and thanked the woman.

The next car Darby thought would bring him a few dollars. It was a Cadillac and Darby seemed to be honored to wash the windows on such a car. He peeked in the windows admiring the features, asking about the sound system. He went to great pains to make sure he did a good job on it and even though he'd finished it while the owner was in the store he acted as if he was polishing chrome when the owner came out. The man just said, "Thanks man," got in his car and drove away.

"Doesn't that make you mad?" I asked.

"He probably forgot he hadn't given me anything yet," Darby responded.

"Dude, he just took advantage of you, that's all," I said, but Darby refused to admit people took advantage of other people.

His most successful window job was a car belonging to a middle class black woman with three kids in tow. She gave him a five dollar bill and before she took off she shut off her engine again and jumped out of her car.

"Here, this was in the pocket of my car. It isn't much, but I don't like the change rattling around in there."

"Thanks," Darby said. "And God bless you."

"You too," she said and off she went.

Darby opened up his hand. She'd given him another eighty-eight cents. He could now afford dinner.

Forgive me, I tend to ramble. The trip to the library opened up a whole new layer of society to me. Darby asked me to drop him off where he could wash windows, but still be within walking distance of his camp. Walking distance was about a mile. He'd make it home okay, make a couple of dollars and I'd be able to find him, or at least leave word that I'd been looking for him.

I went home and parked the Escort next to the Jaguar. I stood in front of the two cars. If someone had walked by and offered to buy the Jaguar I would have sold it. Anybody want a ten dollar Jaguar? But I didn't want to sell it bad enough to actually seek out a buyer. I just considered it an uncomfortable reminder that I was not measuring up to any of the standards I had been raised to. The Escort did not create any guilt trips. I was a mess.

I took the elevator to the tenth floor, got off and walked to the end of the hall. The end apartment was more expensive than the apartments along the hallway. I only had neighbors on one side of me and I had more windows overlooking the city. The disadvantage was that the walk to my door was longer. I couldn't complain. The view was spectacular and the apartment was roomy. My living room had a panorama view and the view continued into the bedroom, but I kept the bedroom blinds closed most of the time. I'd been surprised by a window washer, which was only slightly embarrassing, but I didn't want to repeat the experience. They simply looked at me as if they wished I was female and naked. I waved to them on the way to the shower and made sure to close the door. When I came out they were gone and I closed the blinds.

The living room was much too large for my liking. I had a contemporary style sofa and recliner, a coffee table and a large screen TV. The room looked vast in comparison to its contents, but I didn't have the creativity to make it into a more comfortable and pleasant place to live.

I'd brought a few girls home. They seemed uncomfortable. I wondered if a few candles would help, but I really didn't like the smell of most of them. They were too strong. I didn't even like walking down the candle aisle at a store.

The kitchen was formidable and minimal at the same time. I was sure a gourmet cook would love it, but I didn't eat at home much. I'd never been taught to cook. Why cook when you can buy whatever meal you feel like? So I had cold cereal and milk, beer, ice cream and money. My mother had made sure I had a few cooking pots, utensils and kitchen towels, but most of them had never been used. I used the kitchen towels if I washed my hands. I ran the dishwasher when I ran out of bowls or spoons. My laundry was picked up once a week by a service except for the clothes I kept rumpled for my trips to the camp.

I stood in my living room and looked around. Sterile, that's what my home was. And in more ways than one. Not enough happened here to cause germs to grow. It was stark and nearly lifeless, even when I was home. I did not want to spend the rest of my life here. I thought some travel might tell me what it was that I did enjoy. Maybe if I brought some of that knowledge home with me I could begin to build on this foundation. I went to my office. Yes, I had an office, even though I didn't have a job. It contained a desk, computer, tablet computer, laptop, a shelf of books, a fancy sound system, and a picture of my mother and father that was taken in Italy while they were celebrating some big anniversary. It was taken on a balcony overlooking a very old part of a city. The sun was setting and they leaned together, each holding up a glass of red wine. It looked like a travel poster.

I turned on the computer, then changed my mind and grabbed the laptop. I took it to the living room and sat in the recliner watching the lights come on in the city below. A city that never sleeps. I brought up the geocaching web page and tried to look at a map but I had to sign in and it asked for my geocaching name. Ironically, *No Name* and *No Name Yet* were taken. I finally typed in *The Earl of Nothing* because it was how I felt about life at the time, and it accepted that. With a user name and password I could view the map, though the site warned me that I was not seeing all the caches out there. To view all the caches I had to become a premium member and I debated about subscribing. I decided that Darby couldn't afford the membership fee and he expected me to be too broke to afford it too, so I accepted the limitations of the free account.

First I looked for caches near my building. There were plenty of them, but I did not want to search for those. I typed in my parents' address since there were hills and parks nearby. There were several around their neighborhood, too. I clicked here and there, experimenting. The oldest cache close by had been there several years. The newest was only a few days old. I clicked on it just to see what it said. The entry said, "FTF! WoooHooooo! This doesn't happen very often! I lucked out that I was in the neighborhood when the notice arrived!"

This was puzzling to me. A notice? And what did FTF mean? I also noticed that geocachers really liked the caches around Hollywood Hills. They probably liked the variety of homes, the proximity of the Hollywood sign. I had to admit even after all these years that I loved the little winding streets and the odd homes all scrunched together. You could find a little bungalow right next door to a walled fort-like structure. I had tried to visit the neighbor in the fort, but you had to have a code to get through the iron gate. Doctors, lawyers, actors, sports legends… they lived in Hollywood Hills. Tourists crowded in to see the sign and try to catch a glimpse of a movie star. I couldn't download any caches, because I didn't have a GPS so I determined the next day I would go buy one.

Chapter 3

I chose a sporting goods store in Santa Monica so I could walk the pier and eat at a seafood restaurant afterwards. I drove the Jaguar because I enjoyed the speed and the service at valet parking was great if you had a Jaguar. I tipped them well, then wondered why I tipped well and let Darby get by on six bucks a day.

I walked into the store and saw that I was very lucky I had good genes. All the clothes were for physically fit people, and yet I didn't have any problem finding something that I could wear. I had never thought about the number of different outdoor activities before. I wandered from one department to another watching for a glass counter. I found a few of them. One sold fishing reels, another sold sunglasses and binoculars. It took me a few minutes to find the counter where they sold GPS receivers.

"May I help you?" the salesman asked politely.

"Yes, I guess I could use some help. I'm in search of a hand held GPS."

"All righty, sir. We have several models. What type do you need?"

"A portable one."

"And what will you be using this unit for?"

"Geocaching," I said.

"Ahh, okay." He opened the sliding door on the back of the case and pulled out several models. I could tell they were much better units than Darby could ever hope to own. I could pay cash for any of them, but I didn't think I should and, being entirely new to the hobby gave me an excuse to start out small.

"I've only been geocaching once," I said. "But my friend would like me to get more interested in the hobby, so I thought if I had my own GPS it would make it more fun. He has this one," I said indicating the simplest unit on the counter.

"A lot of geocaching parents buy those for their kids. It's inexpensive and nearly shock proof. That helps a lot when you have kids in the field."

"I think I'd like one a little more sophisticated than that but I don't want to sink a lot of money into this in case I turn out to be lousy at it."

"I understand, sir."

The model he showed me was under two hundred dollars. It had basic maps. It would hold a few thousand caches and it was a very basic model.

"I'm warning you," the salesman said. "If you're the techie type and you find you enjoy geocaching you'll want to upgrade as soon as possible."

"That's fine," I told him. "I don't want to show up my friend. I just want to be able to see a screen, instead of just being told to look within fifty feet of one spot on the earth. If I have my own GPS maybe I can find a few before he does."

He nodded, "So can I interest you in batteries, a lanyard? Space pen?"

"What's a space pen?" I asked.

"A pen that writes in any direction and on wet surfaces so you can sign logs under almost any circumstances."

"If I upgrade, remind me," I said. Darby wouldn't have a space pen and if we got more involved in the hobby I would have to tell him the truth before I upgraded. In that case he would know I could afford a space pen. Maybe I'd buy him one, too. "I'll take some batteries."

"You'll want extras," he said.

"And I'll keep a few of the batteries for my friend's GPS on hand, too."

"Very well, sir. Will that be all?"

"For now, yes."

I took the bag to my car then drove to the pier. I left the car in valet parking again and walked to a restaurant. I took the bag with me again so I could read the user's manual while I waited for my meal.

The device looked simple enough. It had a joystick button in the middle and buttons for back, menu and zoom. I put two batteries in it and turned it on. I waited, and waited. After a while it stated that it could not find a signal. I wished I had a table by the window but I was in the lower story of a two story building so it didn't surprise me at all that it couldn't find a signal. I hit the back button and looked at the other features. Surprisingly there was a list of caches already in the memory. The caches were all over the world. Why would they sell me a GPS with caches in South America, Europe, and Australia in it? I was curious if there were any nearby caches in it but it didn't know where I was to put the caches in order. Looking at the device itself only told me that I knew very little about geocaching and GPS technology.

My catch-of-the-day arrived and it tasted all right, but it was just food. I enjoyed a dollar menu burger with Darby and Henry more than I did sitting in a restaurant overlooking the ocean by myself. Something was wrong with this picture. I wondered what would happen in camp if I showed up with parmesan encrusted halibut dinners for everyone. Fish and steamed vegetables get cold fast. The dinners would probably be lousy by the time I got there. But a lousy gourmet dinner might be wonderful to them. The sharp contrast grated on me.

Instead of going back to the valet stand I walked the beach and waited for the GPS to find a satellite.

Surprisingly enough, the GPS had a few local caches. I guess, if you don't know what country a GPS might be sent to, you included a few from the major geocaching meccas. I had to read the book to find out I simply had to toggle right to get a screen with a map. There were two icons on the screen. I assumed one was me and the other was the cache. It was still a crude map, but I could see I needed to go south. I turned around and began walking the beach south. When I had walked fifteen minutes and made no progress toward the cache I looked closer at the screen. Oh. I needed to go several miles south. Okay. Time to get the car.

Trying to drive and navigate using the little GPS screen was impossible. I thought the GPS on the car would help more but I couldn't tell the car to go looking for a geocache. I needed an address, or coordinates. And I had to learn how to input coordinates into the built in GPS. Then I decided that if I was going to be geocaching with Darby I couldn't use this car. I had to use the old car. So I had to learn how to use the handheld GPS whether I wanted to or not.

Eventually, after many starts, stops, U-turns and route corrections I pulled into Long Beach. Surface streets blipped into place on my screen. Now I know that I was trying to do the hardest geocaching possible. LA is not the easiest place to geocache in. There are streets doing all kinds of odd things, traffic flowing in weird patterns, pedestrians everywhere, parking nonexistent or hidden away in little parking garages. All I could do was get as close as possible and park anywhere possible, then walk. There was a parking garage fairly close to the cache so I left the car there and exited the garage. I blinked in the sunshine and tried to figure out where I was. Having grown up in Hollywood I knew my way around LA and the surrounding area pretty well, but I had never done it on a two inch black and yellow screen before. I felt like a total nerd walking down a crowded pedestrian walkway, eyes glued to the GPS. I almost ran into several people because of my distraction. They stepped around me and stared at my retreating back. Finally I stopped and tried to figure out how far away the cache was. It took me a moment to find the little number that told me the distance. One hundred and twenty-three feet. Oh! I should be able to see where it is, I thought. I stood there in the middle of the sidewalk staring at the screen and then looking about me. The cache should be just ahead… and… to my… right… at about one o'clock. Oh shoot. The place that was hundred feet away and a little to my right was a restaurant with an outdoor dining area. How in the world was I supposed to find a cache in these conditions? How did they even manage to hide it without being seen? Three tables full of lunch diners looked at me like I had a screw loose. I smiled at them and kept walking. They watched me walk down the street. On the screen the number shrunk as I got closer to the cache and then grew as I passed it. I sat down on a bench just past the cache and stewed about it. I wondered what Darby would do if confronted with a restaurant full of people and a cache hidden literally in their midst. I didn't see any way to find it.

I studied the exterior of the restaurant. There was a railing, a patio, and a small tree. Around the top of the restaurant was a decorative ledge. There was a roof over the tables and posts holding the roof up. Listing all the attributes of the patio didn't help me decide anything about the cache, though. I watched the patio and decided this cache was just impossible. Unless I came back well after last call this place was going to be crawling with people all day and well into the night. I had failed. My first geocache search and I came up empty.

Chapter 4

Darby laughed at me. Unfortunately he was very impressed with the GPS. I actually drove him all the way from Pasadena to Long Beach and showed him the restaurant.

"You were right to pass it up. Come back before any of these shops open," he advised. "Why did you choose this one?"

"It was already in my GPS."

"Let me see."

I handed the unit back to him and he clicked through the screens, then laughed again. "These logs are two years old!" he exclaimed.

"How can they be two years old? I just bought this yesterday."

"They added the caches to the unit at the factory. I guess this one is at least a year old. I suggest you delete them and start with more recent, local caches."

"And how do I do that?" I asked.

"Download them from the website. You remember the website, don't you?"

"Of course."

"Find some that look interesting and we'll go look for them tomorrow afternoon."

"Why afternoon?"

"I need to mow a few lawns."

"For dinner?"

He didn't answer.

"If you'll teach me how to geocache I'll take care of your dinner."

"Really?"

"Yeah."

"All right!" he said brightly as if it was a load off his shoulders.

I went home with a new purpose. I was going to download some geocaches. I didn't know exactly how to do that, but I thought I could figure it out. I worked at the desk top computer since the screen was large and the mouse was easier to use. The GPS came with a cord. One end was little and fit into the GPS unit. The other end was larger, like the one on my memory stick, so I plugged it into the USB port. It fit. So far so good. I turned on the GPS and brought up the geocaching website. I waited for the GPS and the computer to make contact with each other. When I got a message that said they had connected I began looking for local caches that sounded interesting. I found out that downloading caches was easy. There was a link that said, "Send to My GPS" and when I clicked it it downloaded. I then had a cache in my GPS. One random cache. No. One random cache plus those other 200 caches around the world. Hmmm. Well, no worries about those other caches, I thought. I can get rid of them later. Since the process was so simple I typed in my address, put in a radius of five miles, and clicked the Go link. Bam, I had hundreds of caches to choose from. However, as I began reading the descriptions and, more importantly, the logs, I found I didn't want to just start downloading the caches near home and work my way out. Some of them had been missing for months and some were just very uninteresting. I tried ones near my parents' house. Those had looked more promising before. I found out the parks around there had a few geocacaches and Griffith Park had several. I was reading about one cache that claimed to be a set from an old TV show when I noticed a number on the page. Wow this one had lots of what they called Favorite Points. Favorite points had to be a good sign, so I was determined that we would find this cache the next day. I thought Darby would enjoy a trip to the park. It would be much easier to geocache there than in a busy downtown shopping area.

"I can tell by that smile that you found a good one," Darby said as I walked up to the camp the next day.

"I hope so. It should at least be easier to look for than that last one."

"Where is it?"

"Griffith Park," I said.

"You figured out the download process okay?"

"Yeah. Click, download."

"There's a better way, but that'll do for now. How many did you find?"

"Hundreds, but I only downloaded about twenty."

"Are you driving?"

"Unless you want to."

"I can drive?"

"Do you know where we're going?"

"No."

"Then let me drive. I don't mind you driving my car, but I know this part of town."

"Shit, you do know this part of town," Darby said as I zipped around seemingly blind corners.

"Sorry. I drove these streets when I was sixteen."

The road went uphill and uphill some more. Frequently in LA a street would look like an older neighborhood street and then continue right up into a woodsy area. That's the way this part of Griffith Park was. There was a house right next to the park gate.

"You're passing a geocache," Darby said.

"Maybe we'll get it on the way out."

"I never expected you to be star struck enough to want to see a movie set."

"I'm not. Only… it just sounds cool. It's where the Batmobile comes out of the Batcave in the old TV show."

"I've never seen Batman. It was on TV before I was born."

"Me, too, but I've seen the part where the Batmobile comes out of the cave. And I get the theme song stuck in my head all the time."

The park didn't look busy but there was no parking. It wasn't a park where people got out of their cars and could be found nearby at picnic tables and playgrounds. This was a big park inviting hikers and joggers to get out of the busyness of the city. Like usual I had to circle around until I saw a family packing up. Then I had to block traffic while they loaded up. Some people got irritated, but people who frequented the city parks were used to it. Finally a family with two kids approached a car and began tossing backpacks, a stroller, jackets and sweaters into the trunk.

"Why did they need those coats?" Darby asked. "I bet they roasted."

"You never know when you go out here. It can look sunny and then a cold wind comes up. On the other hand it can be the middle of January and people are walking around in shorts."

The dad closed the trunk and took a look to see if he had enough space to back up, so I put the car in reverse and backed up until the car behind me beeped his horn in warning. The dad barely managed to back out and I pulled into his parking place as soon as there was space to sneak through. The guy behind me was not happy to pass the parking place but he was glad I was out of the way so he could circle around some more.

"Lots of people at the park today," Darby observed.

"It's a big park."

"Yeah, I guess."

"Come on, let's go find us a bat cave."

A pretty girl jogged by with a large Golden Retriever on a leash. An elderly couple walked past the parking lot hand in hand. A group of Asian hikers headed up the nearest trail talking a mile a minute in a language I couldn't understand.

"Hey, this is Hollywood isn't it?" Darby asked.

"Yeah."

"Maybe we'll see a movie star!"

"Maybe. If we do I won't recognize them," I said. "I've been conditioned since day one that you leave famous people alone."

"Why? They should be used to it."

I was going to say that it was common courtesy in the neighborhood, but he didn't know I lived there. We knew a few famous people, but to us they were just neighbors, just like we were just their neighbors. Famous people are just unlucky regular folks. They happened to be good at something that put them in the limelight. Some enjoyed it. Some did not. But I was always taught that you don't assume a star wants to be a star 24/7.

"Well, I doubt if we see Batman," I said. "He's got to be eighty by now."

"At least. Though there have been newer Batmans, too."

"This is cool," I said showing him the GPS. "It's just like yours, in that you follow the arrow, but you can see yourself and the cache on the same screen."

"So where's the cache? Have you learned how to read the screen?" he asked.

"Only a little. I looked for that cache in Long Beach. That was my first attempt to use it. I know to follow the map and I realize this number up here tells me how far away the cache is."

He pointed to another number. "This is your heading. Here is your scale. You've got fully charged batteries. Move the cursor."

I pushed the little joy stick and a little plus sign moved. A sign popped up by the plus sign. It also showed a distance and a heading.

"This is a lot more information than I need about one geocache," I said.

"Right now. As you learn more about it you'll use most of it."

"Why would I care what my heading is as long as I'm not lost?" I asked.

"You'll see."

We couldn't walk directly to the cache. There was a road leading up the side of the hill and, though the GPS pointed to our left, we followed the road and passed a locked gate. It was obvious the gate was only meant to block cars. Hikers had used the road repeatedly. It was interesting to me that even a dirt road leading basically nowhere still had enough tracks on it to mimic a shopping mall at Christmas. There were so many tracks that they made a fascinating study of layers and people and dogs. I wondered how old the least distinguishable tracks were.

It wasn't a long walk. The road curved around and the cave appeared suddenly before us.

"Whoa, it isn't a cave at all!" Darby said in surprise.

"They must have had the angles all figured out to make it look like a cave," I surmised.

Actually the Batcave was a tunnel through a hillside. It forked and on the other side of the hill there were three smaller openings. Darby and I walked through it and talked about its uses as a Hollywood set.

"These little cave openings would have worked great in old western films," he said.

"I bet they were. It's a handy location. I also bet we'd be surprised at the number of movies and TV shows it appears in. The description only talks about the Batcave but it could be used in lots of different ways."

"There was this one scene. Oh, I can't remember what movie it was in. But it looks like the guy is climbing something really tall and on the DVD they had a special 'making of' film and it shows the guy climbing, climbing and then it pulls back to show him gripping a single rock near a parking lot in Malibu."

"Figures."

"Those were the days."

"Which days?"

"The days when I had a home and a TV."

"If you could get it back, would you?" I asked.

"Where is the geocache?" he said to avoid the topic.

"I don't know. I forgot about it there for a bit."

I had to walk out of the cave and let the GPS figure out which way I was going.

"It says it's only twenty feet away."

"Okay, so we should be nearly on top of it."

There weren't any hiding places close that I could see. And it seemed like a bad place to hide a cache. Too many people frequented the cave. I walked closer to where the GPS said the cache was but it kept saying it was farther until I couldn't go farther without climbing the hill.

"What do we do when the GPS says it's farther and we can't go farther?" I asked.

"We go further anyway," he replied. "There's almost an unwritten rule about geocaching. You spend a lot of time trying to find a way to the cache and then you find a very simple way back. It never fails. I bet if we climb up there we'll find a trail leading right back down to the mouth of the cave again."

"Then why not look for the trail to begin with?" I asked.

"Because for some odd reason the trail never appears until the cache is found."

"So, should we climb up there?" I asked.

"It can't hurt to look for a trail. I doubt the cache owner had in mind for us to climb up the rocks."

We did find a trail but it was one a mountain goat or a ten year old boy would scale easily. This thirty-two year old man had a little trouble with it. The weeds had grown over the trail and I had to crouch and push my way through the branches. I stood at the top huffing and puffing and thinking I was much farther than ten feet from where I stood at the bottom, but when I looked at the GPS it said I was right on top of the cache.

"Three feet!" I proclaimed aloud.

There were plenty of places to hide a cache up on the hill. There were trees and bushes, rocks and weeds. There as a very odd rock. It had holes all over it, but not natural holes, they had been bored by a very heavy auger or drill of some kind.

"Hey, look!" Darby said.

"Did you find it?" I asked.

"No! Look!" he said excitedly pointing off into the distance. He'd spotted the Hollywood sign. To me it was just an old landmark that attracted too many tourists. To him it was iconic. "How close do they let people get to it?"

"There's a trail that goes under it," I said. "I've walked it many times. I wonder if I passed any caches on the way."

"Can we go look?" he asked.

"Sure."

We searched the top of the hill for half an hour. Every once in a while we would hear voices and if we looked down the hill we eventually saw tourists come out of the tunnel. The reactions to the tunnel were mixed.

"Awww it's not a bat cave at all!" said one boy.

"You mean this was here way back when Grandpa was little?" said another child.

"Of course it was here," the mother said. "Hills don't sprout up overnight, you know."

Except in southern California, I thought.

Someone who had seen the opening of the TV show or one of the movies sang the theme song as he walked through the tunnel and I grumbled about having the tune stuck in my head for the rest of the day.

"How big is this one?" Darby asked.

"I don't know."

"What's the hint?"

"Hint?"

"Let me see your GPS."

"How do you know how to use my GPS?" I asked. "I don't even know how to use it."

"I know several people with GPSrs. And when they see mine they let me try theirs. I sure wish I could upgrade but I'm lucky to have this. The cache is a small one."

"How small is small?"

"Well, different people see the sizes differently. I've seen small caches that were pill bottles but I generally think of them as the size of my fist."

I held up my fist. "So we're looking for something this big?"

"Maybe. And it could be camouflaged."

"But there's hundreds of places something that small could be."

"Exactly." He saw my frustration and added, "But hey! We're out in the open air, a stone's throw from the Hollywood sign. I'd never know about the cave or the old Batman or Griffith Park except for this cache. So I kind of like it."

I had seen Bronson Cave and the Hollywood sign many times but his enthusiasm was contagious. My family had just called this place Bronson Canyon but the addition of the geocache made it feel different. Like it had been holding out on me all these years.

"How long has geocaching been around?" I asked.

"I think since the year 2000," he answered. "Though I didn't hear about it until 2010. Life was too busy when I had a job and a family to take care of."

"You have a family?"

"Yeah, I mean…" He sat down on the holey rock. "When I lost my job we did okay for about six months. We had savings. We had to be careful. But when the landlord forced us to move and we had no income… she took the baby to her mom's and… I haven't seen them since."

"Why didn't you go too?"

"Earl… it's not that simple. Sometimes relationships don't hold through tough times. We fought. I hated the yelling. Her yelling threats that if I didn't find work she was out of there until one day she was. I woke up to find her packing and when I called her at her mom's house her the first question was always where I was working. I sold my car. I sold my furniture. And when I didn't have transportation the job hunt went downhill further. Hell, I can't even afford a divorce. I can live without a wife, but I do miss Adele. Her smile could brighten any day. And she's grown so fast."

I sat down on the ground, stunned that a man's world could get so out of hand so fast. I wanted to say, "Better to have loved and lost…" but I wasn't sure anymore it was true.

"If you had a job and place to live, what would you do?" I asked.

He stood up and looked off the hill at the city of LA. "How many people are out there?" he asked.

"A couple million?"

"Most of them have jobs and a place to live. Are they happy?"

"I don't know Darby. I'm having a bit of hard time deciding that, too."

"What about you? Are you happy?"

"Me? No. I don't think so. I mean, I'm not miserable. I'm doing okay. But happy? Actually, I went looking for happiness and that's when I walked into your camp."

"Would you go back?" he asked.

"Dar…" Shit should I tell him? I was tired of living a lie. "You might say I'm looking for a place to prevent me from going back."

He wasn't sure he understood what I was saying even though all the words made sense.

"Well, I think we came up here to find a geocache," I said. "Do you think it's still here?"

He gave the GPS a few clicks and said, "Yeah, it's been found recently. It's here."

We looked high and low for that cache talking about the locale, the weather, the number of people in the park, the Hollywood sign. I told him about the canyon once being a gravel pit long before I was born. This topic came up because of the odd rock full of holes. The holes were manmade and I assumed explosives were put in some of the holes to blast away part of the hillside to extract more gravel.

"Then why didn't they make this rock into gravel?" Darby asked.

I didn't have an answer for that question.

"I'm about ready to give up," I said.

"You want your first hunt to be a DNF?" he asked.

"What's a DNF?"

"Did Not Find."

"No. I don't. But I also don't want to spend all day looking fruitlessly through weeds and brush for something that seems to prefer to remain unfound."

He huffed with frustration, like logging a DNF would tarnish his record. His record? What about mine? I'd start out with a 100% rate of failure. Dang, I didn't want to do that.

"Okay, keep looking. By the way, do I have to be the one to find it to claim I found it?" I asked.

"Generally, the rule is you have to sign the log. If you are in a group and somebody else finds the cache make sure you sign the log. But I recommend at least seeing where every cache is hidden. You don't develop geosenses unless you see the hide."

That made sense, though it still seemed unfair to claim you found something if somebody else found it. So I asked Darby, "Why can I claim a find if I didn't find a cache?"

"Convenience. They could never enforce a strict rule and it makes no sense for each individual in a group to rehide the cache just to have the next person pull it out again. So my rule is that I have to actually see the cache and sign the log."

"Okay, guess I'm just a stickler," I said but didn't add that it probably resulted from balancing books to the penny.

He added, "Online they have no way of knowing if you really found a cache or not, but some of the cache owners require you to sign the log. If you don't sign the log they will delete your find."

That seemed a fair compromise, though the system seemed flawed a bit. I could claim to have found any cache? Why... I could be an arm chair geocacher and maybe a handful of my finds would get deleted but why would I care? If they were not real finds I would have no right to object. Maybe I was over-thinking this hobby a little bit. I hadn't actually found a cache on my own yet so I decided I needed to put in my time before I began making judgment calls.

Ten minutes of searching the brush for a cache was beginning to show wear and tear on the bushes. I normally didn't notice the condition of the bushes around me, but since I had been bending branches and tromping on weeds I began to notice that I was knocking the leaves off and flattening the grass.

"Maybe we should give up," I said.

"All right. I agree. We've spent too much time on this hill."

I sighed and we looked down the hill and as we looked down the hill a gray line caught my eye. At first I shook it off. What importance was a gray line? There were lots of gray things on the hill: Bark, sticks, the rock, more rocks, old papers that had blown into the weeds. But I thought it couldn't hurt to look so I reached down and grabbed the gray line only to find that it was not a line at all but a box.

"Finally!" Darby said.

"You mean you knew where it was all along?" I asked.

"No, but I did want you to find it and not me. There's just something about being the finder that I wanted you to experience."

"And what is that?" I asked.

"I don't know. But you'll figure it out. If you don't, maybe geocaching isn't your thing."

I held the box in my hand. I hefted it to guess its contents but it was very light. Darby and I squashed more grass as we sat and I opened up the box.

Inside I found eight business cards, a flyer for a Mexican food restaurant, a Batman patch, a tiny toy camera, a plastic bracelet, a foam batarang, and three dirty erasers. There was also a small notepad, cut to fit inside the box. I put the tiny camera up to my eye and clicked through four views of cartoon characters.

"This is it?" I asked. "This is a real geocache?"

"Yeah. Did you bring a pen?"

"I always have a pen," I said though it was for signing charge receipts and when I thought about the pen I realized I needed to buy a cheap pen. Mine was given to me by a client who wanted to impress. It was a silver pen made to fit well in the hand and it wrote in gel ink. I couldn't sign the log without taking it out and I already admitted to having one so I pulled out the pen hoping Darby couldn't recognize quality when he saw it. I signed the log and handed the log to Darby. He waited for the pen so I handed it over, too. Thankfully, he corrected me gently.

"You don't want to keep this pen for geocaching," he said. "It takes too long for the ink to dry and it'll leave spots on the pages it touches. If you're out in the elements you don't want to sit around waiting for ink to dry, so get another pen."

"Okay."

"I find pens in the trash. People give up on them or figure they've had one forever, it must be close to dry. Usually they keep working for me."

I made a mental note to buy cheap pens.

"Did you bring something to trade?" He asked.

"No. I really just wanted to see a geocache and see where they would have hidden one at this hill I'd seen so many times."

"Well, there you go," he said. "If you want to trade you're supposed to trade up. Put in something of equal or greater value than the thing you take out. If I could afford it, I'd make sure each cache was well stocked. As it is I can only trade if I find something that another person might want. Sometimes I trade something I took from another cache, just to trade. I don't actually keep any of the swag. But it's fun to trade."

"Swag?"

"Stuff we all get. Though people will say it doesn't stand for that. It's the little tradeable things you see in there. Some people trade, some people don't. Some people actually collect the stuff. It varies a lot. The point is that if you do trade at least keep the cache interesting."

All right, so geocaching lesson number one was complete. Box checked.

Chapter 5

It was the next cache that really caught my attention and it wasn't because of the contents. It was sneaky. It was almost invisible. And it was at a spot I had passed a hundred times.

Since Darby wanted to see the trail under the Hollywood sign I drove to one end of the trail and parked. We sat in the car and Darby looked on my GPS to see if there was a cache nearby. I only had about twenty caches downloaded but they were all in this neighborhood so I knew I did have the Hollywood sign caches in my GPS.

"Two hundred six feet," he read. "Over there. Shit it's right next to that house."

"It's okay," I answered. "That's where the trail is."

"Oh, good. Maybe the people in that house are used to people passing by every so often."

"I'm sure they are," I said, though I hoped they didn't recognize me.

As it turned out the cache was right over the fence from the yard and people were outside. It was rather unnerving knowing I could be spotted in a moment and have to answer questions about my parents. They probably knew more about my parents than I did, but I couldn't admit it.

One of the wonderful things about the beginning of the trail didn't disappoint me this time and, since we were looking for a geocache I actually was able to enjoy it even more. Both sides of the trail were covered with thin, spindly trees and the trees were full of little chirping birds. The birds would not hold still for a second. As soon as I thought I spotted one, off it would fly again. When I came here to walk the trail I barely caught a glimpse of them, but this time they flew about as if they knew where the cache was. I never saw them long enough to distinguish any markings, but at least I got to enjoy their company longer than if I had been hiking. As we looked for the cache probably a dozen people walked by to have their picture taken with the Hollywood sign in the background. A few people actually asked me to take a group photo, which I did. It was a normal part of walking the trail. I had taken dozens of similar pictures in the past. However, this geocache proved to be even more difficult than the one at the cave. The birds, I thought, must know where it is. They are chirping out clues, but we just don't understand them. Darby looked in the oddest places. He even looked inside the pipes that made it so the trail could be blocked. But the cache was nowhere to be seen. Once again, it was just an odd little bit of different color that drew my attention and I reached in to find a very small cache attached to it.

"I found it!" I proclaimed and Darby glared at me with disapproval of my outburst.

He waited until some hikers had passed before saying, "Take a muggle count before you tell all the world the cache is here."

"A muggle count?"

"We don't advertise where caches are located. If muggles know about a cache they might come back to see what it is."

"And the muggles are… those people?" I asked.

"A muggle is anybody who is not a geocacher."

"Ah, evil creatures, these muggles," I said mockingly.

"Just keep it in mind."

"Okay."

Then he smiled, "It is a cool hide though. Great cammo. The muggles would never spot it. I approve."

I felt like I was learning a foreign language.

We signed the log between groups of hikers, then waited for a couple to pass before slipping the cache back in its hiding spot.

"There!" I said.

"Earl! Earl! Yooohooo! Earl! What are you doing here? Do you want a ride?"

Oh no! I looked up and there was my mother sitting in her idling, shiny white Mercedes Benz.

"Uh, no! No, I don't," I replied. "We're just going to hike the trail."

"Well, stop by later!" she replied and drove away.

"Who was that?" Darby asked. "And do you regularly get hit on by rich, old women?"

"No," I said dodging the first question. I pushed buttons on the GPS until Darby took it from me, and with a few clicks brought up the next cache.

"It's just down the trail," he said. "And it's a regular size."

"How big is a regular size?"

"Oh, think of… a shoe box, or a large peanut butter jar. About that size."

"We ought to be able to spot that," I said in an effort to point him down the trail. "Let's go."

As we hiked we met two more groups of people who wanted their picture taken. I used to think of them as tourists but I think just as many locals brought people to the spot and had their picture taken over and over again with different family members and friends. Taking a picture of a person in front of the sign was always a bit tricky. I had to balance the picture in such a way that I got the sign, but captured as much detail about the person as I could. I also never knew if they wanted the antennas on top of the hill to show. So usually I tried to cut off the antennas, and include the whole sign, and as much of the people as possible.

The trail was very spacious and easy to walk on. It had to be because sometimes large groups hiked the trail. It wasn't too bad when we were there, though individuals and small groups passed by from both directions. I wondered about the people walking towards us because I knew the parking that direction was limited even more than the end we started at. As we closed in on the geocache I was relieved to discover that it was not right on the trail. However, when I looked at the spot it had to be in I didn't see a way to get to it. It appeared to be a terrible tangle of brush.

"It can't be up there," I said.

"It can," Darby said. "Come on, there's got to be a way in. Or maybe the GPS is playing tricks on us. Maybe if we move around we can get a better reading."

We moved off the trail and looked for a way into the brush but it was thick and the only way I could see to get to the cache was to army crawl. I wasn't quite ready to do that. It seemed impossible for army crawling through scrub to be a requirement for finding a cache. If it was, I didn't think my patience would last through many geocache hunts. While we were off the trail the people on the trail didn't bother us much. But eventually Darby and I considered the fact that we were not going to get to it from the south or east. The only way in had to be from the trail.

"How are we going to do that?" I asked. "The muggles will see us."

"Where's that camera that you had?"

"I didn't bring it."

"What? With the Hollywood sign right up there on the hill?"

"To me it's as much of a landmark as Bob's Liquor store on the corner. I wouldn't take a picture of Bob's."

"Well, carry it. People can't question why you might want a picture of a bird or a bug or the Hollywood sign, and taking pictures makes a good stall tactic and helps you fit in where you might stand out."

We waited until the tourists were further away and then made our way down the trail until we saw a tunnel through the brush.

"Geotrail," Darby said. "Too bad we didn't see this in the first place."

We waited for a man and his dog to pass by and then we ducked into the brush.

I have to admit that I never noticed how interesting the trunks of bushes could be. They were twisted and gnarly and old despite the low growth. The bushes took on an aged appearance and I could easily envision a whole elf village under the canopy.

Once we started up the hill the cache wasn't difficult to find at all and I learned another geocaching lesson. The cache had three odd things in it that Darby called Travel Bugs.

"Bugs, like bugs that crawl around on the ground?" I asked.

"Well, yes and no," he said. He found one with a silver tag and showed me the logo on it. It looked like a dung beetle made out of scanner code. "Technically this is a Travel Bug, but the term really applies to anything that a travel tag is attached to that is meant to travel from cache to cache by way of geocachers. The first ones were these metal Travel Bugs. Later different designs came out but we still call them Travel Bugs. See the code?"

"Yeah."

"There are three things the code is used for. This bug belongs to a geocacher. It travels from cache to cache and the owner can track its travels. If you just want to tell the owner that you saw it you *discover* it. If you take it with you *pick it up* or *retrieve* it from a cache. Then when you leave it in a different cache you *drop* it."

"And if I take it?"

"You promise to help it fulfill its mission."

"I what?"

"When you log that you have it you can read what its mission is. Some have no mission and you can drop it into any cache it will fit into, but some have very specific missions. If a Travel Bug has a mission you should either help it along, or put it in a Travel Bug hotel."

I was beginning to scratch my head with all these trivial and odd sounding terms.

"Too bad we don't have a smart phone. We might be able to read the missions."

"Are you going to take one?" I asked.

"Me? No. Sadly, I don't know how long it will be until I can find a safe place to drop it."

"Should I?"

He thought for a moment. "Take one just so you can look it up later. If you can't help it fulfill its mission let me know and I'll help you find a cache to drop it in."

"Which one should I take?" I asked.

He looked over the three Travel Bugs. One was a rock with a hole through it and a metal dolphin tag attached. The one with the old style Travel Bug had a very large, green fishing lure on it. The hooks had been cut off. The third was a red, metal racecar with Mickey Mouse at the wheel and a tag of a red pirate parrot attached by a light chain.

"Well, just looking at them I'd say the lure and the rock were sent out by adults and Mickey Mouse was probably sent out by a kid. Kids are less likely to have a specific or difficult mission in mind. The lure might want to visit fishing places. The rock might want to visit geologic places. You choose."

I felt a little silly helping an inanimate object to fulfill its mission. But I chose the Mickey Mouse because I thought a kid would be easier to please.

"So, what do you think of geocaching?" Darby asked as we hiked back to the car.

"I feel like I've been drinking out of a fire hose," I said.

"Oh, too much geospeak?"

"You could say that."

"Well, what did you think of the activity without the drinking part?"

"I liked the little one."

"Small."

"Yeah. I caught a glimpse of what you were talking about. Even if there was nothing in it. There was just that second when my brain went *ding!* And I knew I'd discovered something."

"Do you want to go again?" he asked.

"Let me go home and see what this Travel Bug's mission is. I might have to. But first, I promised you dinner. Where do you want to go?"

"Oh I… I couldn't ask you to do that," he stammered.

"Nonsense. I made you miss a day of work, so the least I can do is make sure you eat. What haven't you had in a while?"

He had to think and I have to give him credit. He really tried to think of a place that had something he wanted but didn't cost too much. It made me feel guilty.

"Darby, are we good enough friends for me to tell you something without being judged and have you hate me for it?"

He stopped and so I told him to sit down. We found a spot by the side of the trail and sat cross legged on the ground.

"I'm not as broke as you think," I began. "That 'old lady' that asked me if I wanted a ride? That was my mom and she thought I left my car at her house, which is two blocks away."

"You mean one of those houses that we passed… you grew up in?"

"Yes, that's what I mean, though we didn't pass her house."

"She's rich and she lets you live…"

"However I please," I added. "It's not like this," I said indicating the million dollar homes below the sign. "But it's too comfortable for my liking which is why I ended up at your camp. I thought if rich people are so miserable being rich what must it be like for poor people? I went looking for a homeless camp. I didn't know what I would do or find. I found out that everybody has a story and poor folks have the biggest hearts and they don't judge a man by his belongings. They judge them by their character. And to be honest, I don't feel like I measure up. Not in my world or yours. I'm a misfit. But I can definitely afford to buy you dinner."

He just sat there and stared at the ground.

"Are you okay?" I asked.

"Yeah," he barely choked out.

"Darby, I'm sorry. I'm tired of living a lie, but you don't have to worry. I…"

"I won't ask for money," he said.

"Darby, forget the money issue."

That statement failed miserably. He then thought I was withholding something from him.

"Stop," I said. "Stop and listen to me. I know you've got your pride. I know you don't want to ask for money. And I also know that you have a need. Can we talk about this on a factual level?"

"Talk about what?"

"I want you for my friend no matter where you live. If you want off the streets I can help, without damaging your pride. If you want to stay on the streets that's fine. That is strictly your choice. One of the first things I learned from you and Henry is that people like different lives. I doubt Henry would leave camp even if I went around handing out money. He's entitled to his life on the road. Just like you are if that's what you want. But if you want out I have a temporary solution that could bring about a permanent solution. All I ask is that you accept my company while we figure this out."

"Figure what out?"

I was taking a great leap of faith in the human race.

"I want to hire you to teach me about geocaching. I want to travel and see the world. My mother suggested Paris, but I don't want to see the Paris she wants me to see. I want to see Paris through geocaching. I'll pay your way. Your room and board will be covered. You'll be paid basic wages on top of that. You can save it for housing when we get back or you can spend it all on booze. As long as it doesn't interfere with our travels that's up to you. Think about it. Paris first. Then? Who knows? We'll have to see what the future brings. Now, can I buy you dinner?"

He didn't answer for a long time. He sat there just trying to gather his thoughts. He wouldn't look at me. When he did speak, he almost whispered and I knew it wasn't me he was talking to. "Adele, I'll try baby. I'll try."

Chapter 6

I swallowed hard.

"Dinner first. Then we have some planning to do. Later, a passport."

"You're sure?" he asked.

"If you will go with me? Yeah. If you don't want to go, all I can ask is your forgiveness and friendship. But, yes, I'm sure. We can even go visit that old lady who was hitting on me."

"You mean go into one of these houses?" he asked.

"Sure, only be prepared to be insulted. She won't like you. But she's living in another world. You have to remember that."

"No, I guess I'd rather be spared that," he said. "But you can point out the house to me as we go by."

"Okay, I don't blame you one bit for passing up that fine chance to be insulted. She does the same thing to me without intending to."

"Her own son?"

"I keep looking for that silver spoon," I said and opened my mouth. "Ith I coul find it… I'd shpith it outh."

When we walked up to the Escort Darby quipped, "Nice car!"

"If you'll drop me off at my building tonight you can borrow it to help you get ready for the trip. You'll have to gather some records, get a copy of your birth certificate, apply for your passport at the post office, get your picture taken, get copies made of your driver's license. I'll give you an allowance to cover the passport and paperwork. If there's some left over use it for travel clothes, a suitcase and stuff you'll need for the trip. I think we better make a list of the things you will need."

We went to the coast for dinner. On the coast people dressed casually. They might have even taken a dunking in the ocean fully clothed. So it didn't matter as much what you wore at a restaurant by the beach. These were also restaurants where Darby could order whatever he wanted and get something half way nutritious. He looked uncomfortable.

"You don't mind this?" he asked.

"It depends on what this is," I said.

"The restaurant? The wine glasses on the tables? The expense?"

"The only thing that I mind is you worrying about it."

"Sorry."

"Maybe we should make that list. Let's see. Paper, paper, I need something to write on."

I ended up writing on the napkin my drink was sitting on. Birth certificate, driver's license, passport, picture...

"What address do I use?"

"Mine. I'll write it down. And if they ask for a utility bill to prove you live there I'll give you one and you can tell them that the bills all go to your roommate. Let me know when your passport arrives and then we'll make travel plans."

"You'll know when my passport arrives because it will go to your house."

"Oh, yeah. Then I'll come tell you. If you end up too short on cash to get a good suitcase let me know. They take a beating and you want one that will stand up to it. Make sure it has wheels. It will be infinitely easier to get around airports if your luggage has wheels. There are a thousand things that will help you but we don't need to get into that now. Do you think you need a new GPS for a trip like this?"

"Earl, I'm not going to ask you for anything. Got that? Anything."

"Got it," I said and made a mental note to include a suitcase and GPS in his requirements.

"Is your dinner okay?" I asked.

"It's great," he said. "Do you know how long it's been since I've done this?"

"No."

"Years! I think, now that I stop to figure it out, it's been three years. Last time I went to a restaurant like this was for my anniversary. Right before everything went south."

"Well, get used to it," I told him. "This is the only way to eat while we're traveling."

"So, what do I call you?" he asked. "Are you my boss?"

"I'm your friend. While we are traveling together we are just two guys with roughly the same plans."

"But if you tell me to do something."

"Take it as a friend. You know one of my greatest fears ever?"

"What?"

"My greatest fear was that if you and Henry found out I really had money that you would disown me. You'd call me a liar and ask me not to come back."

He looked me in the eye, "We have friends with and some without. You'll not be judged by your possessions but by your willingness. Henry told me that when I first came to camp."

"And that's why I was worried. I had withheld my willingness. But I did watch for opportunities. I just never got the impression that money was the solution."

"To what?"

"I didn't think a gift of money would help. A gift of friendship seemed more valued."

"And it still is."

"But I need someone to travel with, someone who can show me the ropes and get me started. I don't want to take the trip my parents envision. I want to discover something new."

"Surely you have rich friends."

"I have business associates. I have acquaintances. I have advisors. I have no friends."

"I wonder what the cachers in Europe use for swag," He mused aloud.

"I don't know. I guess we'll find out. Should we travel first class or do we want to ride as the peons?"

"That's your call, boss."

"I think it depends on the flight schedules. First class is much more desirable on long flights. I think you should fly first class once in your life. And I should try coach just to see what it's like."

"Uh oh, do you have a laptop?" he asked.

"Yeah."

"I wonder if hotels have the right hookups. I wonder if they have free internet access."

"Now you're talking. I can get adapters but I'm going to need some help. You can judge a cache by its description."

"No I can't. It's the logs that distinguish a good cache from a lousy cache. The logs and favorite points."

"See? I need your help."

And so it seemed as if I had my traveling partner. At first he seemed a bit standoffish, but as the idea of geocaching in Europe took hold of him he began to see the trip in a new light. He would be able to travel, earn an income and pursue his favorite hobby all at the same time.

It took a little poking around but I finally figured out how to check the Travel Bug's mission. I had to type the number on the back of the tag into a search field, but the number was all letters: ARCBWX. It seemed to have its own web page and there was a host of information about it if one cared to sit and read a while. There was a map of its travels, a picture, a description of the bug and a mission. It did belong to a little boy just as Darby had guessed. The boy was eight years old. He wanted his travel bug to visit theme parks. So far the Travel Bug had made a jump from New Hampshire to Colorado. Then it bounced around the south west United States before another geocacher brought it from Quartzsite, Arizona to Los Angeles. The log said, "I'm not going to any kiddie parks but maybe you can find a ride from here."

I read through the other logs and it seemed the geocachers hadn't given the boy much hope of his travel bug ever reaching a theme park except that last one who went by the name of Grandpa12. I thought it was stupid of me but I felt sorry for it. The Travel Bug was eight months old and still hadn't fulfilled even part of its mission. When I posted that I picked it up I promised to take it at least to the front gate of a theme park. Maybe I would take a picture at the sign, or maybe drop it into the nearest large cache.

I walked into camp the next day ready for opposition or bitterness. It was much quieter than usual, but they greeted me warmly. "Darby, do you want to fulfill a Travel Bug's mission?" I asked.

"What's it want to do?" he asked.

"Visit amusement parks."

His eyes lit up and just as quickly went sad.

"Earl, I'd like to, but... I can't. I can't do something like that without Adele. It wouldn't be fair."

"Would her mother let her go?"

"With us? No. She would be very suspicious if we just showed up at her door and asked for Adele."

"Rats. Okay, I guess I can understand that."

"Earl," Henry said. "Is it true?"

I was going to go to the theme park by myself but I thought it might be more important to talk to Henry. Henry was close to eighty years old. He reminded me of the men who sang *I've Been Working on the Railroad*. He looked like a train conductor and he spoke like a man used to hard labor. He was wise and he was caring. But he considered the camp to be his family and he was fiercely loyal to his family. His eyes were in a semi squint from living outdoors so long and his gray hair was always unruly because he couldn't afford haircuts. I wondered what he would look like with a haircut and a shave. Unrecognizable, I think. Still, he was a father figure to many.

"Yeah, Henry, it's true. Some random rich guy walked into your camp to see what it was like and he found out that he liked the people at the homeless camp better than his investment advisors."

Henry's eyes narrowed. "I gotta think about this," he said.

"Okay, if you have any questions let me know."

"Can we sleep in your car?"

"The one Darby has? Ask Darby. He needs it to do a few things for me."

"What are *you* driving?" Henry asked.

"My other car. It's a couple of blocks away."

"Why? Are you ashamed of it?" he asked. "You think we might do something to it?"

"No, Henry. I was worried that you would think badly of me having more than you."

He burst out laughing. "This is LA! Everybody has more than us folks here. We cain't hate 'em. They're everywhere! You know what they say, 'if you cain't beat 'em, join 'em.' I wish I sure as hell could, but not enough to actually do it. So do I hate you cause you got money and a fancy car? No! Just like I cain't hate the rest of the city. We get by here, Earl, you know we get by."

"You could get by better," I pointed out.

He looked at me as if I was talking gibberish.

"I get by as well as I want to get by. If I really, truly need help, maybe I'll ask. But if I ask you better have that fancy cell phone handy 'cause it might be you need to call 911."

"Don't wait that long," I told him. "We want you to be around for a long time."

"I already been around a long time," he reminded me. "I hear you're taking away our Darby boy."

"He wants to be able to provide for his daughter. You got a problem with that?"

"Me? No, no, I ain't got a problem with that. He knows his way back if he wants to come back," Henry said. "And you do, too."

"We'll be around a while before we leave and after we leave, we'll be back."

"You wouldn't happen to need your lawn mowed," he said.

"Sorry, I don't have grass."

"Man's gotta have grass. What do you do? That fancy xeriscaping?"

"I live in an apartment and there is no yard. But if I did have one you could mow it every day."

Chapter 7

I felt a little silly standing out in the parking lot trying to hold the Travel Bug up where I could get a good picture of it with the amusement park sign in the background. I found a shopping area where I could take pictures without going into the park, but I kept seeing families of bouncy youngsters flocking to the gate and I couldn't help but wonder why I hadn't been one of them in all the years I was growing up. So I paid the admission price and went in. I walked around the park, hands in pockets fingering the little Mickey Mouse toy with its attached metal tag, thinking about why somebody would send a toy out into geocaches to be picked up and moved around. Maybe it was the muggle in me at the time. Maybe I was entrenched in high society too much, but I didn't understand why anybody would care to track a toy's travels around the world. What difference did it make where Jeremy's Park Hopper was or what it was doing? And then I thought it was no more trivial than my endless financial decisions. A stock gains or loses a point in a day. What difference does it make in the grand scheme of things? As much difference as where Jeremy's little Mickey Mouse Travel Bug is hiding today.

Kids rushed past me calling out "I wants" to their parents and the parents pushed strollers around trying to keep up. Looking around I began to feel very Scrooge-like. It wasn't that I resented them having fun or that I didn't want to have fun myself. I wondered if I even knew how to have fun. I stepped into a line to get on a ride. I stood in line for an hour and half to get on a jerky kids' ride just to see what they were so excited about. We were whisked through a maze of animated figures. I took a picture of Mickey Mouse while we were in the dark and nobody would notice a grown man taking pictures of a toy.

"That was soooo fun!" a little boy said as he jumped up and down on his way out the exit.

I sat on a bench in the middle of the park and studied my surroundings. Kids would run up and oooh and ah at the grand sight of the castle rising above them. Families stopped and took pictures.

"It must be a gazillion feet tall!" a little girl proclaimed.

It's an optical illusion, I thought.

"So, are you totally lost?" a young woman said as she plopped down beside me on the bench.

"No, I'm not lost. You can't really be lost if you have no destination."

"Ah, but you can," she said. "Are you waiting for somebody?"

"No, I'm here by myself."

"Really!" she said as if she didn't believe me. "Me, too. Well, I was supposed to meet my brother and his kids here but little Lindy got sick. I showed up and then I found out! So here I am in a park full of happy people looking for somebody to sight see with. I'm Jo."

"I'm pleased to meet you Jo. I'm Earl."

"Like the Earl of Sandwich?" she asked.

"I am the earl of nothing," I said.

"Do you want to go on a ride?"

"I did that."

"Oh come on, there's more than one, you know. Pick one! I'm up for just about anything."

I doubted that, but I had no doubt she would enjoy a ride so I stood up and started walking. She followed happily and I thought that was a good sign so we found a ride. It was a happy ride, with happy animated figures. Jo did enjoy every minute of it, laughing and pointing to the figures that caught her eye. She skipped down the ramp at the exit ready to find another.

"What's wrong?" she asked as we exited the ride.

"Nothing's wrong," I said. "That was fun."

She pouted at me. It was a cute pout.

"Do you want to help me fulfill a promise?" I asked.

"What kind of promise?" she asked.

"Well, it's going to sound silly, but I promised this kid that his toy would have its picture taken at a theme park." I pulled out Mickey Mouse with his metal tag. She took it and turned it this way and that wondering what the tag was for. "The pictures are going to be on a web page, so maybe you'd rather not be in them, but could you just hold it up so I can get the travel... the toy in the picture with buildings or a ride or something like that?"

"Well," she said. "At least you're easy going enough to make a promise to a kid. Sure! And I'm on social media. My pictures are everywhere, so I don't care about being in them."

"Would you like some mouse ears?" I joked.

"Oh! Yes!" she squealed. "That would be so cool!"

We went to the nearest souvenir shop and she began looking around. Mouse ears are about the easiest thing to find but she looked at sunglasses, scarves, purses, postcards, toys. She blew me a kiss wearing red and white polka dot sunglasses and a black and white striped scarf. I had to smile, though I didn't take the kiss seriously.

"You did it! You smiled! I can't believe it! You smiled!" she took the sunglasses and the scarf to the check register and I grabbed some mouse ears and followed her. I stuck my card on the counter before she could pay. She glared at me playfully.

She carried Mickey as we walked the park and rode her favorite rides. The candid pictures mostly showed Mickey but occasionally a photo spot would draw her attention and she would pose wearing the sunglasses, scarf and ears with Mickey Mouse perched on her hand. I really wished she would take the sunglasses off. She really had very pretty eyes. She hadn't dressed to spend the day with a man, but I could imagine what she might wear if she had. She was a bit of a flirt though she couldn't really decide if I was worth her time. I decided she must have been a cheerleader in high school. When she posed she didn't just stand there and hold Mickey up so I could focus on him. She stood on a bench with her feet apart and her hands raised high in the air. I could easily imagine pompoms in her hands and a short uniform creeping up her backside when she raised her arms. She didn't step timidly down from the bench, either, she leaped down ready to move on to the next ride, landmark or photo spot. I really only needed a couple of good pictures but Jo seemed to have taken the task to hand and as long as she was willing to pose I was willing to take pictures.

"Well," she finally said. "I need to think about finding some dinner. When Brad, Melissa and the kids didn't show up, I really only planned on shopping a little and going home, but this was fun."

"Thank you," I said. "You made my day much better."

"It was nice to meet you Earl."

"Likewise," I said.

"Well…"

"If you'd like to eat dinner here I'll buy."

"Really?"

"Or if you'd like to go somewhere else that would work, too."

She pouted again, then brightened.

"I've always wanted to eat at that underground restaurant. Did you see the diners while we were riding?"

"I did."

"Maybe they'll give us a table on the water! And Mickey really needs to see the parade. You have to take his picture at the parade. And in front of the fireworks."

The restaurant was very crowded but we had to expect that. There were not very many fine dining spots in the park and it was tourist season. I tried bribing the maître d but it didn't work. While we were waiting, the usual introductory questions were batted back and forth like a ping pong ball. What do you do for a living? Invest. She worked at a department store selling lingerie.

"You'd be amazed how some women have no clue was really looks good on them," she said. I wondered if she knew what looked good on her.

Where are you from? California native. She was born in Nebraska but her family moved to the area when she was young so she considered herself a California native, too.

What do you like to do? I didn't know. I told her I was still trying to figure that out. I told her about the geocaching. She thought it involved rocks. It was awkward explaining the hobby to her while I was still trying to learn about it myself.

"Mickey was in a geocache," I explained. "Supposedly he is a Travel Bug. He's got a web page online. On it this kid says the Travel Bug wants to visit theme parks. It had already traveled around the US without visiting a theme park, so I brought it here to fulfill its mission. If the kid is patient maybe I'll take it with me to Paris. Not that a kid cares about Paris."

"But there are parks there, too!" she said.

"Then maybe I'll drop it off in Paris," I said.

"Why are you going to Paris?"

"I'm not sure. Well, mostly I am going there because my mother wants me to see it. But after that I'm not sure where I will end up. Maybe back in Hollywood. Who knows?"

"You act like you're taking a bus ride to the zoo but you don't like animals," she said.

"I suppose that's true."

"What do you *want* to do?"

"I want to discover for myself what I want to do. I just happen to be lucky enough to be able to do that."

"You don't sound lucky."

"I know. And I don't feel lucky either, but feelings aside, I *can* climb a mountain just because it's there. So I'm flying to Paris, just because it's there."

We had a long time to stand there and chat and in our chatting we learned a little about each other. When we were finally led to a table she gazed out over the water watching for ride boats to come by.

"Somehow I keep thinking they will be pirate ships and then they turn out to be boat loads of Californian tourists," she said.

"At least they won't shoot at us."

"The tourists won't. You never know about the Californians."

"I've never met a violent Californian yet," I said.

"Me neither. Well, aside from insane customers. But they are just used to getting what they want and I can't help it if it's not in my store."

"You're kidding. Since when are women that determined to shop for lingerie?"

"Oh, wow. Some of them are monsters! But most of them are really nice."

"What do you like about your job?"

"Helping people. The nice ones. I have to say the difficult ones are hard to deal with and it can get crazy but when a woman walks in and she just wants a special something... it's fun."

"What about men?"

"There's not a whole lot we can do. Since they usually don't know the size, we show them what they want to see and tell them to save the receipt."

"Do they?"

"I don't know. We do get a lot of exchanges, but it's the wife that comes back, not the husband... or boyfriend."

"What job would you have if you could be anything you wanted?" I asked.

"I'd train for the Olympics," she said.

"Really? What event?"

"Umm, hm, maybe gymnastics? Beach volleyball?"

I laughed. "You don't even have an event but you want to train for the Olympics?"

"I didn't say I'd make it."

"May I suggest beach volleyball then?"

"We should get Mickey's picture down here. Even if the kid doesn't care, his parents would like to see it."

We set up Mickey with a fork and a bite with the ride boats going by in the background. After Mickey had his picture taken she pulled a pen out of her purse, wrote her phone number down on a coaster and stuck it in my shirt pocket. I didn't know what to say.

"Call me when you get back from Paris," she said.

"Okay."

Mickey had his picture taken at the parade. Jo clapped her hands when she saw the picture. "That's the one you should post!" she said. "He looks so happy there!"

The fireworks show was better than any I had seen. It was midnight before I realized I'd spent twelve hours at a theme park. I walked Jo to her car and there was an uncomfortable pause as we both wondered if the day or our time together merited a kiss. I figured if we were both waiting and wondering it was worth a try.

"Thank you for turning my day around one hundred percent," I said.

"Thank you for the glasses, the scarf, and the ears," she answered. "And for dinner!"

"You're welcome."

The kiss was polite. I didn't get dragged into her car or end up at her place or anything like that but I patted the coaster in my pocket and said, "Thank you Mickey," as I walked the half mile to my own car.

It was well past 1 a.m. when I finally got home and uploaded the pictures to my computer. I flipped through the pictures one by one. A few hadn't turned out but a few of Jo were stunning. I mean, she was stunning. And a few of Mickey were worth posting so I figured out how to post pictures to the Travel Bug's photo gallery. I left the coaster beside my computer keyboard as a reminder to call Jo when my travels were over.

Chapter 8

"Thank you," I said as I approached camp early the next morning.

"Why?" Darby asked.

"I spent the whole day with a girl who wants to grow up and be a beach volleyball player and sells lingerie at the mall."

"Wow. You're kidding!"

"No! Her name's Jo. She gave me her number."

"Did you try it?" Darby asked.

"No. She knows I am going to Paris and she said to call her when I get back."

"Dude, we're not even leaving until I get my passport and then we'll be gone who knows how long. She's going to forget you even exist. You should call her just to chat. Maybe she'll go out with you again."

I sat there staring at the phone for a long time. I picked up the coaster and entered Jo's number into my contacts list. When the only information to input was Jo and a number I thought perhaps she pulled a fast one on me. I didn't even know her full name. I thought it was kind of stupid that I would call a stock broker in New York City I had never met, but I was scared to call a girl I had spent half a day with.

There was only one way to find out if the number worked and that was to call it. No, there wasn't only one way. I could do a search for it online. So I typed the number into the search field and came up with a name. JoReilly James. Wow, it just might work. JoReilly sounded like an energetic lingerie saleswoman from Nebraska.

I decided if I called the very next day I would sound desperate so I waited a day and tried the number. It connected to an answering machine. I had to think quick.

"Hello? Jo? This is Earl, the man you met at the park. My travel has been postponed and I was hoping you would accept an invitation to dinner. I'll try back later or you can reach me at…" and I left my number.

I didn't hear anything for several days and kicked myself for getting my hopes up. Darby was having a hard time reaching his parents to get a copy of his birth certificate. He knew where his father was born but he only knew what state his mother was born in. His driver's license was expired. A process that was simple for me was very complicated for a man whose belongings fit into a backpack.

When I did hear from Jo it lifted my spirits immensely.

"I'm sorry for taking so long to call back," the message said. "I volunteered to work evenings since I have no social life. I don't get off until nine and then I have to help close. My weekend is usually Monday and Tuesday if that works for you."

So she hadn't written me off completely. I called back the next morning, giving her plenty of time to oversleep if she wanted to.

"Hello!" she said brightly.

"I thought we were going to end up in an ongoing telephone tag," I replied.

There was a small dog yapping in the background.

"Sorry," she said.

"It's okay. I bet there are advantages to having a different weekend than most people. There will be less waiting at a restaurant."

"That's true."

"So… can I pick you up and buy you dinner?"

"Tuesday?"

"Sure."

"Sixish?"

"That works for me."

She gave me her address and I hung up and did a little victory dance.

In the meantime Darby had declared I needed to go to geocaching boot camp if I was going to go geocaching in Europe. He had never been geocaching in Europe either but he imagined crowded streets and the need for stealth. He also told me that I needed to develop some geosenses and geocaching techniques to make the search easier. So he took me on a tour of LA to find some caches that he had already found so he would know what we were looking for. We found guardrail caches, fence post caches, magnetic nanos, hanging caches, LPCs. He seemed to dislike LPCs and when I'd found a few I couldn't argue, but he said it was a hide I needed to know about. And he told me my goal before we flew off to Europe was to find that cache at the restaurant in Long Beach.

I picked up Jo on Tuesday. I was surprised that she lived in a house. A retail clerk couldn't afford a house in LA. It was small and in a crowded neighborhood, but it was a house. A little white dog greeted me at the door. She unlocked the security door and smiled, then scolded the dog.

"She thinks she rules the place," she explained. "And she has no idea she only weighs seven pounds. She thinks she's a guard dog."

"You look beautiful," I said.

"Thank you. You too. I mean… you look great. Very handsome."

She did indeed know what looked good on her. I was used to being around nicely dressed women, but they dressed for business. Jo was shapely. She had plenty of make-up but she only used it to enhance her already fine features. I never thought about gray eyes being so sexy. I decided she hadn't dressed to attract sexual advances, though it was still tempting.

"What kind of a place do you like?" I asked. "Quiet and intimate? Loud and boisterous?"

"No sub sandwiches," she said. "I eat one every work day and I am thinking there's got to be a better solution for a quick lunch."

"Okay, no subs, it's a deal. Can you deal with a little geocaching reconnaissance expedition?" I asked.

"Ooo, sounds adventurous!"

"Well, it's at a microbrewery. I walked past on the sidewalk but I need a closer look. There are too many people around for me to find it. Maybe if we eat on the patio I can narrow down the hiding places."

"I think you need to explain this odd hobby a bit more."

"Okay, though it isn't really a hobby yet. I'm still deciding if it's worth pursuing."

She was a little taken aback by the Jaguar. I thought in her line of work she would meet a lot of people who drive luxury cars. She settled herself in the passenger's seat and ran her hands over the leather, then settled back to see what the night would bring. I pulled up to valet parking and we got out. I guess valet parking was just a habit. My parents had always used it. It left more time for talking and we saw fewer greasy parking garages.

We walked down the sidewalk until the brewery came in sight. I stepped out of the flow of traffic.

"Somewhere within reach of the sidewalk a container is hidden on the front of that restaurant," I explained.

"Really?"

"Yeah. So, what do you think? Would going in help or hinder the search?"

"We would definitely need a patio table."

"Is it too chilly?"

"No! I'm fine. What kind of container is it?"

"I don't know. Small. I can't imagine it being any larger than a deck of cards."

"And why are you looking for it?"

"Because it's my graduation from geocaching boot camp."

"Earl… you're speaking in mysteries."

"I know. The sport is a bit of a mystery to me, too. So, if you were going to hide something on the front of that building where would you put it?"

"I wouldn't."

"I know, but somebody did, and I've got to find it before I go to Paris."

"Why?"

"Because this cache is similar to ones I might encounter in France."

"Earl... this quest of yours... it seems a bit strange."

I sat down on a bench and sighed, "Look, you saw the car. My apartment is similar. I am tired of being high society. It is empty. I've never had a dog, never sat by a fire, never just stood outside and looked at the stars. When I went to the amusement park I was looking for something. I wanted to see how other people enjoy life. You helped in that department. I just... there has to be more and I know it won't be found in financial offices or in skyscrapers. It will be little things. Big things have disappointed me, so maybe I'll find joy in the little things. Darby has been teaching me to find these containers and I've seen little unknown corners all over this city. I can see the two worlds I live in inching closer together, but I'm still stuck in the middle. Someday, maybe, just maybe, the two worlds will join and I'll be able to walk in the world as a normal person, enjoying the sights around me, the people, the little yappy dogs, the cold in the morning and the sunshine of the afternoon."

"And this container..."

"Is a challenge. It's taken my mind off the stock market. That's good."

She didn't run away. I thought I was beginning to sound a bit unbalanced, but perhaps she could tell that balance was what I was searching for.

"Do you think it's in the tree?" she asked.

"I think it would be too easy to spot there."

"That ledge?"

"Too high. Maybe if we get a table we can get a different angle on it."

It wasn't the best second impression she could have gotten. We spent the time gazing in the rafters of the patio, speculating about how to hide an object in a public place. But it was really detracting from what a date really should have been. And, though I had a few places I could check out after business hours, I was no closer to Jo than I had been before.

"Next time *you* choose the place," I said. "I apologize for letting my puzzle interfere with your night out."

"That's okay. How long until your trip?"

"I don't know. It depends on the offices sending the documents we need."

I got another kiss out of it but I went home feeling like there might not be a third date. I turned on my computer and read logs for the cache at the brewery. It seemed many people gave up just because of the high number of people. Some came back, even sneaking in during the night, and had no success. The pictures helped. I thought people were not supposed to post spoilers but some of the pictures clearly showed the cache. It helped to know what I might be looking for. It was slim, easy to slide behind a larger object. Many of the pictures just showed tables full of diners. Others showed the street the restaurant was on. So many pictures and very little real information. I felt like a discouraged detective trying to crack a cold case.

"So, how did it go?" Darby asked when I brought his mail to the camp.

"Just for your information," I said. "Dating and geocaching do not mix."

"That's what you get for dating a muggle," Henry said.

"I'll never find that one at the restaurant. I looked. She looked. We even ate there and we couldn't spot it."

"No clues at all?" Darby asked.

"If you want to go back and get stopped by the police in the middle of the night, yes, but I don't really want to post bail to avoid jail time."

I handed the mail over to Darby. He opened the business sized envelope and pulled out several sheets of paper and began reading. His brow furrowed. He scowled and stomped out of camp. I caught up with him as he walked quickly down the grimy street.

"What happened?" I asked.

He didn't answer, just kept walking.

"Darby... come on man. You can talk to me."

He scowled again, reached down and pick up a small rock from the sidewalk. "This!" he said as he turned around indicating the dilapidated, graffiti-ravaged part of LA. He threw the rock as hard as he could and it bounced off the asphalt and rolled into the gutter. "This city! This life! This... this... everything! They've robbed me! Robbed me of a life. I got the fucking papers."

"But?"

"Earl, while I was out of touch..." he stalked off again, just raw emotions he didn't want on display for another man to see driving his feet. "She prayed for me every day. Praying I'd find a way off the streets. I thought she was praying, even today, yesterday, the day before. Shit. Earl, my dad said she's been gone for months. My mom. She believed in me. She would have taken me in any time but I told her I'd be fine. She praised me for sticking close to Adele. But she prayed I'd find a way off the street. I failed her. I failed her and her prayers were for nothing."

"No, they weren't. You will find a way. If you want it. We can make it happen."

"I'm not accepting charity."

"It's not charity. You're going to work your butt off. And your expenses will be minimal. You can save it all, find a place to live, find a job. You can beat this city. You can take hold of your life."

"But she'll never see it."

"She sees you every day. Now she's where she *can* see you. You never know what Adele's doing but your mom can find you whenever she wants to now."

I didn't know if there was an afterlife. I didn't know if Darby's mom could see him, but I knew some people believed in stuff like that.

"And she sees… this. A life thrown in the trash. A gutter life."

"And she sees that there's only one way you can go. So go that direction. Prove yourself. Show your mom that you can go from the street to being a dad again and even farther than she ever dreamed."

It's funny what a man can come up with in the heat of a problem. I had no idea if Darby could pull himself up by his bootstraps. Some homeless people settle into the life and they are content. Like Henry. I was beginning to think Darby was not meant to be homeless. I could picture him as a business man, in slacks and a polo shirt, dealing with the public. He could do it. If I could just figure out how to unravel his mistakes and darn them back to cover the hole he'd dug.

"Make your mom proud. Go to the top of the Eiffel Tower and send her a promise that you will not go back."

"I can't do that."

"Why?"

"I don't see a way out."

"One day at a time. What papers did you get?"

"My dad told me where he and my mom were born, the basic information I was waiting on. He sent my birth certificate. It's typed on a typewriter," he laughed.

"How old *are you*?" I asked.

"There were computers then. It was just a backwards town I guess."

"I'm sorry about your mom," I said. "Is there anything I can do?"

"No. It's over. She's gone. Nothing can bring me to her bedside or to the funeral. I just curse this life, that I didn't even know. I might have been there, had I known. My dad would have sent bus fare… but I didn't know because I was fighting for a meal."

"You want a beer?" I asked. "Come on, let's go check out that brewery. I'll buy you a beer or two." Or three, I thought. Sometimes a guy just needs to sit at a bar and forget things.

And so we found ourselves sitting in that same restaurant I'd visited with Jo the night before. We started out at the bar because it was too early for a meal, then we drank enough that we needed to walk it off, so we ended up sitting outside the restaurant blearily studying it for signs of a geocache. It was between meals so there were not many people inside and the shoppers seemed to be on their way elsewhere.

"Jo and I agreed the tree would be a lousy hiding place."

"Agreed. Is it magnetic?"

"I'd never even thought of that. But… no… I've seen a picture of it. It doesn't look magnetic."

"It's not a nano?"

"No. It's about four inches long and an inch in diameter."

"Like a match container?"

"Longer."

"What is it? It isn't matching up with any caches I've seen."

"I know, me too."

"Where'd you see the picture?"

"On the web page."

"In the gallery?"

"Yeah."

"Why didn't you show me?"

"I thought you could look if you wanted a spoiler."

"Oh! Oh! I got it!" he said. "Was it a preform?"

"What's a preform?"

"It's a… hmm, I think it's a two liter bottle before it gets blown up to bottle size. It looks like a large test tube with a soda lid on it."

"I… don't know. I've never seen one. But this is brown. Are they brown?"

"No. But it could be painted."

"The picture didn't show the lid. But it sounds like it could be."

"That would just be cruel if they put it up there," he said.

"Yup. I ruled that out just for that reason."

"How can we look up there for a legitimate reason?" he asked.

"I've got an idea," I said.

"Oh no. We are not climbing up there."

"We need to go shopping."

"How will shopping help us look on top of that ledge?"

"Come on," I said. "Pretty soon diners are going to start showing up."

"What are we shopping for?" He asked as he followed me down the street.

"I don't know yet."

It had to be something that two half-drunk guys would be tossing around, but want back if it landed on the ledge. A wallet? Why would they be tossing around a wallet? A ball? Nah, not worth the trouble. A Frisbee? Still not worth the trouble. I found the nearly perfect solution, and I blame the beer, but hey it worked! It cost me forty bucks but it was worth it for the memories it created.

"What are you doing!" Darby asked as I set the remote control helicopter and roll of tape on the counter.

"Reconnaissance mission in the making!" I said.

He stared at the box not quite believing what he imagined me trying to do. We pocketed the receipt, took the helicopter and tape out to the sidewalk. I opened the box and carefully removed the helicopter.

"Shoot. Do you have batteries?" I asked. I ran back into the store and bought batteries.

Within a few minutes we had the helicopter hovering over the sidewalk.

"Too bad they don't make helicams," I said.

"That would be cool," Darby admitted. "What's the tape for?"

"Let's see if it will fly with the tape on."

"You've got to be kidding."

"No! If we balance it right it should fly. After all it came with a hook so it could pick up rings. It can take a little weight."

"But what's the tape for?"

"To stick to the cache!"

"Oh shit. You are not sending the helicopter up onto that ledge."

"Why not?"

It was a very delicate maneuver. The ledge was narrow and if I allowed the helicopter to stray too close the blades would hit the wall and break. Add to that the fact that the cache would probably be laid against the wall and there was little hope of finding it. Over and over we attempted to get the helicopter up onto the ledge and over and over we chickened out. Finally I needed a break from the fine motor skills so I just flew it around hoping it wouldn't crash on any shoppers. People would stop and watch the mini helicopter flying around and look for the man at the controls. When they spotted me they just smiled, waved and continued on their way. It was a fluke really, that we found the cache at all. Darby shifted on the bench we were sitting on and he jarred me a bit which caused the helicopter to dart low.

"Whoa! Watch it!" Darby said, but then as the helicopter continued on higher his eyes stayed fixed on one spot.

"What?" I asked.

"Land the copter," he said.

He stood and walked to the railing of the restaurant. I followed his gaze up into the supports of the patio cover. Maybe! Maybe that was it! Darby looked both ways but there were shoppers walking down the sidewalk.

"Do you see it?" he asked.

"I think so."

"How do we get it? The helicopter can't get in there."

"No, but either one of us could reach it if no one was looking."

We looked both ways again.

"Create a distraction," he said.

"Okay."

I eased the helicopter into the air and made it fly circles around the bench. I buzzed a few shoppers. They swatted around their heads. Then a little boy saw the helicopter.

"Mommy! Look! A toy helicopter! It's sooo cool!"

He jogged over and asked to try it.

"Do you know how?" I asked.

I got so busy trying to explain the workings of the helicopter that when Darby came over with a smug expression I didn't even realize he had the cache.

The little boy tried to fly the helicopter and nearly crashed it so the mom took the controller away, handed it to me, and continued down the sidewalk with a squalling kid in tow.

"Can you put it back?" I asked.

He nodded. We sat down on the bench and signed the log.

"Thanks for the distraction, partner!" he said as we rose to put the cache back.

"Need another one?" I asked.

"Nah, it's easy once you know where it is." He looked both ways, spotted a shopper and said, "Dang! What is that!" The shopper turned to see what he was looking at and he slipped the cache in slick as a whistle.

"Nice move," I said and we took our helicopter back to the car.

I have to admit the helicopter looks very cool cruising through my apartment with the city lights behind it. I can picture the scene as part of an action movie. But there is something a bit lonely about a man recreating action movie scenes in his living room when he should be out on the town talking to a beautiful woman or hunting for little hidden containers in the big city.

Chapter 9

Jo and I managed to have one more date before Darby and I departed for Paris. I let her choose the restaurant this time. I could tell when I picked her up that she had chosen someplace that was special to her. She wore a dress this time with high heeled shoes. Her blonde hair tumbled down her back in wavy cascades contrasting with the blue of her dress. She had gorgeous legs.

"Where would you like to go?" I asked.

"I can choose any place?"

"Yes, of course."

"I've always wondered what it was like. Can we go to Horatio's?"

It seemed a curious place to me because it was a popular restaurant to take important business contacts if you wanted to impress them. I had been there several times. In fact, my father had a table there that overlooked the city. Horatio's was located in a bank building, a very tall bank building. A few of the floors were rented by law firms and Hollywood plastic surgeons. There was also a less pricey restaurant on a lower floor that appealed to the bank employees.

"Horatio's is great," I told her.

It was almost like my car knew where it was going. My usual parking spot was open and it was close to an elevator. The parking spot was not really mine, but it was usually free because it was higher up in the parking garage. We glided to a stop and I opened the door for Jo. She waited for me to come around the car, another small hint that she was testing the waters. Usually women opened the door themselves and stepped out before I could reach the other side, but I noticed Jo waited. All these subtle clues were starting to add up. She was asking for a date to remember. Hey, I could play that game.

The interior of the elevators were elegant polished brass, and mirrors. It always seemed a relief after the gray of the parking garage. It was quite a maze to get to Horatio's but I led her through it with ease.

"All the hallways look alike," she said.

"I know. It's this way."

The whole of downtown LA was before us as we entered the restaurant. A tank of tropical fish lay against one wall. Blue and gold carpeting drew the eye toward large, plate glass windows. The skyline twinkled, bright and promising, a stark contrast to the version of LA that Darby lived in. The tables were covered in white, starched tablecloths. A gold-rimmed bread plate and a wine glass adorned each table. The napkins matched the blue of the carpeting.

"Oh my! I never thought of LA as beautiful before. I mean, it has beautiful areas but I've never seen it quite like this."

"The view from my apartment is almost this good," I said.

The maître d' stepped up.

"Is Mr. O'Connor expected tonight?" I asked.

"No, sir. Would you like his table?"

"That would be nice."

"Who is Mr. O'Connor?" Jo asked.

"My father."

"Your… and he has a table? Here?"

"Yes. You'll like it."

"And they know you here?" she asked.

"I've been here on business and with my father."

"And your mother?" she asked.

"Yes, I've been here with both parents. They are so busy they frequently lead separate lives, but we've been here as a family. We didn't eat at my dad's table, because it's a table for two."

"How can they stand it?" she asked.

"They have always been that way. They enjoy each other's company when they are together. They share a house. But they each have their own circles and business endeavors."

"And you?"

"I respect their lifestyle. But… I think they are missing out on something. I do not want to follow too closely in their shoes. Right now I am and I don't enjoy it. You could say I am trying to break free from affluence."

"Will you ever marry?"

"I hope so. What about you?"

"I… I'm not sure."

That answer somewhat surprised me. Though she didn't seem like the type of woman that would enjoy backyard barbecues and camping with the kids, she did seem like the kind that would like to share her home with family and friends.

"Why? Bad luck so far?" I asked.

"You could say that," she said shortly.

"I earnestly hope I don't add to your bad luck."

I ordered a bottle of wine and the stuffed tiger shrimp appetizer.

"I won't be able to eat dinner at the rate we're going," she teased, but there were only four shrimp in the appetizer. They were stuffed with crab and lobster and wrapped with bacon.

The waiter set down the shrimp and walked away when there were voices at the front of the restaurant. I didn't hear the maître d' but I did hear a familiar voice say, "That's okay, Juan. Let me just say hi."

There were quiet steps across the navy and gold carpeting and my father stood over the table.

"It does my heart good to see you enjoying an evening out," he said. "And what lovely company you keep!"

"Thanks, Dad. Jo," I said as I stood up. "This is my father, Ashton O'Connor. Dad, this is Jo…"

"JoReilly James," Jo said as she extended her hand in greeting. I cracked a smile at her accent, which I hadn't noticed until her own name didn't match the spelling I'd read.

"A pleasure to make your acquaintance," my father said as he gently shook hands. "Well, I won't take over your evening. Enjoy the table."

"Thanks."

"He seems a charming man," Jo said as he walked away.

"Should I tell him that?"

She shrugged. "What do you think of kids?"

"I doubt I get to find out," I admitted. "I have no nieces and nephews like you do. I have nothing against kids. But time is running out for me."

"Nonsense. People are waiting longer these days."

I glanced over at the table my father sat at. "If it's in my future to have children, I hope they teach me how to see the world. I have no lofty goals for children. I'd like to come down to their level rather than whisking them through life to success. Sometimes it's the journey and not the destination that matters."

She glanced at my father, noticed the exotic fish in the tank again and sighed at the scene of the city again. "I look around and think *what am I doing here?*"

"Why?"

"I never dreamed of actually being able to find this place and here I am with wine and appetizers…"

"What are you going to order?" I asked.

"I don't know. It all looks so good."

"Then may I recommend the Hightower Sampler?"

"What's that?"

"It's all Mariano's specialties in sample size portions. You'll probably get another one of the shrimp as well as his crab cake, Cajun prawns, a light salad with the house dressing, a miniature filet mignon and, oddly enough, some chicken nuggets. These are not your ordinary chicken nuggets, though. They are tender white meat encrusted in a cashew and parmesan cheese combination that makes you forget all about chicken."

"What are you going to order?" she asked.

"I think I'll go directly for the prawns, but ordering the sampler will show you what you like for next time."

"Next..."

"If you'd like to come back."

"Earl I... I'd love to. When are you going to Paris?"

"I don't know yet. As soon as my friend gets his passport."

"And you?"

"Me? I've always had one. International travel is nothing new to me. Taking a trip for other than business reasons is the part that will be odd for me. How will I fill my time if not in business meetings? I need to start planning my itinerary so I know my days will be full."

"And your friend?"

"He's never traveled. And he's in need of a helping hand. I need his knowledge, and he needs a paycheck. It works out well for both of us. Just two guys off on a grand adventure."

"What does your friend do?"

"He works for me. He is teaching me how to become a world class geocacher. By the way, that cache at the microbrewery? We found it! Darby and I went back the next day and he finally found it. After three tries in broad daylight. Actually it helped to go before the lunch hour. There were only the early shoppers around."

"Where was it?"

"Just in an out of the way spot where it wouldn't be noticed."

"Does geocaching enter every conversation you have?" she asked.

"No, at least I don't think so. How could it? I barely know what geocaching is."

"But you get so animated when you mention it."

"I do?"

"Yes... you do."

She had a little bit of trouble deciding how to eat her dinner. Mariano believes that presentation is a large part of the dining experience and some of his entrees can look like sculptures. It takes a little disassembling to eat dinner at Horatio's, but I have never had a meal there that I didn't enjoy. Having somebody to enjoy it with made it even better.

"Don't laugh at me," Jo said in an awkward moment.

"I'm not. I know precisely how you feel. I've told Mariano that disassembly should not be required to eat one's dinner but he... speaking of which, smile and tell him it's wonderful."

"Good evening, sir, madam!" Mariano boomed. "How is your evening? Your meal?"

"It's superb," I told Mariano. "As always."

"Muy bueno!" He nearly shouted. I don't think Mariano ever learned how to talk quietly. He probably got kicked out of a lot of libraries as a student. "And the beautiful lady! You like the Hightower?"

"I do!" Jo beamed. "It's wonderful."

"Whata you like the most?"

"Well, I don't know. I haven't finished it yet. I loved the stuffed shrimp and the crab cake."

Those were the two that were easiest to figure out.

"I'm sure the rest of them are perfect as well," she added.

"Magnifique!" He went on to my father's table. "Ah Mr. O'Connor!"

"Good evening, Mariano."

"You letta your son steal your favorite table tonight. Why you not join them?"

"I can see he's busy," Dad said. "And I wish him the best of luck."

Jo blushed scarlet, not that she was shy. I imagined she'd be amazing if I got lucky, but I didn't think we were to that point in our relationship yet.

"Ignore him. He's a guy."

I suppose the date was successful. When I took her home and walked her to the door she seemed uncomfortable and I thought a kiss might be out of line until she said, "I don't want to pretend with you. Earl, would you come in. I want you to see who I really am. I'm not sure you understand..." She unlocked the security door, then the front door. I was glad she had deadbolts on both. "Come in. And welcome to my little home."

The dog barked and jumped around my feet as I stepped into heaven. It was like being wrapped in a warm blanket. I stood there and took a deep breath. She had an old overstuffed country style sofa and a ratty arm chair facing an analog TV. There were pictures on the walls and a mirror by the front door that I thought she used to check her makeup before work every afternoon.

She picked up the dog and then picked up a dog toy that had been stuffed between the sofa cushions. She set the dog and the toy down in a tiny dog bed. It scratched around in the bed, then lay down and huffed disapproval.

"It's beautiful," I said. "It's everything I never had in a home. Do you mind if I walk around?"

"Mind? No."

I walked to the back of the house and she started to stop me. When I reached the kitchen I could tell why. There were a few dirty dishes next to the sink. The refrigerator had children's drawings stuck to it with magnets. The dining table was worn. Some of the chairs had pads, some did not.

"You can't know how good this feels," I said.

"You're kidding."

"No. I'm not. The TV could use an upgrade. But I'd trade you in a heartbeat."

"I thought you said you had an apartment with a view of the city."

"I do. But it's nothing like this. It's… lifeless. This house belongs to a real person. A real person who loves animals. Who curls up with a good book and watches game shows and reality TV and soaps without HD. It's a house where real life happens. Did Lindy draw the pictures on the fridge?"

"Yeah, you remember?"

"Of course I remember. Looks like she has a colorful personality."

"Most of my family does."

"Does she come here often?"

"No, not often. The pictures she sent me in letters. The letters are only a few sentences on penmanship paper, but she tries."

"Do you answer her letters?"

"Oh yes! I do. The very next day. But I never have much news. Next time I will, though. I'll tell her that a handsome man took me out for a fabulous dinner in a fancy restaurant."

"You're so lucky. I mean that you have kids in your life and they care about you."

"Your father…"

"I have a father and a mother and I suppose they do care about me, but it's in such a highbrow way that it never comes across as love. I am just another one of their responsibilities. I am out in the world on my own, financially stable, so they can check that little box off. They wish me the best and they toil endlessly at making my inheritance larger. I don't need their money. They started me out with an investment portfolio that most people only dream of. I have no need to work. No need to do anything I don't want to. But the problem with having every need met is there is nothing to apply oneself to. I am in limbo. No one to provide for. No one to care for. Whenever I get on a plane it reminds me of my life. Just hanging in the sky and waiting to land. The plane lands. I go to meetings but my life never lands. It's still up there somewhere."

"Aw, Earl. You will land. One of these days you'll find your place. At least you are looking!" And she hugged me. It took me a second to hug her back. "Can we take a quick picture so I can email it to her?"

"Sure."

"Just a quick selfie."

She went to find her purse and got out her cell phone.

"Okay, smile!" Click! She looked at the picture. "Aw, we can do better than that. My eyes look puffy."

It took three tries. We finally resorted to using the mirror beside the front door to tell us when the picture was framed right.

"At least we didn't have to resort to the bathroom mirror," she quipped.

Women have no idea how good they look and feel to a man. When they sit with the city lights illuminating their features or when they scrunch together for a picture it leaves a guy wanting just a little more. But I had to be content. At least she invited me in. And she liked me enough to send a picture to her niece.

"When I get back from Paris I'll show you my place and you'll see why your house is so comfortable to me," I told her.

"I bet it just needs a few pictures on the walls," she said.

"I think it needs a new tenant. But I'll go to Paris and see if I can land long enough to find a few caches. My mom said to visit Paris but I don't think she quite had my idea of recreation in mind. I'll send her a postcard of the Eiffel Tower and she'll think I'm going to operas and walking through art galleries."

"And you will really be…?"

"Tromping through the city streets looking for small hidden containers. Would you like me to bring something back for you?"

"Oh, Earl, you already said you were not going there to shop. Don't worry about me."

"I'm not worried about you. I'd love to buy you something while I am gone. It will give me something to do."

"I couldn't…"

"Couldn't what? Accept a gift?"

"I'll tell you what. If you find a Christmas tree ornament that reminds you of me, get that. Just a little one."

"Thank you. You got it," I said. I was so afraid she wouldn't accept a gift from me. At least I knew there was one thing she wanted. I gave her a hug, and a kiss, and grudgingly left her wonderfully warm home and stepped back into my life of luxury.

Chapter 10

When I walked into my apartment I looked across the room at the lights below, then I walked around looking at my walls. They were painted white. Each wall had a large picture on it. One, large, picture. Each time I had spent more than a week in a large city I sought out a picture and had it shipped back to arrive after I returned home again. I had one of the New York City skyline, the watery streets of Venice, a market street in Shanghai, a Japanese garden, and a boat in a bay near Hong Kong. My house looked like a swanky travel office. The Shanghai one appealed me the most. There were people in it. Busy people. People with lives to lead, places to go, and people to visit.

When another letter came for Darby I was relieved. I wanted to get the trip over with. Despite our three dates I still thought that Jo would take the opportunity to see other men while I was gone and I'd be another number in her little black book when I returned. After all, a girl bold enough to walk up to a complete stranger at an amusement park and spend the day with him was bold enough to get picked up nearly any place she went.

I brought the letter to camp but Darby wasn't there.

"He'll be along in a few hours. Windows to wash. Lawns to mow. Now that he has your car he can find yards father away."

"How does he buy gas?" I asked.

"Farther he can go the more lawns he can mow, the more gas he can buy," Henry said.

I sat down on a dirty blanket they had stretched out on the ground.

"Henry, have you ever been married?" I asked.

"Shore 'nuf."

"What was your wife's name?"

"Winifred. She was a dear. The cancer took her. We had a home then. A little house, not much to it, but she made it a home. She was a good cook. Man I miss her cookin'. Real meals that'll stick to your ribs, you know what I mean?"

"Yes, and no."

"You, who never been hungry?"

"I admit I've never been particularly hungry, but all the meals I eat are only meant to keep me from starving for three or four hours. They never look like they would stick to my ribs. You want a meal? I'll bring you a meal."

"Naw, Earl, a man's gotta do for hisself or he don't amount to a hill o' beans."

"How about a hill of beans?" I asked.

"We don't need no gas powered folks, neither."

"Still beans are food. Add a little ham or bacon."

"Quit it," he snapped in a friendly way. "You's making me hungry. Winifred was like Darby's mom. He was sittin' right where you are, tellin' me 'bout his mom. Gooood woman she was, prayin' for her son to come home. You think he can do it?"

"Yeah, he can do it, if he'll swallow his pride."

"You see to it," Henry said. "I'll back ya. That guy's gonna have a shorter than normal life if he don't do somethin' soon."

I came back nearer to dinner time. Sometimes the camp would pool their resources and cook one meal in a pot and so I thought I might catch Darby at camp at dinner time. I wasn't disappointed.

"Sit down, Earl. Did you bring a spoon?" Henry said.

"No, I didn't. I brought mail for Darby."

"Did it come?" Darby asked.

"I think so. It's your mail. You open it."

He tore open the envelope and pulled the passport out.

"This little book, empty as it is, cost me a whole month's food," he said.

"Hopefully it'll feed you for longer. When do you think we can go?"

He pulled his allowance out of his pocket. "I've got this much left to buy a suitcase, and clothes."

"How much is there?" I asked.

"Almost three hundred dollars."

"You've been very careful," I said.

"That's what you *got left?* After all that finagling you did?" Henry asked.

"It's not my money," Darby said.

"It's to be used for whatever you need for the trip," I told him. "I'll buy the tickets. We'll plan to leave next week unless the tickets aren't available."

I tied up some loose ends, attended a few meetings at my father's company, and bought the tickets. Then I found out that it was a lot easier to tie up loose ends, attend meetings and buy tickets than get a homeless man ready for international travel. The few clothes he had hadn't been washed in weeks. He had bought two pairs of pants, two shirts, all new socks and underwear, but he was so glad to have new clothes that he wore those and they needed washing as well. We didn't know how long we would be gone and two new outfits were not going to last long on the road. One whole day would be taken up flying. We had a four hour layover in Moscow before flying all the way across Europe. We were going to arrive in Paris dead on our feet, check into a hotel and sleep twelve hours straight. He'd arrive in Paris with half his wearable clothes on his body and the other half would only last him one day, maybe two if we only found easy caches. I laugh at that now. Easy caches. Having only found big city caches I had no idea what I was in for. The Batman cache was the dirtiest one yet. I got a little dusty but I just threw my clothes in the bin and the laundry service picked them up, washed them, and delivered them the next day.

Another thing that I found difficult was downloading caches. There seemed to be plenty of them in Paris, but half the descriptions were in French. Some of the cache owners, knowing they had caches in areas frequented by tourists, had short versions of their descriptions in several languages. I was downloading caches one by one when I noticed the site had perks for members who upgraded their membership. Cool! A membership was cheap, so I tried it and then I found I could make lists and upload the whole list to my GPS at one time. This helped a lot. I began building lists for Paris and other nearby towns. Then I checked to see if there were any near the airport in Moscow. I think I got a bit carried away.

Two days before the flight I brought Darby home to get his packing done. It was a good thing I did because he looked at what I was packing and laughed.

"Earl, what do you think you're going to be doing on this trip?"

"Geocaching."

"Those clothes are going to get ruined. Where are your hiking boots?"

"I don't own a pair."

"Well, you better get some."

"Why? You don't wear them."

"That's because last time I needed shoes Goodwill didn't have any in my size. I'd have bought some two sizes too large but they didn't have those either. You want sturdy shoes. The slacks won't do. You need jeans or cargo pants. You'll want to layer your clothes."

We had to go shopping and whatever I bought for myself I also bought for Darby. He argued, but it only seemed fair. He walked straighter and taller in his new boots.

"Hiking boots shouldn't look like this," he said. "We need to break them in."

So he wore them everywhere, trying to get a little dust on them and work the soles so they moved with his feet. They weren't broken in but it made me smile when I saw him watching his feet. He hadn't had new shoes in several years.

I bought myself a better GPS and gave my nearly unused one to Darby. He insisted on sleeping on the couch. The night before our flight took off I made a quick stop at Jo's house.

Ding, dong! The doorbell chimed cheerily.

The door opened. "Oh! Earl! What are you doing here?" she said clearly embarrassed to be caught unprepared.

"I just wanted to stop by and say goodbye. My flight leaves in the morning. Early. Don't worry. You look wonderful."

She smoothed out some wrinkles and that's when I saw it. Her upper arms were covered with bruises.

"Jo, what happened to you?" I asked.

"Nothing! Nothing at all."

I opened the security door past the wide crack she had opened it and she began looking for an easy escape.

"This doesn't happen without cause," I said.

"Don't worry. It'll go away," she assured me.

"I want to know who."

"No. It's better if you don't."

"This… is wrong," I said, anger flaring. "Anybody who would grasp you that roughly has gone too far."

"It'll be all right. I can't talk right now. I'll see you when you get back."

"I can cancel," I suggested.

"No!"

"If you protect this scumbag you're only asking for more."

"I… I know. It'll be okay. Really."

She seemed anxious to get rid of me and I can't really blame her. In her eyes I could only stir up trouble.

"I really can cancel my flight," I insisted gently. "If you need someone here."

"No, go on. Have a great time."

That last statement left a bitter taste in my mouth. How could I have a good time when some girl back in LA was getting pushed around against her will? Turning my back on that door was one of the hardest things I have ever done. It made me feel like a scumbag myself.

I barged into the apartment, making Darby jump.

"Sorry," I said.

"What's up?"

"Nothing."

He didn't believe me. I walked to the panorama widow and looked out over the city.

"Somewhere down there is a man who needs to be arrested," I said.

"There's a thousand of them, Earl."

"There is one in particular, but I can't do anything about it. How can I fly off to another country when he's loose out there?"

"You want to stay home?"

"No, I want that creep hauled on his ass and..." I sighed, "I don't even know who he is. Anyone who would treat a woman that way..."

"Jo?"

"How could I not see the signs?"

"What signs?"

I thought back but I couldn't think of any. Yet I didn't think this was a first. No. From her answers to my questions I thought she had dealings with this guy in the past. I sat down on the couch and watched the city below as if I could spot him from ten stories up, then got up and walked right up to the window.

"I can't do that," Darby said. "It's too far down."

"You'd get used to it after a while. Most of my business occurs high off the ground."

"I still can't believe you live like this. You seemed so normal before."

"I think the man who walked into your camp every couple of days is more like the man I'd like to be. This," I said indicating the apartment around us. "Is space. Just space. Expensive space. But it's no life for me. I want to be down there."

"So move."

"I think I will. I'm hoping the trip and the next few months will tell me where to move. Would you mind putting off the trip?"

"I don't know what's in your craw, but Jo's life is her own. It has been for a long time. And whatever she's dealing with is none of your business."

"What if the day I met her she wasn't looking for somebody to sight see with. What if she was looking for someone to help her?"

I turned the situation over and over in my mind. Jo had told me to go to Paris. If she wanted my help she would have accepted my offer to stay.

Standing in the airport the next day I knew I was sunk. I dreaded that plane taxiing to the gate. I knew as soon I handed my ticket to the agent and entered the tunnel that I was leaving Jo's fate in the hands of a man I didn't know and didn't trust. It wasn't the fear I'd feel for just anybody. We see people in the news meeting unthinkable trials and it's always somebody else's problem. No, this was my heart on the line and the line appeared to be a boarding gate.

"Dude, relax," Darby said. "You look as scared of flying as I feel. I thought you'd done this before lots of times!"

"I have. You didn't tell me you were scared of flying."

"Petrified."

"Why?"

"I've never flown before and the thought of being a thousand feet off the ground... Na uh, no way, no how, am I ever doing that. But... it's part of the job, so here I am shaking in my boots."

"At least you *do* have boots," I joked. "Just keep telling yourself it's all going to be all right. This is nothing. We will survive just like all those thousands of people who have flown over the ocean before us."

I didn't tell him it was more like 30,000 feet and millions had flown over the ocean. Some of them had even crashed terrifyingly into the ocean. But I wasn't afraid to fly. Air travel felt much safer than driving in LA. I was more afraid of what might happen to Jo in her own, safe, ideal house.

I sat with my back to the window just so I wouldn't see the plane coming. They'd just tell us when to board and I'd get on the plane and it would whisk me into the sky and after the wheels left the ground... I'd have no choice. I'd be Paris bound. I know men are not supposed to talk about their feelings, and I kind of stuck to that unspoken rule, but it was because I had very few feelings until I realized Jo meant more to me than any of my one night stands had. I brought out the laptop, signed onto the one social media website that I checked often. I looked up JoReilly James but she wasn't a member so I tried one of the more popular ones. I was thankful she had an unusual first name. There were several Joe Reilly James but they definitely didn't look like Jo. It took some clicking and reading but I finally found her profile page so I sent a friend request.

"I miss you already and I can't help but worry. Keep in touch," I typed into the message box.

"Earl, you're sunk," Darby said.

"I know."

"If you went back would you propose?"

"No. She's not ready for that yet. There's something going on that I know nothing about. It affects all her relationships with men. I think I need to take my time. But it's okay. If I can have patience and figure out why, maybe I can help her through it."

"And then what?"

"Then... we'll be free to pursue our own relationship."

"Then why are we going to Paris just to hunt for frustrating little containers hidden all over the city?"

"Bad timing," I said. "Just very bad timing."

The plane did arrive and the announcement came over the intercom that families with children and first class passengers could board. I had bought first class seats but I waited. I knew Jo wouldn't call, but I waited anyway. When, at last, we did board it was like taking a trip to outer space to me. I gathered my things and boarded after most of the other passengers. It was a large plane with many passengers. I usually don't notice when they close the door on a plane, but this time the sound echoed in my mind. I was Paris bound.

"Wow," Darby said when he saw our seats. "I thought flying was supposed to be like getting stuffed in a sardine can."

"The sardine can is behind that curtain."

"This is nice."

"And much more comfortable. Do you want the window or the aisle?"

"You're the boss. You pick your seat."

"Then I'll take the aisle. There's more space to use the laptop. Are you okay?"

"Yeah."

"You don't look too worried," I pointed out.

"Thanks."

"Are you scared?"

"I think I'll be okay till we get off the ground."

I didn't tell him that most jet accidents take place during takeoffs and landings.

He buckled up and sat looking important. He took the magazine out of the pocket in front of him.

"It's going to be a long flight. Take your time with that," I said.

"Sound machines," he said as he leafed through the ads. "It makes white noise. What is white noise?"

"It creates a sound that drowns out noises that irritate you. Like the air conditioners and heaters in hotels."

"But what does it sound like?"

"Like a TV when the channel goes away."

"People would rather listen to that than a heater?"

"Yes. Some people."

It had been years since he had been to a mall and the products available had changed tremendously.

"Don't look out the window," I advised him as the plane began taxiing toward the runway.

"Why?"

"If you don't like the view from my apartment what makes you think you want to see the view from an airplane?"

"How high up is your apartment?"

"Oh, ten floors, ten feet per floor, probably a little over a hundred feet."

"A hundred. Dang, I don't even like being that high up! What am I doing in this flimsy, tin box that's fixin' to whisk me up into the clouds?" he asked.

"Close your eyes. Wait for the plane to stabilize and it'll be just like sitting in a buoyant chair at home."

It took a while for the plane to get a chance to take off, as it always does, and Darby began hyperventilating.

"Dar... it's not that big a deal. Here. Breathe into this," I said as I handed him the bag from the seat pocket normally reserved for other uses.

I was a little irritated with Darby, but I also thanked him silently for distracting me from my own fears. I'd rather deal with a little aerophobia than worry about the happenings in LA. He put the bag down and grabbed the armrests white-knuckled as the plane sped up. He closed his eyes tightly and I almost handed him the bag again, but thought he'd be better off with his eyes closed. People began staring.

"First flight," I explained.

An elderly man across the aisle said, "This is easy, son. Now taking off from an aircraft carrier. That was a bit dicey. You had the length of one ship to get up to speed, then *zing*! Up you go into the wild blue yonder. It was called the Air Corps back then. Yes sirree. Served three years. Taking off and landing in god-awful conditions. Under fire."

"World War II?" I asked.

"No, I was a little too late for that. Korean War."

The conversation seemed to help Darby focus on something besides the engine noise. He began to relax but every time the plane jostled he felt it in the pit of his stomach and grabbed the armrests again.

"Just think," I told him. "A layover in Moscow and then landing in Paris. So two landings and one takeoff to go."

"Why did I ever let you talk me into this," he said.

"After we level off you can have a drink. But I suggest waiting to see how your stomach takes to air travel."

He did okay after we leveled off but he kept the window closed for the entire flight. I read books on my notepad computer and played solitaire. After a while I noticed Darby watching over my shoulder.

"Do you want a device to play on?" I asked.

"No, I don't want to use up your batteries."

"We've got three: my phone, the notepad and laptop."

"How long do the batteries last?"

"A few hours."

"It's okay. Go ahead. It's long flight."

"You can listen to music," I offered.

"I don't want to."

"They will hand out ear buds in a little while. There will be a movie soon."

The movie helped distract Darby and by the time it was over he had released the arm rests.

"I haven't seen a movie in years," he said.

"Oh? Which one was it?"

"You didn't even watch it enough to know?"

"No, I don't watch much TV. I have to be home to do that and I try not to be home much."

"You could go to a theater," he said.

"By myself? No thanks."

"When did computers replace people?"

"A long time ago."

"When did computers replace real explosions?"

"Even longer ago. Surely you've seen CGI explosions and characters in movies."

"I've been so broke for so long... I haven't seen anything but work, the freeway, and the streets since I was old enough to have a job."

Darby had worked at a fast food take out window. He had sold shoes at a discount shoe store, tried an apprenticeship with a mechanic and sold movie tickets at a theater. All of them temporary and dead end jobs. His longest stint was at the shoe store. The theater showed foreign films and old classics and the big bucks chain came in and put it out of business. When he lost one job he immediately went looking for another, but luck was not on his side. I was hoping I could turn his luck around, but I didn't know how.

Moscow. A four hour layover. Could we get to a geocache, find it and make it back through security to catch the next flight? I hesitated to try but only because of the foreignness of the land. If we were confronted I wouldn't know the language. I kept picturing landing in a Russian jail.

I thought I had read the cache description carefully. It did give directions to the cache, but inside the airport we didn't know where we were allowed to go and where we would meet opposition. We sat down and brought up the cache description again.

"Let me try. When the library wasn't busy I tried to do some puzzle caches. A friend taught me some tricks. One of them is to check every link and scan the coding used to write the page."

We began another reading of the page, clicking every link we found. One simply led to a web page that told about the airport. However, traveling geocachers had helped the cache owner and posted detailed instructions complete with pictures. We viewed each picture and we still wondered if we would be stopped and questioned.

"Aw, come on, we sunk nearly five hundred dollars into this one smiley! We can't pass it up!" Darby said.

"It was just visa fees. We don't have to do it."

"You paid to go get this cache. We should do it. I don't know how often you come to Russia but this is my only chance to get a smiley in this country. How risky can it be? You hired me to get the right documents. Now I've got the right documents. What can they do?"

"You told me yourself that geocaching can look like suspicious activity. So we should do that here. Right?"

"No! We don't have to look suspicious at all. If they ask we say we're lost tourists. Then we ask where we can rent a car. They send us back to the airport. It's easy! Plus, if they arrest us you can bribe them!"

"You have to be careful with bribes. Too little and you get charges added. Too much and they think you're really up to something illegal worth much more than a large bribe."

By the time we talked ourselves into looking for the cache most of the people from our plane were through security and things looked relatively quiet.

We followed the pictures to the security checkpoint and they looked over our passports, asked all the usual questions and then looked over our visa. When they asked why we were visiting Moscow I'd written that we were visiting a friend. When the officials read that they checked our plane ticket.

"You have not the time," the security guard said.

"We promised we would try," I said. "So we must try. It is a family member whom I have never met. He wishes to see his great nephew in person."

"O'Connor?"

"A great uncle on my mother's side," I explained. I had discovered that if you give officials too much information and they got tired of hearing chit chat they would dismiss you.

"Good luck," he said.

Darby was ecstatic when they pointed us down the corridor to the next terminal.

"Okay, watch for a big corridor with weird dots from the lights everywhere."

When we found the corridor he said, "Watch for signs for a car park."

On and on we went, following each picture. They led us deeper and deeper into the airport and I began to wonder if we'd ever find our way back in time to catch the plane. I began to feel like the spy I might be mistaken for. Somehow looking for a geocache redefined the word tourist. Yes, officer, I came here to sight see, I just like parking garages and fallen trees.

After we were outside, conditions became both better and worse. Our GPSrs now worked but we had quite a walk ahead of us and we still felt as if somebody should stop us and question us. The further we got from the corridors of the airport the more foreign the signs became, too.

"Cut in here," Darby said and we ducked into the trees.

I wish I could detail the search for the cache. I can say there were plenty of places for a geocache to hide and we did our best to search without looking like we were searching. There were a lot of places to look, especially since we didn't know for sure if the coordinates were precise. I was relieved when Darby finally announced that he had found the container and he showed me where it was. To be unobtrusive we sat on the ground to open the cache. The container itself was unremarkable. We were astounded by the number of Travel Bugs inside. Tags from several different countries. Simple tags, fancy tags, and plain tags with all kinds of attachments to them.

"TB hotel, I'd say. Wow, there's lots of travelers in here! And even a geocoin!" Darby said. "People don't release these into the wild every day. Look, isn't this cool!"

I shooed some mosquitoes away and took the coin. It was large, and heavy. It wasn't round. It looked more ornamental than a typical coin. Being raised to think in financial terms I looked for a denomination, but there was none. The front depicted a cartoon frog on a toboggan, and the coin was shaped more like a snowflake. On the back I found a snowy scene and there was an empty oval where a word was etched.

"Okay… so what is it?" I asked.

"See this number?" he asked. "It makes this coin trackable."

"You mean the word here?" I asked.

"It's a word? Normally it is a number with letters in it, like a code."

"It says SGW0RD," I said.

"That's the coin's tracking number. It makes it so you can log it into and out of the geocaches like a Travel Bug. And the owner can follow its travels online. Think of it like a lost UPS package. You can go online to find out where it is."

"You mean where it's been and where it was supposed to go."

"Right! Except usually these things don't have a final destination. They travel around and geocachers log them so the owner can track it. I'd consider it to be really cool to find out my geocoin was in Moscow!"

"Do you have any of these?"

He laughed as if it was an absurd idea.

"What?" I asked.

"That coin probably cost its owner fifteen or twenty bucks. You think I'm going to shell out that kind of money only to drop it in a cache?"

"I guess not," I said as I turned the coin over and over in my hand. Fifteen dollars for one coin. It looked to be brass. "What do we do with it?" I asked.

"Sadly, I think we should leave it," he said.

"Okay, why?"

"Well, because it's at the airport. It might have just landed and it hasn't seen Russia yet."

"But that could be true of any of these. These look like the same thing, except with toys attached."

"True, they are. Did you bring Mickey along?"

"Yeah! I thought I'd leave it in Paris so somebody could take it to the park there."

"Well, these are just like Mickey."

"But… if the people who put them here had just gotten off the plane they would have taken them to see the country. Maybe they were put here by people who just took off."

"Then why didn't they take them along?"

"I think what we are deciding is, no matter what we do, we have a 50/50 chance of doing the right thing."

"Yup."

"Okay, well, we need to decide something."

"What time is it?"

"We have time, but we shouldn't be slow about it either. We've already used up an hour. It could take longer to get back depending on how slow security is."

"Right. Well, I think we should cross our fingers and take two. There's five here. That leaves some for other travelers but it allows a few of them to travel."

"Okay. So… which ones get to take the flight to Paris?"

"This one," he said pulling a Russian nesting doll from the cache.

"Why?"

"It looks like it's from Russia so maybe it's looking for a ride out."

"That makes sense."

"We can also claim it's a souvenir if they ask us about the odd things in our carry on."

"I'd like to take the coin," I said.

"Okay, why that one?"

"I don't know. It just triggered something in my mind. Maybe if I take it I'll figure out why it brings questions to mind."

I think I was meant to find that coin, though I didn't know it at the time. I dropped it into my laptop case and we made our way back into the airport. Unfortunately, we got lost because we entered the building in an atypical way. We tried referring back to the pictures but we were going the other direction. We found a car park and a parking garage and eventually an airport entrance but we were beginning to get nervous. Time was slipping away and we still had to get back through security.

"When I become a rich world traveler I'm going to buy fancy slip on shoes so I can get through security quicker," Darby said as he worked his way back into this hiking boots.

"At least you broke in your boots more. Slip-ons aren't the best shoes for tromping around in the woods. When I took my shoes out of the bin they had to dump the mud and sticks into the trash."

"I hope Paris has fewer mosquitoes."

"Me, too."

We checked the flight schedules and gate numbers, then the time.

"I never took up jogging," I admitted as we hurried toward our gate. "And I'm glad we got first class seats. We might have missed lunch but they'll serve a meal on the plane. I was going to ride in coach on the way home just to see what it's like but I think I'll upgrade so we don't have to worry about meals."

"I'm going to get fat hanging around with you," Darby complained.

"Nobody's forcing you to eat."

"But it's all so good," he said as the gate appeared in the distance. "After eating mostly canned goods and fast food for three years, restaurant food is… I feel guilty eating it, knowing Henry's back at camp eating canned stew."

"I know. I felt the same way. But Henry won't change. I talked to him. He'd like you to, but he feels like the camp is his place."

"After you live like that a while it gets to be normal, and finding a job and a place to live looks impossible. So many things need to be overcome. The problems increase and the will to fight them wears away with time. After a while surviving just becomes the job instead of searching for one. Do you think I can make it?"

"Yeah, you can make it."

We stopped when we suddenly saw the gate before us. We were both breathing a little heavy from exertion when he said, a bit choked up, "When I told Adele that I had a job and maybe I'd see her real soon do you know what she said?"

"No, of course not."

"She said, 'can we have a house? A real house?' Earl… I couldn't tell her no. I couldn't make promises but I told her I hoped so. And I can't let her down."

We stood there nose to nose, snobby rich guy and his friend, the street urchin.

"You'll make it."

Chapter 11

That coin began a conversation that lasted most our travels.

"Where do people get these coins?" I asked after we boarded the plane and we had time to get bored.

"Mail order," he answered.

"Why a frog?"

"He's like the geocaching mascot. But there are coins with all kinds of different pictures on them. I don't see them often because they tend to be collector's items more than trackable items."

"People collect these things?"

"Sure."

"But the tags…"

"You're more likely to find Travel Bugs in caches, because they are cheaper and more disposable."

"How much does a Travel Bug cost?"

"I haven't looked recently. I'd guess five bucks."

"Then they add the toy."

"The hitchhiker," he corrected me.

"Adds a dollar or two."

"Or more. It just depends on what appeals to the person who sends it out."

"What did you mean by disposable?" I asked.

"If you send one of these out don't attach anything to it that means a lot to you because eventually it is going to vanish and you will never see it again. That's what I mean by disposable."

"What happens to them?"

"A cache gets muggled, or the person who picks it up loses it, or it gets stolen. Lots of things can go wrong in a Travel Bug's journey. A hundred miles? A thousand? Ten thousand? Eventually it is going to get lost."

"And people mail order these things?"

"Yeah."

"There's no place to just shop for stuff like that?"

"No."

"You're telling me there is no physical geocaching store."

"Yes… well, I guess that would be lying. There is one."

It was astounding to me that there was this whole marketing niche and they didn't have a store for it. If they had stores that sold nothing but candles, or model railroad stuff, then surely a geocaching store could make it. Yet so far there was only one? Darby's future was beginning to look brighter. I decided to slowly expand my geocaching education and explore my options when I got home.

"How far do these things travel in a lifetime?" I asked.

"It varies a lot. Some never make it to their second cache. Some have been all over the world. How many miles did Mickey have on him when you looked it up?"

"I didn't know I could check."

"We'll look when we log our cache find and the travelers we picked up," he said.

We talked. We slept. Night and day became fuzzy. I learned a lot about geocaching just by asking a continual stream of questions. I learned that geocaches have ratings for difficulty and terrain. Darby had found some difficult caches but he had never met difficult terrain so he only speculated that a difficult terrain would involve a strenuous hike or a drive down a four wheel drive road. My rich guy status perked up at the thought that I might need a four wheel drive vehicle to explore further afield than the city limits of Los Angeles. I had driven the Jaguar up into the mountains and looked out into the barren desert to the east of LA. The car drove like a dream, but I had tried driving into a couple of campgrounds and ended up driving through a car wash on the way home. The thought of driving on the many dirt roads and possibly seeing some wildlife appealed to me. Then I wondered how much wildlife lives in civilized Southern California.

I learned that many geocachers carry a trash bag with them so they can clean up the landscape as they geocache. The idea both appealed to me and repulsed me. I'd never really gotten my hands dirty working before so it wasn't a practice I thought I would easily add to my geocaching, but I did see the value of it. There were many places in LA that could use some trash removal.

I learned that there were several types of geocaches, though Darby only had experience with what he called traditional caches. There were also puzzle caches, challenge caches, multi caches, earth caches, virtual caches and event caches.

"Will we find any of those in Paris?" I asked.

"Not unless we make a point of it. Did you download any?"

"I don't know. I just downloaded them based on my interest level."

"Well, then we might. Earth caches and virtual caches are usually located at points of interest, and there is no container so be prepared for some different kind of hunting."

"What do you mean?"

"There isn't a container but there is a quiz at the end. Sometimes what you take from a cache is a little education."

"And these puzzle caches. What are they?" I asked.

"I never had time to pursue them. You have to solve a puzzle to get the coordinates to the cache. Since I usually downloaded caches at the library I was limited to about half an hour of computer time. That includes emailing Adele. The easy ones require some figuring. The hard ones I've known people to work for weeks trying to solve one cache. With so many traditional caches around I don't see any reason to struggle for one smiley."

"And event caches?"

"I've never been to an event, but all you have to do is sign in when you go, then log it like a regular cache."

I didn't ask why he hadn't been to an event. I knew he hadn't gone because he looked too obviously homeless.

Darby coped better with the landing and takeoff at Moscow. He hadn't noticed we were landing until the plane began dipping on the descent and then we talked about geocaching. It wasn't until he heard the wheels touchdown and the flaps open that the fear kicked in. When we took off he was still recovering from almost missing our flight. He still grabbed the armrests tightly, but he was glad to be on the plane.

"If we'd missed it we'd have been stuck and I would have had *hours* to worry about it," he said later.

"Hours," I agreed. "I wonder how many flights go from Moscow to Paris in a day."

"It might be worth five hundred dollars to you to be able to snag one smiley, but it's not worth spending hours worried about the next flight out. No way. One thing the street life has spoiled me to is worry. When all you have to worry about is the next meal you lower your worry threshold."

"Did you ever go a whole day without eating?" I asked.

"Almost. Henry takes care of his own. Sometimes our camp stew got mighty thin but we always had one meal."

"And to think I thought it would be ostentatious to bring in a real meal. I thought the camp would ostracize me if they knew I wasn't one of them. You can't know how much I puzzled over what I could do to help without giving away my identity. So I tried to bring what any homeless person would bring. Sometimes I ended up falling short because I didn't have things on me that a homeless person might. It's amazing how resourceful they are."

"You couldn't fool Henry anyway. He wondered where you went to at night. He was honest enough not to follow you to your car, but he knew something was amiss. Honesty is what he values most. You talked with him a lot. He trusted you."

"And, amazingly, I think he still does. Why?"

"Because money does not make a man."

"Maybe not, but it certainly affects them."

"And that's how he could tell you were not homeless."

"I owe you and Henry my thanks," I said. "You taught me more than I could ever learn without sitting around the camp stove."

"Like what?"

"Like... it's the little things in life that count. Just being able to meet everyday needs. My needs have shrunk. I no longer need to see that little plus sign on my investments. When I look at a plate of food I think how much it would add to the camp stew. One of my meals would feed the whole camp for a day. I'd like to simplify my life."

"No running off to Paris just to find geocaches?" he asked.

"When I met you I was looking to see what life across the tracks was like. I found out there are advantages to both. Admit it, you'd rather ride in here than in coach," I said. "But I can't help but think, that if I was back there I could talk to a housewife and learn what it's like to live in Russia."

"Or you could sit back there trying to figure out how to say hello in Russian," he said.

"True, but I've found foreigners more schooled in English than Americans are in foreign languages." I looked around, found a gentleman who was dressed slightly differently, and nudged his shoulder. "Sir, do you speak English?" I asked.

"A little," he said without even a hint of an accent.

"I was telling my friend that foreigners speak English better than Americans speak your language."

"True," he said and then spoke something in his native language.

"See?" I said to Darby and the gentleman. "You prove my point perfectly, thank you."

"You're welcome," he said.

"What did he say?" Darby asked.

"My guess is he asked me if I speak his language. Either that or he said 'crazy Americans.'"

"Actually," the gentleman said. "I said, 'We speak English where I come from, too.'"

"And where is that?" I asked.

"Zuni Pueblo," he answered.

I couldn't help but laugh. I'd judged that man just by his clothing and he was dressed as a businessman. A slightly quirky businessman but his suit was immaculate. Only his shoes and slightly longish hair distinguished him as being different. His black hair was gray at the temples and at first glance I had thought he was Mongolian, though I'd never met any Mongolian businessmen. I wondered what industries Mongolia had.

"And you're flying to Paris?" I asked.

"Yes, I am attending an international conference on cancer research."

"Wow," said Darby.

"And your friend is right, in Paris you should have no trouble communicating," he said to Darby. "We'll have multiple interpreters at the conference, but for everyday business most people will speak English for you."

When we arrived in Paris it was light outside but we had no clue what time it really was. We flagged down a taxi. I handed him my reservations and he dropped us off at an ancient, but grand hotel.

"I wonder how we got these reservations if there's an international conference going on," I said.

"Paris is a big city," Darby answered.

"Usually the good rooms go first so don't get your hopes up."

"Hey, I'm the one who sleeps under overpasses. If it's got furniture at all I'll be happy. By the way, when does my job kick in? I have hardly lifted a finger this trip."

"It began the moment we left for the airport in LA. I owe you two days wages."

"Two days? All we did was fly from LA to Paris."

"And we jumped ahead a day in the process," I pointed out.

"You can't pay me... for a time change," he said.

"Then I suggest you plan our day tomorrow. For now I want to get a drink, find my bed and sleep for several hours."

I didn't have any use for my own personal secretary, but my dad's secretary didn't mind doing odd jobs for me, like making travel plans, and I paid her extra for it. Her daughter had special needs and she always had more bills than paycheck so the extra work was welcome. She also found me some great hotels since she booked them with my dad in mind. This was not the first hotel I'd stayed at that had ancient carvings in their exercise room, but it always felt incongruous to be walking on a treadmill with a gargoyle standing over me. I'd have to check out the other facilities after a long nap. It didn't surprise me one bit to walk into a suite with a sitting room. I wondered what Darby's room was like. It didn't take long for me to find out. He knocked on the door before I was half way undressed.

"Dude, I think there's been a mistake. I got me a fuckin' suite!" he said.

"It's not a mistake. This happens a lot when Bernadette makes my reservations."

"But it's like a whole house! A fancy one!"

"It's better to have some space to spread out."

"How rich *are you*?" he asked.

"Too rich for my own good," I said. "Enjoy the room. The bed should be comfortable, too. That's what really counts right?"

"Uh, right."

I finished undressing and lay down but I couldn't fall asleep. I kept wondering how Jo was doing. I tried calling her and she answered tentatively.

"Hello?"

"I was just thinking about you, wondering how you were doing."

"Earl?"

"Yeah. How are you?"

"I'm…I shouldn't talk to you right now," she said rather abruptly.

"Okay, can I call back later?"

"I don't know. Let me call you."

The conversation didn't ease my mind at all. I lay there staring at the ceiling wondering what the hell I was doing in Europe when Jo might need help. But then I wondered if she would call me. She had never called me before. She had always dealt with her problems on her own. But she shouldn't have to, I kept telling myself. Somebody has got to stick up for her. Somebody. Me? What was I doing in France? I should go back. But I was here and eventually my argument spiraled into a fitful sleep and I found a little rest.

Chapter 12

Darby took his job seriously. I guess he thought he needed to earn every penny I gave him because after a few hours he called me and said that if we wanted to find a cache or two before dinner we better get busy.

"Now remember we're already seen as different here and we have to try not to stand out. It's okay to look dumb, because they expect us to not know where we are going, but we can't make people think we're doing anything suspicious or we might get questioned."

"Great."

"See all those people out there?"

"Yeah."

"Muggles. Every one of them."

"So how do we search if we have to look like them?"

"I don't know. I've never geocached like this before. Back home it's easy. They see me, they look away. I have no idea how to find a geocache on a crowded sidewalk in the middle of rush hour."

"Oh, good," I said a bit worriedly.

"All we can do is follow the GPS and see where it leads us. My suggestion? We follow the GPS and take mental notes. Then we pass the cache completely and compare what we both think. We make multiple long passes."

"Okay, I think I can do that."

We joined the press of people walking down the sidewalk. I should have been used to this, having walked many an LA sidewalk to go to lunch or from one appointment to another, but I wasn't used to having to find a micro cache somewhere in that constant flow of people. As the distance narrowed between us and the cache I began looking for hiding spots. I wasn't very experienced at finding geocaches so the bush, light pole, newsstand and trash can did not stand out except that I was looking for anything that could hide something small.

"What do you think?" I asked Darby as we passed the hiding spot and the numbers representing the distance to the cache increased.

"Work your way to the side so we can let a few people pass. Then we'll turn around," he instructed. "It's not the trash can. They get banged up too much. It would be too easy to lose it. The newspaper box is a possibility. It would be in the inner workings of the box so a geocacher could snag the cache while they buy a paper."

"I can't even read the paper," I pointed out.

"So? Just because you put a buck in the machine doesn't mean you have to take a paper."

"I hope it isn't in the bush. That would take some stopping and searching."

"Right, we'd rather do that with fewer people around. The light post is an option though if it's there it'll take several passes to spot it."

After we found a spot to stop Darby said, "I'm ruling out the newspaper box, too. We're not supposed to have to spend money to get to the cache."

"What if it's a free real estate listing like back home?"

"Then it'll take another pass to be sure, but I doubt it. Folks look pretty settled here. Ain't a lot of house selling and buying here."

"You'd be surprised."

"Well, I say it's the light post but it'll take a sharp eye to see it."

Two more passes and we still were not sure, though we added the grate around the base of the bush as a likely spot.

"Wouldn't it get wet when the bushes are watered?" I asked.

"Who says they water bushes here? They might have real rain here."

"Still, water is water."

"Geocaches are supposed be at least a little waterproof. If it isn't it wouldn't last."

"Why put one here?" I asked. "Why a difficult place like this?"

"Good question," Darby said. "Want to go back to the room and see?"

"How would that help us?"

"It wouldn't unless the description was in English, too. But maybe folks posted pictures."

"I'd rather not go back," I said. "We're out here. We can come back later. This is only two blocks from the hotel. Maybe it'll be less crowded on our way back to the room."

"Well, we have to pass it one more time just to get to the next cache. It's over thataway."

I always enjoyed walking down foreign streets listening to the flow of language around me. It leant a flavor to the day and put me in my place. It was refreshing being unable to understand any of the signs or talk around me. I didn't have to process it. It felt like an informational vacation, a break from the constant inflow of words and numbers. I laughed and Darby asked me what was so funny.

"Even the distance signs mean nothing to me!" I said cheerily.

I don't think he understood why it made any difference at all, but he didn't live in a world of investments and stock points. I almost wished I didn't know the value of a euro, so I could walk around in total oblivion.

As it turned out the next cache we were looking for brought me back to earth in a different way. The cache was in a little park with a large wall in it. At first I thought the wall was written on and I was perturbed at the sight of graffiti even in Paris, but as we got closer to it we could see that it wasn't graffiti at all. It took a little searching to realize all the phrases on the wall said one thing, "I Love You." I shrugged back the word, trying not to remember my hesitation about leaving the country, but it was no use. Memories of Jo came back and with them my concern for her safety.

"I remember this one from our searches," Darby said. "It has over a hundred favorite points! Cool! I wonder where the cache is."

This started him reading the description and logs. He found the cache within minutes but he stood off a ways and let me do my own search.

"It says we should post a picture of ourselves in front of our language. I don't think it's a requirement, but since we have a camera we might as well," he added as I searched.

It seemed a waste to have my picture taken in front of the wall of love by myself, but I submitted to having my picture taken just in case I was able to share it with Jo later. Darby took great joy in being able to add pictures to his logs. Since he never had a digital camera or a computer of his own he had simply been logging his finds as often as he could while at the library, but his online count was off and he had never posted pictures before. When I saw how much he enjoyed adding pictures to his geocaching I gave him free reign of the camera and only took it back for certain pictures I wanted for myself. We took each other's picture in front of the I Love You Wall and then, when I finally located the cache, we pretended to take a picture at a different angle so we could grab the cache without people noticing. There were a lot of tourists out and the wall was a popular attraction. Couples would walk up to the wall and gaze about at it until they found their particular language and then look around. I learned to recognize the phrase, "Excuse me, could you..." in French but it was easier to just read the body language. I took pictures of four couples and Darby pretended to take a picture of me while he put the cache back.

"You know, this would have earned a favorite point from me if I could have had my wife here," Darby said.

"Maybe you can bring her here someday," I said, but he only replied with, "Yeah, right."

"I guess if it would have gotten a point from me under different circumstances then it feasibly earned one."

"You would know more about it than I."

"Well, you have to admit making your girlfriend geocache with you and then ending up at the I Love You Wall would have at least earned you a kiss. So I'm willing to give any cache a point if it leads to more kissing."

"In public?"

"Hey, this is the I Love You Wall. All the couples were kissing."

"True."

What a way to end my first geocaching day in Paris, with a reminder of why I shouldn't be there.

"You seem bummed out," Darby pointed out while we were waiting for our food to arrive at dinner.

"I can't help but worry."

"About what?"

"Jo. Last time I saw her, her arms were covered in bruises and when I called to check up on her she acted like she couldn't talk."

"Maybe she had something else going on."

"Yeah, but what was going on worries me."

"What? You think she's cheating on you?"

"I don't know what to think."

"Are you two… you know."

"No. She has every right to date whomever she pleases. I just get the feeling that she needs an escape."

"From what?"

"An unhealthy relationship."

"And you think she can't get out if she wants out?"

"I think she should want out. Anybody who would put bruises on a woman like the ones I saw needs to be stopped. I'd like to get my hands on the SOB."

"What would you do, if you could?" Darby asked.

"I don't know. I've never hit a man in my life. That's one reason I can't see the sense in using violence on a woman. If you don't like a woman enough to be civil why stick around?"

He didn't have an answer but my quiet rant had produced a melancholy feeling in both of us: me worrying about Jo and Darby wishing he could bring his own family together again. I quit complaining about my own worries and decided instead, that Darby's family would be united again if there was any way for me to allow him to do it himself. That sounds contradictory but in fact it wasn't. I had a plan in mind. I just needed to learn more about geocaching so I could implement it.

Chapter 13

You can't visit Paris without taking a ride to the top of the Eiffel Tower. It's just a rule. If you have the means it's almost a rite of passage. If you've been to Paris people will ask you if you've been to the top of the Eiffel Tower and you better be able to say you have. And so, even though I'd gone up there when I was five and pretended I was Superman flying through the sky because the wind was strong and I felt like I was flying, I went up again. This time the tourists were not as irritated with my actions. I noticed that Darby tried to act casual, but he always had a hand on a railing or wall except when he took my picture.

The geocache that had been there was archived long ago but it was hinted at in the logs that somebody was thinking of making a virtual cache out of it. So we took each other's pictures just in case we were able to log it as a virtual find and we walked around speculating about where the cache had been hidden when it was active.

"Wow," said Darby. "I never dreamed I would ever visit a foreign country and now here I am at the top of the Eiffel Tower. I'm going to send a postcard to Adele and show her where we were."

I thought it was a good sign that Darby was willing to splurge on postcards. He was shedding his hopeless view of life and enjoying the moment. I also thought that if he wanted to find postcards I might be able to look for a Christmas ornament for Jo.

"I can see the next cache from here," Darby said.

"Yeah? Where?" I didn't think he could actually see the cache, but he certainly might have been able to see the location.

"Right there," he said pointing. There were a lot of hiding places within the scope of that single point.

"Are you ready to find it?" I asked.

"Yeah, I don't like being this high up."

"Did you say hi to your mom?"

"No," he said, then looked out at the city and up at the sky. I don't know what was going through his head. I hoped he was telling her he was going to beat homelessness. He was going to get an apartment, find his wife and daughter, and live happily ever after, but I doubted it went that far. Darby was a realist.

Darby stomped his feet on the ground feeling the good old terra firma on his boots when we stepped back into the park and got our bearings.

"Whew, at least I did it once, but once is enough," Darby said.

The next cache gave us a good look at the ground. It was hidden in a cemetery. I didn't spend much of my time in cemeteries. In the busyness of the city I tended to forget cemeteries exist. So far I'd never attended a funeral and I never saw cemeteries in the city. This one was in the center of Paris and very old. Finding our way into the cemetery was harder than actually finding the cache, but the cemetery was fascinating. I walked the cobblestone walkways between the tombs and graves with a feeling of foreboding and wonder. Had I been an imaginative child I would have thought I had landed in a very old, miniaturized village. Some of the tombs looked like little stone houses. And the trees lent the whole place a dappled, mysterious air, like we had stepped back in time and were giants walking in the midst of the land of elves. Moss coated some of the tombs like ivy on a cottage. I found myself wandering, just taking in the feeling of the place.

"What kind of a geocacher are you?" Darby asked as he held up his GPS.

"I believe you now," I said almost in a whisper, because this felt like a quiet place.

"About what?"

"About geocaching being more of a journey than a hobby."

"Good, it's about time."

"This is fantastic."

"And old and creepy," he added.

"I don't find it creepy. I find it enchanting. It seems odd that I'd love to show Jo a cemetery, but I would. If I brought her to Paris, I'd be sure to show her this place."

Darby was more interested in finding the geocache.

"At least there are no muggles," he said as he walked down a narrow walkway between the tombs. "This reminds me of a place in San Diego. There's this little cemetery, only the city didn't know the cemetery was there and they built right over it so they have grave markers on the sidewalks and streets. How'd you like to be laying dead under a street?"

"I don't think I'd care, if I was dead," I answered.

"I wonder if this place is haunted," Darby said.

"It doesn't feel haunted, but I bet there are some interesting stories from people who visited this place in the dark and had too much bad wine."

"Speak for yourself. I still say it's creepy and I've heard the wine is great here."

"I wouldn't have taken you for a wine connoisseur," I said.

"I'm not. But I might be persuaded to try it here."

In my family we had wine with most meals. It was what you drank at dinner. I wasn't exactly a connoisseur but I'd drank my share. I'd had wine with dinner the previous night without noticing what Darby ordered.

"Feel free to order what you want," I said. "This is a chance to experience a new country. Take advantage of it."

"I'm not going to take advantage of you. Just because you have deep pockets doesn't mean I should drink expensive wine every night."

"Then I'll order a bottle and you are welcome to try it, too."

There were a lot of hiding places but the cache was not hard to find. The cemetery seemed to be visited only rarely. We only saw two other people, also tourists, roaming the paths. It was a relief to geocache without worrying about who might see us.

"I think I will leave Mickey here," I said. "I'll post a picture of the Eiffel Tower, not the graves. I don't know how many medium sized caches I will find in the city. I have to take advantage of the first safe cache I can find."

So Mickey and I parted ways, but not before I stood him on a tomb with the Eiffel Tower in the background and took his picture. I hoped he would be picked up by a family who would take him to Disney Paris. I didn't think a child would like to think about their travel bug sitting in a cemetery. So I kept my log online light and only showed the tower and left them hopeful that another part of its mission might be accomplished.

Darby and I walked past the geocache near our hotel again and again watching for anything different.

"I think we need to try it at night, when there's no one around," Darby said.

"If we can't spot it in the daylight, what makes us think we can find it in the dark?"

"We should have done it when we first came in, since we were wired from flying and being in a new place anyway," he said. "But we didn't know it was there."

"Why are you determined to find this particular one? There are hundreds."

"It's challenging me to a geocaching duel," he said. "I will find that sucker."

"What do you log if you can't find a cache?" I asked.

"It's called a DNF and it's a shame on your record, only… sometimes you just gotta do it, because how's a cache owner to know something is wrong with his cache if you never tell them it wasn't there, or wasn't findable, or just impossible, or that you just suck at geocaching."

I laughed at his explanation. "So if you log a DNF it means you're a bad geocacher?"

"Yeah, I mean... no. I mean... there are people with tens of thousands of finds that still DNF caches, but I personally hate to do it. I only log a DNF if I think it serves a useful purpose."

"And this one? Will you log a DNF?"

"Only if it beats me the whole time we're in Paris."

"Do you think Paris has a geocaching store?" I asked.

"Nah, I wouldn't expect to find one here. If you want to shop for geocaching stuff look online."

With the subject broached I asked Darby what a geocaching store should stock and I got a long list of items from four dollar travel tags and replacement logs to six hundred dollar GPS receivers. He told me I should look through the online shops and see what they had.

"What do you think the chances are of a geocaching store staying in business in LA?" I asked.

"Depends on how well it's stocked, how knowledgeable the staff is and how well known it is. One thing for sure, it has to have a very spectacular cache hidden at it."

"Why?"

"Look, if you go into a train store what do you expect? You expect train buffs. You want to be able to tell them about your layout and have them know what the hell you're saying, right?"

"Right."

"Same goes for geocachers. They love to talk geocaching. Going to a geocaching store should be like attending a meet and greet. Whoever works at a geocaching store should have some good stories up his sleeve and know all about everything in the store, not so's they can sell it but so's they can talk."

"The salesmen are not salesmen?"

"Well... they are, but... a good story buys a friend. And a friend will keep coming back, just to talk, and when they come back just to talk they buy stuff. So as long as you can talk geocaching you'll have good customers."

I took notes as Darby examined the light pole again as we walked past it.

"That sucker is mocking me every time we walk by," he said.

"We'll come back at night, though I'm warning you Paris has a very active night life."

Twice more we walked past it and Darby's glances were becoming too obvious. I began looking away so I wouldn't be adding to the obvious interest in the lamppost. When I did that I began noticing something else. It was a small rectangle on the side of a windowsill behind the bush. The corner of it was tan and the cement it was on was gray. I smiled to myself, followed Darby and waited for night.

I convinced Darby to try a different area so we went back to the hotel and had the concierge call a taxi for us. The driver was more than a little puzzled when we didn't know where exactly we wanted to be dropped off. The best we could do was a description.

"Can you take us to the bridge near Rue Claude Monet?"

"De bridge? Sir, there is many bridges."

"Okay, hold on," Darby said. He held his hand out for my GPS because mine had maps. He clicked through the screens like a pro, zoomed in until he could read street names.

"Can you take us to the intersection of Rue Claude Monet and A14?"

"Ah, yes sir, but parking…"

"We'll be ready, you just drop us off," Darby said, not at all familiar with how taxi cabs were really paid. These days they took a card, but it took a moment to do the transaction. Perhaps the traffic there would make that difficult. I took out my wallet so I could just pay cash.

I have to say I was rather pleased with the location. I had thought the intersection would be crowded with buildings and tourists but the taxi driver turned onto what I thought was our destination, but he had to wind back to it to find the precise spot we had requested. When he stopped the Seine River was on one side of the road and a field was on the other side. No muggles! I looked to Darby.

"So… how close are we?" I asked.

"A ways, but we ought to be fine."

"Okay, we will get out here," I said.

"Here? But what you do?"

"We would like to see the river," I answered.

"But de river, she is much nicer…"

"It's okay. We prefer a peaceful walk. How much do I owe you?"

He gave me a figure and I paid him before stepping out of the cab.

"This is a side of Paris I never expected to see," I commented. "This is great! We can hike and geocache and call another taxi when we get tired."

We had been dropped off at one end of a long string of geocaches that followed the river. I couldn't read any of the descriptions because they were in French, but I could follow the GPS, and that was good enough for me. It wasn't important to me to find all of them. I just wanted to get away from the crowds, add to my find count, have a chance to talk to Darby and just enjoy the day. We locked onto the closest cache and began walking.

"If you had a geocaching store what kind of cache would you have to bring geocachers to the store?" I asked.

"Well, I've heard the one in Florida is a huge ammo can. It's got to be huge, or creative or technical or something."

"If I were to put you in charge of coming up with one could you do it?" I asked. "I'd pay for the container…"

"Or the pieces to build it?"

"Certainly."

He grinned broadly. "Now that is a problem I could wrap my brain around!"

As we walked he spouted out ideas, "People like big caches. How about the world's largest travel bug hotel?"

Later, "An evil micro would be… evil, but if it was done right… hmm."

And still later, "You can't put it inside. There's a rule about that."

Then in the middle of the walking path he stopped, turned to me and said, "Are you thinking of opening a west coast geocaching store?"

"Uh, yeah, I was thinking about it. If you'd like to have the job of overseeing the process."

"Oh, man! I didn't see that coming."

"What do you mean you didn't see it coming? You asked me if that's what I was thinking of. So you must have had some inkling."

"Really? You want to open a geocaching store?"

"I'm willing to sink some spare cash into the venture. How long do you think it would take to turn a profit?"

"I haven't the foggiest notion."

"If I did that, do you want the job?"

"A job?" He said it like it was a dream. Like little kids who dream of being an astronaut. Something way out there, unobtainable but worth fantasizing about, just in case everything happened to line up just right, turn out to be easier than expected, the kid turned out to be smarter than they thought they were, and be able to take a few risks.

"Yes, a job. It takes time and dedication to open up a new business. Do you think you can do it?"

"If it means getting Adele back I'll even lay the bricks and do the plumbing to code," he said.

I noticed he didn't add his wife to the statement but didn't write her off.

"Then I need some advice," I said.

All during our time in France he would come up with little bits of advice that I could never keep track of or remember but I was glad to see his mind busy on a task that could get him off the streets.

"I think the geocachers would like a travel bug hotel that was really, truly safe," he said.

"You can't keep new geocachers from taking a travel bug," I pointed out.

"No, but you can educate them a little while they are there. And you can ask folks to log them in and out so they make a conscience decision to follow through. And it should be big. And well organized. You don't want travel bugs getting lost in there."

I let him think.

The road we had chosen was pleasant and interesting. I had thought we would be geocaching along the Seine River, and we were, but soon we encountered a cache at a house. I was uneasy, thinking people were watching us, but the area was quiet. Another was at a dock. Swans floated majestically in the river and ducks paddled up asking for a handout. Still another was at a little bridge. It was a curious sight and I never really understood what we were looking at. Water drained under the bridge, of that I was sure, but there appeared to be circular... ponds? Fountains? I never did decide. If the circular structures were fountains they were not functioning while we were there. Still, it was a pleasant hunt and trying to figure out the use of the place kept us interested and talking. The ducks followed us even though we didn't have anything to feed them.

After a while we began to notice a group of three younger men following us. They kept at a respectful distance but if we took a long time to find a cache I felt guilty making them wait. They were obviously European.

"Do you think they're geocachers?" I asked Darby as we walked along.

"Could be, though they hide it well. We're being kind of obvious, so they are probably asking the same questions about us."

"Should we ask them?"

"Nah, if they want to know they'll ask us."

"But will we understand them?"

"Geocachers are a breed all their own. Even if we can't speak the same language they will be glad to talk geocaching."

"So we should talk to them."

"Sure, it can't hurt."

We stopped at the next cache and began searching, the three men hanging back. We kept looking back at them and they kept standing around acting like they were admiring the view of the river. I think the presence of the three men made Darby nervous because he began singing to himself, "I'm siiiigning on the Seine. I'm signing on the Seine. I must be insaaane to be siiigning on the Seine."

"I agree," I said. "Except that we have to find the cache to be signing on the Seine."

We looked around in the bushes nearby. We looked next to the cobblestone path. We ducked down to see if we could get under the bridge.

"Avez-vous trouvé?"

We both stood up and the three men stood around us.

"Sorry, we don't speak French," Darby said.

The three men exchanged glances and a different man spoke to us. I was guessing he was the one who spoke the best English.

"Have you found it?" he asked.

"Not yet, but these have been pretty easy," Darby said.

"You are... American?" he asked.

"Yes, from California," Darby said.

"How long will you be in Paris?"

Darby looked to me for an answer.

"A week," I said, though I wasn't really sure.

"Check the listing," the man said. "There is a small event tomorrow. Will we see you there?"

"That would be cool," Darby said to me. "I've never been to an event before. Do you want to go?"

"Sure!" I said. "We will try to find it."

"Sometimes there are new caches published so be ready to race," he said.

"Race?" I asked.

"For the FTF," Darby explained.

"We have no hope of winning a race," I said to Darby. "We have to rely on taxis and everybody else will know the route."

"So? It's the challenge of it."

I shrugged. I had no plan except to see Paris from a geocacher's point of view and what better way to do that than attend an event?

"Will you be there?" I asked.

"Why, of course!"

"We will look for you," I said.

"Good, good. My name is Remy, and this is Christophe and Marc. We will see you there. It's always very good to have visitors. Some stories from other lands will be most interesting."

"Earl," I said indicating myself. "And Darby." We shook hands. Remy found the cache but we all signed the log and the group went on ahead.

"We, uh... we better start thinking up some good stories," Darby said as we parted ways with the French men.

"I don't have any," I said. "I am still new to this."

"Well, we do have one doozie," Darby said. "I bet none of them have geocached by remote control helicopter."

"Yeah, and we can really build it up with all the false starts, too," I added. "Good thinking."

"I wonder why they didn't tell us their geocaching names," Darby said.

"Maybe they thought we wouldn't remember them."

"Probably true."

We geocached until we reached the next major street and then we called the taxi service again. The driver seemed puzzled. He began asking a question in French and we told him we didn't speak French.

"You tired of walking?" he asked.

"Yes," I said, though it wasn't really true. Geocaching down a nice flat cobblestoned path is not a very strenuous task. We mostly didn't know the way back to the hotel and we knew the taxi drivers were experts in navigating the city.

He dropped us off at the hotel but I nudged Darby toward the light post that he was getting increasingly frustrated with.

"What? You want to walk by it *again*? Folks are trying to get home from work."

"Okay, we can wait," I said.

"You really want to?"

"Yeah, then we can eat dinner."

"Okay, you're the boss. I don't know how I'm earning my keep on this trip. The least I can do is walk past a post even though it's useless."

We began walking down the street. Every once in a while I shook my foot, as if I had a rock in my shoe. But as we neared the post Darby decided to check the other side of it and when I made my way to the edge of the sidewalk to fix my shoe he walked right past the light post and kept going. I pretended to fix my shoe and then stood up and grabbed the gray box I had seen earlier. It was a hide-a-key and it was magnetic, but the hiding spot was not metal so the plastic box had Velcro stuck to the bottom and the other side of the Velcro was attached, not very successfully, to the side of the windowsill. If I'd seen how precarious the hide a key was attached I would have been more careful. The side of the Velcro on the windowsill was dangling. Only the container kept it flat.

I held the little hide-a-key victoriously. I'd found it! I slid the cover open.

"There you are!" Darby said. "You didn't tell me you were stopping!"

"Sorry."

"Hey, what's that?" Darby asked.

I removed the log sheet and handed the hide a key to Darby.

"You found it!" he said.

"Yeah, I thought I spotted it last time but I couldn't get to it. I needed a plan so I could grab it inconspicuously."

"I guess you came up with one," he answered. "I didn't even see you do anything."

I signed my geocaching name and handed the log sheet to Darby.

"Where was it?"

I pointed to the loose piece of Velcro.

He glared at the lamppost as if it had tricked him.

"Sometimes our preconceived ideas stop us from finding a cache. That's one way newbies have an advantage. They don't know the typical hides so they just look everywhere," he said.

He pretended to be stretching and when he brought his hands down he slapped the cache back into place where the loose Velcro slid a bit. We waited to see if it would hold before we went back to the hotel to log our caches.

"I sure am glad we got that one behind us," Darby said. "To have a DNF in France would drive me up the wall. At least in LA I can go back and attempt to revenge the DNF."

"Do you have any outstanding DNFs?" I asked.

"Not right now, though there were some that took two or three trips to find."

At dinner I ordered a bottle of wine so Darby wouldn't have to choose one and feel like he was taking advantage of me.

"Do you think we will be able to understand a word that is said at that event?" Darby asked.

"I think so. I bet all three of those guys knew some English."

"But, what about geocaching? How do they say DNF and FTF and stuff like that if the letters don't match their words?"

"Don't worry about it."

When we logged our caches we looked up the event, but the description was in French. We logged a note that said we would be there and I wrote down the address so we could just hand it to the taxi driver the next day. We downloaded the coordinates so we could go the rest of the way on foot.

Chapter 14

Event day. Neither Darby nor I had ever been to a geocaching event. We had barely met other geocachers at all. Darby knew a few other homeless people who played the game and they talked when they ran into each other. The only other person I knew who even understood the lingo was Henry. He'd found a few caches with Darby and one or two on his own, but he couldn't walk as far as Darby could. His patriarch status at the camp was pretty well sealed. He felt responsible for the people who came and went from camp whether they stopped in for a chat or needed a spot to roll out a sleeping bag for a more extended stay.

I thought it was strange that I was completely comfortable walking into a meeting about a subject that I had very little knowledge of, in a foreign country. I contrasted that with a high power financial meeting in LA. The tensions would be high. I wondered what the difference was.

We were in the taxi heading to the event after finding a few very ordinary caches at famous landmarks. I took pictures of them all to prove to my mother than I had truly seen Paris. She would ask me about the museums but I hoped she would not press the matter when I told her they didn't allow photography in the museums. Maybe, if I was lucky, she would think I knew about the photography rule because I had actually visited a museum and been told not to take pictures.

"Here we are," the taxi driver said as he pulled to the curb.

I thanked and paid the driver and we stepped out onto another busy sidewalk.

"Six hundred feet that way," Darby said.

"That would put it in the middle of a building," I said.

"It's probably around the other side of the block," Darby answered.

"Nope. If it was the taxi driver would have dropped us off there."

"Well, we have an address, not just coordinates," he said.

"We'll never know until we go look."

Actually it did take some looking because European geocachers appear very much like normal people. There were no signs. Nobody was holding a GPS and all the talk was in a language we didn't understand. We made our way down a busy street to a little sidewalk café. We walked around looking puzzled until Remy pushed his chair out and maneuvered his way through the tables and chairs to one corner of the patio area.

"My American friends, welcome!"

"Thank you," I replied.

"Are you ready for the race?"

"Uh, no, we don't have a car."

"Ah, but you can ride with me! Geocaching in a group is much fun. But first the others."

I was right about never remembering their geocaching names. Only a few of them made sense to me. There was one name that I think meant Night Cat and another that I thought meant something like Stealthy Cacher. Some of the names incorporated a last name coupled with a geocaching term. But after three or four introductions I was lost. It was hard to tell who was a geocacher and who was just stopping for lunch. Remy took us from table to table and we met approximately twenty other geocachers.

"What kind of race are you talking about?" Darby asked Remy.

"It is not really a race. All can win. Is just that the more who win the more we celebrate the winners! Wait, for the announcement."

"How can more than one person, or group, be FTF?"

"Ahh, that race! We get the coordinates to those after we return."

"Attention! Attention please, welcome everybody. Welcome our American vistors," a man in one corner of the assembly said.

"Thank you," I responded unobtrusively.

Then he said the same thing again in French and a few of the geocachers glanced around and waved in our direction.

"Today we have an objective. We will find four puzzle caches so I recommend sitting in groups that will travel together, unless you happen to be a supersleuth yourself. If not, I suggest finding someone who is to join your group."

"See?" Remy said. "You are supersleuth, right?"

"Oh man..." Darby said. "I am useless at this."

"I like them, so we are in luck," Remy assured us.

"Oh good," Darby said. "I appoint you our official group supersleuth."

"Do you like puzzles?" Remy asked me.

"I'll give it a try," I answered. "Can't say I'm very experienced, but I work with numbers a lot."

Darby began clicking through the screens on his GPS.

"What are you doing?" I asked him.

"Well, the answers to the puzzles are coordinates. I gotta know where we are so's I know what kinds of numbers I am watching for."

"Makes sense to me," I replied.

He began whispering to himself the longitude and latitude of our current position.

People began grouping together depending on the size of the vehicles the drivers had. I noticed that usually meant four people to a group.

Talk about a crash course in geocaching! We not only had to solve the puzzles, we had to find our way to the cache location and figure out clues from our surroundings, too. I became immensely thankful that Remy had taken the time to help two ignorant tourists. Each group was given a sheaf of papers. Remy took ours and flipped through the sheets, then handed Darby and I each a single sheet of paper. Each page was a printout of the description of a puzzle cache.

"They are supposed to be random, and easily solved by the average person," Remy said.

I looked at my puzzle. It seemed to be simple enough except for one small problem. It was an acrostic and to solve an acrostic I needed to know a little bit about the French language.

"Remy," I said. "I don't speak French. Can you get me started here?"

"I did this one already. It's entirely geocaching words."

But I barely speak geocaching, too, I thought.

"How are you at speaking geocaching?" I asked Darby.

"Pretty good. What is it?"

"Acrostic," I said. "What did you get?"

"Sudoku," he said.

"Do you want to trade?"

"I don't know. What's an acrostic?"

"You've got blanks with numbers. The number consistently matches the same letter. So if you reason out one word you know where those letters go in the rest of the puzzle."

"Give me a for instance."

"O… kay, for instance you have a three letter word and they give you a free D. You have to think of what three letter word begins with D. If you choose dog then you plug the O and the G into the rest of the puzzle and see if it makes sense."

"There's a hell of a lot of three letter D words," Darby said.

"Remy said they are geocaching words. So what geocaching term is three letters and starts with D?"

"Okay, I got an idea, give me that one."

I handed over the acrostic and took the Sudoku. After a while Marc sat with us and Remy handed him a puzzle, too. He asked a question in French and received an answer from Remy. When Darby and I looked at the puzzle he had received it only showed a picture of a piece of sheet music. No word of explanation, nothing.

I worked my way through the Sudoku and Darby frowned over the acrostic. I hoped the acrostic was as straight forward as my number puzzle. Some of the squares in my puzzle had a little number in the corner and I thought if I took those squares and wrote the numbers from the boxes in the right order I'd end up with coordinates. I was perhaps two thirds of the way through my Sudoku puzzle when a group of five left the café on the run.

"They are always the first," Remy said.

"Almost," Marc agreed.

"Is okay, just so we find them," Remy said.

"If you've already done this one, why are we doing it again?" Darby asked.

"Because, you have not," Marc said.

For some reason the answer made sense to Darby so he returned to his puzzle.

I completed the Sudoku and took a short break. I think I put more concentration and effort into that one puzzle than I did in a financial meeting with my accountant. He would throw numbers around and I would usually agree with him. Occasionally we butted heads but it was usually because I was willing to risk more than he thought I should. That resulted from an ambivalent attitude about my money. As long as there was enough of it to pay the bills I was willing to risk it just to see what happened. Sometimes it paid off, sometimes it didn't. But it paid off often enough that I still risked. I was unconcerned about my income, but I did care about finding this cache. When all the numbers fit neatly into the Sudoku I found the little numbers in the corners of the squares and put the numbers in order. Then I looked at the coordinates on my GPS to see where the gaps might fit to make real coordinates out of the numbers from the puzzle. I thought it was odd to have a set of coordinates without zeros in it. Back home it wasn't unusual to have zeros in coordinates. Then I thought that all one would have to do to eliminate zeros was to choose a new hiding spot.

Darby still appeared to be stuck on his puzzle so I looked over his shoulder.

"Every letter you fill in should give you a different clue to find the next one," I told him. "Ask yourself questions and answer them to the best of your ability and the answers will sometimes be right. Fill in the ones that sound likely."

"Okay," he said as his eyebrows furrowed. "What is this gibberish? How the hell should I know? It isn't working."

"Maybe more specific questions," I suggested.

I had to admit the first few attempts at solving acrostics were a bit confusing, but once a strategy was worked out it generally went together pretty quick. I was sure the cache owner was not a master puzzle creator himself, so it should be very solvable. I sat down and walked Darby through the process as we solved the puzzle together.

"Want me to work on yours?" he asked.

I handed him my page and at first he grinned thinking he would show me up. Then he saw that mine was finished.

"You got DFand N. Just keep going like that," I said as I searched for the next logical geocaching word. "Where might some vowels be?"

"Well, this here, if it's an acronym might be an O. For UPOR or UPOS."

"Then try it along with the U and P, too."

"Do you folks have UPOS in the city?" Darby asked Remy.

"Maybe an unnatural pile of bricks would be more likely," he said.

"Is that a hint?" Darby asked.

"No."

It didn't take me long to figure out that we didn't need to solve the coordinates following the DNF acronym because we were not supposed to find the cache there. The second line contained the coordinates we were supposed to go to. This cut down on our solving time immensely. We had the second line about half solved when my cell phone went off. I grumbled about my financial advisor as I pulled the phone from my pocket, but the call was from Jo.

"Excuse me," I said as I quickly pushed my chair back and worked my way through the crowd, while answering the phone. "Hello?"

"Earl, I'm sorry," she began.

"It's okay! Really!" I said. "You can call me any time!"

"I mean, I'm sorry, I really shouldn't call again. Something is coming up and... well... I feel terrible about leading you on. I was hoping... I don't know what I was hoping but I can't change what's happened. Just know that I didn't mean to hurt you..."

"What's going on?" I asked.

"Or take advantage of you," she said, her emotions beginning to get the upper hand.

The doorbell rang and she opened the door. Somebody came in carrying something. It sounded like they bumped the door jamb. The voice was male, "Who are you talking to?"

"Just a minute," Jo said as she rushed out the door.

"I can't talk," Jo said into the phone.

"I said, who are you talking to," the man said. The phone was pulled from her grasp. "Hello?"

I didn't know what to do. If I spoke he would know Jo had called a male friend. Judging by the bruises on Jo's arms I could do more harm than good by talking to this man. My heart and my mind were fighting it out. I'd just been dumped, but what could I do to better the situation? I guess it was a good thing she got interrupted. I was more worried about Jo, than I was crushed over the breakup.

"Who is this?" the man said to Jo.

"Just a friend," she told him.

The tension in the voices was palpable. He was irritated and she was scared. I could only make things worse by speaking.

"Why won't they talk to me?" the man asked. "There's only one reason I can think of."

"Jarrod, it's not what you think."

I thought I should hear what happened if I stuck around, but the longer I did the more he'd jump to conclusions. I wanted to talk to Jo, find out exactly what was going on, but now was not the time. I didn't know if I'd ever find out, but I did get one last hint.

"You're making wedding plans at the same time you're..." and then there was a crash as the phone hit a wall or sidewalk and went dead.

I stood there with the phone in my hand.

"Earl?" Darby said.

"I'll be right there," I answered, though I wanted to do almost anything but concentrate on a silly puzzle. I wanted to go back to the hotel and sulk. I wanted to call Jo back. I wanted to drink myself into oblivion and wallow in the results of my mistake. None of those options were available to me. The café did serve wine, but I thought a tighter rein on my brain was needed and wine wouldn't help. I sat dejectedly and tried to get interested in Darby's puzzle, but I'd lost the ability to concentrate.

"What's up?" Darby asked.

"Jo's getting married," I answered.

"Aw, dude. Don't that just..."

"No. I've got to stop her."

"An' how're you going to do that?"

"I don't know."

I flip flopped back and forth between wanting to jump on the first flight home and sucker punching myself into reality. The fact was I was in France and she had made up her mind. If she hadn't, she wouldn't have called. But somebody had to stop her. No matter how I felt, she was making a mistake. And I was in Paris.

Despite Darby taking a long time to figure out the acrostic, the page with the music on it had us all stumped for a much longer time.

"I can tell you what the notes are, but that doesn't help," I offered. "I can tell you which are quarter notes, eighth notes, etcetera. There are 9 notes in a scale but that doesn't help because we don't know which scale they are using."

"What key has two sharps?" Marc asked.

"I can play a harmonica, but I can't read music," Darby said.

"That would be D major, or B minor," I said.

"Well, lookie who's so ediccated," Darby said.

"I had to take violin and piano in school," I explained.

"So, if we start with D being one, E being 2 and so forth, what coordinates do we get?" I asked.

The beginning of the piece did not match any coordinates for the area.

"What's this thing?" Darby asked.

"It's a coda."

"A coda, like a mysterious geocaching code?"

"It tells you to go back to a certain spot in the music and repeat it," I explained.

"Go back? Like people go back again and again to a cache?"

I shrugged. It was a stretch to jump to that conclusion, but when we looked at the portion of the music that the coda pointed to it did, in fact, lead to coordinates that made sense.

"Wahoo!" Darby said. "We're in business!"

We all packed into Remy's little Fiat and he put the pedal to the metal. He seemed to know every twist and turn of the streets of Paris. I just held on and stewed about the conversation, and lack thereof, with Jo. She must have had some doubts about this engagement if she had accepted my invitations. I wasn't angry about the dates and the cost. I was hurt. I wanted to punch a certain man named Jarrod in the nose, but I'd never struck a man in my life and I knew it wasn't a solution. It would just invite a fight and I'd lose.

If Darby had known where the first cache was he wouldn't have been in such a hurry to find it. We found the French take their geocaching very seriously. Remy parked in a little lot at the head of a trail. The trail led into a forest. The walking was easy on hard packed soil. The forest closed around and we walked in shade all the way to the cache. We all watched our GPSrs and it soon became obvious that the cache was not going to be right on the trail. It was off trail a little bit. Then up ahead we saw a curious sight. Darby and I thought a bike rally or a marathon was going on because there was a tent set up beside the trail.

"Muggles? Way out here?" I asked Darby.

Marc and Remy were used to this. As soon as they saw the tent they put their GPSrs away. Darby and I followed. It also appeared that our team wasn't the only one to have this puzzle because there were several people gathered around the tent. Darby and I looked over the table that was set up under the tent. It held a mound of straps. And ropes.

We were greeted in French and we just smiled and shook hands still wondering what we had gotten ourselves into.

"Oh shit," Darby said. "No, no, no, I ain't doing that."

I followed his gaze up into the trees where a man was being lowered to the ground. He had to be fifty feet in the air. He wore a harness and helmet and he held tightly to the rope. His smile lit up the forest.

"I wonder if you can just sign the book…" I began, but Remy interrupted.

"The log stays in the tree," he said.

"Earl…"

"I'll give it a try but I want to see how it's done first," I told him.

"Can you sign it for me?" Darby asked. He got stern looks from the Frenchmen.

"It's part of the game. You climb the tree, you sign the log," I said.

"Oh shoot, oh shoot."

"Is a five terrain," Remy pointed out.

"I CAN SEE THAT!" Darby said in a slightly panicky voice.

"Watch a few climbers. The hide should be obvious after a climber or two."

"The hide isn't what worries me," he said.

"Just don't look down," I told him. "Just pretend it's a step ladder at home."

"A looong skinny, white barked, leaf shedding, step ladder. Yeah, right."

"You can do it," I said. "You're more athletic than I am."

"My athleticism isn't the question," he said.

"You can't fall. You'll be in a harness and there's a man on the other end of the rope."

"Falling isn't what I'm worried about."

"Then what are you worried about?" I asked.

"Heart attacks," he said matter-of-factly.

"Fear doesn't cause heart attacks," I pointed out.

"There's always a first," he said. He was getting more worked up about it by the minute, but he needed to see that it could be done before he'd agree to try it.

I watched a couple of climbers and it seemed easy enough, if someone manned the rope. The bottom of the tree was impossible to climb so all I had to do was get lifted into the air until I could make contact with some branches. I think the team work involved was the reason for the high terrain rating.

Darby was shaking in his boots so I decided it was time for me to take the plunge.

"Can I try it?" I asked.

"The American!" Remy said.

I better succeed, I thought, if I represent my country.

"Take a couple of pictures," I said to Darby. It would give him a chance to focus on something besides the height of the tree.

The man stationed at the base of the tree didn't speak much English but he knew how the gear worked. Through hand motions and the simplicity of the straps I was soon outfitted for a belay up into a tree. As my feet left the ground the man at the end of the rope said something about de l'eau. It wasn't until I was about ten feet off the ground that I noticed the rope had swung me out over a small river. Oh, shoot. Darby wasn't going to like that either. The stream was flowing bank to bank and I wondered if it was deep enough to cushion a fall. Up, up into the tree I went until I found a branch to grab hold of. There was a shout from below and Remy translated.

"Tell us when you are ready for less tension."

"Okay," I called down. Suddenly I began lowering. "Wait! I mean okay, I'll tell you!"

The rope tightened again and I looked for a foot hold on the tree. I looked up and saw that I still had about ten feet to climb under my own power. I grabbed hold of a sturdy branch and reached with my foot and found a stable place to stand and choose a path up the tree.

"Okay, ready!" I called down.

The rope eased up and I began my climb. It was a little disconcerting seeing how small the men below appeared. I noticed Darby had backed off from the group trying to get a picture of just how high up I was in the tree. Green leaves quivered in the breeze around my head and I began watching for a geocache. I thought it had to be near the pulley at the top of the tree. I wished I had the camera with me because the view was one to remember, both out across the forest to the city and down where the geocachers all craned their necks to see if I was finding the cache.

There didn't seem to be many hiding places in the tree. I had watched two other climbers and so I climbed toward a thick branch with a knobby protrusion on it. It was about five feet above a branch that had been stood upon many times. I was very tempted to sign the log for Darby, but I knew Remy and Marc would climb the tree after me. They would know whether or not Darby had climbed the tree. As much as I wished Darby could get credit for this find I couldn't sign it for him.

It wasn't easy juggling the cache, lid, log, and pen. Then after I signed the log I decided I should trade for something. I didn't have any swag with me, but I did have my wallet, so like foreigners sometimes left banknotes from their own country in American caches, I left a five dollar bill and chose a little metal pencil sharpener shaped like a castle.

After I closed up the cache and replaced it in the knot hole I called down, "Ready!" and began the descent. When I ran out of branches I watched for a go ahead from below before I slowly rappelled down the trunk of the tree to the ground below.

"It's pretty stable up there," I told Darby. "If you don't look down it should be easy."

"Easy for you to say," he said.

"You can get a souvenir of your climb to prove that you really did it," I countered as I held out the little castle.

"Ah, Carcassonne," Remy said. "A very interesting place if you extend your stay."

The phrase fell flat. Extend my stay? I wanted to fly home that instant, but I knew there was no use in it.

"Darby, you next," Remy announced.

"Me?" Darby nearly squeaked. "Ain't nothing can make me go up there!"

"It's perfectly safe," I said.

While we were standing there trying to persuade Darby to overcome his fear for just ten minutes a kid of about seven piped up in French and if I could have guessed just by his tone of voice he wanted to go next. I didn't understand what the people around me were saying but the child was determined to climb that tree and the adults were telling him how high up it was and questioning whether he could reach the branches to climb the last little bit. I wondered the same thing, but the geocaching event hosts seemed to think everybody should have a fair chance at finding the cache and they seemed to be assuring the parents that they would hoist the boy all the way to the cache if necessary. At last the boy won his case and he was outfitted for the climb. All this time Darby was fretting and grumbling. If a seven year old boy could do it, he felt he had to climb the tree, too. He had no excuse except for his own bull headed fears. So much for nothing being able to make him climb the tree. He might have irrational fears, but he also had irrational justifications to overcome them. Too bad pride wasn't stronger than fear for more people.

The boy was ecstatic about being so high in the air. It made me want to learn French just so I could share in his joy.

Remy sensed Darby's hesitation so as soon as the boy was on his way down Remy treated Darby as if he was next and he was going up and before

Darby knew it he found himself putting his feet into the harness and buckling on the helmet. *Click!* And he was on the rope.

"Now wait a minute! I didn't agree to this! I didn't sign the form! If I fall I'm going to sue you for every penny! I might anyway for... for... aw shit, aw heck, don't look down, don't look down. Just sign the log and give the signal."

I thought the leaves on the tree Darby was climbing were shaking more than the leaves on the other trees. After watching him on the plane flight I could easily believe he was literally shaking with fear up there. Would his signature in the log book even be legible? I suppose it didn't matter. Everybody had seen him, mad as he was, up in the tree. No matter what his signature looked like everybody knew he did it. I took pictures, partly so he would have them and partly so I could use them later if his fear surfaced again. I felt a little sorry for him but I also thought a fear of heights would be a good one to get over. Little did I know that the tree climb was sissy stuff compared to the other puzzles.

Chapter 15

I was glad we were in the company of seasoned geocachers and that Remy was basically acting as a tour guide. He had explored all these places already but went along with the event just to socialize with geocachers. He knew a helpless American tourist when he saw one. My climb up Mount Everest had been much the same. I had a guide along who told me exactly what to do and when to do it. When I reached the top all I could see was clouds and mountain peaks, and the victory was more a sense of relief that I had made it. The next cache was not a tree climb.

As I stood before the doorway in France I thought I had entered an Indiana Jones movie. It was dark in there. Moss coated the stone of the entryway. Beyond that I had no idea what I was stepping into. Darby looked inside with a sense of adventure. It didn't involve heights yet so he was ready to enter the darkness. Remy handed out "lamps". We called them flashlights. I thought it interesting that the headlamp was called a headlamp but the flashlights were called lamps.

I expected to enter the fort and feel claustrophobic. In general I do not suffer from claustrophobia. I am used to putting my life into the hands of elevators. I've even been stuck in one once during an earthquake. I thought the darkness would close in on me when I entered the fort, but that didn't happen either. Instead I felt immersed… in history. I didn't know why the fort had been built, or why it was underground, or what had transpired there, but the place oozed fears and pain that I could not imagine. A musty scent permeated the air, like moisture and age and rot had formed into one never ending process to bring the fort down despite its history in the war. Mother Nature works where even man cannot.

We were the only ones in the area but even Remy spoke in hushed tones. It was almost as if the place had heard enough screams and shouts. It seemed wrong to yell.

"You can explore, but be careful," Remy instructed. "There are many things to trip on. The ground is not level."

"Where are we going?" I asked. "The GPS is useless down here."

"Read the instructions," he said. "I know the route."

"Route? You mean it's not in this room?" I asked.

He just smiled knowingly. "That way," he said.

"Now wait a minute," Darby said a little too loudly. He was in his element now and he wanted to savor the adventure. "We gotta do this for ourselves." I agreed, though I was willing to follow Remy if that's how things worked out. I realized this event had a time limit. We were to meet up at the café after dark and we had three more caches to find. I doubted we would find them all if they were all as involved as tree climbing and fort exploring. So perhaps having a leader would help.

Darby worked his way over to a wall, but he quickly found the room to be just that, a room, perhaps just an entryway. I didn't expect large rooms in a place that needed to be defendable.

I switched my GPS to the description and when I saw how long it was I handed the GPS to Darby so he could see that this was not going to be a simple find. It was very involved... and written in French, so we were forced to follow Remy and Marc.

When we left the first room and entered a narrow corridor I imagined a battle raging. There was absolutely no space to fight a battle inside this place. I could easily touch both walls, though I didn't want to. I had seen spider webs and lizards already. I didn't know what else might live within these walls. The lizards were small and brown with stripes that ran head to tail. They were quick and ran away at the first sight of us, but I still didn't want to surprise one in the darkness.

Marc asked Remy a question in French and Remy replied in the affirmative. Another question passed between them and they laughed.

"A quick side trip," Remy said. "Because Darby wants to explore."

"Oh, good!" Darby said.

The two Frenchmen nodded and I was prepared for a scare, but they turned a corner and entered another room.

"Be careful the chains," Remy said, but what he wanted to show us was not the inch thick chains bolted to the floor. "Shhh," he said. "Can you hear it?"

We all silenced our breathing and listened closely. There was a sound. A very soft sound. A sound of movement, but soft movement. Not like the rattling of sticks or flutter of leaves. Whatever made the noise was very quiet and soft.

"Above," Remy said quietly.

We shined our lights at the ceiling.

"Ahhhaaiii!" Darby yelled without thinking.

Hundreds of bats hung upside down until they heard Darby's yell. Some of them startled and flew away, causing Darby and I to duck. I had never seen bats before. I wasn't afraid of them, yet I didn't want to come into contact with them either. I shined my light up at the colony and beady eyes blinked down at me. Leathery ears made them look almost comical. When they became uncomfortable they would stretch out a wing and hook onto another part of the ceiling and then let go with their other claws and swing over to the new spot. The ceiling must have had rough patches because the bats moved upside down with awkward ease. I know that sounds like an oxymoron, but picture a child born without feet. They are used to moving about and it looks awkward to us, yet they move easily and naturally because it is all they know. This is what the bats resembled. They had little hooked claws and they used them very efficiently, yet they could barely walk using wings and feet.

"Them critters give me the willies!" Darby said.

"Yeah, cool," I said. "Thanks for showing them to us."

Remy led us deep into the fort. I call it a fort because it was just fortress-like to me. Later I began to think it was a prison, but nobody actually told me what the structure used to be. We saw rusted cell doors and rooms that I couldn't identify. Dampness hung in the air but I didn't actually see any running water. I began debating if age and damp felt the same. At the same time that I sensed dampness our footsteps stirred up little dust clouds. Everything about the place caused conflicting sensations. Sound and silence. Dark and light. Dampness and dryness. Age and decay. Past and present. Deep and deeper. The silence was only broken by occasional instructions by Remy.

"Don't hit your head," he said.

"Why would the roof be so low?"

"Shifting of the land."

We had to step around several square stones that had fallen out of the wall.

"Is this place safe?" Darby asked.

"As safe as any other place," Remy said.

"We're from LA so that's not saying much," Darby said.

A lizard skittered over the side of the one of the rocks and peeked around the side to make sure we were leaving.

"How deep are we?" I asked.

"I don't know," Remy said. "Not very. But wait."

"It feels like there must be a whole hill above us," I said.

"It is level here, so, I doubt it is very deep. Follow, it will go a little deeper."

"Who explored this place enough to place a cache here?" I asked.

"Many people. Sometimes we meet others down here."

I cringed when I saw where we had to go down. It was a trap door, or rather, it looked like a trap door used to cover a hole in the floor. Our flashlights revealed... nothing. Even shining our lamps into the hole, all we saw was the top of a rusty ladder. The ladder disappeared into total blackness.

"I doubt this cache gets muggled often," Darby observed.

It was easier to climb down the ladder with the flashlights off and stowed. Marc shined the light on the top of the ladder until the three of us climbed down. It felt like a long descent but it was hard to judge the distance in the dark.

"Are there bats down here?" Darby asked as we stepped down and down again and again.

"I don't see bats," Remy answered.

"Very funny," Darby said.

Marc waited until we were all the way down and then Remy shined his flashlight up, giving Marc something to focus on as he climbed into the darkness. The beam barely reached, only giving Marc a hazy glimpse of the rusty rungs. We stood in the dark, tiny pinpricks of light for Marc to climb down to. When we all stood at the bottom of the ladder I worried a little bit about leaving the ladder. We couldn't see anything, even with the flashlights shining brightly, except the floor and the ladder. The floor was bare stone. We still needed to walk to find the cache and to walk meant leaving the ladder.

"How the hell are we supposed to see a cache in all this... dark?" Darby said.

"I don't know, but I hope we brought extra batteries," I said.

The room seemed to swallow the light. The air was still and I was tempted to scuff my feet just to stir up some dust and give the light something to shine on. I couldn't help but compare the bleakness of the room to the way I felt without Jo. It was dark and I couldn't see where to go. I knew there was a life outside the darkness, but it felt very far away.

Remy read the description and then translated it into English for Darby and me, but we really didn't need it translated because as soon as Marc heard the French version he began feeling his way forward, shining his flashlight on the rough stone floor. However, we did get a couple of good hints. The container was painted to match its surroundings and it was a cigar tin. I wasn't sure if it was painted to match the stone, or black as the inside of an Egyptian pyramid, or an ancient French fort.

Remy just waited. The few times I shined my flashlight on him his expression changed and I imagined it changing in the dark as we got closer or further away from the cache. I brought the beam back to Remy to get a clue.

"Are you standing on the cache?" I asked.

"No," he said. "That is impossible."

Ah, a clue. I began searching higher but when I checked Remy's expression he was amused that he had given me a clue and tricked me at the same time. I began thinking. How could you hide a cache down low that could not be stood on?

"Are we even in the right part of the room?" I asked.

"Perhaps it isn't in the room at all."

Another clue. How could it not be in the room? The room was encased in the earth. If the cache wasn't in this room he would have led us further. Maybe it just wasn't technically in the room. This thinking led me to look for a gap in the wall near Remy. The beam only illuminated a small section of wall and it all looked normal to me.

"This is impossible!" Darby said.

"When I found it my caching partner brought a bright lamp. This cache is much talked about. So he knew to bring a bright lantern."

"Then why didn't you bring one?" Darby asked.

"It was a most difficult thing to carry around while we explored. I also think it made the final finding of the cache too easy."

"So this thing is recognizable in the light," I surmised.

"How do you take everything he says as a hint?" Darby asked me.

"I'm used to high powered financial meetings. If you listen very carefully and read between the lines it generally pays off. Ask Remy. He's been handing out hints whenever we want."

Darby shined his flashlight on Remy who didn't have to say a thing. His smug expression confirmed that he knew where the cache was and had not led us astray.

Darby huffed. "Okay, so what hints did we get?"

"The cache is painted to blend in with its surroundings. It cannot be stood on. It is not in this room, and it is recognizable in the light," I said.

The wall looked perfectly normal so I went on to another wall but when I checked Remy's expression I realized I was further away from the cache. I decided I had the right idea so I went back to the wall near Remy and began tapping the wall. I thought my knuckles would be raw by the time I accidentally hit the wall with the toe of my boot and was rewarded with a hollow sound and the clank of a metal object hitting the rock behind it. I knelt down and shined the light on the base of the wall. The tin fit the space where a stone brick was missing. Perhaps the gap around it was a bit wider than the mortar between the rocks, but the tin looked amazingly like a rock. Nobody seemed to have noticed that I found the cache. I kept seeing flashlight beams wandering the room. Remy knew of course, but he didn't say anything as I opened the cache as quietly as I could, signed the log and rehid the tin where I had found it. I joined Remy in watching the others.

"Do you think they will find it on their own?" I asked quietly.

"Marc will. But he has found these kind before."

"I don't know about Darby. We don't have caches like this in LA. Everything is modern and well lit."

"How did *you* find it?"

"I listened to you."

"Did I reveal too much?"

"No, I think just enough. Darby is used to plain talk."

"I am not! I can listen to fancy talk with the best of them," Darby said.

"Then follow the hints," I suggested.

"How did you open it without rattling anything?" Remy asked me.

"Carefully."

"Do that always when you geocache and you will be a formidable geocacher."

"French geocachers seem to enjoy the adventure," I pointed out.

"Yes. Some. We have some very ordinary caches. The difficult ones, I think, are more so here."

"I think so," I agreed, though I hadn't really looked for difficult caches yet. "Are there any so difficult that they go unfound?"

"Oh, yes! Of course," he said as if this was an ordinary thing.

"Would you stop yacking and start looking?" Darby said.

"Okay," I said as I moved about a little bit. I made a point to shine the flashlight right on the cache and occasionally kick it just enough to cause a sound, but Darby seemed oblivious.

"Sometimes caches are placed during mountain climbing expeditions. Some are years old and still no FTF."

"Really? Is there one you have been tempted to find?" I asked.

"Of course!"

"What stops you?"

He chose his words carefully. "My sense of safety is larger than my sense of adventure."

"Ah, I see. Darby!"

"Yeah?"

"When I asked you what I should be when I grow up, what did you tell me?" I asked.

"I don't know! It was just a flippant answer," he said.

"He told me to be a lion tamer," I told Remy. "He said, 'what's life without a little risk?'"

"And what did you do?" Remy asked.

"We flew to Paris instead. But why stop in Paris? Where is this cache you haven't found?"

I wished I could see his eyes. A long pause made me think he was considering his answer.

"Perhaps… maybe…" he didn't commit. It made me wonder where this cache was that made him question going to look for it.

I nudged the cache again making a scraping, grinding sound.

"Would whoever is doing that stop?" Darby said. "It makes me think there's something in here with us. And I don't want to see what makes that much noise. It's almost like a… uh, is that you Remy?"

"No! It's not me," Remy said.

"Earl?"

"No, it's not me. It's the cache."

"You found it?" Darby asked.

Remy and I both laughed.

"Then where is it?" Darby asked.

"Follow the sound," I told him.

I nudged the cache every once in a while until I saw him nearby, then I stopped. "It cannot be stood on. It's not in the room. It's painted to blend in. And it sounds like…" *Scrape… grind…*

"How can it be in the room but not in the room?" Darby asked.

"Perhaps," said Remy, "It is part of the room."

"Use your ears," I added.

He grumbled quietly as he searched the area around where Remy and I were standing so we stepped aside. It took him several more minutes and a few subtle hints before either Darby or Marc tapped the cigar box.

"All riiiight!" Darby shouted. It echoed off the walls of the room and we all cringed at the outburst. I imagined all the lizards startling and freezing in place until the intrusion faded and soaked into the rocks and the silence resumed.

This time, since we all knew where it was we were able to slow down and get a good look inside the cache. It was rectangular, spray painted black with tan, random spots to break up the view and it fit nearly perfectly into the spot where a brick had worked loose. There was originally a picture of a man on a horse stamped into the metal and even the shadows of the stamping helped the container blend in. I thought Remy was right; finding it in the dark, with minimal help was more enjoyable than lighting up the whole room and simply spotting it.

While the cache was open we all looked through the swag. It was a bit difficult to do in the dark, but the cache was well stocked. Once again I didn't have anything except money to trade and I decided no matter what I had planned the next day I had to buy some swag. However, this cache had plenty of travelers, those little metal tags attached to a "hitchhiker" because geocachers thought this was a safe place to leave them. We found four of the tags and two geocoins. This reminded me that I still had the frog coin that I picked up in Russia. I decided to leave it in this cache. I thought maybe the owner of the coin would like to read about the cache his coin was visiting. I traded the frog coin for a tiny coin of an artist gnome. I also took an aluminum tag shaped like a badger. It was attached to a chipmunk riding a skateboard, but the skateboard was made out of a bottle opener. Marc traded travelers, too.

"This one wants to visit spooky places," he said as he dropped it in. "I can write about the bats in the log."

"And the dark," Darby added.

We closed up the cache and replaced it in the wall with a sense of accomplishment. We stood around in a circle, the lights flickering off our faces. We looked like a band of modern day pirates. Remy looked each of us in the eye before saying ominously, "I found one more place. There is no cache. Do you want to see it? It is deeper into the ruins and we must be cautious."

"No more bats," Darby said.

Chapter 16

Remy shined his flashlight along the walls as he led us deeper into the fort. He pointed out brackets on the walls that were made for holding torches. I could not imagine maintaining burning torches, or what these narrow corridors had smelled like with torches burning in them for hours at a time. How old was this place?

Deeper still we went until we didn't even startle lizards anymore.

"Stop," Remy said. "Don't step where you cannot see the floor."

"Why?" Darby asked.

"If a geocache was hidden here it would be a... ten/ten. Be very careful. Very."

I think Darby began sweating at this point. A ten/ten was infeasible and any place that nobody would even consider putting a cache he did not want to see.

"I will find it," Remy offered and the three of us stood in one spot while Remy advanced. He didn't walk far and he as extremely careful to only step where he could see. When he stopped he said. "Okay. Now come forward. I think this is the first. And we will not proceed further. Shine your light on the ground to be sure."

Marc and I followed as instructed. Darby didn't move. When Remy, Marc and I were standing in one area, Remy said, "Now wait. Don't move."

Remy shined his flashlight until the beam reached a hole. The light sank like a rock in the ocean. Remy began removing his pack. Inside he had a rope.

"Who wants to go down?" he asked.

"You have a harness?" I asked.

He did.

"How will you secure it?" I asked. He shined his light on a rusty metal loop.

"What is this place?" I asked.

"An oubliette."

"What is that in English?"

"I believe the word is the same. It means a place of forgetting."

"But what is it?" I asked. Being a financial investor I didn't have much experience with ancient French architecture.

"It is a... a cell. At the bottom of a... shaft." He was having a little more trouble finding English words to describe French things.

"Like a prison cell," I said.

"Yes!" He said, glad that he was explaining things clear enough.

"Like solitary confinement," I added.

"No way," Darby said. "Earl... don't."

But I was curious. What was this oubliette? I had wanted to see Paris, even the littlest, dustiest corners of it. We were not in Paris proper but I still wanted to see what was down there.

"Okay, I'll go," I said. "Marc?"

"One at a time," Marc said.

"Have you done this before?" I asked.

"No, I have never been to this place before," he answered.

"Remy?" I asked.

"I have."

"And?"

"Just be happy you are not forgotten."

I strapped on the harness and used the aluminum clip at the waist to fasten myself to a loop on the end of Remy's stout climbing rope.

"Do you do this a lot?" I asked Remy.

"No, but when I do it I am prepared," he answered.

"Are all the groups looking for caches this difficult?" I asked.

"No, I chose these puzzles because I knew where they led."

"Are you going to any you haven't found yet?"

"No, but that's okay. Today I am the guide. Next time another will host."

So that's how it worked.

Remy threaded the rope through the loop.

"Ready?" he asked.

"How do I do this?" I asked.

"Put your feet in the hole and lower yourself down. Marc?"

Marc grabbed the rope behind Remy as an extra precaution. I stuck my feet into the hole and scooted forward. I propped myself up on my hands as I lowered my body through the hole. I imagined trying to get an uncooperative prisoner through the hole. It would be difficult. Yet at the same time it was a little difficult going through willingly, too. The walls of the shaft were close enough to touch.

"Shine your lamp down," Remy nearly yelled down to me. "If you see water tell me."

Oh, great. I shined the light down but the beam didn't hit anything yet. They lowered me further into the blackness. I turned the beam to the wall and it was black with age and perhaps soot and grime. I shined it down again and the floor looked dark, but not muddy or watery.

"I think it's okay," I called up to Remy.

"If you want to come up, just pull the rope twice."

"Okay."

The shaft ended and space opened up around me. I shined the light down. I still had about ten feet to go.

"I think it's dry enough," I said. It was right about then that things went wrong. I heard a noise and I dropped, suddenly freefalling. My stomach leaped to my chest and a moment of panic overwhelmed me. I didn't know how to land and didn't really have time to worry about it. I reached out with my hands, which was a big mistake. My flashlight fell and my hand hit it as I crashed to the floor. The flashlight rolled, twisting my hand painfully. Then the rest of me landed with a crash and everything went black.

When I came to I expected to hear voices but an eerie silence enveloped me. I tried moving and found my right hand to be useless. My head pounded in time with my pulse. I felt my head and there was a large lump on the back of my skull. I felt around with my left hand for the flashlight. The lens and bulb had broken in the fall. I was sore from head to toe but my wrist was the most painful part of me. I stood and tried walking but I quickly ran into a solid stone wall.

"Yeeeeoow!" I cried when the collision caused me to bring my hand up and I bashed it into the rock. "Remy? Marc?"

At this point I remembered the rope. I found the clip and, left handed, pulled the rope until I concluded that the end had fallen into the shaft with me.

"Earl?" Marc said.

I was so relieved to hear another voice that I nearly cried. I wasn't scared. I don't know why my emotions reacted the way they did but just knowing I was not totally alone brought a joy that I cannot describe.

"Yeah," I said.

"How are you?" he asked.

"I think I'll survive, but I injured my wrist. How long was I out?"

"Out?"

"Unconscious," I corrected myself.

"Remy and Darby went to get another rope. Perhaps… ten minutes."

"They've been gone ten minutes or I've been out ten minutes?"

"Perhaps he has a rope in his car. If he does not he will call for help," he said.

I guess it didn't matter how long I'd been unconscious, so I didn't press for an answer.

"Thanks for staying," I said.

"Your friend is loyal," Marc said.

"Oh?"

"He argued that he should stay."

"He would have been terrified."

"That's why we made him go."

"How in the world did I fall?" I asked.

"The metal broke," he said.

"The loop? But it was solid iron!"

"It was solid... how do you say it."

"Rust?"

"I think so. The break was sudden."

"Yeah, it felt sudden."

Marc and I talked for a long time but after a while the strain of trying to think in English made him cut his sentences shorter and shorter until we fell into uncomfortably long silences and then I sat in the dark thinking. I remembered my conversation with Jo and her boyfriend interrupting. He'd mentioned a wedding. I didn't think Jo was really the type of girl to cheat on her boyfriend. There had to be a reason she agreed to see me.

"Marc?"

"Yes."

"Why would a woman go out with a man if she was engaged to be married?"

There was a long silence.

"Are you the groom to be or the other?"

"The other."

"My father has a saying. I think your American version is, it's not over till it's over."

"But that doesn't explain why."

"That is a matter of great import. The why... you may never know... the fact is she sees in you what she does not see in another."

"Thanks."

"This woman. She is... beautiful?"

"Yes. Very."

"Then why do you play the tourist?"

"My plans were made. She knew it."

"So you turn your back and while you are away... Go back. To go back will tell her she is more important than your travel. More important than..."

"I think she is more sensible than that."

"You are sensible, are you not?"

"I hope so."

"Then you tell me, if this beautiful woman should appear at your hotel you would... get the message, would you not?"

"Most definitely."

"Then..."

I had asked myself the same thing. Why was I in Paris when I could make a difference back home? Then I told myself that Jo had made a decision. She had called me. I had no say in her future plans.

It's not over till it's over.

She called me. It's over.

Maybe you think it's over, but it's not over until she takes that final step to make it truly over.

So it's nearly over.

I thought the oubliette was an appropriate place for me at the time. Los Angeles felt a million miles away. Dang, Paris felt a million miles away. I might as well have been on the moon and Marc was Houston.

Marc and I were stuck in the fort for hours. Even if I hadn't been trapped in the oubliette I doubt we could have found our way out. Eventually I stood and felt my way around the cell. The walls were very rough. The rock was jagged and unfinished. It was easy to bash my head or just run smack dab into the rock because I couldn't see a thing. The cell at the bottom seemed to be about three paces long and four paces wide. The walls curved up into the shaft above my head and beyond my reach. If anybody had ideas about how to climb up out of the cell they could forget them. It wouldn't work.

Eventually I grew thirsty, so Marc dropped a water bottle to me. We worried that dropping it from such a height would break the bottle so he shined his flashlight straight down the shaft. A tiny smudge of light reached the floor. He dropped the bottle straight down the beam so I could try to catch it, or cushion its fall. It ended up glancing off my arm and rolling across the cell but I eventually found it by feeling around. I didn't want to think about what else might be down there. It occurred to me, when I thought I found a stick that it could just as easily be a bone. But then when I felt around I didn't feel other things that felt like bones, so that eased my mind a little. Still, it felt like a very hopeless place to be. The cell felt as if it had soaked up decades of pain, loneliness and despair. Worrying about Jo didn't help either. Thinking of the fight just to get a person down the shaft reminded me of the bruises on Jo's arms and my anger burned. Jarrod. That was the guy's name. An oubliette was a good place for him.

During the hour or so of silence when I got tired of calling up to Marc and he got tired of figuring out responses in English, I sat in pitch black silence so deep that I thought I could imagine what it felt like to be pressed into a diamond. The walls closed in, the darkness pressing upon me. The silence made my ears strain until I thought I could hear ringing even though no sound was present. Everything focused down on me, even my thoughts and emotions until I felt as if I must be compressed by it. I could easily see how a man might go mad down there. I, at least, had hope of rescue in a short while. Others who shared my circumstances had not been so lucky.

I heard voices above but to really be understood they would have to talk down the shaft.

"Earl?" Remy called down.

"Yeah!"

"Are you finished with the tour of the oubliette?"

"Yes sir, I believe I am. Now, if I could get a lift out."

"We're working on it," he called down.

There was more talk above and then Remy called down, "Stand aside. Help is coming."

I hoped they didn't send much help because not very many people could fit in the confines of the cell. Several minutes later the hole at the top of the shaft became illuminated and shortly thereafter the light was blocked by an object, then nearly totally blocked out by a person. I stepped out of the way of whatever they were sending down. First I heard a clunk, like a large plastic object softly hitting the rock floor, then very soon after that the sounds of a man's clothing and gear filled the cell. They were soft sounds and yet the confines of the cell seemed to magnify their significance. When the man's head appeared I was blinded by the light from his helmet.

After my eyes adjusted I realized the man was dressed in rescue gear, which meant he wore a uniform consisting of cargo pants, matching shirt complete with official looking patches and bright, yellow reflective strips, a helmet and boots. He looked like a soldier. His immediate concern seemed to be my health.

"Sir?"

"Earl O'Connor. Thanks for the help."

"Have a seat," he said.

"You're American?" I asked.

"Yes sir."

"What's an American EMT doing in an ancient French fort rescuing stupid tourists from the folly of their ways?"

"I'd thank you, but it might encourage you," he said. "I've heard stories about this place and I wanted to explore it, but it was always somebody else who got the call."

"I don't recommend exploring on your own. And bring plenty of rope," I said as we attempted to sit in the cell without bashing ourselves on the rocks.

"Yes sir."

"Look, you can drop the formalities."

While we talked he opened a tool box and took out a blood pressure cuff. He took my pulse and blood pressure in the light of a headlamp. He seemed to come to the conclusion that I wasn't in immediate danger because he put the cuff away.

"Coming down!" a voice above said and the EMT stood and accepted the package that was being lowered down the shaft.

"It's going to be bright," he said as he turned on a lantern that would have lit up half the fort had it been needed. "I was told you were unconscious for several minutes, so let's take a look at you."

He felt around on my head until he hit the bump and I winced.

"Hmm," he said.

"I didn't land on my head. My right hand hit first. I think I sprained my wrist."

"Well, your head did hit something," he said. "What were you doing in here?"

"Here? Just exploring. I'd never seen an oubliette. I was curious."

"Maybe you should take it easy for the remainder of your trip."

He shined a light into my eyes to check the dilation. Next he went on to my wrist, which we could immediately see was bright purple and slightly swollen. He squeezed gently but it hurt like crazy. He checked the rest of my arm for broken bones. As he did I took the chance to look around the cell. The thing I thought was a stick was the dried out handle of a tool. However, it was shaped differently than manmade tools today. It was too straight and it was unfinished wood, more like an old broom handle. At least it wasn't a bone, I thought.

"How do you feel in general?" he asked.

"Sore. I suppose the wrist needs an x-ray."

"Yes sir, we're going to splint it, then I think we can get out of here. Can you walk out?"

"Yeah, I've been walking around the cell. I'll have to go slow on the ladder," I said.

"I think if that's the most we have to worry about we can count this as a successful rescue," he said. "From the initial report we thought we would be carrying you out on a stretcher. When we arrived we weren't certain the stretcher would fit down the hole."

"It's a bit of a squeeze," I admitted.

He fit a splint around my wrist. It was odd how my wrist felt both better and worse with the splint on. I thought perhaps I would be able to handle the ladder better. The splint seemed to immobilize the wrist enough to allow me to use my fingers.

He wouldn't allow me to clip on until he went through the blood pressure check and shined the light in my eyes again.

"How far did you fall?" he asked.

"I think I was at the bottom of the shaft. It had opened up a bit before the bracket broke."

We both looked up to get an idea of the height of the cell and guessed I had fallen about eight feet. The cell was built to be impossible to climb out of so the ceiling had to be out of reach of even the tallest prisoner.

"You were very lucky," said the man I had begun calling Gilmore because of the patch on his uniform.

Gilmore clipped the rope to my harness.

"It's going to look like an army up there," He warned me. "They're only there to help."

"Okay, why the huge turnout just to help one guy out of a predicament?"

"After your experience you can understand… this was almost like a cave rescue. When people get lost in caves it takes a team. There are specialists up there so no matter what we encounter there will be a man for the job. Are you ready? Grab the rope. Okay. Ready?"

"Ready."

"Okay!" he called to his comrades. "Tension…" the rope tightened and I readied myself for liftoff. "Okay," he told me, "going up!"

He wasn't kidding. If he hadn't warned me I would have expected to end up in a more modern French prison, but they really were there just to make sure I was found and transported to a local hospital. I could see Darby behind the scenes, worry etched in every line of his face. I gave him a thumbs up to let him know I was okay.

The fort was twice as interesting on the way out because everybody had professional grade lights. I was able to see places that I had felt my way through the first time. I was surrounded by ETMs, all able military trained men. It was rather humbling and a bit embarrassing. I could not have injured myself further if I tried. I was told where to walk, how to climb the ladder safely and when we walked out of the fort and into the light the sun was setting and the forest chill was settling in. We had missed the conclusion of the event completely.

"I'm sorry, guys," I told Remy, Marc and Darby.

"We will see you later," Remy said. "We have much to discuss."

"Will do," I said.

I thought about what we had to discuss as I was driven to the hospital. It was then that I remembered there were a few old caches out there that Remy said had never been found. What other surprises did this country have to offer?

I was in for a painful couple of hours while they x-rayed my wrist and skull, then declared the wrist badly sprained. I had also cracked my arm, so I ended up in a cast and sling. I called Darby as soon as I was released.

"Hey, where are you?" I asked.

"Remy dropped me off at the hotel. How are you?"

"I'm okay. I say we take it easy tomorrow. Maybe do some shopping, meet up with Remy and talk about that FTF."

"I don't think that's such a good idea. I already talked to Remy about that."

"We'll talk about it later. I need to find a ride back. Did you get dinner okay?"

"Don't worry about me. What do you want me to do? So far my job today involved geocaching and talking to Remy for hours and hours."

"See if the hotel has an American bacon cheeseburger and fries. Tell them to put it on our room tab."

Darby showed up at my room with a hamburger and chips shortly after I got back to my room, which meant he had spent an hour looking for one. At least he felt like he had done his job. It didn't have bacon, but I was too tired to care. I dug the tiny coin and the travel tag out of my pocket and we looked up their missions. The coin was so small Darby had to read the code to me.

"It says GFGY4M," He said as he squinted at the back of it. He flipped it over. "I never seen a coin like this before. Looks like it would get lost really easy."

I typed in the code and read the mission.

"It's collecting pictures that are worthy of painting," I read. "I'm sure we can help in that department. What's a GIFF event?"

"Ooo, oo, I know that one. What was it? I never been to it, 'cause it's a popular event. I think it's a film festival for geocachers. That would account for the FF. G would be geocaching."

It sounded reasonable so I accepted his explanation and decided to look it up later. The other one, the badger, was code number CABFFN and it wanted to visit other animals. I didn't have a dog but I could drop it off near the LA Zoo.

"You are not going after that FTF," Darby said.

"Why?"

"One, it requires a boat ride up river. Then the person that hid it was a mountain climber. And hiker. Dude could walk forever. Then the forest grew up and covered over the path. It will take a couple of strenuous days to reach that cache and you've got a... cast. Is it broke?"

"Sprained wrist, cracked ulna."

"I think your head is cracked, too."

"You'll feel better in the morning. Other than falling into the oubliette, I thought it was a great day and it would have gotten better if we hadn't spent the day trying to extract me from the center of the earth."

We sat around the small dining table in my room.

"So what was it like down there?" Darby asked.

"Bleak. It will make you appreciate sunshine, that's for sure."

"I think I can appreciate it just fine without going down there."

"Can you open this?" I asked Darby.

He easily turned the little lid on the pill bottle.

"Wow, so what do they hand out for pain in French hospitals?" he asked.

"I don't know. But I plan to have a good night's rest."

"How much did you have to whine to get these?" he asked.

"A lot," I answered.

"I wonder if the dosage goes up the more you whine."

"I don't know. Why did I ask for a meal I have to eat with two hands?"

"I thought you were in American food withdrawal. Sorry there isn't bacon."

"It's okay. I wonder what the sauce is."

"French ketchup?"

"I wonder if the kitchenette has a fork."

"I'll look."

He got up and walked to the little kitchen unit in the corner of my room.

"So why don't you want to go on a boat ride and climb a mountain?" I asked.

"You ever bushwhacked your way to a cache?"

"No."

"It isn't the best way to spend a weekend."

"But it's an FTF. You used to brag about getting an FTF. How old is this one?"

"Three years. Usually if a cache is going to be found it's found within hours. If it's really, really tough it might take a few days. That cache might not even be out there."

"Mountain climbing. Did Remy say what the elevation is?"

"No, I didn't think to ask."

"France has some big mountains."

"No shit."

"We've done the city geocaching. Let's go see what roughing it is like."

"Dude, you just broke your arm."

"But I didn't break my legs and my shoulders will still support a pack."

"Sleep on it. You might feel different in the morning."

"Okay, I need to do a little shopping tomorrow anyway. I need swag and I promised Jo I'd watch for a Christmas ornament."

That night I lay awake for a long time, waiting for the pain killers to take effect. And I wondered why I should buy Jo a Christmas ornament if I was never going to see her again. But I'd promised and it was a small thing.

Oh, Jo, what are you doing? You can't marry that guy. Even if I never see you... please... be safe. I don't know if it was me or the drugs doing the thinking. It was a rough night.

Chapter 17

The sun oozed though the crack in my curtains. It brightened. I tried to pretend it was still dark. I felt like I had been run over by a Mack truck. I was glad my wrist was immobilized because anything that moved ached. The bed was comfortable and I sure didn't look forward to walking, showering and dressing. I remembered the struggle trying to find ID, insurance cards, filling in the paperwork at the hospital and paying the bill predominately left handed and it made even shopping look like a chore. I wondered what Darby would do with a day off. When I quit making excuses and began thinking, I decided I better get up and distract myself before I allowed Jo to overshadow my thoughts. Maybe a hot shower would ease some of the aches.

I rolled out of bed and forced my body to assume a normal standing position. I wondered if the hotel had a hot tub. Maybe if I walked around a bit my muscles would loosen up. I looked for a book that told about the facilities at the hotel but there were too many places to search and I was too sore to care. I didn't want to walk the hotel looking for the hot tub anyway. I turned on the hot water and steamed up the bathroom, then attempted to shower without getting the cast wet. I made a mental note to buy tape. I could tape the hotel laundry sack over my cast next time I showered.

It was awkward getting dressed and my arm hurt when I tried to button my shirt. Maybe I should buy some t-shirts, too. I debated about calling Darby. Then I decided he was probably a step or two ahead of me anyway.

"You're alive!" he said when he answered his phone.

"Yeah, I'm alive. I discovered a few things I need in order to live with this cast. Do you have some simple caches downloaded around town near shopping?"

"Maybe. Do you want to download caches before we go or hope there are some nearby?"

"Let's just hope there are some nearby. This better be an easy day."

"You got it."

"Really cushy, like, let me do the driving."

"Uh, you're going to drive? Like that?"

"No, and I'm not going to hail taxis either. Meet me at the concierge's desk."

"I'd like to hire a driver for the day," I said.

"Yes sir, and what would you like to do?"

"Just some shopping, eat out, maybe meet a friend and find a geocache or two."

"A geo... what?"

"Don't worry, I'll tie it in with the rest of the activities."

"Yes sir."

I asked the driver to take us to the tourist shops first.

"What are the chances of finding a Christmas ornament in June?" I asked.

"Don't look for one. Just look for anything that could hang on a tree," Darby said.

"I don't know why I'm looking anyway. Jo called and said she couldn't see me again. I just said I would buy one if I saw it, so here I am shopping for a Christmas ornament."

I found dozens of different versions of the Eiffel Tower. Many of them could be hung on a Christmas tree, but I didn't want to buy the typical Paris souvenir.

The shopping area was captivating. Trees shaded the streets and the river flowed lazily past. Benches lined the river, providing romantic sitting spots. I couldn't look around without wishing Jo was there with me. Flower boxes hung from the windows and vines covered the storefronts. It was in a charming little shop with arched windows that I found an ornament for Jo. The vines climbed trellises that framed the windows and pink flowers framed the scene of the river outside. Sunlight streamed through the windows illuminating three dimensional, stained glass sun catchers. But these were not the typical cheap plastic sun catchers. These were etched crystal. There were hummingbirds, daffodils, irises, crosses, Eiffel towers, snowflakes, stars, gondolas and cathedrals. The churches had windows etched in them. The snowflakes were adorned with smaller snowflakes in a beautiful pattern making the snowflake shimmer like blue ice. Each sun catcher's etching matched to the overall design. The star caught my eye. It was a four pointed star and the etching caught the light and twinkled with bright cheerfulness. The design just appealed to me. Jo made my heart twinkle and she lit up my life. I had very mixed feelings buying the ornament. I knew I would probably never get to give it to her and then what would I do with it? I couldn't keep it. Nor could I give it to anybody else. So I bought it with a heavy heart. In France you don't just go to a shop to buy something. My mother had schooled me in such things and it usually did pay off in any foreign country to exchange a few pleasantries with the shop owner before getting down to business. I chatted with the woman at the checkout counter about the weather, postcards for Darby to send, and her splendid selection of merchandise in the store as she wrapped the ornament very carefully with stylish tissue paper.

Even the tissue paper had Eiffel towers on it. Then she placed the ornament into a silver and gold gift bag.

"Do you know where I can buy package tape?" I asked the woman.

"We would be happy to ship your purchase to anywhere in the world," she said.

"No, I don't need the ornament shipped. I just need some heavy duty tape."

She thought for a moment, then gave me directions to a market, however I thought I'd have about the same luck asking our driver the same question.

"Thank you," I told her.

"There's a geocache four blocks up," Darby said when I exited the shop. He had looked around the shop for a few minutes before deciding the river was more interesting.

"If you see something you want to buy for Adele, go ahead and get it," I told him.

"I can't," he said. "She knows I don't got money for gifts."

It occurred to me with this statement that Darby's grammar degraded when he felt like a loser. If he was in charge and talking about something he knew about, he dropped the poor grammar. I made a mental note to pay attention to his manner of speech. I also thought that Darby had better start earning his keep or he would refuse the pay. My sore arm gave me the perfect excuse to ask him to do things for me.

"Let's walk down and see if we can find that cache. What's it called?"

"It doesn't matter. I don't know what it means."

"Right. Me, too. I wonder if having a French dictionary would help."

The cache made me think perhaps a French dictionary might be helpful. We couldn't read the name of the cache or the description. It was another place with many people around, but they all seemed to be strolling, sightseeing and shopping. They didn't seem to worry about two Americans with a special interest in one tree. It was a mature tree, frequently pruned. It stood in a little spot of soil surrounded by walkways. Bricks were laid in attractive patterns and there was a decorative metal fence around each tree. The branches of the trees nearly touched making the area shady and comfortable. Here, too, there were plenty of benches. It seemed the people of Paris did a lot of sitting.

"There isn't a place on this tree to hide anything," Darby said.

"All the recent pruning is just maintenance. The basic shape of the tree is mature. So it's got to be someplace they don't need to prune anymore."

"They'd still see it," Darby pointed out.

"Maybe it's magnetic. Maybe it's on the fence."

"Naw, the metal is too fine."

"You told me to look where an ant would look," I reminded him.

"Okay, then look on the fence, but I'm telling you it isn't there."

"I wish we could read the description. Any hint would help."

"Ask the driver," he suggested.

"He's probably taking a nap. We've been gone for an hour."

"Still, he's working for us. He should be able to answer a simple question. What's his number?"

I clicked down to the driver's number and handed Darby the phone.

"Yes, hello? Hello? This is Darby. Earl and I are having a little trouble and we want to know what a couple of words mean in English." There was a pause and then he read off the GPS, guessing at the pronunciation, "Aspeerator a gonzesses." There was another pause much too long for a three word translation. Darby looked at me and said, "He's laughing like crazy. He wants to know where we are and can he join the party."

"Why?" I asked. "There's no party here."

"He wants us to get the girl's number."

"Well, what does it mean?" I asked.

"Yeah, what does it mean?" he asked the driver. There was a short pause. "Thanks, I think. We'll tell you about it when we get through." He ended the call.

"Well?"

"It uh… it means playboy."

"What's that got to do with a tree?"

"How should I know!"

"There's got to be more to it than that. Maybe you said it wrong."

"Probably so. I don't exactly have a French accent. Hold on. I got an idea."

He called the driver back. "Can you use those words in a sentence and then translate the sentence?" He listened for a moment and he grew more puzzled, but then the meaning dawned on him and he laughed out loud. "HA HA hahahaha, I got it now! That's funny. That helps a lot. And there's no party going on. We aren't getting picked up by any playgirl French beauties."

He ended the call again and said, "He was disappointed. Turns out the title does mean playboy, as in chick magnet. So look for something having to do with baby birds."

Darby found the cache. I could tell because he was laughing again. Way up almost beyond reach was a nest. It was held in place by some stout nails and the cache was inside the nest, a magnetic bison tube. There was also a fake bird but we left that there.

"I wonder if that's a pun in French," Darby said. "Seems like it would be weird for the humor to cross from one language to another."

"I agree, but maybe it's just a title."

"I guess you can't argue with a title. I see plenty of paintings where the title doesn't match the picture at all."

We signed the log, replaced the cache and continued our stroll.

"Look, the path opens up. Maybe those booths over there sell something to eat."

"Could be."

We entered a large park-like area. Off in the distance, as always, we could see the Eiffel Tower.

"If it's food you want, there you go," Darby said as he pointed toward a nearby street. People were lined up five deep by a large red truck. We hadn't had breakfast so we headed that direction.

When we stepped up to the menu Darby said, "Ah, here's where I should have looked for that bacon cheeseburger."

The truck had about fifteen different variations of the hamburger, but what drew my attention was a sandwich made with French ingredients: thick meat that resembled bacon, some crumbly cheese and greens that I took to be spinach. Many of the dishes had corresponding pictures. The deserts looked interesting, too. People walked away from the truck with little paper baskets containing pastries topped with custard or whipped cream and chocolate drizzled over them. It helped that each picture had a number, so it was almost like ordering fast food back home. I ordered the bacon/spinach/cheese sandwich just to see what it was and added one of the pastry desserts so Darby would feel comfortable ordering dessert, too. We took our baskets to a nearby bench to eat.

"What kind of meat is that?" Darby asked.

"I don't know. It looked like bacon in the picture."

"It doesn't look like bacon now."

"I agree."

I took a bite. It was good, but it wasn't bacon.

"So what is it?" Darby asked.

"I still don't know. It's been marinated."

"Are you going to eat it?"

"Sure, why not?"

"I don't eat anything unless I know what I am sticking in my mouth."

"Even Henry's stew? You never asked what was in that."

"That's cause it was always real food. Poor folks can't afford all those weird things I wouldn't eat. It was potatoes, carrots and chicken, or beef, or chicken and beef, if we were lucky. Sometimes it ran out of meat and only had the flavor of meat in it."

"So what's in your burger?" I asked.

"Beef," he answered.

"Are you sure?"

"Of course I'm sure!"

"Okay, because the descriptions have odd names. You could be eating bison or veal or mutton."

"I think we really should buy a French dictionary. What's veal?"

"You're kidding, right?"

"No."

"You'll be glad to hear it's beef."

"Why don't they just call it beef then?"

"Because it's veal."

"Then what's mutton?"

"Lamb."

"And what's bison?"

"Uh… buffalo? Are they the same thing?"

"You'd have to ask a scientist. They don't have buffalo in France, do they?"

"They have anything they want to buy," I said.

"Imported buffalo?"

"Sure."

"From a food truck?"

"This is a pretty good sandwich considering it came from a food truck," I observed. "It wouldn't surprise me to find out that the hamburgers were different kinds of meat."

"Now you got me thinking I might be eating something weird."

"Sorry. It doesn't bother me to not know what I am eating."

"So what are some weird things that you've tried?"

"How should I know?"

"Well, what did you eat that you couldn't guess what it was?"

"This."

"Aw come on, there's got to be more."

"I try not to worry about it. When you dine out with business associates in foreign countries you just be polite and clean your plate."

He crinkled his nose at the thought. "You could be eating dog, or squid."

"Meat's meat."

"I think I'll become a vegetarian," he declared.

"Dessert it usually safe," I said as I turned my attention to the pastry.

I picked up the pastry and made sure it had some custard and chocolate sauce on it, then took a bite. The chocolate didn't taste like chocolate. I decided not to question it. The pastry was light and sweet. The custard was heavy and sweet. The sauce was sweet and salty. The flavors blended in interesting ways, like putting salted peanuts on an ice cream sundae. When we were finished I asked Darby to locate the nearest cache while I took our trash back to the food truck's trash can.

"By the way," I said to the cashier. "What was that sauce on the pastries?"

The cashier asked the cook and then in a very thick accent said, "Eel sauce."

After I thought about my many visits to sushi bars I had to agree, but I wasn't going to tell Darby.

Chapter 18

I was trying to find Darby again when I happened to run across an old man who was trying to sell his artwork in the park. I stopped to admire this work and I was amazed at the amount of detail he was able to achieve with a few simple brush strokes. His paintings looked like they could come alive at any moment. He sat at an easel working on his latest creation. I made my way to his side. He was facing the Eiffel Tower and I expected to see a grand landscape on his canvas. The park itself would make an interesting painting but the tower dominated everything. However, when I saw his painting I realized he wasn't painting the tower at all. And when I looked back at his other works none of them were paintings of the Eiffel Tower either. One was of an elderly couple holding hands on a park bench. Another depicted a child running down the sidewalk, pigeons flying out of the way. There was a street scene with a sidewalk café and tourist shops. In fact it looked much like the street I had shopped at earlier in the day. I was amused by one painting that showed two people walking dogs. The woman in the picture had a large unruly dog with muddy paws and the man walked a freshly groomed French Poodle.

"Where I come from everybody expects a man to have a large dog," I commented.

"Uhhgn," the painter said as he concentrated on a detail on the canvas. When he got it right he put his brushes down and ambled over. "This? I paint what I see."

"You mean these people really were walking dogs in the park?"

"Most definitely."

"And these other people?"

"Yes. I like to watch. I watch. I paint."

"Why don't you paint the tower?" I asked. "Surely many tourists would buy a painting of the tower to help them remember their trip to Paris."

"Nah," he said as if it was a distasteful thing to do. "I no see the tower. Always it is there pulling the eye up. Always up. I see… life. I keep de eye on the level. That's where de life of the city lies. I paint what I see and I see de life of everyday."

"You've got a good eye," I said as I walked over to see the painting he had been working on. It was of the woman at the flower stand just a little ways away. She had armloads of elegant flowers held in buckets of water and people would pass by and choose flowers for a bouquet. "A very good eye," I added.

"Thank you," he said with flare. "You like to buy?"

"It would be difficult to bring one home," I answered.

He looked disappointed and I began noticing that his jacket was worn out and his shoes were very old. His driver's cap was sweat stained and his easel was covered with paint smudges. Everything about the display, except the paintings themselves were old and nearly worn out. I looked at the price of his paintings and saw that they were not unreasonably priced.

"I tell you what," I said. "I need a small painting. Very small. Maybe 4 inches max."

"Eenches..." he said.

"About the size of a hand," I said as I held out my hand, palm open. "If I come back tomorrow can you have a small painting for me to buy? It is for a very special lady."

"Just so," he said as he held his hand up.

"Very good. I'll come back tomorrow."

"What you like me paint?" he asked.

"Something a very special lady would like," I answered.

"You like dis?" he asked.

"Yes, I like it very much."

"Very good."

I found Darby back at the bench we had been sitting at.

"There you are!" he said.

"What do you say we call Remy and see about the FTF?" I asked.

Remy was at work, but he promised to meet us for dinner. He gave us the address of a restaurant near his home.

"Hey, Remy," Darby said. "Can you read this menu to us?"

"Why of course! Anything for my geocaching friends."

"You can skip any of the weird stuff," Darby told him.

"Okay," Remy said smiling. Then he began reading and translating the menu in a way that he thought Darby could understand but it just sounded like different meats and vegetables with "red French sauce" or "white French sauce".

"So if it says blanc it's chicken or fish and if it's rouge it's beef," Darby summed it up.

Remy shrugged thinking Darby could make his decision with the information given.

"Earl?" Remy said.

I glanced up from my menu.

"You understand?"

"Enough to order."

"Okay."

"What's this banner thing at the top?" Darby asked.

"It proclaims National Escargot Day to be prolonged throughout the month."

"National Escargot Day?" Darby asked. "You have a National Escargot Day?"

"Why of course!"

"What is this escargot?"

"Ahhh, it is the most delectable French dish..."

"You don't want it," I said.

"Now wait a minute, Earl. How do you know what I might want? This is a national delicacy we're talking about here. A whole country cannot be wrong."

"You said you didn't want to hear about anything weird. You would consider escargot to be weird."

"Have you tried it?" he asked me.

"Yes, once."

"Did you like it?"

Before I could answer Remy launched into the different merits of escargot preparation. He had eaten at this restaurant frequently and knew all the dishes. "... But the garlic butter variety is most scrumptious with a good Chardonnay."

"Good. I'll have that."

I wish I had a video camera when our meals arrived. Darby looked down on the escargot swimming in butter with minced garlic, rice, and steamed vegetables.

"What is it?" He asked.

"Try it," Remy said. "Is most delicious."

Darby scooped up one of the snails and placed it in his mouth. The garlic flavor was pretty good so he began chewing. His expression grew puzzled.

"What is this? Meat flavored bubble gum?" he asked.

"Ahhh," said Remy as he swallowed a snail. "Is most delicious."

Darby was still chewing the first bite, but he decided to cut one in half to see what the inside looked like. He sawed until the bite was cut in two then looked at the half the fork was in. He couldn't figure out what he was seeing. I laughed to myself. I was a little worried about what would happen if he found out exactly what escargot was. Had he really been on the streets eating Henry's stew so long that he had never heard of escargot?

"How come your plate's got shells on it?" Darby asked Remy.

"It is just another way to prepare them. You chose well. Is best to try the garlic first." Remy pulled a snail out of its shell, appraised it, and popped it into his mouth.

"Uh, did you just... I mean, this isn't..."

"I told you so," I said.

"Those shells," Darby said to me. "What lives in those shells?"

"Escargot," I said.

"My brain is telling me one thing and my stomach refuses to believe I'd do that to it," he said worriedly.

"You can listen to your brain," I said.

"You mean escargot is..."

"Snails."

"Oooohhh noooo, no, no, no, no" he said as he scooted his chair back. He looked around feverishly for a restroom sign then hurried away.

"What happened?" Remy asked.

"Darby is not used to foreign foods," I said. "I think we better find him something more traditional."

"It *is* traditional. A national celebration of a delicacy!"

"Perhaps something closer to American food," I said. "Maybe he'll trade with me." I had ordered a beef dish expecting Darby to question his choice.

It wasn't easy for Darby to admit he'd made a mistake and an embarrassing one to boot. I was glad he didn't realize the cost of his mistake. He never did figure out how Euros worked. I paid him in Euros while we were traveling and we would convert them back to dollars later, but he had no idea how expensive things were when he spent money. For that reason he didn't buy much. He worried about wasting any money that might go toward getting on his feet again. I'd pay for our dinner, and Remy's, too.

"Remy, where do you go to buy geocaching supplies?" I asked.

"The GPSrs we buy at the sports store. Anything else we use what we have or we order online. Why?"

"I was just wondering."

Darby came back to the table carrying a salad.

"This oughta be safe," he said.

"If you landed in a major city and were going to be there for a few days, and they had a geocaching store, would you visit it?"

His expression brightened. "Most certainly!"

"Darby," I said. "I think I have a proposition for you."

"Oh? Does it involve eating snails?"

"No."

"Okay, what is it?"

"When we get home I want hire you to find a store front property in a good location for geocaching."

"I think that fall done something to his head," Darby said to Remy. "Do you know how much it cost to start a new business? You got to get a lease, there's rent, inventory, utilities…" he began slowing down.

"Yes, I know. It'll take a year or so. But that gives us time to think of what we really want in a geocaching store."

"You got the money to sink into a brand new business?" Darby asked.

"I might have to cash in a few investments," I admitted.

"Dang."

"Where is this place?" Remy asked.

"It would have to be in southern California somewhere," I said. "Right by the airport might be hard to accomplish. It's a busy down town area. But there are pleasant coastal areas very near."

"Speaking of risks. I have been trying to think of a way to apologize," Remy said.

"What for?"

"I put your life in great danger."

"I chose to go down the oubliette. You only showed me a place to explore."

"But still, it was I. And I would like to show you a different adventure. One that is safer."

"You want to go for the FTF?" I asked hopefully.

"No. I would like to take you geocaching where is a… treat for the eyes! I had the plan even before we met. Is perfect!"

How could I say no? He seemed so earnest and wanted to show us a good time after the trauma of being dropped, literally into the pit of despair. I had put the fall behind me, except for the inconvenience of the cast on my arm. He noticed my uncertainty.

"You have other plans? No?"

"No, we don't have other plans. I thought you had to work."

"Tomorrow, yes, then… freeee!"

"What about you, Darby? Are you ready to try something new?"

"I don't have to climb trees? I ain't going to break my arm?"

"No," Remy said. "Though your eyes might pop out of your head."

"That works for me," I said. "I have to pick up a gift from a local artist but other than that we are free to come and go as we please."

"Very good, so… after we eat we go upstairs and I give you de caches."

Remy lived two blocks from the restaurant in an apartment building that looked like every other building on the block. We entered a small hallway that led to an elevator. For some reason I was surprised to find an elevator that close to downtown Paris. To me the downtown area seemed quaint and old. It looked like the building had been built long before elevators were commonplace, but his apartment building did have one, right next to a very dark and narrow stairway. We went to the fourth floor. I noticed very quickly that the doors were not far apart. It was almost like looking for a motel room and when we entered his apartment it was almost like entering a hotel room, except that we entered the living room. The whole apartment couldn't have been a thousand square feet. The living room and kitchen were one room with a breakfast bar separating them. Stairs next to the front door led to a bedroom and bathroom. The whole apartment was smaller than my hotel suite, though the kitchen was more useful. There was a small table in a nook in the kitchen where Remy used his laptop computer. It looked like he also ate his meals there. A half full cup of cold coffee sat beside the mouse pad and a plate of crumbs waited to be put in the dishwasher. He cleared away the dishes and pulled out two chairs on either side of the table.

"I already get the pocket query. All we need to do is huke it up."

"You got the cable?" Darby asked.

"Let's see."

He brought up the query and Darby said, "Holy smokes! How many caches you got there?"

"Many," Remy admitted. "It's a long drive. There are many caches between here and Montalivet."

"Montalivet?" I asked.

"Every year I go. My brother lives nearby. I go camping, visit my brother. To be sure we will see the country and you will like it. You have been camping, no?"

I had only been camping in Henry's camp and I didn't think that counted, but I nodded affirmatively anyway. Darby, of course, had been camping. The last few years were nothing but camping. I'm sure he would rather stay in Paris at the cushy hotel, but he was willing to go anywhere I went and I didn't want to refuse Remy.

"Before geocaching I would fly, but… now I drive to find the caches along the road."

"How far is it?" Darby asked.

"Five hundred and forty kilometers," Remy said.

"Oh, that tells me a lot," he said a bit sarcastically.

"All day driving and geocaching," Remy said to give Darby a better idea how far it was.

"Dang. I haven't traveled that far in years."

"You're in Europe!" Remy pointed out.

"Yeah, and that's weird, too. Now I'm driving all over a foreign country."

I have to admit I didn't know what I was getting into. Remy wanted to visit his brother and he was willing to allow two Americans to come along. He felt bad and wanted to make my trip to France memorable in a more positive way. Remy gave us instructions to pack clothing for four days. He loaded the caches into our GPSrs. Later we Googled Montalivet and Darby let out a low whistle.

"My wife ain't ever going to hear about this, right?" he pleaded.

"Not from me," I said. "So… you want to try being a naturist?"

"I don't know. When you live on the streets you ain't never naked, not even for baths!"

I smiled but I wasn't exactly comfortable with the idea either. I thought back to when the window washers were working on my bedroom window when I got up in the morning. I hadn't been uncomfortable then, just surprised. I decided I could do this.

First I had to pay a visit to the park to pick up the painting for Jo.

"De painting, she is finished!" the artist said.

"Wonderful!"

"I show you!"

I really didn't want to look too closely at the painting. I wanted to save it and see it in detail with Jo, not that I would ever see Jo again.

"It looks fantastic!" I said without really looking at the painting. "I'm sure she will love it. Can you wrap it up so it will survive an airplane ride home?"

"Is what you say… acrylic so she dries faster. De oils, they dry too slow, weeks, months. You not have de time. This," he said as he flicked the painting with his fingernail. "She dry, she no stick."

"Perfect. I'm sure she will love it."

"Ahh, for a special lady! I wrap it very gude."

He took the painting behind his easel and wrote something on the back then wrapped it in several layers of tissue paper and taped it closed. He put it in a plain brown sack. It looked as if he brought the sack just for this purchase because I didn't see any other sacks around. His other paintings were too large to fit in a bag. I paid him and thanked him for creating a painting just for me, then after I left I wondered again if I would ever be able to give it to Jo.

"You'd like that guy's paintings if you stopped to look at them," I said to Darby when I caught up to him.

"I kind of lost my appreciation for art when it got limited to the graffiti on bridges," he said. "Gee, that world feels a thousand miles away."

"That's because it is," I said.

"Naw, I mean figuratively."

"You don't have to go back," I said.

He stuffed his hands into his pockets and stared at the ground. "Want to find a cool cache?" he said, deliberately changing the subject.

"Sure." What was it about guys communicating? I wanted to ask him why the idea of getting off the street made him uncomfortable, but that's not something you ask a man. Men are used to being in control of their lives and to ask them to analyze their status in life is to question their manhood. So I didn't press. I got the feeling Darby was getting a taste of life off the streets and going back was going to be tough, but having things handed to him was distasteful too. He was stuck between an emotional rock and a hard place. Either way was going to wound his pride. "Remember Remy's car?" I asked as he got out his GPS.

"Sure. Little one, Fiat?"

"The point is I don't think our suitcases and a bunch of camping gear will fit into it. We need to find a way to pack light for the next few days."

"Right. How're we going to do that?"

"I suggest duffle bags with minimal clothes and toiletries."

He nodded and we made a point of watching for a shop that might carry duffle bags. When we found one, they also had a rack of tacky tourist trinkets: Key chains, luggage tags, collector spoons, shot glasses all with Eiffel Towers pictured on them. Despite my disappointment with the souvenir companies, I bought several of the trinkets to add to caches farther from Paris.

"I should have brought a bunch of this stuff from California," I commented to Darby as I checked out. Darby had chosen a blue nylon duffle and I chose a black leather one, only to discover later it was a women's bag and had a rhinestone Eiffel Tower on the pocket. I picked at the rhinestones to see if they came off easily. They didn't. I decided I would just carry the bag so the logo wouldn't show and make the best of it.

"Where is this really cool cache?" I asked. "Does it require a taxi?"

"Well, here's the thing," Darby said, which told me we should find a bench because he had some explaining to do that involved the map. "The cache is a mile away. We got some close to us but this one sounds way cool. I want to try it even if we don't find it. You don't mind that, do you? If we just look for things based on the coolness factor?"

"No, that's what we're here for."

"Okay, cause it sounds cool. I wouldn't waste your money on a lousy cache."

"That's what it's there for," I answered.

"For the finding, yeah," he said.

"No," I corrected him, "for the wasting."

He started to ask a question, stopped, started again and gave up. He wasn't used to having money for wasting. We hailed a taxi and Darby gave him the street names where we wanted to be dropped off. On the way he gave me a lesson in cache page reading.

"To find a cool cache first you look for favorite points. But if it's a new cache it might not have a bunch of points yet, so you read the logs. Sometimes the description will make the cache stand out but more likely the logs will tell you. Folks can't come out and talk about the cache itself, cause that would be a spoiler. You gotta pick up on words like *cool cammo*, *very clever*, *nice hide*, stuff like that. If a cache has lots of long logs it's a good sign that the cache is a good one. Folks don't go on and on telling a story about a lousy cache…"

"So what drew your attention on this one?" I asked.

"Folks went on and on about it. I couldn't read the logs, 'cause they were in French. But it seems this one has multiple stages, what we call a multicache, so people wrote about each stage."

The taxi came to a stop in a residential neighborhood. I paid the taxi driver and we got out and looked around.

"Wow, rich folks," Darby observed.

The houses were two story and each house seemed to have a semi wild garden. If I had seen the same flowers back home I would have thought the house was weedy, but here the flowers gave the yards an airy, romantic look that I wished Jo could see.

"Six hundred feet," Darby reported. I found the cache on my GPS list and locked on to the cache so I could use my own GPSr in the hunt. We followed the sidewalk past iron fences and creaky gates until the sidewalk ended. "Still a hundred twenty feet," Darby added.

At the end of the sidewalk was a woodsy area. We stepped off the sidewalk into the brush and followed the map to a tree.

"Usually in a multicache the first stages are small with only a sheet of paper in them that has the coordinates to the next stage," Darby explained. "So look for something small."

I began examining the tree, but Darby went on to another tree.

"Dude, I think I found it," he said quickly. "Take a look at this."

I walked over to the other tree where I found him squatted down and looking at the base of the tree. On the trunk of the tree somebody had added a little arched door complete with decorative rock trim and a little window. There was a window on the side of the trunk, too, making it look like a little gnome home.

"It doesn't open," he said of the door. He lifted up the rock that served as a little porch or stoop. The cache wasn't there.

"Try the doorbell," I said.

"You think?"

"Can't hurt."

"Okay." He pushed the doorbell and off in the woods, back towards the houses, we heard a classic *ding dooong*. "It's got to be stage two," Darby surmised. "Walk over thataway until you find it." He rang the doorbell to give me an idea which direction to walk. *Ding dong, ding dong.*

"Okay, enough," I said. "We don't want to scare away all the wildlife in the area."

I had my eye on a tree near the fence line of the house. I walked to the tree before calling back. "Okay, try it again."

Ding, dong. It wasn't at the tree. I moved around the tree and spotted it.

"Found it!" I called back.

Just then I heard voices from the house. Oh, no, muggles. There was a man waving at me from a balcony. I waved back reluctantly. There were more French phrases but I recognized the word Americans in the stream of conversation on the balcony. A woman appeared, brightened and waved.

"Do you mind if we join you?" the man shouted.

"I think they're geocachers," I said to Darby. "They recognized us as the Americans."

"Dude, we reek of America, can't you see that?"

"No, I think they know who we are, at least vaguely."

The man walked quickly across his lawn smiling broadly, "Welcome! Welcome to our little corner of the city!"

"Thank you," I said.

"We watch for the geocachers," he said as his wife caught up to us huffing and puffing a little bit. They were older than Darby and I, with gray hair and glasses. "I am Edouard, this is Jolie, and this..." he said indicating the multicache, "is our creation for your geocaching enjoyment."

"You did this?" Darby asked.

Edouard nodded.

"Cool!"

"Jolie made the homes and I created the sound effects."

"We are kind of new to geocaching," I explained. "I've never done a multicache before."

"We made it simple," he explained. "Just so people enjoy each home. The first sound was simply to see if the idea of using sound would work. Then I learned how to record different sounds. Most are not true. It is simply what we imagine you would find at the next stage so, listen to the sounds and it will give you a clue what to look for."

"So where is it?" Darby asked.

"Right here," I told him. "On this post."

The bird house was painted in the colors from the geocaching logo. It also had a doorbell next to the door. This time when we pushed the button we heard a chattering sound.

"Look for another tree," I said. "That sounds like a squirrel."

The squirrel's house was a hollow full of fake nuts.

"We tried real nuts, but the squirrels took them!" Edouard said.

The windows of the squirrel's house made it look like the squirrel sat by a fireplace reading newspapers with his feet up on a large acorn hassock. The doorbell made a *whoo, whoo* sound so we knew to look for another tree. The owl's house had windows revealing a large library. It even had a crooked chimney snaking up the side of the tree. The door was larger than on the other homes and had a door knob so I tried pulling it and it swung open. Two large yellow eyes looked back out at me and the *whoo, whoo* sounded again.

"Very clever!" I said. "I love your attention to detail."

"One more home," Edouard said.

Darby pushed the owl's doorbell and we heard… We had to listen carefully. The sound blended in with the forest noises so well that we had to press the button several times quickly to get the sound to stand out. When we did that we thought we heard crickets.

"Well, Earl, what did I tell you about searching for geocaches like an ant would?" Darby asked.

The cricket's house was not as small as it could have been. The cricket lived in a hollowed out log that was furnished into a shop that repaired violins. There was a toy sized counter where a few broken violins lay and there was a wall with either new, or fixed violins hanging, complete with little tags on them. The shop had a cricket proprietor. When I pushed the doorbell at the violin shop we heard a tune that sounded like cricket chirps, except they were chirping Pachelbel's Canon. I wondered where they found a cricket sized cash register. A sheet of plastic closed off the log so moisture wouldn't ruin the scene.

"Wow," said Darby. "I ain't never found caches like these before. No wonder it got tons of favorite points. How do you keep it from being muggled?"

"The land has been in our family for many years. People walk the path to the river, but not many wander in the woods."

"How did you get the crickets to follow a tune?" Darby asked. I thought he was joking but he seemed very serious.

"I found a sound clip of a cricket and we have an electronic piano that will take recorded sounds and play the sound instead of a note. So all we had to do was use that clip, play the canon, and record the results."

"You play the piano, too?" Darby asked.

"I don't think we've found the log book yet," I pointed out.

There was a sign on the front of the log that I thought was the fictional name of the shop. And there was a sign lower down on the log that said something else in French. Had this been America the lower sign might have read *Handicapped Parking*, or *Please use other door*, or *Parking in rear*. With that in mind I walked around to find that the log also had a back door. It was plainer and less noticeable, like the back door on most businesses, but it had a little door knob so I pulled the door open and behind the door was a black cash box.

Jolie clapped politely and said something that I loosely translated incorrectly into, "Good job!" or maybe just "Goodie!"

Inside we found several travel bugs, probably because people felt a muticache was a safe place to leave them and only dedicated geocachers would find them. It seemed Edouard kept careful tabs on the contents because he plucked one from the box and said, "Take this one. It wishes to travel to the see the sports. It has been to football, what you call soccer, polo, tennis. America would be a good place for it to visit American football and baseball."

"And basketball," Darby added. "Can't forget them Lakers!"

Since the cache owners were present I felt a little pressured to trade for something from the cache, but I was glad to trade when I saw that Jolie had the cache well stocked with little handmade souvenirs. Edouard had cut branches into half inch thicknesses and Jolie had burned into them little pictures of birds, owls, squirrels and crickets. There was regular swag, too, because geocachers had traded before us, but I made sure to take one of Jolie's creations. I took one with a little bird on it because I thought it might end up as a Christmas ornament in the future, but later, I kicked myself when I realized I was unconsciously hoping to see Jo again. And that wasn't going to happen.

"This cache has had visitors from eleven different countries!" Edouard proclaimed.

"Are we the first Americans?" Darby asked.

"No, but you are just as welcome nonetheless," Edouard said.

"I guess the favorite points are a nice draw," Darby added.

"And we try to greet each geocacher," Eduoard said.

"Well, it's been great meeting you both," I said. "I wish we had been able to attend the closing of the event, but we got tied up on one of the cache finds."

"Yes, we heard. All the geocachers were told," Eduoard said.

"And we all waited expectantly for good news," Jolie added.

"It was quite an adventure," I admitted. "But I will be fine. I only regret it was such a huge undertaking to extricate me from the oubliette."

Jolie gasped at the mention of the oubliette. To me it was just a piece of history, but I wondered if it meant more to her.

Darby looked longingly at the wood burned creations. It wasn't every day we found handmade swag. I tossed him one of the souvenirs I'd bought at the tourist shop.

"I don't want to take your swag," he said.

"It's not mine. It's ours. It's for geocaching, so trade already."

I'd put him on the spot so he felt he had to trade. He traded for the wood burning of the squirrel.

"Thanks," he said. "That'll be a conversation piece so's I can tell people about this cache."

I thought it was something more but I was willing to accept his explanation. He didn't talk about his wife much, but I knew he still held hope of reconciling with her for his daughter's sake if nothing else. We thanked Eduoard and Jolie for their excellent cache and for their visit and walked back up the street as if we were looking for the next cache. We really had no idea where we were going.

"Was that a cool cache, or what?" Darby asked.

"That was a cool cache," I admitted.

"See? I told you that grungy reflector in LA was not like most geocaches."

"Neither was that one."

"True. What next?" he asked.

"I don't know. Where's the closest one?"

"Six tenths of a mile. You don't want to walk that, do you?"

"As the crow flies?"

"Yeah. Hold on, let's see how weird the streets are. That could be the deciding factor."

The streets were confusing but I decided to walk anyway. If we got tired or frustrated we could always call a taxi later. I'd programmed the taxi company's number into my cell phone.

We started out talking about the shop.

"What do you think a geocaching shop should have in it?" I asked.

"Everything," he said.

"It can't have everything. I don't even know what everything is yet. I have to know about it to order it. Besides, I wasn't talking about the stock so much as how the store should be laid out. What kind of a store front would attract geocachers?"

"I don't know, but it's gotta have a cache hidden outside, that's a given."

"Be thinking of a cool way to hide a creative cache," I said. "Jolie has given us a benchmark. It's going to be hard to come up with something creative like that."

"We could build the world's largest ammo can," he suggested.

"Somebody else would just build a bigger one to best us," I said.

"I wonder... how much extra is floor space?" he asked.

"I have no idea, but it's bound to cost more for a bigger shop. What are you thinking of?"

"I think the shop itself should be small so's people don't get lost in it and so's they end up talking. But maybe you could have a bigger room in the back that would hold... oh... fifty people or so. It don't have to be fancy. In fact I think it should be barebones. Just a plain room with cafeteria tables, a podium, and plain walls so's you can fancy them up for special occasions."

"And what are these special occasions? Geocaching doesn't have special occasions."

"Sure they do! They got 12-12-12, Leap Day, Pi Day, any day that's a nerdy number can be made into an event and you might want to host events. You give the geocachers a regular place to meet and they will flock in. You'll see."

"I don't know how to host an event," I said.

"You don't have to. All you got to do is invite everybody. Once you get to know the local geocachers they'll be glad to ask for stuff, probably pizza. And you'll probably end up giving stuff away. A door prize will bring folks in. Or maybe you should locate right next to Dominoes. That would do it. Then people could get a pizza and come over and talk."

"Geocachers like pizza?"

"Geocachers like food and they like to talk. And they like to eat and talk. And when they get through with that they talk and eat."

"I'd like to go to an event where I can understand all the talk. I didn't learn a whole lot listening to half an event in French."

"You're picking up the lingo pretty good."

"Thanks, I think."

"I wonder if there's a little beachy strip mall with two vacancies between the airport and the coastal communities."

"Even if there isn't we could buy them out," I said.

"You're kidding, right?"

"No. I just mean to make it worth their while to move."

"You're still kidding, right?"

"No. I don't mean to drive them out. Just make them an offer they can't refuse."

"So you're not kidding? You could really do that?"

"We'll look around. Maybe it won't come to that."

We fell silent for a while. The neighborhood we were in looked old but Eduoard and Jolie made me think it was still modern. They didn't seem to be the type that would do without conveniences. They were technologically astute and, even though the houses we walked past looked like they had been there at the founding of the city, I was willing to bet the insides were very different. Everybody seemed to have a garden and the flowers were abundant. Winding walkways led to almost villa like homes.

"So, you wanna move to Paris?" Darby asked.

"No, yes, no. I'd like to live some place homier than my apartment. But Paris? No."

This reminded me of Jo and her house.

"Oh, no. What did I do?" Darby asked.

"Nothing," I answered.

"Dang, dude, why so glum? We're geocaching!"

"Does it really show that much?" I asked.

"Something's eating at you and you gotta do something about it."

"I can't. It's final. All I can do is forget about it."

"Who says it's final?" he asked.

I had to think back to the conversation and I didn't like doing that.

"Jo's boyfriend," I answered.

"Oh man… but Jo herself didn't?"

"Well, yeah, sort of. She said she shouldn't talk to me anymore."

Now he was bummed out, too.

"But did she say it like she meant it? Or did she say it like she had to say it?"

"They're getting married. I'm not going to break up an engagement!"

"Something isn't adding up right. The guy mistreats her, but she's marryin' him, so she can't see you and he says it's over."

"Right."

"Dude, that don't sound over to me."

"Why?"

"It ain't over until she's sealed the deal. And it ain't sealed yet, is it?"

"I don't know."

"What do you mean you don't know?" he said stopping and turning to me.

"I don't know when the wedding is."

"Then what are you doing *here*?"

"I'm… sinking."

"No, you're flushing a perfectly good thing down the drain when all you got to do is stop pushing the handle. Dude, the girl likes you. And she's got second thoughts or she wouldn't have two timed the guy! You turn your back on the situation and you're good as gone."

"If she said she couldn't talk to me anymore and I show up at her door, then I'm just as bad as he is, forcing myself on her."

"You think a woman means everything she says? Women. You got to see into their minds. They say things hoping you don't believe them. Trust me. I've got a wife. I know how it is. You ask what's wrong and they say 'nothing' but they expect you to fix it anyway. Jo wasn't saying you shouldn't call her, she was saying, 'if you care enough you'll call.'"

"No. I can't accept that. If I call and this Jarrod what's his name finds out, he'll get mad and... no. I can't risk hurting her like that. Even if I lose her I can't endanger her. I don't know how many times it has happened but he's put bruises on her once in the short time I've known her. So I won't call. I can't."

I was sinking and I was using the geocaching as a distraction. But how long would it take to sink too far? Would I find a way to rise above this before my heart broke? And what would I do if I didn't?

I kicked at a nonexistent rock and continued walking down the sidewalk to find a mysterious box hidden in France. When I set out I doubted I'd walk the whole way but I needed something to do. Sitting in a taxi would just leave me time to think. I didn't want to think. So we ended up walking over a mile down winding Paris streets trying to follow a sketchy map on a tiny screen. The guy at the store had been right. I wanted an upgrade.

Chapter 19

Finding the closest caches taught me more about typical geocache hides. Finding the favorite ones was interesting but didn't teach what to look for on a typical geocache hunt. The cache we walked over a mile to was only worth the hike because it taught me one more tidbit of geocaching information. Darby and I searched that tree for half an hour and Darby spotted it first. I didn't have much experience with camouflage. Even the most basic Duck Tape made the little bottle invisible in the leaves of a tree. The lights and darks moved and tricked the eyes. A thousand people could walk past the tree and never guess there was a container hidden there. Even knowing it was there didn't help much. Darby pointed out the container and it took me a minute to see it. The wire was what I spotted first.

"Wow."

"Yeah, hanging caches are not my favorite but they're common back home, so you might as well get used to them."

When I asked him what the common hides were back home I got a string of cryptic acronyms.

The tree was only a little taller than Darby and I. We had searched so diligently for that cache that we had forgotten to look around. The tree the cache was in was planted on the outside of a fence, and beyond the fence was a fairytale cottage, much smaller and older than the grand houses around it. It almost appeared to be leaning. None of the angles on it looked correct. And yet, it appeared perfectly normal, too. I almost expected a bent old man or Mother Goose herself to step out and ask what we were doing there, but a young woman exited spryly, got into a very modern, little car and sped away.

"I wonder if she knows she lives in a storybook house," I said.

"Course she does," Darby said. "You cain't live in house that looks like hers and not notice. What I wonder is how come she bought it."

"Maybe she reads a lot of fantasy books," I speculated.

"Yeah, it looks like a wizard's house," Darby added. "I wonder if that's why the cache owner put a cache here. So's we could see this house."

"After a multicache, a one mile hike and a half hour search, I think I'm ready for lunch," I said.

"Okay… only… the next cache is only three tenths of a mile away."

"Three tenths? How far is that?"

"Look on your GPS. It's just a few blocks."

I clicked to the list of caches, found the nearest one and navigated back to the map screen.

"It's just over there, two blocks down and one block to the right," I said.

"Okay. But after that I'll definitely be hungry."

"Me, too. It's a one/one and a half."

The neighborhood was like walking through a historical movie except for the modern cars. Wrought iron balconies provided charming views of wide lawns and rambling gardens. The yards were enclosed in decorative fencing, sometimes with climbing roses leaning out over the sidewalk. The roses were smaller than I was used to seeing. I was guessing they were more like wild roses, smaller and less regal, but whimsical and very thorny. We had to walk around the stickery vines a time or two before turning onto the street with the cache on it. As we walked I watched the screen and I became puzzled.

"Usually by now I can tell which side of the street a cache is on," I said. "But this makes it look like it's right in the middle of the street."

"Lemme see that," Darby said.

I handed him my GPSr and he squinted at the screen. "Shore nuf," he admitted. "And it's only two hundred feet away. Maybe the coordinates are off."

The coordinates were not wrong. We stood on the sidewalk and stared into the middle of the street as cars went by. Traffic was at a leisurely pace, but there were too many cars for us to walk out into the middle of the street and look around.

"I can't see any way for it to be there from where we are. Maybe we can from the other side," Darby suggested.

"Right."

We waited for a break in traffic and then jogged across.

"We shoulda stepped on it on our way across and I didn't see nothin'."

"You mean you didn't see anything."

"Yeah, that, too."

"Me, too, but I forgot to look. I was just crossing the street."

We turned around and looked back to the middle of the pavement. It just looked like a typical French street, slightly rougher than the pavement back home, but I didn't see any way to hide a cache in the middle of the street. Streets are swept and torn up and repaved. I didn't see any way the cache could be in the middle of the street.

"I got it," Darby said.

"No you don't. What have you got?" I asked.

"How the cache can be in the middle of the street. Look. The yard on this side of the street isn't a yard. It's a little hill. And look what's here."

I looked down the little hill and there was a drain under the street.

"You're kidding. Would they really do that?" I asked.

"Sure, why not?"

We descended the hill until we could see inside the culvert. There was a metal grate over the hole, but it was hinged and could be raised given a little muscle.

"Okay," I sighed. "Who is going in and who is keeping watch?"

"It's your nickel," Darby said.

"I think I'd rather go in than stand out here watching cars go by," I answered.

"Go for it, dude," Darby said. "I doubt you'll need your GPS in there."

I left all my belongings outside except for a small flashlight. Darby took a quick muggle count before lifting the grate.

"Go dude! Go!" he urged me. I stooped down and entered the dark drainage space beneath the street. The first thing I found was very wet, slippery footing. Green slimy plants grew on the bottom of the culvert and I slipped, barely catching myself with my left hand. Water splashed around and soaked the bottoms of my pants legs.

"You okay in there?" Darby asked.

"Yeah. It's just slippery."

The flashlight was almost useless. The sides of the culvert seemed to suck the light in. I could hear a trickle of water and the rush of traffic overhead. I couldn't stand up. Had I driven to this cache and was taking my own car home I would have crawled through the water but I didn't want to get wet.

"Muggle alert," Darby said. At least I think that's what he said. It echoed a bit in the tunnel. "Howdy," he said to somebody walking by. There was an answer in French, but it sounded like a momentary greeting.

The cache was not hard to find. It was a hide-a-key magnetized to the top of the culvert. However, opening the cache, while holding the flashlight, and signing the log was impossible to do without slipping, so I carried the cache back to the opening.

"Did you find it?" Darby asked.

"Yeah, I just can't sign it in there. Here, hold this," I said as I handed the flashlight through the grate. I opened the cache and handed the hide a key through to Darby, then I signed the log and handed the log and pen through to Darby. He handed back the cache. It felt like a slow game of hot potato. He signed the log and handed it through. I put it back in the hide-a-key and headed back down the culvert.

"Earl! Do you want the flashlight?" he asked.

"No, it only helped me find the cache. It's easier to go by feel."

Boy, did I eat my words fast, two steps into the culvert to replace the cache and I was feeling my way forward. The flashlight had helped more than

I gave it credit for. I slipped and came down heavily on one knee, almost dropping the cache into the running water. I was soaked up to my knees and I was supposed to pass for a tourist in Paris. I thought I might not tell my mother about this particular cache hunt. She would know about my geocaching because eventually I would have to explain what I had done to my arm. At least in that hunt I had been visiting sites of historical significance, though I thought I should probably look up what that significance was. She would ask and I better know as much about the place as a person might if they went on a tour. I pushed myself up to my stooped position and waddled forward until I thought I was halfway through the culvert, then snapped the hide-a-key into place. Darby lifted the grate and I stepped out into daylight again.

"Duuuude, what happened to you?" Darby asked.

"Just a little slip," I said. "In my geocaching store I think I better stock water shoes."

"And swim trunks by the looks of you," he said.

"Maybe we ought to stop by the hotel before lunch," I suggested. "Is geocaching always this dirty?"

"Just think about it for a minute. If you stopped to find a cache on your way to… one of them fancy meetings or… maybe a dressy date, would you really be able to search? If you're wearing a suit you wouldn't even want to lean against a tree or brush against a dusty bush. So even the clean geocaching is a little dirty. How dirty you get is up to you. But I bet the cleaner you stay the more DNFs you'll pick up along the way."

He had a point. I felt dusty after even a little bit of genuine geocaching. I called a taxi and we went back to the hotel to change clothes.

The room was cool, quiet and peaceful. I thought I could easily lie down and take a two hour nap, but the outside bustle contrasted and little hidden containers begged to be found. Darby and I were supposed to meet in the lobby in half an hour. He must have felt the pull of the nap, too, because he was half an hour late and looked like he wasn't quite awake yet.

"Some geocaching teacher I am," he said. "Now I'm starving and I can't think enough to find the door."

"It's that way," I explained.

"Why are we eating lunch three miles away from the hotel when there was a sandwich within walking distance?" Darby asked as we were shown to a table in a bustling restaurant.

When we were seated I said, "Because, I don't know if you can see it, but if you look out that window… nope I can't see it. Our table is too far away. But somewhere out there is another smiley."

"I shoulda guessed."

Darby read and reread the menu. He went to the part of the menu labeled Entrées and counted down five dishes, then tried to pronounce the name of it.

"What are you doing?" I asked.

"Five's my lucky number. I figure it won't let me down and make me eat snails or something weird."

"You've got the logic backwards. Five is a common lucky number so if the restaurant manager is smart he'll put whatever dishes he wants to sell on the luckiest numbers, which I think would be seven, followed by five."

"So… maybe the manager has his favorite dish as number five. If he likes it, maybe I will, too."

"So what would Remy put for number five?" I asked.

"Uh… snails? Then maybe I ought to pick dish number thirteen."

"Maybe we ought to get a French phrase book so you can look up key words."

"What about you? You never have bad luck ordering," he pointed out.

"That's because I'm not picky. I can enjoy just about anything."

"But dude… snails?"

"Don't think about what it is, just think about the way it tastes."

"No. No way. I don't care if you dip them in chocolate. There's no way you're going to make a snail taste good enough for me."

"Okay. Order number five."

"Now you got me leery of lucky numbers!"

"Then order number thirteen."

He huffed and slouched in his chair. My lunch was excellent, while his was consumed with a suspicious air, like the dish was going to trick him.

One thing I like about European countries is you have modern conveniences right next door to ancient ruins. In this case it was a thirteenth century cathedral. We couldn't help but feel the building looming over our geocache search. We followed the sidewalk past the towering structure and turned to see a bridge crossing the river. Paris has many bridges but this one was unusual. It was covered with locks. We followed the GPS until it zeroed in on a spot beside the rail, but we could barely see the rail underneath the layers of locks.

"What is this place?" Darby asked.

I clicked back to the cache listing. "It's the Bridge of Locks," I read, though I didn't know if that was the cache's name or the bridge's. "They wouldn't make a geocache that looks just like a lock would they?"

"Oh man, I sure hope not. That would be evil."

I moved a lock so I could read the notation someone had written on the side. It had two names, not English, nor French, inside a heart. One of the notes on a different lock, written in English said, "Toby and Cammy together forever." Most of the locks had some message written or etched on them. There were layers upon layers of locks. The locks were so thick and numerous that a large lock might have four or five smaller ones locked onto it. Old locks, new locks, cheap locks, ornate locks, any kind of modern lock I could remember ever seeing was represented. How would we find a small cache in the midst of all this? Darby was searching the same way I was. I would move a lock, read the side, discard it, go on to the next. This could take all day.

"I feel like God's watching us and he thinks we look suspicious," Darby said. "Usually I worry about muggles but God... he's, like, big!"

"I think God would approve of geocaching," I said.

"Why?"

"Well... he likes people who search, right? Like for the truth."

He just looked at me as if he never expected me to get philosophical.

"I don't think you need to worry about what God sees," I said. "He sees a lot of worse things than two guys looking for a box near one of his churches."

"But this place is holy," he said of the cathedral. "It has to be to last through the wars. God was watching over it."

"Darby? Are you on some guilt trip or something? I've never seen you worried over religious issues before."

"No, no I ain't. Though I haven't been to church in four years."

"Well, if God has watched over this church for all these years I doubt he sends lightning down this close to it. I bet we will be allowed to find this container."

"Now where the heck is it?" Darby said, but the way he said it he sounded like he was trying his best to not say, "where the hell is it." Maybe we should find a more rural place to geocache.

"Seek and ye shall find. Knock and it shall be opened to you," Darby was mumbling to himself. "I'm seeking. I'm just not finding."

There were tourists all around the grounds so God wasn't the only muggle to worry about. They climbed the steps and entered through huge doors carved by men's hands and centuries of weather. The stained glass windows would be spectacular from inside the church. Even from the outside, the intricacy of them caused me to stop and admire the skill it took to piece them together. I wished I could take little pieces of glass and form them into a huge picture, but I even had trouble seeing the pieces of my income and forming it into an accurate picture of my own standing in life. It was scattered all over the world and came together at the bank. Some of it I kept track of, some I had totally forgotten about. When you have a financial advisor buying and selling hither and yon it's hard to remember which little NASDAQ symbols in the newspaper affect your bank balance. At this point in my thinking I paused. I'd gone from the beauty of a cathedral to stock listings in just a few jumps. I knew I was raised to think in those terms, but it appalled me. I remembered the little stained glass ornament I'd bought for Jo and it reassured me a bit. I was willing to give away my riches for beauty and then I wondered if it was the beauty of the objects or Jo's natural beauty that made me do it. Okay, I thought, this is getting me nowhere. I am geocaching. Just find the box.

"This is impossible," Darby said.

"No kidding," I admitted without telling him exactly what I thought was impossible. "But we have to find it now. I'm determined."

When we had looked for a good, solid half hour we decided to walk around and take a break. Sometimes when you take a break from something and come back to it little things jump out at you that you couldn't see before because you were too focused. So we entered the cathedral. Churches made me feel odd. There is a certain quietness to a church that just kind of envelops me. I am not a religious person and it still happens. Like the quietness of the old fort, but more spiritual in origin. While the fort had a historical quietness the church had a soul reaching quietness. I even thought that things with Jo might work out in the end even if I couldn't see how.

Kids ran up and down the rows and parents, who felt the quietness I did, shushed them as they tried to figure out how to take pictures of the ornate altar and stained glass windows without being a distraction with the glaring flashes from their cameras.

I noticed Darby had gone to the altar and he knelt in prayer. I didn't, though I didn't fault him for it. I thought the future was my own to work out. And that depressed me a little because I couldn't see how it could. Oh, I'd survive all right. I'd go home and be right back where I started. I just didn't want to be right back where I started. Dang, even God had me questioning my status in life. I didn't appreciate him taking the offensive. I could use a little help, but it didn't involve getting down on my knees and asking. I sighed, ready to leave. Maybe I'd feel better outside where God's quietness wasn't so heavy.

I waited for Darby to finish his prayers and we exited the building squinting at the bright sunlight outside.

"Let's try again," I said.

"Okee dokee. You got some new ideas?"

"No, I just hope getting a fresh perspective will help."

"Hey, that smart phone you got... can you access the cache page on it?" Darby asked.

"I don't know. Why?" I asked.

"Cause a place like this, people will take lots of pictures. I bet you downloaded this cause of the favorite points and it's in a picturesque place. It's bound to have favorite points, and there's gotta be a spoiler pic or two."

Not only were there pictures, but after looking through dozens of pictures, we finally found a picture that showed the cache container.

"Wow, that's going to be hard to spot," Darby said. "But at least it isn't a lock! I suggest we trust the coordinates. Lots of people have found this one and it's only a two, so that means the hide is just tedious. It'll take a lot of searching but we can do it. So start at ground zero. You search this side for about eight feet out and I'll search that side starting at the middle and working out."

"Sounds reasonable."

We meticulously made our way through the layers of locks, with me thinking out loud.

"If I was going to hide a cache here I'd make sure it was under the top layer, but not so deep that it would be impossible."

"Then look for groupings of locks."

It wasn't easy to look because people would walk up and begin looking at locks, then stand to have their picture taken. Since it was a photo spot for couples we were asked to take several pictures of couples standing on the bridge with the river in the background and locks on either side of them. One couple who had stopped at the bridge during our first search came back with a lock during our second search and asked me to take their picture as they added their lock to the bridge. They clasped each other in a jubilant hug and joyfully tossed their key into the river.

I hated to intrude on their moment but when they turned to leave I asked them, "Why did you do that? Why toss the key away?"

"It's a tradition. My parents did it when they got engaged. I always loved that old picture," the woman said. "So I decided, if I got engaged I would do the same thing. All these locks were put here by couples to seal their love for each other. You throw the key in the river making it impossible to break the bond between two lovers."

"You're American," I observed. "But you came all the way to Paris to add a lock to the bridge?"

"Yes, it was so important to me. I don't know why."

"Then why have a common tourist snap a picture. Why not hire a photographer to do it right?"

She shrugged. "It's just the tradition. They found somebody to snap their picture."

"Aren't you going to at least look at it and make sure it's the shot you want?"

"Okay." She clicked back through the pictures. "It'll be fine," she said, then showed me the picture. It wasn't professional quality but it had all the fundamental elements in it. "Here, let me show you." She dug through the contents of her purse and produced a very old, slightly creased picture that showed a couple on this same bridge. There were fewer locks but the light in their eyes and the way they stood made it obvious the two were in love. The picture glowed with possibilities.

"Maybe someday I'll be able to bring someone here," I said.

"So what are you doing here?" the man asked.

"We're geocaching," I said.

"Geo... whating?"

"Geocaching. There is a geocache hidden somewhere on this bridge and we are trying to find it."

"I never heard of such a thing," the woman said.

"It's a hobby that's gaining popularity. I'm kind of new to it, so this one is proving to be difficult."

"Impossible!" Darby interjected.

"How interesting!" the woman said. "Well, good luck with that!"

"Thanks. We might need it," I said.

After a while all the locks began looking alike, then add the frequent interruptions and the search was getting frustrating again. I returned to the search never knowing if I started where I had left off. I could be searching the same spot ten times without knowing it. A boat load of tourists went under the bridge and all the people waved up at us.

"What if you're not watching, and you throw your key into a boat?" Darby asked.

I almost felt like that was what I did when I left for Paris. The key was back in LA in another man's hands. The thought was unsettling.

"Are you ready to give up?" I asked.

"You haven't even made it four feet down your section. Then we were supposed to switch off."

"All right," I said getting back to work. Personally, I thought the cache was hidden too well for my inexperienced eyes to spot. Even knowing what the container looked like didn't help much. It didn't look like a lock but it would fit into an extremely sneaky little gap between locks. After perhaps ten minutes of searching Darby asked if I was ready to switch places, so I began again at ground zero and worked my way the other direction. Another boat approached and as it grew closer Darby stood up to wave at the people on board. As the boat passed under the bridge he leaned over the railing to watch it disappear.

"Awwww dude, you'll never guess," he said.

"Did you find it?" I asked.

"If we'd just leaned over sooner we could have seen it an hour ago!"

"Where is it?" I asked with a touch of excitement. I wanted to see where this elusive container was hanging out. I leaned over the rail and Darby pointed down. Even knowing where it was it was hard to spot, just a little rounded dark thing lurking behind a lock.

"Wow, that's a two?" I asked.

"It's a one and a half if you happen to look in the right spot."

It didn't take long to unclip the cache and sign it. Then we were so relieved that we finally found it that we posed for pictures with the cathedral and locks behind us.

"That was one hard earned smiley!" Darby said as we descended the bridge.

"Yeah, this calls for a beer. I'll buy, since you found it."

Chapter 20

When we met Remy the next day he had no camping gear in his little car. He had a carry on sized suitcase and his go bag of geocaching gear. Likewise Darby and I had our duffle bags and smaller geocaching pack.

"Where's the gear?" I asked.

"Christophe has it. I mostly go camping with him and his car is bigger."

"Wasn't Christophe with you when we met?" I asked.

"Yes."

"You remember that stuff?" Darby asked.

"When your livelihood relies on remembering your contacts you tend to develop a system for remembering names."

Riding with other people in a foreign country is always a bit nerve-wracking. Now I knew how Darby had felt as I zipped around Hollywood Hills. It felt like being on Mr. Toad's Wild Ride. I kept expecting to run smack dab into a pedestrian or delivery truck. I couldn't help but picture Remy's car the size of a sardine can with the three of us squashed into an unrecognizable lump inside. Then when we reached the highway I could understand completely Darby's fear of flying. It was all I could do to maintain a calm outer composure. I kept telling myself that it felt faster than it was. I took a glimpse of the speedometer but I didn't have a good feel for how fast thirty-eight kilometers per hour was.

"How many stops do you wish," Remy asked.

"Right here would be great," Darby said.

"You're just not used to French highways," I said, though I agreed wholeheartedly with Darby. "Stop wherever you want to geocache," I added hoping he wanted to do a lot of geocaching on the way.

"Then perhaps another question. Interest or numbers?"

"Considering our record so far, I'd have to go with interest."

"Very well," he said and pressed down harder on the gas pedal.

We passed wide, open, flat lands, farms, villages. Cars whisked by. In the open there were green fields. The fields were outlined by streams and the streams were lined with trees. I couldn't actually see the streams. I was only guessing that they were there until we crossed a little bridge. After Remy left the freeway the roads gradually became more rural. He finally pulled up to a visitor's center. He put the car in park and stretched as much as the little Fiat would allow, then he got out of the car and stretched again.

Darby and I climbed out of the car and Darby looked around in wonder as if he couldn't believe he was still alive.

"Where are we?" Darby asked.

"I think, perhaps, the place should speak for itself. We are... at a multi cache. Wait! We need a piece of paper."

At first the museum seemed to me to be simply a war museum. I imagined hundreds of them scattered around Europe. It wasn't until I found the tower outside, the plaques listing the names of the people killed, and the glass cases of bones that the reality of the display set in. Human bones only identified from city records and memories of friends, neighbors and family members. People reduced to statistics in the blink of an eye. Some not even that. As I walked the streets of the village the war hit home. It was a ghost village. And just like the fort, I couldn't help but see real people where there were burned out doorways. The people I imagined were all French in old style costumes. I know the costumes were not accurate portraits from the time, because I didn't remember at all what villagers wore in the mid 1940's, except for the renditions I viewed in the museum. It was the faces that mattered. In an open doorway I imagined an old woman with a broom. In a field of flowers I imagined a young girl picking wild flowers. Bare stone walls reached toward the heavens and rusted remnants of the past were around every corner. An old car, signs, the crucifix on the church, a sewing machine, fences. It was a charming and macabre village, half dead and half a living memory of a place, a time and lives completely destroyed. And as I made my way from way point to way point the reality set in and the people morphed from people cheerfully going about everyday activities to people living in fear of invasion and finally, when I saw the woods around the village, I pictured people running to take refuge there, fearful they would be discovered by German soldiers and shot to death. I wondered what I would do. And what would I do if I were one of the few who staggered out of the woods days later to see my town, my home, everything I held near and dear to me taken from me. The flowers were knee high, bright, cheerful and dancing in the breeze, but what did it look like to a kid looking for food, or for his toys. There had been a few toys in the museum. They contrasted sharply with toys today. They didn't talk or teach reading or drive mothers to distraction. They were quiet toys from a tumultuous time.

One by one we found the answers to the questions in the multicache but the cache became secondary to the ghosts revealing a story from a long gone time. We checked the answers against the cache description. It didn't really matter if we found all the right answers because Remy had the final coordinates in his GPS so we found the final cache, which was a large plastic container outside the village. It was good practice for future multicaches and virtual caches, which sometimes ask the geocacher to search out answers to questions to log the find.

Remy must have been historically minded. While I was in France the soil oozed history. I wondered why I didn't feel the same about my own country. After all, the United States existed as long as Europe had. Perhaps it wasn't as settled during Europe's early history but it did exist. I finally decided it was the human element that I felt in France. America held a pioneer spirit, but it was a modern pioneer spirit. France had centuries of humanity, generation upon generations invested in their country and their lifestyle. As we passed farms and villages I could see the past melded into the present. A computer repair shop in a five hundred year old building. A café where they made their own cheese and wine just as they did fifty years ago. Cyclers had pulled up to it and they walked around in neon spandex with contoured helmets. They all looked fit. I'd last five minutes doing what they did.

Montalivet. When Remy had said it was a feast for the eyes I wasn't sure what he meant until Darby and I looked it up on the internet. It was unseasonably warm while we were there so, let me just say more people were inclined to try the naturist approach to camping. In some ways Remy was right, it was a feast for the eyes, but watching a hairy man light a camp stove in the nude made me wonder if we ought to keep a pail of water handy.

"Earl? Are you really going to do this?" Darby asked.

I looked around camp, which at this point was just a flat spot.

"I have no problem with the nudity, if that's what you're talking about."

"I don't remember this being in the job description," he said.

"I'm not telling you what to do in the clothing department. Let's help Remy set up camp, then I bet they want to get something to eat, or find a cache. We can do that, right?"

As long as he had a task to do that didn't involve disrobing he kept to the task at hand. He briefed himself about where all the caches were within walking distance and noted the most interesting ones we might have to drive to. I could tell he was keeping occupied thinking about geocaching because he kept making comments like, "I hope the forest around the caches isn't any thicker than this!"

The trees were thick, providing a nice privacy screen between camps, but to find a container in the woods might be a little tricky. Saplings were numerous and crowded the older trees. I, too, eyed the woods wondering how we would maneuver. However, I was not opposed to noticing some of the more entraining things in camp, either. The group at the next camp looked like a beach volleyball team out of uniform. Lithe and lean they seemed to be familiar with the camp setup process. I was not. Even the two nights I spent in Darby's camp we did not use tents. A tent in Los Angeles only attracted attention, so Henry, Darby and Wanda found out of the way places and rolled out their sleeping bags on the ground, or on a mat. They owned a camp tent but only used it in inclement weather. It was small, only big enough for four sleeping bags if they slept very close together. In the morning sleeping bags were rolled or stuffed and strapped to their packs, then the packs were worn or hidden. Usually they spent most of the day in their packs, only taking them off if they got in the way of money making opportunities, cooking, eating and sleeping.

I had plenty of time to learn more about my surroundings while we waited for Christophe to arrive with our gear.

"I smell the ocean," Darby said.

"The beach, you must see," Remy replied.

Darby asked where it was and Remy directed him to the west but Darby hesitated. He didn't even want to see who the campers were next to us. He'd gotten a glimpse of skin and avoided looking that direction. The idea of walking the beach seemed to make him uncomfortable.

"How long will it be until Christophe shows up?" I asked.

"Explore," he said. "Enjoy yourself."

"What do you think?" I asked. "Want to walk down to the beach?"

"I, uh… Remy have you found the caches here?"

"No, we can find them tomorrow," Remy answered. Darby gave me a look that said he would rather look for the geocache than walk the beach but he agreed to go for a walk.

We followed Remy's directions and walked through the woods. We eventually found a trail that led down to a sparkling, white, sandy beach. At first we had to pick our way across stones, but the beach was pleasant and there was a breeze off the ocean. Several people were out walking the beach, all completely naked. I expected Darby to balk at nudity of any sort. He was so used to being overly clothed to live on the streets that I thought it would be hard for him to be naked in public. I wasn't exactly comfortable with the idea, but I also wasn't at all opposed to it and it rather intrigued and interested me. I noticed right away that sexual reactions were uncommon. So I could see why Darby might be worried about being nude. One disadvantage to being male was the obvious indication of sexual arousal. I wondered how I would react myself. The women definitely did draw my eye, though I tried hard not to watch them. I don't know what it was about the place that seemed to have instinctive, but unspoken, rules. I felt the people here were not nude to elicit a response. They were nude because they were comfortable nude. They seemed to expect others to be comfortable here, too. I think it helped Darby, though it was a distraction to me, to have geocaching to focus on instead of the... uh... scenery.

"Geocaching has brought me to some unexpected places but I think this takes the cake," Darby said.

"Yeah, it wins... hands down," I said.

"This trip sure has had its highs and lows," Darby said. "All the way from the top of the Eiffel Tower to the bottom of one of them oobli-ays."

I thought the lowest part of the trip was Jo's phone call, but I didn't bring the topic up again.

The beach was pleasant, the water inviting.

"The geocache is only three tenths of a mile away. We'll walk that far just on the beach."

"Remy wants to find it, too."

"So? We don't have to tell him we found it. We can find it with them, too."

"You just feel uncomfortable being clothed at a nude beach," I pointed out.

"Not as uncomfortable as I would feel nude at a nude beach," he said. "But you're the boss."

I didn't want him to be uncomfortable just for the sake of walking a beach and he was right, Remy would never have to know we'd found the cache, so we headed back into the woods in search of the geocache. It took about thirty seconds for the trees to completely block our view of the beach. I wasn't concerned. The GPS would lead us to the cache. We would know we walked away from the ocean. The beach would lead us back to the campground. The only problem with that logic was that when we got to ground zero and looked for the cache we ended up walking in circles. Sure, we had walked away from the water to get there, but then the ocean had changed in relation to our present position so many times that we no longer knew which direction "behind us" was.

"Dang, even finding it before Remy won't help us to find it again! All these trees look alike!"

"You're right. So which way is the beach?"

"Uhhhh, that way?" He asked.

"I was going to say that way," I said.

"Why do you say that way?"

"Because it feels right. Why did you choose your direction?"

"Because that tree looks familiar."

"They all look familiar. They all look identical except for their circumference."

"So which direction is right?"

"I don't know."

"Tracks! We must have left tracks!"

We sure did, we left hundreds of them, all going in circles. We quickly gave up on tracking ourselves out.

"We could just wait for Remy. He'll turn up at this cache first. It's the closest one to camp."

"Tomorrow. Plus if we wait for him we have to admit we found it without him."

"Oh. Yeah."

"So what do you want to do, boss?"

I didn't really like being reminded that I was the leader of our little group. It made me feel responsible for his safety. On the other hand, I'd hired him as a geocaching guide. I chose not to place our fate on his shoulders.

"Let's try this way," I said as I set off walking through the trees. "Three tenths of a mile is just a few blocks. If we don't reach the beach soon we'll come back to ground zero and try a different direction."

"I guess we can't be lost if we always know where ground zero is, right?" he said.

"Right."

We walked, and walked, and didn't catch a glimpse of the ocean. We turned around and found the cache again. We chose a different direction and tried again. This time when we gave up Darby said, "Way mark this point so we know to avoid it."

"Good idea," I said. "We should have done that last time, too."

After our third trip back to ground zero Darby snacked his forehead and said, "Gimme that thing! Dude, why didn't we think of this an hour ago?"

"What?" I asked as I handed him the GPS.

"We've become so citified we count on city landmarks. All we gotta do is zoom out and it'll show us the caches in town. There won't be any caches in the ocean. We got a map of sorts right in our hands and we aren't using it!"

He zoomed out and the caches in town appeared, then he set a way mark in the direction of the beach.

"There. We walk that way. Follow your GPS and we'll hit the beach eventually."

I zoomed in and there wasn't a road to be seen. I zoomed out and the town appeared. His theory made sense, though, so we walked toward the way point.

When we reached the beach he said, "And when we get back to camp way point that, too!"

After we missed the path from the beach to the campground, I agreed. Way points definitely had their uses when it came to navigating in an unfamiliar place.

"Or we could just follow all the naked people," Darby quipped.

A young woman ahead of us on the trail turned around.

"You're American?" she asked.

"Yeah, straight out of southern California," I admitted.

She was definitely American, too. I was wondering how much a boob job like that cost her. She was tan from head to toe.

"You aren't in California anymore," she quipped.

"We kinda noticed that," Darby said as he tried to nonchalantly look into the tree tops. He might have been looking for birds, but I don't think so.

"Are you going to be around?" she asked.

"For a few days," I answered.

"Look for me in the village. I'll let you buy me a drink."

"I'll keep that in mind," I said, "Though my evening is not entirely planned out at this point."

She gave her bare bottom a little shake as she hurried down the trail.

"Dude!" Darby said. "Do women do that to you often?"

"No. You can look at people when you talk to them," I said.

"I did!"

"For maybe half a second."

"It just doesn't take me long to appreciate the finer points," he said. "Are you going to buy her a drink?"

"If the opportunity presents itself."

Remy and Christophe had the tents almost set up by the time we found the campsite again.

"You walked very far!" Remy said. "You remember my brother."

"Yes," I said. "We do, from the trail by the Seine River."

"Is good to meet you once again," Christophe said.

Both men wore only shoes, but it was obvious why they wore them. The forest was typical French forest which means it had its allotment of stones and sticks on the ground.

"Did you locate the beach?" Remy asked.

"We did. Tell me how I can help."

"Step to the other side," he said as he fed a tent pole through a sleeve of tent fabric. I grabbed the other end. "See the stake?" I had never set up a tent before. He had to tell me each step, but it only took a few minutes to complete the task. In the end we had to two tents and four sleeping bags. Remy and Christophe occupied one tent, Darby and I the other. Christophe had brought food along that we could cook in camp, but the village was much more interesting and only a short drive away. Give three guys the option of cooking burgers on a grill by themselves or drinking a beer with a dozen French beauties walking around half clothed nearby and they will inevitably choose the beer and girls. The food matters little. The village had several restaurants and I really held little hope of the girl from the trail actually tracking me down but she was walking through the restaurant and recognition dawned on both of us at the same time.

"Ehh, buddy," said Darby. "You think she'll take you up on it?"

"You're the one who told me I should be a lion tamer when I grew up."

"Yeah, but I didn't expect to meet any lionesses. Remember, the lionesses are the ones who do the hunting."

She sauntered over, her skirt swishing in interesting ways. She was wearing high heels, which made her legs look even longer than they had appeared while she was unclothed. Her dress was suggestive. She wanted to go home with somebody tonight. Too bad I didn't have any home to bring her to. I doubted she wanted to go sit in camp with four guys and talk about geocaching. I wondered how much commitment one drink meant to her.

She wasn't camping in the woods, that's for sure. She had curled her hair and put on makeup. Her jewelry sparkled as she moved.

"So…" she said. "What do you say?"

"Do you mind?" I asked Remy and Christophe. Their eyebrows raised a notch.

"I shouldn't abandon my hosts completely," I told her as we made our way to the bar. "By the way, I don't think you told me your name."

"Raven," she said. "But I don't think I got yours either."

"Earl," I answered, but as I led the way to the bar I wondered, why me? Back in LA I would assume she noticed my car but she couldn't be after my money here. I looked like a scruffy geocacher and didn't even have my own tent to sleep in that night. "So, what would you like?"

I had to hand it to her. She knew what she wanted and she had good taste. I didn't know a lot about wine but I could read the bartender's expression. She had chosen well and she didn't want to get drunk too early. She wanted to enjoy the evening.

"So, Earl from southern Cali, what are you doing in Montalivet?"

"Actually, I am geocaching," I said. "Though we haven't really begun. We just arrived and barely got our camp set up."

"Ah, the outdoorsy type," she said. When I laughed she asked, "What?"

"Nothing. So what brings you here?"

"Letting my hair down. I come here every year. I get tired of the politics, the striving to get ahead, the business suits and competition, so once a year I come here to just let loose for a change."

"It looks like a good place to do that," I admitted. "What do you do back home?"

"I sell advertising for a fashion magazine."

"Ah, so you're responsible for those perfumed pages that make old men quit breathing in doctors' waiting rooms."

"That's me," she said proudly.

She was charming and beautiful and any guy would consider himself extremely lucky to be hit on by her but... she was trying too hard to impress. I didn't want to be impressed. I lived in a world of constant first impressions. That's one thing I had admired about Jo. She hadn't been trying. She was helping me take pictures, just silly pictures of a toy, but she was real and... and... damn, I was sunk.

"Can I introduce you to my friends?" I asked.

She got into a detailed discussion with Remy about exactly what was the right fragrance for different personality types. Christophe's English was limited, but he tried to keep a conversation going. His sentences always had a, "how do you saaaayyy" in the middle, then he would guess at a word. Sometimes it was right and sometimes Darby and I had to suppress a laugh. Darby and I had to talk slowly so Christophe could hear the individual words and have time to decipher them. If we kept our sentences short and used the words taught in high school English class he understood most of what we said. As with any language, he hesitated to speak because of verb conjugations. I had to give him credit for trying. I wasn't about to try and speak French. Darby had to answer his questions about geocaching because he had more experience in geocaching in the United States, that is until he got around to telling the story of helicopter geocaching in Long Beach. We had to draw a helicopter on the napkin before he understood, then looked at us even more puzzled than before.

"It was a toy. You know... a toy like kids play with," Darby said.

We couldn't use the words *remote controlled helicopter*. We tried talking around the subject but he kept coming back and ask how a toy helped us find a geocache.

"I think it just helped us see the cache. We needed to look up and the helicopter helped us look up."

He finally resorted to asking Remy for a translation. When Remy got the point across Christophe's eyes opened wide.

"Why we not use a heeleochopper for de tree cache!" he said.

Talking with Raven left me homesick for Jo, yet it was a homesickness that had no cure. After the struggle to communicate with Christophe eased, my thoughts strayed back to her situation and I decided that after our excursion to Montalivet we should gather our belongings and find a flight home. I'm afraid the trip to Montalivet, while it was indeed a feast for the eyes, backfired completely. Every woman reminded me of what I would never have and every family reminded me of the family that would never be. I talked to Raven a few more times both clothed and nude. She felt a bit of rejection. I told her, though I didn't believe it, that I thought beginning a new relationship on the rebound was not wise. The truth was, there was still an inkling of hope that I'd see Jo again and things would be miraculously different. I suddenly wanted to get home to see for myself, even if it meant being turned away. I wanted to see it be final with my own eyes.

And so I had to endure two frantic, very physical days of geocaching. Or so I thought...

Chapter 21

Christophe had brought along two bicycles. When I saw the campground I did not question why. It was a beautiful place to ride around. However, his plan did not involve biking around the campground. No, not at all. He drove us to the village where we rented two more.

"How long has it been since you rode a bike?" I asked Darby.

"Years."

"Me, too, I think."

"What do you mean, you think?"

"I mean I don't remember ever riding a bicycle."

"You're kidding!"

"No. I had no use for one growing up. The streets were narrow. We had a car."

"So did I, but how can you grow up without riding a bike?"

"My parents drove me places, or called a cab. They bought me my first car as soon as I got my license just so they would be free of the taxi calling duties."

"Dang. What was it?"

"It was a little Miata. Very nice little car. It handled the narrow streets and curves really well."

"What happened to it?"

"Just like my investments, they made me trade up. Even today I don't keep a car much more than three years."

"And you don't know how to ride a bike?"

"I think I can catch on fast. Distract Remy and Christophe while I figure it out."

"Dude, it takes more than an idea of the mechanics of it. It takes balance and leg muscles. You are going to be sooo sore if you've never ridden a bike."

"I doubt it's any better for you, not having ridden a bike in years."

"Don't remind me. Okay, tips for learning to ride a bike. Now that you're grown up and have plenty of experience tipping over, it's easier to balance the faster you go. So pedal until you get some speed up then work on staying upright. It shouldn't be hard. You know how it works. You know not to fall over and how to stop yourself from falling. You just gotta get used to it."

"That's what I thought."

"Oh and shifting. After you learn how to ride it you gotta learn how to shift it."

"Shift."

"Yeah."

"Like a car."

I should have known that bicycles shift. I'd have to learn the process quickly because Remy and Christophe were experienced cyclers.

Darby helped Christophe unload the bikes at camp and I grabbed one and walked it over to the road. I hopped on. The seat was hard and narrow. It felt like straddling a two by four. I pushed off, wobbled and caught myself with my foot. I pushed off again, harder. I remembered that it was easier to balance if I got up some speed so I pushed several times and got my feet up onto the pedals.

"Try downhill first," Darby called out to me.

I turned the bike around. The road looked pretty level but there as a little bit of a slant to it which helped in the speed department. I pushed off again and found the pedals but it was very wobbly at first. It took several starts and stops to get the hang of it. Campers noticed me wobbling down the road and waved. I couldn't wave back because I was too busy trying to stay upright. I did, however, wave to them on my way back up the road.

"How's it going?" Darby asked as I rode up.

"So far so good," I answered. "Now to see how fast this thing will go."

"Okay, just remember the faster you go the more it hurts to fall. You're lucky that cast only goes up to your elbow. One wipeout and it might just break there."

"Yeah, it's harder to brake with that hand."

I turned around and headed back down the road, this time pedaling hard. Little did I know that I would be pedaling hard all day.

When Remy and Christophe met Darby and I on the bank of the Seine River they had been remarkably patient. Geocaching with them in Montalivet, they were geocaching terrors. Remy laughed out loud when we found the cache in the woods that Darby and I had gotten lost at.

"Tracks everywhere, but the last to sign was two weeks ago!" he laughed. "Oooo DNF, DNF."

"Is *not* difficult," Christophe said, scratching his head with a very puzzled expression on his face.

"Maybe they were new to the hobby," I suggested.

"I wonder how they could have missed it," Darby said in a very poor acting job.

The bike ride to the cache closest to camp was easy, but after that Remy led us north and toward the coast where there was a long trail of caches along a bike path. The woods were thick here and though it was open to the sky it felt like riding through a tunnel. I had never seen forest that thick. Los Angeles had craggy, windswept forest, wide park-like forest and dry, scruffy forest, but I had never encountered forest with trees so close together that I couldn't walk between them.

Christophe was always at the head of our group and he rode fast and hard. Remy rode in a more relaxed manner, yet he kept up with his brother. Darby and I struggled. I was so out of shape, each time we stopped it was a relief just to be off the bike. By the time I caught my breath Christophe and Remy had found the cache and were ready to ride again. I tried to sign the log slowly but no matter how slowly I wrote it doesn't take long to write, "The Earl of Nothing." One of the logs I had to sign was so small I could only fit initials but then Remy asked why I didn't just write 10. It took me a moment to figure out that the initials for The Earl of Nothing could be written TEN. Every time I got on the bike it was harder. My legs burned and my butt was sore.

"It's okay, Earl," Darby said as I hobbled up to yet another late find. "You learned the bike really fast."

"Yeah," I huffed. "Now I just hope I survive the day!"

"Why? What's wrong?"

"I… I still don't understand the shifting and I never get it right. So I either pedal like mad to go nowhere or I strain like crazy just to produce forward motion."

"Let's switch. Mine's somewhere in the middle and I can set yours right on the way to the next cache."

"It's a deal."

Riding Darby's bike helped a lot. I didn't bother trying to shift. I was still sore but I wasn't fighting my wheels. Many of the caches that we found were typical hides. Since I got there late and I was trying to learn geocaching, I tried to be there to see where the cache was hidden and how it was disguised. Most hides were not complicated. It is just a matter of placing the container in the right spot. Sometimes just putting the cache in the right spot made it invisible but sometimes I was told to stack sticks or rocks on top.

One cache made me feel a little smug with myself. I arrived late to the search and found Remy, Christophe and Darby attempting to walk around the trees in search of a container. I joined them but I was equally baffled.

"My GPS says it has to be this tree right here," Darby said.

"Mine keeps sending me back and forth between that tree and one four meters that way," Remy said.

We agreed we were in the right area.

"Maybe the cords are off," Darby said.

"I can't read the logs or the hint," I added. "They're in French."

"Nobody complains about the coordinates," Remy said. "It's a favorite."

That puzzled us even more. When I found it I didn't even know I found it. I noticed a line, just a line or a crack in a log. Many of the sticks and logs had lines on them but this was a perfectly straight line, perpendicular to the grain. I squatted down and ran my fingernail down the line. It was deep and went all the way around the log. I stood and tried to move the end of the log. It didn't move easily. I thought I had traced the line all the way around but when I walked around the log to see the other side there was a little latch. It was just a hook and eye latch but it was small and painted to blend with the bark. This was my chance to rest, so I stepped back and watched the others for a while.

"Earl, you give up too easily," Darby called out to me. "Have you even found one yet?"

"Yup."

"Well, help us with this one. It's a devil of a cache."

"What do we do when we find a cache?" I asked.

"We open it!"

"Aaaannnd?"

"We trade stuff."

"And?"

"We sign it."

"What do we sign?"

"The log."

"Okay, then think log."

He glared at me and walked over. He sat down beside me.

"You found it?" he halfway whispered to me.

"I haven't checked."

"Well, check already!"

"I'm resting. My legs are going to fall off."

He huffed with frustration, then got up to look for a log. There were lots of them around. Even with the obvious hint he didn't see it.

"Look where an ant would look," I told him, but this just brought another glare.

After a few minutes I pushed myself to my feet and hobbled over to the log.

"It would have to be a strong ant," I said to Darby. "Look here."

I flipped the latch.

"Duuude," Darby said when he heard the latch click open. "How's it work?"

"I don't know yet."

"Hey dudes! Guys! Over here!"

"Wha???" Remy said. "Finally!"

After the latch was opened the log still didn't move. We tried pulling up. Then we tried moving it side to side. It finally opened by swiveling the top. A steel rod was used as a hinge and the top swung around to reveal a hollow about the size of a peanut butter jar.

"Wow, talk about muggle resistant caches!" Darby said.

Since the hunt and the find took so long and proved to be creative we took a bigger interest in trading. I took a cardboard beer coaster and left a bottle opener from Paris. I thought I could use the coaster on my computer desk at home.

The rest helped my legs but it also helped Christophe and we rode quickly down the path toward the next cache. The woods were thick, so thick I could barely see into them, so it was easy for things to be just out of sight. Christophe pumped the pedals of his bike furiously when all of a sudden there was a brown blur of movement. Christophe didn't even have time to apply the brakes. It wasn't until he broadsided the thing and flew head over heels over it that we saw it was a huge boar. It was knocked over and it thrashed around in the road until it regained its feet. Hot on the heels of the boar was a farmer who shouted at the beast in French. He stopped and threw his hands in the air as the collision happened right in front of him. The boar was shaken and his coarse hair bristled on the back of his neck. His eyes flashed fear as he rolled to his feet and chose a direction to flee in. I never knew pigs could run that fast. I slammed on my brakes and left my bike on the side of the road as I dashed to see how Christophe had fared in the accident.

Remy had a completely different reaction to the collision. Though he was concerned about his brother he was laughing as he gave Christophe a hand up. He chatted animatedly in French.

Christophe had left the skin from both forearms on the asphalt and his knee was bleeding. We sat him down on the shoulder of the road and I retrieved his bike, which needed a whole new front wheel.

"I was reminding Christophe about a time when we were kids. We rode down a street with a grate over drainage. *Foom!* His tire went straight into the grate and Christophe flipped over! He almost got run over by a car!"

"I roll down de street and stop under a car and I think this car, it's very low. De tire. It was round."

"You mean the tire was flat?" I asked.

"Yes, very almost. It was funny that I crash but all I can think is the tire is flat."

"So what did you notice this time?" Darby asked.

"De ground. She is hard."

"Put pressure on the wound," I advised. "Do we have anything to soak up the blood?"

"De boar, he is one mean peeg," Christophe said. "Like a wall."

Christophe would be fine, but we had one useless bicycle. Remy began asking Christophe questions in French to which Christophe replied. If I had to guess the questions were things like, "Is anything broken? Sprained? Do you want to continue? Can you walk?" Finally Remy stood up and announced, "Okay. A new tire! I will return!"

Darby and I questioned him regarding where he would go and how long he would be gone. He replied that, at worst, he would have to return to the village where we rented the bicycles and it wouldn't take long. He would ride quickly and return as soon as possible.

The farmer shook his fist at the boar and yelled at it. I couldn't understand him but he seemed to be telling the boar that it got precisely what it deserved and good riddance. Christophe partially verified my guess by saying. "De peegs very... how you say... destructive... dey deeg."

"De peegs, dey deeg, the big fat peeg. De swine dey dine on roots and vines. De boar, dey bore. ... uh sorry," Darby said. "Dumb songs pop into my brain at the most random times."

While Remy was gone Christophe and I did our best to stop the bleeding. It wasn't a serious wound, though Christophe occasionally picked tiny rocks from his arms. By the time Remy returned with a new wheel strapped to his back Christophe's scrapes had scabbed over. However, the scabs had formed as he sat on the ground and when he stood to meet his brother he received a rude awakening when the scabs were stretched in different directions and opened again. Remy replaced the front wheel of Christophe's bike, but pedaling wasn't easy. Christophe grimaced with every turn of the pedals. We biked to the next cache just because the trail had little shelters along it. Each shelter consisted of a wooden bench and a trash can under a rough wooden roof with walls on three sides. Being good geocachers, the brothers wouldn't leave the broken bike tire behind and we threw it in the trash can before finding the nearby cache. Bike repairs finished, we decided to find some lunch. Remy and Christophe seemed to have a goal in mind and this setback irked them.

The afternoon saw a reversal of sorts. The out of shape guy with the broken arm and the banged up battered and bruised guy rode side by side as Darby pulled ahead and joined Remy.

Five caches later, Christophe and I were ready to revolt. Remy was disappointed. He wanted to geocache the whole bike trail.

"I say the FTF on the mountain top sounds easier than geocaching this whole bike trail," I said.

"No, no, you don't understand," Remy said. "De FTF, I think, is no more."

"If it's as remote as you say it is what could possibly make it disappear?" Darby asked.

Remy folded his arms. "It's not a matter of whether it is there or not. The journey is…"

"What if we could remove the tough part?" I asked.

"Is impossible. The ice, the snow… The bushes are grown taller."

"How can it be impossible if we have the coordinates?" I asked.

Remy searched for the right word. "The forest. It is wild. You cannot hike there. What do you say in America? You must…"

"Bushwhack?" Darby offered.

"Yes! But I have not the tools."

"So what do you recommend?" I asked.

"We forget it."

"We obviously can't," I pointed out.

"I can," Remy said. "I have for years."

"But it still bothers you," I said. "Or you wouldn't be so adamant about it."

"I think the CO was crazy. I think anybody who would attempt to find it… is crazy. So it should be archived."

"How hard is it to get something archived?" I asked.

"This one… The reviewer has to contact the owner."

"And?"

He sighed, "The owner insists it is still there. He argues that some people like a challenge."

"So it is still active and still findable," I pointed out. "Finding it would give you bragging rights at the local events for a long time."

"These 'bragging rights' are not worth risking my life over," Remy added. "You don't want to ride a bicycle but you would like to ride a boat, climb an icy mountain and fight angry insects and impenetrable brush instead?"

"No," I said. "I'm thinking we hire a pilot."

Chapter 22

"No," said Darby. "You ain't getting me up in the air again until we fly home."

"It's completely safe," I said.

"Completely safe as in… how?"

"They take tourists up all the time. We just happen to have a particular destination in mind instead of just wanting to see the city from above."

"So tell me, how do we get from the helicopter to the ground?" Darby asked.

"Rappel!" Remy said enthusiastically. It seemed this turn of events had piqued Remy's interest.

"Maybe they can land," I suggested.

"Chris?" Remy asked. "What do you say?"

"To be truthful… I do not like the sound of sleeping on the ground."

"But the FTF…" Remy sort of asked.

This prompted a string of French from Christophe. From his tone of voice he agreed the FTF probably did not exist, but they could prove it by looking for it. A slight brotherly argument ensued. Remy wanted to camp. Christophe was tired of roughing it. His legs were bloodied, though not dangerously so. It was painful and inconvenient to ride a bike, get on and off and hunt for geocaches. I think there was a little name calling as Remy pointed out to his brother that if he would watch where he was going he would not be missing large patches of skin or be bleeding on the flora of the French countryside. This brought on some angry words about the boars in France. Remy suddenly turned to me and, remembering to switch to English said, "How? How do you propose to fly to this cache?"

"Is there a place where we can hire a pilot?"

"No way," Darby said. "First I had to fly in a jet. Then I had to go to the top of the Eiffel Tower. Then I had to climb a tree! I am keeping my feet on the good old terra firma."

We stood beside the bike trail in a circle. Remy had a vote for camping, Christophe wanted to do anything besides bike riding, Darby was willing to go for the FTF if he could stay on the ground. And I… I was intrigued by this cache sitting on a mountain that had never been found.

"What is the easiest way to get there?" I asked.

"Helicopter," Remy said.

"Or how you say… balloon?" Christophe added.

"Hot air balloon?" I asked, fascinated by the prospect. "You have hot air balloons here?"

"But of course!" Christophe said.

"And how are we *expected* to get there?" I questioned further.

"A boat ride upriver followed by a two day hike."

"I thought you said two day bushwhack," Darby said.

"Eh, could be," Remy said.

"If it was just a hike that cache would have been found right off," Darby said.

"There is a little mountain climbing involved, too," Remy added.

"How much is a little bit?" Darby asked.

"If I knew that, I would know if the cache is there," Remy said.

"Is there any reason we can't fly there?" I asked.

"It is not... typical," Remy said. "But I suppose it isn't against the rules. Hiring a pilot, whether it be helicopter or balloon, would be nearly as troublesome as taking the boat and walking. It is only less physically demanding."

"Flying is probably safer than bushwhacking and mountain climbing," I thought aloud.

"According to who?" Darby asked.

We ended up biking back towards camp, finding a few geocaches on the way, then ending the day with beers and dinner in town, the brothers still at odds about the next day. After a few beers the conversation turned to mostly French.

"So what's the big deal about being FTF? So you're the first to find... Is there a reason you want to be first?" I asked.

"Us? No, not really, except for bragging rights about being the first to locate a remote cache that hadn't been found in two years."

"Bragging rights. There's no prize?"

"No. Well, there might be a small one, but not one to make it worth the trouble to pay our way on a boat ride and bushwhack up a mountain."

"But... it'd make quite a story."

"Sure... if you had a place to tell it."

I was thinking of the store. If I was able to open a geocaching store I'd want a tale or two to give me something to talk about to the customers. The story of the FTF hunt might be worth the trouble in the long run. In that case the harder or more unusual we made it the better the tale would be.

"Just think," I told Remy. "At the next event you could tell everybody you found that cache."

"How? There is no way to get to it!"

"We could make a way. Tell me, how would you do it, if you could choose?"

"The helicopter idea... it is cheating."

"Thank goodness!" Darby interjected.

"Is too easy. They drop us off, we hunt in the rocks, we board the helicopter. No. Is too easy. The balloon... is cheating, too. I don't know why it appears to be more acceptable. The boat... is the expected approach, but the brush is too thick. I have no machete and would not use one. Too destructive. I try to leave no signs of my passing. I will not bushwack my way in. So..."

"The balloon?" I asked.

"And how do you propose we do that?"

"I don't know. Let's look and see if there is a company that gives balloon rides. Maybe we can bribe them into taking us there."

"Oh, no, no way," Darby said.

"You don't want to go?" I asked.

"Want? No, I don't want to go up in the sky a gazillion feet from any safe height and look down to see busses the size of ants and... no."

"Okay, I'll give you the day off."

In the end the mysterious container was more of a draw to the two brothers than some caches found many times on a peaceful bike trail. The next day very early we packed up camp into Christophe's larger car and drove back to Remy's apartment. We stood huddled over his computer researching balloon ride companies.

Chapter 23

"This one is closer to ground zero," Remy said as he read the screen. "But this one can take four passengers."

"How many can the first one take?" I asked.

"Two. I think two is the expected number. Nobody wants to ride a balloon with a stranger. Couples, friends, yes. So two is standard."

"But we need four, so do you know where this company is with the extra large capacity baskets is?"

"If I can find a geocache, I can certainly find a building."

"Three. You only need three to go up," Darby reminded me.

"I want to leave you the option of going. It's an FTF, on a mountain top, in France. You don't want to try?"

"No."

"Then I'd enjoy a little extra space in the basket. But, yes, we want go together, so ask about the package for four."

"Extra space? No," Remy said. "I think we should be better prepared. This is no simple undertaking. We should be prepared to spend most of the day there. We will need food and water."

"We have that in the camping gear," I pointed out.

"Okay, Christophe and Earl, sort out the camping supplies. I will call the balloon company."

Remy called the phone number on the web page. Occasionally he came in to get answers to questions. I don't know what eighty kilograms works out to but I think that was Remy's guess about my weight.

"Darby, are you certain?" Remy came in with a final question.

"Do they speak English?" Darby asked.

Remy inquired as to their English speaking abilities and handed the phone over to Darby.

While Darby questioned the balloon company representative, Remy finalized a few things.

"You know balloon flights are at dawn and conditions in the sky only permit morning flights, yes?"

"Uh, sort of."

"It is possible for maybe an afternoon attempt to return us to the village, but they will not guarantee."

"So we should bring tents as well."

"Yes."

"And it would be better to plan on spending the night on the mountain and being picked up the next day."

"Yes."

"Is very expensive, one, for a private flight, and two, for special flight requirements."

"I know. It's okay."

"I am... not so sure. This is unexpected."

"Don't worry about it. How much is it?"

"A hundred fifty Euros per person. One way."

A little over two hundred dollars each?" I asked. "No problem."

"And Darby?"

"I think he'd be better off staying behind, though I'd like him to go."

I kept catching phrases from Darby like, "And there ain't no way to fall out... or catch fire... or see down... or freak out and jump?" Apparently the representative was pretty convincing because Darby looked very worried when he handed the phone back to Remy.

"Dang, she had the answer to every question!" Darby said. "They ain't never had an accident, never had a customer freak on them. She said I'd feel like I was standing on a platform on the ground! Heck, that's impossible. Not when my brain is telling me I'm floatin' in the clouds! I don't know. I don't know, Earl."

"It's up to you. I'm not going to force you. I just think the more times you go up the more you will see that you really have nothing to worry about. You'll be okay in town for a day?"

"Yeah, sure."

"Remy will let you use his apartment as home base. You can call a taxi to take you anywhere you want for meals. You can geocache, anything you want."

"Earl? When are we going home?"

"As soon as I can find a flight. I think we've accomplished what we came here for. When I get back we'll find a flight home."

"Shi-it. Then I gotta fly agin."

"Yup, if you want to go home."

"I wish I could talk to Henry."

"What would Henry tell you, if you asked for his advice?" I asked.

"He'd say... he'd say to pray about it and trust God."

That kind of took me aback. I never knew Henry, Wanda and Darby were religious in any way. I could understand their need to place their fates in the hands of a more powerful being, and I understood how they could have a faith and yet not go to church. I wondered if there was a church for the homeless. But Darby's answer still surprised me.

"Then pray," I said. "And if God doesn't think you should go, you don't have to."

Actually, I thought it couldn't hurt to pray about it. It's like the age old coin toss. Most people think they do a coin toss to decide something that could go either way, but as soon as that coin is in the air a real decision pops into your mind before the coin is caught. Then when you see whether the coin is heads or tails you hope it lands your way. That's the way I thought it would be with Darby's prayers. He'd send a prayer up and he'd hope for an answer and when we looked at the results of his prayer toss he'd know whether he was going to trust God to hold up a balloon, or trust his fears and stay on the ground. I wasn't going to make that decision for him.

Darby paced the floor as Remy made arrangements for our balloon trip the next day. I couldn't tell if Darby was praying or just worrying. I knew prayer took many forms. If Darby was praying he was used to doing it on his feet, but then a lot of Darby's life was spent on his feet. I left the decision to him.

We debated whether Darby and I should go back to our hotel but it was ultimately decided that we were in this FTF hunt together and it would be much easier to just stay at Remy's apartment so we wouldn't need to regroup. Darby and I slept in the sleeping bags on the floor. We each offered the couch to the other, but neither of us wanted to deprive the other of the comfort. It mattered little because it was a very short night. We stayed up late speculating about the chances of the cache actually being there and discussing all the things that could happen to a container left in the wilds for two years. Because I came from the city and I didn't have experience searching amongst rocks and trees, it never occurred to me that the container could be completely invisible, buried under two years of sticks, leaves and dirt, or that repeated snows and intense sunshine could take a toll on a container's life expectancy. I was told to watch for anything, anything unusual at all. Anything that might be a piece of swag or log book needed to be examined to determine if it used to be part of a cache. Our FTF hunt was looking less promising, but there was still only one way to find out if it would pay off and that was to go see.

Three a.m. Remy flips on the lights and sings cheerfully, "Off we go, into the wild dark niiiight, flying high up in the sky!"

"Uhhhh, he butchers an American classic," Darby mumbled.

"The balloon! She rises at dawn!" Christophe said.

"Okay, I'm getting up, I'm getting up," I said and rolled out of the sleeping bag. I forgot I was on the floor and thought I was rolling off the edge of a mattress, so I hit the coffee table instead of the floor. I stumbled through a quick semi-normal morning routine wishing coffee was in the very near future, but knowing the coffee shops wouldn't open until we were far away from Paris. It wasn't until we were ready to leave the apartment that I noticed Darby had risen and gotten ready with the rest of us.

"You decided to go?" I asked.

"It's an FTF," he said. "Don't matter what I want. It's out there and it's gotta be found."

"All right!"

"You look like something the cat drug in."

Chapter 24

We didn't stop for coffee at all, but the little balloon airport was used to dealing with people who were half awake and running on empty. There was a large urn of very strong coffee and a box of pastries on a table beside the check in desk. Great, caffeine and carbs. At least it would stave off the hunger. By the time we got checked in I was looking forward to the flight, but Darby... was barely functioning. He didn't need coffee either. He needed a chill pill. It didn't help that the airport had posters on the walls of colorful hot air balloons floating peacefully in the sky far above the green mountains or bustling cities far below. All the balloons were bright and cheerful. All the people were smiling. All the posters were ads and that fact wasn't lost on Darby. He knew sitting in the corner of one of those baskets was one person who was scared to death to stand up and smile, who thought they might not land, might fall screaming through the atmosphere until they landed in a splat upon the earth, who expected to hit trees or power lines and have the whole balloon burst into flames around them. Today he was that person.

I walked over and started asking him geocaching questions, hoping to get his mind off his fears. "So how many FTFs do you have?"

"Only a couple. I never got notifications so I had to check the webpage for new caches and then hope they were close enough to walk to."

"Why don't you get the notifications?" I asked.

"You gotta be a premium member."

"Oh. We'll take care of that when we open the store."

"Take care of what?"

"Every worker will be a premium member. You have to be to keep up with the clientele. Would you hire a car guy to sell cars who didn't know how to drive?"

"This'll be one hell of an FTF if we can get it."

"Have you ever taken Adele geocaching?" I asked.

"Nah, my wife won't let me take Adele anyplace. She thinks being on the streets will damage her for life. If I see her I have to go visit her at home, and then I get a lecture, and it turns into a fight."

"Does your wife work?"

"Oh yeah, she works, but not doing anything that would support a family. So she pays a little rent to her folks and keeps her and Adele clothed. She just don't include me in any of that. Her mom calls it tough love. Yeah, right. Her mom don't know what tough is. Tough is seeing your family happy and leaving you in the gutter."

"You'll get out of that gutter. You'll see."

"I can't blame Sherry. You gotta do the best you can and the best she can is at her mom's house. I'm glad Adele's got a roof over her head, a mom, a grandma and granddad. I just wish I could be the man I'm supposed to be, you know what I mean?"

"To do that you just need an opportunity and we're going to try to create one. All we have to do is commit to it and put in the hard work to make it happen. Now, how about you take on a job for me? We want to document this FTF hunt and I appoint you the group photographer. You don't have to shoot down. Look for the geocaching aspects of the trip."

Darby took the camera and wandered out to the "runway." Maybe it's a float way? A launch pad? Though he came back even more worried I was astounded by his artistic eye when I saw the pictures much later. If I had seen the pictures I never would have guessed that his first statement when we met up again was, "You're trusting your life to a hunk of material and a fire?"

"A controlled fire," I corrected him.

"Dude, they got propane!"

"And I'm sure it burns quite well."

"That lady on the phone sounded so sure this was an easy thing to do. She said I'd hardly be able to tell I was flying at all. She made it sound like an easy elevator ride. The only hitch in the plan is a lack of steering. She said, judging from our destination we could be dropped off half a mile from the cache, but we would be above all the brush so I thought it sounded great! Now I see this setup and I say no way is this going to work."

"Half a mile is pretty close. It was the bush whacking that we were trying to avoid."

"Yeah, but this ballooning thing… I don't know. It's like… way out there, you know what I mean?"

"Relax. The worst that will happen is we'll get off track they'll find a nice field to land in and we'll be brought back here. So it's a DNF. We can try a different approach."

"In our case the DNF might be Did Not Float."

The balloon was laying on its side when we walked out to the take-off area. They were blowing air into it and it was maybe half inflated. The breeze would catch the fabric and make it look like something was inside feeling around for a way out. The pattern on the balloon was a spiral of colorful diamonds. Darby walked around taking pictures from all angles. He wasn't a professional photographer so he just took lots of pictures hoping maybe one of them would be good. There was very little he could do wrong. The green rolling hills with woods in the background and the colorful balloon standing at anchor made a beautiful sight.

Boarding the balloon was somewhat like getting on a motorcycle. We slid a foot into a little step and swung a leg over the side. The other leg followed and we maneuvered to make room for the others. Christophe handed the camping gear over the side.

"Darby! Load up!" I called. He was still walking around taking pictures, probably putting off the inevitable. I thought if I was afraid of going up I'd be the first one in so I could claim the most stable spot, but he seemed to be procrastinating.

The noise from the burners was loud but Darby walked worriedly our direction.

"Oh man, the things I'll do for a smiley," he grumbled as he figured out how to board. I guess he had been so busy taking pictures he hadn't seen the rest of us board.

"Use the step," I told him. "Swing your leg over. There you go."

"This ain't so bad," he said as he stood at the basket's side.

The pilot asked Remy if everybody was ready. Remy glanced around to see if we had all the gear and took a head count then gave the pilot a thumbs up. The fires roared to life, the balloon rose and Darby quickly backed away from the side of the basket. He eventually ended up sitting on the pack where he couldn't see anything.

I learned a lot about atmospheric conditions on that flight. For instance looking straight up I would never guess that different layers of air are traveling in different directions. While on the ground it feels as if all the air is moving the same direction, that is only because all the air around you is moving in one direction. At first the balloon follows the breeze close to the ground, but as it rises it enters different air currents and so we drifted in the wrong direction for a while before entering a different current which carried us in the general direction we needed to go. I took over the photography to get shots of the countryside going by and my fellow travelers. The pilot would point out landmarks below in French and Remy translated for me. We passed a castle and followed a river. In general the French countryside was very green and heavily forested. Unlike the only rivers I had seen in California, the river here flowed bank to bank. In California the term *river* could mean a boulder strewn ditch, a trickle of water with a ticket to the Pacific Ocean, or, rarely, a tumbling rushing expanse of water. I tried to remember if I had ever actually seen a typical river in California but I could only remember seeing one from the air when we were flying from LAX to Seattle for a business meeting. We had a layover in Denver so I think it was the Colorado River, which technically was only half in California. I always wondered why the airline companies flew to Denver when they were trying to get to Seattle, but you can't argue with the system. I can say I do not own stock in the airline industry.

We discovered just how skilled balloon pilots had to be when the air currents near the mountains changed and we had to rise and fall to stay on track. This was particularly nerve wracking to Darby. As the mountains grew close he worried about hitting them but Guillaume, our pilot, seemed to know what he was doing as he confidently maneuvered the air waves. As we grew closer to the cache the stream of French between Remy, Christophe, and Guillaume was constant. Remy talked and pointed. Guillaume shook his head and spoke. Remy's brow furrowed and he asked another question which seemed to get a better response. I could only trust Remy to get us as close to the cache as he could.

Darby stood up to get an update but quickly closed his eyes and turned around. It looked like we were going to slam into a mountain, but the balloon was moving very slowly and very deliberately, carefully guided by Guillaume's experienced hands.

I will never forget the sound of hot air balloons rising and falling. There is just something about the noise that cannot be mistaken for anything else. If I had to close my eyes and say what I picture it would be a giant robot smoking a cigar, but that's silly. There are bursts of heat, releasing of flaps, roaring air, and the balloon goes down, rides a current, goes down. Precision takes time. While it is happening there is a strange mixture of wanting to watch the proceedings longer and excitement about reaching the destination. The balloon can only fly while the outside air is cool so the flight could not last all morning. We hit the mountain with a bump that startled Darby and made us all grab for a steadying hold on the basket. Guillaume and Remy exchanged instructions for the pick up as I handed the camping gear over the side of the basket to Christophe.

Darby nearly leaped over the wall of the basket, but it was he that pointed out, as the balloon began rising into the blue sky, "Now how are we going to get all this stuff to the cache?"

We all stood in a circle around the pile of gear in disbelief that we had overlooked the simple fact that we needed to carry our camping gear over the mountain to the cache. It was impossible. There was just too much gear. Each man had a sleeping bag and a bag with a change of clothes. The containers of food contained enough to keep us fed for a two days, but it was too bulky to carry. We had a small cook stove and two tents to transport as well.

Everything was packed well, but it was packed for car camping, not geocaching.

"How far is the cache? And which direction?" Darby asked.

"Two kilometers," Remy said.

"How far is that?" I asked.

"Two thousand forty meters."

"Anybody got miles?" I asked.

Darby read the distance off his GPS "One point two seven miles. That's as close as they could get?" Darby said incredulously.

"The wind was blowing that way," Remy said pointing in the direction of the wind. "The cache is that way. To continue on would only take us farther away."

"Okay," I said. "Let's set up camp at the closest flat spot we can find. One point two miles isn't that far. We can set up a quick camp, hike to the cache and put in an afternoon searching for it."

Darby shrugged. It sounded doable for macho geocacher men.

"You know," Darby said as we were setting up tents, "We gotta get all this stuff to the balloon when it comes back."

"We'll worry about that in the morning," I said.

When the tents stood on the mountainside and the cooking spot was arranged we stepped back wondering if everything was secure, but it wasn't as if it was going to get raided while we were gone. We could stand at camp and look in any direction and see for miles. There were no trees, just windswept grassy mountainsides. If a person was out there we would see them.

"Dang," Darby said. "We should be able to see the beacon from here! The cache is thataway. I don't see any hiding places that way."

"Distances can be deceiving," I said.

"It's already after noon," Remy said. "We have a backpack. Perhaps, lunch on the hike?"

"Works for me," I said. "Then we can search for the cache and be back for dinner."

"What if we don't find it?" Remy asked.

"Then we have to forget the FTF. The balloon will be here whether we find it or not. We have to get camp packed up and more transportable before the balloon arrives."

"Perhaps we could have prepared better," Remy said.

"Well, this is what we have to work with. Everyone make sure you have something to eat and a bottle of water."

Darby was in his element hiking to the cache. He was used to walking, but there seemed to be more to his hiking than just an enjoyment of what he was doing. I think the fear of flying was working its way out his feet. Add to that the spectacular views, the foreignness of the setting, the pleasant breeze and the promise of exploring the mountain tops, and I couldn't really blame him. His enthusiasm was contagious, so the first half mile went quickly. The heights were invigorating, the balloon ride had been fun and scenic, now here we were hiking off to an FTF hunt. Tomorrow at this time we'd be back in town celebrating our determination and fortitude.

While we were hiking we spotted some kind of goats I had never seen before. They were the color of rock and looked wild. We all stopped and watched the herd as they crossed a hill nearby. I am not a wildlife expert. To me they were goats because goats have weird expressions and these animals' eyes were weird even from a distance. They also had horns. Sheep don't have horns. Oh, yes they do. The rams do. But sheep are fuzzy and these were definitely not fuzzy. I will call them goats for lack of a better word. The herd went over the hill except for one youngster. He hung back for a minute before scampering to catch up.

"Did you get a picture of that?" I asked.

"I hope so," Darby answered. "I was fiddling with some of the features so I'm not sure."

As it turned out he did get a few good pictures. They showed the goats' odd horns and quirky expressions from a distance. A few of the photos only showed retreating rear ends.

The goats liked the mountains, especially the rocky areas. We didn't know the terrain we were about to encounter was the goats' natural environment. We followed the GPSrs, Remy and Darby were ahead and I ended up hiking with Christophe. We called ourselves the Walking Wounded, he with his scrapes and bruises from the bike wreck and I with my cast on my arm. Free of the confines of naturist expectations and his fear of flying, Darby hiked enthusiastically across the mountainside reminding me of the movie *The Sound of Music*. He wasn't singing but the thrill of the hunt was visible in every move. We walked at a good, steady pace until Remy and Darby screeched to a halt. We were hiking cross country and there were no trails so Christophe and I had to catch up before we discovered what caused the sudden stop.

"They climbed up to place the cache," Darby said. "But that's still a long ways down." We'd reached our first stumbling block and it was a doozy.

The river was barely visible in the valley below and the cache owner had disembarked the river boat, camped and then hiked into the wilderness to place the container in its hiding place. Maybe we should have looked at the satellite images more carefully before being dropped off on the mountain. However, judging by the angle of the rocks we might not have seen it from above anyway. Perhaps a topo map would have shown us had we owned one or known how to read it.

"What direction is the cache?" Remy asked, though he had his own GPSr in his hand. Everybody who was carrying a GPS agreed that the cache was straight out from the cliff. We looked at the lay of the land, which was pretty easy to do as high up as we were.

"I say we go north," Remy said pointing. "The mountain slopes and we can walk across level ground instead of trying to descend. Then when we get to that valley the walking will be easy enough to hike down."

The valley he was talking about was simply the cut between two hills but I could see what he meant.

"Looks good to me. We'll need to remember to retrace our steps to get back to camp," I said.

"We don't want to climb down those rocks," Christophe said. "Or climb back up them without ropes."

"I didn't think about bringing a rope," Remy said.

"Uh, guys, speaking of bringing something, does anybody have a pen?" Darby asked.

Remy and Christophe looked at him as if he was insane, as if to say, "We are *geocachers*! Of course we have a *pen*!"

"Okay! Just asking," Darby said.

As frequently happens our one point two miles turned to two point two and I began to lose track of where camp was when we lost sight of it behind the mountain. I memorized the rocks of the cliff so I'd recognize it to find our way back. I wasn't used to navigating in the mountains. I was used to addresses and buildings and easy to identify landmarks. All we had here to use for landmarks were rocks and hills until our GPSrs led us back down into the forest. Then all the trees looked alike. As I followed Remy and Darby I kept telling myself that a person cannot get lost in two miles. I pictured two miles in the city and everything was very straightforward. A couple of neighborhoods, or downtown LA, or the length of two large mall parking lots. Two miles. Simple. But as I looked around and only saw trees I thought camp could be in any one of several directions. Pick the wrong one and we'd be walking the wrong direction and completely miss it. Up. I knew we would have to go up and then perhaps we would be able to see the familiar mountainside we had been dropped off on. In the forest I couldn't even see the mountain we had just descended. We tromped through the woods like a herd of buffalo scaring away every animal within half a mile. I became grateful for the cast when the mosquitoes settled in for a banquet. At least they couldn't bite through plaster and gauze. We hiked and slapped at mosquitoes and cursed the river which attracted them to the area. We switched the GPSrs from hand to hand to slap at different parts of our anatomy. I learned that squashing a mosquito with the screen of a GPS only makes navigation more difficult and there's always another mosquito to take its place. We found ourselves jogging through the woods to put an end to our misery quicker. We should have been counting our blessing with the mosquitoes. A breeze came up and the mosquitoes eased up. The breeze increased and the branches of the trees shook and danced above our heads. The sky darkened and I understood why Guillaume was in a hurry to get back. What I didn't understand was why we were not warned about the possibility of a storm. None of us had rain gear and were dressed in t-shirts and jeans, except for Remy who wore light weight cargo pants. When the rain started we became chilled very quickly. All except Darby. I wondered if he had developed extreme weather tolerance from living on the streets, but the streets of LA had very little inclement weather. Still, he seemed unnaturally comfortable. The trees sheltered us a little, but at the same time the leaves held rain until they bent under the weight and then they released a huge drop that felt like being smacked with a water balloon. If they struck our clothes it wasn't so bad but occasionally one would go straight down the collar of my shirt or splat on the very top of my head.

"How much are we willing to endure for an FTF?" I asked, but I was just met with blank stares. I guess we didn't travel the length of France just to give up within a half mile of the cache. "It's still a quarter of a mile away and I'm sinking ankle deep in wet leaves."

"Yeah? So?" Darby said.

All right, press on, I told myself. The spoiled rich kid needed to learn a thing or two about real work. I decided to just follow and not complain. Cold shirt clinging to my skin, hair plastered down my head, water dripping off my nose, I followed. The leaves began sticking to me and if we hit a branch it caused a cascade effect and drenched whatever body part was closest.

The further into the woods we hiked the thicker the undergrowth was until we were squeezing through brambles. I thought we came this way to avoid bushwhacking but I refused to say anything. Remy came to a halt in shoulder high brush.

"The cache is that way," he said pointing.

"There's no way to go that direction," I said.

"We must return the way we came and try a different approach."

We were getting close, but the rain was incessant, the brush thick. The woods were quiet except for our huffing and puffing, fighting to wade in damp leaves through thick brush. Again and again we close in on ground zero but were held back by the vegetation. It was already late afternoon, hunger was setting in and we still had to hike back to camp, but we hadn't reached ground zero yet.

Christophe said something to Remy in French and Remy shrugged.

"He wants to try army crawling under the branches to reach the cache," Remy explained.

"What if you get stuck?" I asked.

"I can always do the reverse," Christophe said.

Reverse sounded harder than army crawling but it did look doable. I just didn't think Christophe should be the one to do it because his arms were already scraped up from the bike crash. I began looking for a way through. Pretty soon my investigation led to a slow crawl through the brush. It was a tight squeeze in spots. I even had to turn sideways and wriggle my way through. The branches caught on my clothes and I had to untangle myself frequently to gain any forward motion. I was slow as a slug and felt like one, too. I had to stop frequently to check my direction with the arrow of the GPS. There was no way to stand up. I looked at the screen. Fifty-two feet. Fifty-two feet of army crawling under bushes? I must be nuts.

"Can we get through?" Remy shouted.

"If I can do it, you can do it, but I don't recommend starting until I see if it's even possible," I shouted back. "It's going to be kind of hard to look if we can't even stand up."

"You can't even stand?" Darby asked.

"I've got sticks poking me in the back and I'm not even on my hands and knees," I said.

I ducked under another spindly branch and pulled myself forward. The leaves rustled off to my right and I stopped.

"Remy?"

"Yes?"

"What animals live in these woods?" I asked.

"Many do."

"Anything I should worry about?"

"Can you see it?"

"No. What animal would brave this rain?"

"Us."

Something moved in the brush. The brush here was more like small trees with low branches.

"What would come this close to me?" I asked.

"How close?" Remy asked.

"I don't know. Not far. A couple dozen feet?"

I continued crawling through the leaves and the thing watched from above. I craned my head trying to see what it was but it was only a blur that stayed just out of my line of vision. It was a little disconcerting being watched by an unknown animal. I was certain, though, that Remy would warn me of any animal I should be worried about.

"Can you guys see it?" I asked

"You're kidding, right?" said Darby. "We can barely see *you*."

The creature rarely descended to the ground. It seemed perfectly comfortable in the trees.

"You don't have monkeys here?" I asked.

"No. Not wild, or in the woods," Remy answered.

"It doesn't move like a monkey anyway. It's more like a raccoon."

"No," he said. "Raccoon dogs are not like monkeys."

"Raccoons in America are good tree climbers."

"Perhaps a genet?" Remy suggested.

"What's a genet?"

"It has spots and a striped tail."

"I don't know. It's staying mostly out of sight. I just wonder why it's so interested in me."

"If it's a genet you have no worries. They eat mice and steal chickens."

I looked at the GPS again. Eighteen feet.

"Bad news, guys," I said. "I'm down to eighteen feet and I still cannot stand up."

"Do you see any beacons?" Darby asked.

"Oh. Wait. There is something in here. Hold on."

I crawled through the trees into grass. The grass bordered a small pool of water. A spring in the forest?

"Can you crawl this far?" I called back. "I can stand up now and I think the cache is nearby."

First I looked around for the creature that had been following me, but I couldn't see it. Next I looked at the GPS to see where the cache might be. I felt like I ought to wait for the rest of the guys, but I also had nothing better to do than look for the cache. The coordinates led to the other side of the pool, which was only the size of a small pond. One side had a rock outcropping and I headed toward that thinking there would be hiding spots there.

With the proximity of water, the rocks were covered with a fuzzy green moss. The rain had awaked the moss, too, and it stood like a miniature forest on the bare rock. While I was searching the rocks I noticed a wall. It was only about two feet tall and covered by more of the moss. The brush was thick around the wall, but I didn't have to crawl to it. When I reached the wall I could see another wall through the brush. I think we had stumbled on an ancient village, long abandoned in the woods. I would have loved to find the other walls of the village, but we needed to find this cache and make our way out of the woods before the sun set. Even after we left the woods behind we had a long hike ahead of us. I went back to the spring and the rocks and began to search in earnest. If I found the cache I could always let the other guys search, too. But time was not on our side. We didn't come all this distance and put all this effort into hiking through the rain and crawling through the leaves to not find the cache, so I was going to look, even if I had to give away the glory of finding the cache. We had already agreed we were a team. I wasn't so prideful that I had to be the one at the top of the log. Our number one goal in my book was to prove we could do it, we could find this long forgotten cache in the woods. Secondly we wanted to put the cache back on the map so other geocachers would come look for it, too. And thirdly we wanted our names on that log as the intrepid explorers willing to brave the rough terrain to find it.

"We are insane," Darby said as he army crawled through the brush following my very obvious trail.

"Did you see the animal?" I asked.

"No. If it was smart it ran away."

"I'd like a picture of it but I know that's hard to do even if an animal cooperates."

When all four of us stood around the spring we compared GPS readings.

"These trees don't help at all," Darby said.

"It's still worth using the GPSrs," I pointed out. "What does yours say?"

"Eighteen feet."

"Remy?"

"Twelve meters."

"Christophe?"

"Fifteen meters."

"Mine says twenty five feet," I said. "I found some rock walls. I think the cache owner brought us to a village. Keep that in mind while you are searching. He might have had a specific place in mind when he hid it. So watch for ruins."

As we picked our way through the brush we discovered colorful geckos and sunken walls. One of the walls looked like it was once a round tower and I kept expecting to find old weapons and rusted out farm tools. In the United States old ruins were so picked over it was impossible to find remnants of the people who lived there but I didn't know about what might be found in France so my imagination was free to make things up. It soon became apparent that the cache could be buried deep under ferns, and forest litter. The coordinates could easily be off considering the thick canopy of trees. Our task was beginning to look daunting. It was during this search while I was peeling plants away from a rock wall, soaked to the skin by rain, checking my GPS frequently, that I thought I was a real geocacher. I had arrived. I may not be the most experienced geocacher, nor did I know how to find the elusive containers, but I felt like I was really geocaching. I'd gone from tentative bystander to explorer in one walk in the woods.

"Dude, is that the critter?" Darby asked quietly as he pointed into the trees.

I had to follow his point.

"Yeah, I think so. Can you get a picture of it?" I asked.

It looked like a cat of some kind. It had a pointy face and enormous ears. Its coat was spotted and its striped tail gave away its agitated state. However, even with all the tail thrashing it gazed down on us tipping its head as if it was curious what these two legged creatures were.

"It is a genet," Remy said. "And hungry. Usually they run away from people."

"It won't attack, will it?" I asked like a typical foreigner.

"We are too big. It knows we are not mice," Remy answered.

It crawled higher into the branches when it saw it was the focus of our attention and Darby swore as his shot was ruined. He began following the genet trying to get a good picture but he only managed to chase it away.

"The geckos are colorful," I suggested to Darby so he'd concentrate his efforts closer to the ground.

"This place is like a jungle," Christophe complained as he worked his way through the vegetation. I had to agree.

Most of the forest I had seen in France had been thick with trees, but not so much so that we couldn't walk around. This forest was much older and neglected so the trees had actually become too crowded. The spring kept them watered and at the moment there was even a little creek that led from the spring downhill and I could only assume the creek ended at the river. After we had given the area a cursory search we regrouped.

"I think we should concentrate on ground zero," Remy said.

"With all these trees?" Darby asked.

"Yes. A true geocacher will not use the first coordinates his unit shows him. He will write down the coordinates several times to decide the exact spot. And when he gets home he will try to find the spot on satellite images. Then, even if his coordinates are bad he can correct them."

"So you're saying there should be a landmark," I said.

Remy nodded.

"Even when all you can see from above is trees?"

He nodded again.

There was no reason not to find ground zero so we all walked around until our GPSrs had narrowed down where they thought ground zero was. We ended up about ten feet apart but no two of us were standing at the same spot.

We began again but speculations began flying.

"They wouldn't hang it would they?"

"This place is so remote. There's no reason to make it tough."

"Did anybody read the hint?"

"No hint."

"That means they want it to be really hard or it's so easy it doesn't need one."

"Yeah, right."

"In two years it could be buried."

"That's why we wanted to find ground zero. So we'd know where to dig."

"It could be camouflaged."

"It could be gone."

On and on the comments flew back and forth. The possibility of it being buried under years of fallen leaves kept coming back to me until I was convinced it had to be true.

"No one brought a shovel?"

"No."

"I haven't even seen dirt since we got here," Darby said.

"Dirt isn't the only thing that can be shoveled," I pointed out.

"It wouldn't be in the water," I thought aloud.

"It could," Darby said as he approached the spring. He gazed into its depths. "There are lots of underwater caches."

"How deep do you think it is?" I asked.

"No telling. I don't see bottom. Do you?"

"No, it's too small to swim in, though."

"How far is it from ground zero?"

"Only twelve feet."

"Mine says six feet."

The number varied because we were standing in different spots but it was obvious that the spring had to be considered a possible hiding spot.

"If it was in the spring, the description should say something. They shouldn't make somebody come all the way up here unprepared."

This caused us all to click back to the description but Darby and I soon found the description was useless to us. It was written in French.

"Not in the water," Christophe concluded.

"It doesn't say that," Remy confirmed. "It says the pond is here, and it was central to the life of the village. It says nothing about the cache in the water. I think, if it was under the water, the description would tell us."

"So we're assuming the cache is on land."

"We need to think like a cache hider. They had quite a hike just to get up here. They happened on a spring and the ruins, thought it would be a cool place to put a cache. They didn't have time to rig up something clever. They just wanted other people to find this place, too. So it's not going to be something fancy," Darby said.

"And," I continued. "We have to consider what the forest has done to the hiding spot after the cache was left here."

"The base of trees and the walls," Christophe said.

We all agreed to look close to ground zero, checking walls and tree trunks. When I began looking closer at the tree trunks I realized there was a couple of feet of leaves around most of the trunks. We really needed some tools to make short work of it, but I didn't even think about needing rakes or shovels on a geocache hunt.

Looking back on previous geocache hunts we usually found the cache within ten minutes of honest to goodness searching. As long as we were focused on making a find we usually found the cache quickly. After about fifteen minutes frustrations set in. And so with this search we began cycles of searching, frustration, resting, regrouping and searching again. However, each time we stopped to regroup there was less determination to keep looking. Each time we regrouped there were more doubts about the cache's existence.

"We can't afford to put much more time into this cache," I said. "We're going to run out of light and if we aren't at camp when it gets dark we won't be able to find it."

"I keep asking myself what could happen to a cache in a place this remote," Darby said. "I can't think of anything to make a cache unfindable except that it's covered over and can't be seen."

"How careful have you guys been when you search?"

"Careful?"

"Are you digging recklessly?"

"No! Of course not!"

The two Frenchmen acted as if I had insulted them, but I had to admit that I was not digging carefully. I was just moving leaves. I had been watching for the cache, but forest litter was deemed unimportant and shoved aside. The forest looked as if a pack of boars had descended on the area with news of a scrumptious boar delicacy that could be found at the roots of trees. Leaves were scattered, sometimes in large piles. It appeared as if our search had failed but I couldn't go back without at least spreading out the leaves in case the cache had been moved from its hiding place accidentally and never spotted.

I walked around kicking and pushing the leaves back into place. Darby followed my example and Remy and Christophe sighed with resignation. Remy clicked back through his GPS screens looking for anything that might help, while Christophe went to look at something outside our search area that had caught his attention earlier. There was no way Darby and I were going to make this section of forest look natural again. Only time, wind and gravity could accomplish that. I found the sun to be on the brink of dusk and decided we had to stop the search before camp became inaccessible. Remy noticed our actions and called his brother.

"Christophe!"

"Oui!" shouted Christophe from behind a wall. He appeared around the end of the wall and froze. "The cache. She is box. Is she not?"

"We don't know," I said. "If you see anything manmade it is worth checking out."

"Recently manmade," Darby corrected me. "As in the past hundred years or so."

Of course Christophe knew to check out anything unusual at all. He was fifty feet from ground zero so he didn't expect to find the cache there.

"Take a picture first!" Darby said. "So's we can remember just how it was when we found it."

We all hurried to where Christophe continued to stand and stare at the same spot as if the cache might run away if he didn't keep track of it. Darby got there first and snapped a couple of pictures. His expression was one of excitement so Remy and I hurried faster.

The four of us stood in a line staring at a single red corner of a plastic box. I don't know how Christophe ever spotted it. Had we searched this far from ground zero we might have discovered it, but to just spot it seemed impossible. The corner was only visible for an inch or so though the leaves.

"Well?" I said. "Christophe, you found it. You should check it out."

"We are a team. We sign together."

"Okay, man, but dig it out already," Darby said.

Christophe stepped forward and we all paused for effect, or maybe because we couldn't believe we'd actually found it. Time stood still for the two seconds it took Christophe to test the corner, then returned to normal time as he discovered it didn't move. We all dove for the spot of red, except for Darby who now felt like he needed to capture the moment. We pulled leaves back until we uncovered the plastic box. The sheltered part of the box had been spray painted green but the paint had been scratched away. It was looking more like a cache after the leaves were removed. Now I know that the container was called an Otter Box. They are used in marine activities because they have a rubber seal. While we were in France, though, I didn't know that. The box seemed very tough and ordinary. Christophe snapped open the latch and we might as well have had music behind our actions building to a climactic ending to our search. We held our breath as the box lid opened and we looked down into a very typical geocache.

"The log! The log!" Darby called out, camera still aimed at the container.

Christophe pulled the logbook out. It was a small notebook with the name of the cache printed clearly on the front. Christophe flipped the notebook open. I leaned over his shoulder to get a glimpse. Christophe showed the log book to the camera. We heard a click of the shutter.

"Wait! I don't know if that one was sharp!" Click again and once again. "Okay, I think I got it. First time I've taken a picture of a blank piece of paper before."

"First to find! First to find!" Christophe yelled triumphantly.

Indeed it was. The log was completely blank.

"WooHooo!" Darby yelled. "We did it! Way to go dude!"

All the geckos dived for cover. Christophe signed the log and we quickly passed the book from man to man until Darby signed it and took a picture of our names in the formerly blank book.

Ironically the cache container contained a return ticket for the boat. The ticket expired a month after it was issued and was useless but I liked the ticket, which I thought dated our find, plus it had a picture of the boat on the river on it. So I traded for that. There was a travel tag for the FTF prize and we insisted Christophe should keep it. The swag was mostly soccer themed, though there was a fancy women's fan, too. We found a small plastic soccer ball, a team France jersey refrigerator magnet, a soccer shoe key chain, and sweat bands. Darby traded for the key chain. We took a group photo to remember our victory, then looked for the sun. It was gone. The forest was dim.

"We've got to get out of here," Darby said.

Chapter 25

"There's no way we're going to find those tents," Darby said.

"The GPSrs will lead us back," Remy said.

"Oh, yeah, right," Darby said, though he wasn't completely convinced.

"Everybody check to see if you have the coordinates of the camp," Remy said. "If the batteries lose power we will have extras."

"Good idea," Darby said and we all checked our GPS units. I needed to update my GPS because I set out thinking a little too optimistically. I had no doubts we would get back to camp in plenty of time.

When we all had updated coordinates we took a reading and hiked as quickly as we could to the hole in the impenetrable brush. The brush seemed to snag us even more on the way back and foliage blocked what little light there was left. It was dark by the time we reached the edge of the forest and the mountain loomed ahead of us. An owl circled above watching for dinner, seemingly reminding us that night time had truly fallen.

"Okay, only two miles to go," I said. "Open ground. Then dinner."

"Yeah. Dinner. I'm hungry," said Darby, then he laughed. "Hey! I'm hungry! I'm hungry!"

"Yes, we know," Remy said.

"Used to be it was remarkable if I was full. You're spoiling me Earl."

The only thing that kept us warm was our fast pace. If we stopped to rest we became chilled. Living in LA I had no concept of what hypothermia might feel like. At the time it never even occurred to me. Our clothes were damp and we became even colder when we stopped. Then we hit the rocks.

In the dark we knew we would have to go uphill to find the place where the rocks and hillside met, but we didn't know how far it was nor how steep it would be to climb. Scaling the rock face looked impossible in the dark. We could find a few hand holds and foot holds at the base but as soon as we put away our GPSrs we lost the light from the illuminated screen and the holds vanished, so we didn't try very hard to climb the rocks. Remy and Christophe seemed to have a little rock climbing experience but Darby and I were strictly city dwellers. I thought I better change that if I was going to continue geocaching. Finding our way up the little valley between the hills was not easy. Rock had fallen from the cliff side and we had to navigate around the stones and boulders. Occasionally we would hear scurrying noises in the brush or something we had assumed was a rock would suddenly dart away. I tried taking a picture of one of the rock shapes but when I looked back at my picture it was indeed a rock. I took the time to notice things because it seemed to stave off the worry that we wouldn't find camp. If I was taking pictures of rocks hoping they were rabbits at least I wasn't worrying about hiking on a dark mountain with little idea of where I was going. The valley seemed much longer than it was when we hiked down it, but I decided it only seemed that way because we couldn't walk as quickly, we had to be careful where we stepped and perhaps we hit the cliff further down the mountain because of our GPS leading us in a straight line.

"Maybe we climbed down rocks on our way to the cache," Darby speculated when we had been following the cliff for close to half an hour. "But it was so easy we didn't think about it."

"If so it wasn't more than six or eight feet and the angle was manageable. This is too steep," I said. "It couldn't have been here. We should be able to see the top even in the dark."

Time after time we stopped and speculated about how to get up the cliff to the hill beyond. Once we reached the top of the cliff it would just be a quick hike to camp.

We followed the rocks, and they went on seemingly forever but we finally reached a rough rock that bordered on firm ground and we knew we had reached the top of the valley. We consulted our GPSrs and two of them had run out of batteries. We didn't worry because there were still two GPS units functioning. However, we had ascended the valley much higher than we had descended and so we had a longer hike across the mountain. We spotted the moon reflecting off the tops of the tents and staggered into camp with a sigh of relief. Darby was hungry enough to cook dinner but I was too tired to care about eating. I left the food to those who wanted it and fell asleep as soon my head hit the pillow.

In the morning we were all very excited about getting back to Remy's apartment and logging our FTF. The entire group was abuzz tossing back and forth the parts of the trip that they were going to include in their log. We cooked a quick breakfast and packed up camp, then dragged all the gear to a higher vantage point so it would be easier to load into the basket of the balloon. Since the balloon was dependent on the air currents we might have to carry our gear quite a distance. We decided we would rather lug it downhill so we pulled it to the highest spot we thought the balloon would land.

The only problem was the balloon never arrived.

Chapter 26

We sat on the mountain waiting and watching expectantly. Any moment we thought we would see the balloon arise on the cool morning breeze and slowly drift our direction, but it never happened. We knew it could take a while. After all, we had lifted off at dawn and landed at camp at ten in the morning. So the fact that it was late didn't bother us, but we also knew that it couldn't lift off and maintain altitude after the air warmed up, so as the morning progressed we had to admit we were not getting off the mountain that day.

"So, where's the nearest geocache?" Darby joked. "We could find that."

"At the boat dock on the river," Remy reported. "Five kilometers down the mountain."

"Through the forest," Christophe added.

"Hey, we could hide our own," Darby said.

"Yes, maybe it will be found in two years," Remy replied.

"We could look for them billy goats."

"Darby, I believe billy goats are tame," Remy said. "What we saw yesterday were ibex."

"Ibex? Like they got at the zoo?"

"Maybe."

"For some reason I never expect to see zoo animals loose in the wild."

"Perhaps your American zoo has ibex just as our zoo has white tailed deer."

"They do?"

"In your country the deer are common are they not?"

"Uh, I don't know. I never seen one. We got mule deer."

"I think white tailed deer are more common in the northeastern part of the U.S." I said.

"So, you see? Just because a creature is found in a zoo does not make it unusual."

"Wait'll I tell Henry I saw an ibex. I bet he never even heard of one."

"Henry's been around," I said. "He knows more than one would think."

"So, what're we going to do about the balloon not showing?" Darby asked.

"Maybe conditions in town are making liftoffs impossible," I offered.

"Should we set up camp again and wait? The balloon company knows where we are. They will come according to our agreement when they can," Remy said.

"How much food in the pack?" Christophe asked.

"Not much," Darby said. "But I doubt if we starve."

Darby was used to getting by on very little. The rest of us might have a harder time adjusting to our situation.

Remy gazed at the valley below.

"I see nothing to prevent the balloon from departing."

"It's too late in the day. The air temperature has warmed up. Remember? Guillaume was anxious to land after he dropped us off because it was getting too late to fly."

"So tomorrow morning is the first he might arrive. What will we do?"

"I suggest taking an inventory of our supplies and I wouldn't mind exploring the mountain."

"You seem calm."

"It's a business. If they want to stay in business they will keep their customers happy. After leaving us up here an extra day I expect them up here early with profuse apologies and an offer for a free ride in the future," I said.

"No thanks," Darby interjected. "I'm kind of glad they didn't show up."

Since we were trying to cut down on the weight of our gear we had very little food left. We did have one extra package of freeze dried chicken and stir fry vegetables, but other than that we were down to small individual servings of snacks. We saved the dinner to split later and divvied up the snacks leaving it up to each man how he would make use of it.

We set up camp in a spot where we could watch for the balloon and be more sheltered than we were the previous night. Some of us scrambled over the rocks until Remy reminded us that the more we explored the hungrier we were going to get.

When the sun began setting we lit the little stove and cooked our last complete meal, then split it four ways.

I set my internal alarm for dawn and sat shivering on the mountain willing the balloon to make an early appearance. I still had a small bag of granola and dried fruit but it wasn't even close to being a meal. I was tempted to eat it since I expected to see the balloon appear in the valley below any minute. But I waited and shivered and watched hopefully. One by one the other guys woke up and joined me. The minutes ticked by slower than I had ever known them to. We kept looking at our GPSrs and watches and frowning. Ever so slowly the sun climbed in the sky. None of us had much energy for exploring that morning and we were all hungry.

"It ain't comin'," Darby said dejectedly.

"Why wouldn't it come back for us? We had an agreement. Remy, you did make sure they knew we needed a ride back, didn't you?" I asked.

"But of course!" he said confidently.

"We can't walk out. What if they do show up and they can't find us?" I said.

"Then they will begin a search."

"We don't want that to happen. I've already been rescued by them once on this trip," I said.

"We can't wait here forever, either," Darby said. "We're out of food. I say they aren't coming."

Had we known the balloon was not returning we could have been back quicker. But we had no way of knowing that Guillaume had met up with electrical lines and the balloon was a tangled heap of fabric next to a road. Guillaume was in the hospital and had no record of dropping us off. Instead of worrying about four geocachers left up on a mountain the balloon company was worried about almost losing one of their more experienced pilots, not to mention the loss of one of their more profitable balloons. However, being stuck on top of the mountain, we did not know that. We got into an argument about whether we should try to hike out ourselves or wait. Darby didn't want a balloon ride if he could avoid it so he was arguing pretty convincingly that we should hike out.

"The river's five kilometers? Heck, they have 5K races all the time. We can hike 5 kilometers."

"It's not the distance, it's the terrain," I said. "Five K is a long ways to crawl under bushes."

"So you're just gonna sit here waiting for a random balloon to blow by?"

"Our gear is packed for car camping. How are we going to transport it?"

We wasted a good hour arguing about a plan of action. We never came to blows or divisions but we certainly aired all the options we could think of. I have to say the only one of us truly adamant about their point of view was Darby, but in the end his experience actually helped us.

"We go through our gear, find what we think we'll need, bundle them in the tent and use the cords to make us a backpack. We can carry what we need. All we have to do is make it more portable."

We took the stove, the tents, flashlights, what food and water we had left, and a knife. We put any extra batteries we found into the GPSrs and flashlights. Darby fashioned the tents into backpacks with our essentials just inside the zipper door. The packs were not very heavy but we took turns carrying the two bundles. We set our course for the river, since water was our main concern. Remy thought we could hike up or down river to a dock and flag down a ride to town where we could catch a taxi. The only problems facing us were the elevation, rocks and the thick forest.

Just for the record, five kilometers of cross country travel through impenetrable forest is not a walk in the park. It means multitudes of scratches, walking, backtracking to find a better route, and getting lost from walking in circles. The more we walked the more water we drank, the lighter our pack became, and the more the river seemed important to reach before nightfall. We turned off all the GPSrs so we would always have one with some battery power left. The cache Christophe had told us about was not loaded into the GPRs but we still felt like we had a better handle on our location if we could glance at a screen occasionally. For some reason I felt that keeping our spirits up was more important than our food and water situation. It was easy to get discouraged and testy when we were surrounded by thorny bushes with no idea how to make our situation easier.

"Where is that village we visited yesterday? The woods were less thick there," Darby said.

"It's that direction," Remy said. "We came this way because it brought us to the river sooner."

"Soon shmoon, this forest is impossible!"

We were hot, sweaty, and irritable when we almost tripped over a tiny stream.

"Wait! We should fill our water bottles while we are here," Remy said. "It will give us more time to reach the river."

"I agree," I said. "We can't have too much water."

We all filled our water bottles but there was one problem. The little stream ran away from our route to the river. The others didn't seem to notice.

"I thought the river was that way," I said pointing in the direction we had been traveling.

"It is," said Christophe.

"Then why is the stream flowing that way?"

We all stood there in a line staring at the water and scratching our heads.

"I say we follow this stream," I said.

"But the GPSr says the river is that direction," Remy said.

"You can't argue with gadgets," Darby said.

"You can't argue with physics," I countered.

"Fizics?" said Christophe.

"The laws of nature," I said in an attempt to simplify the vocabulary. "Water flows downhill. So it has to lead to the river."

"Well," Darby reasoned. "We won't be without water if we follow the creek."

"Right."

"Though I might starve to death or die of poisoning from chewing on some of these plants."

"You can get by for a week without food if you have to," I reminded him.

"Dang, and I thought the streets of LA were rough."

And so we followed the creek… until it vanished underground and left us standing in the middle of the woods with no idea where we were.

Darby very nearly freaked out. Remy and Christophe were pissed that they had listened to my reasoning instead of obeying their instincts. With all these varying emotions flying around all I could think was, "How am I going to get these guys to focus on the problem at hand?"

"Okay, first things first. Make sure your water bottles are full," I said. "Next we check the GPSr. Just stay calm and focus on the next reasonable thing to try. Sit down. Cool off. Conserve your resources."

"What makes you the leader?" Christophe barked.

Instinct made me step back and see his attitude for more than it seemed. I decided to keep an eye on Christophe. Something was eating at him and I needed to pin down what it was.

"You can lead if you like," I told him. "As soon as my advice is poor."

He thought about my suggestion but he couldn't find fault with it even if he didn't understand every word of what I said. I thought he understood more than he could communicate back. I was thankful to have Remy along to act as a go between.

I was frustrated by the GPS units. If we zoomed in enough to know where we were we couldn't see the big picture. It just showed an orange triangle in the middle of nowhere. We already knew we were in the middle of nowhere. If we zoomed out to get the big picture we lost all roads, rivers, towns. Essentially, no matter what we did we appeared to be in the middle of nowhere. I turned my own GPS off, declaring it useless. However, always the planner and schemer in the financial world, I turned my thinking to our present situation.

"Remy, when you added the FTF to your device, did you clear your previous cache finds?"

"No… Uh… I think perhaps three months ago."

"But your device does have more caches in it than mine or Darby's," I surmised.

"Yes, perhaps."

"Power it up."

We rested while Remy's unit booted up. I watched the guys. Remy was tired but fit. Darby was doing well because he was used to walking and doing without. Christophe sat frowning and rubbing at his leg. After an initial washing we really had done very little doctoring on the massive scrapes on Christophe's arms and legs. Now was not the time to single him out but I made a note to try and figure out if Christophe was reacting to difficulties due to his injuries. And me? I was very hungry and very tired but I tried not to think about it. I had dirt, sweat and forest litter under the top edge of my cast. It itched and I tried to dig out anything that irritated but I also thought that casts were not made for comfort and I should concentrate on finding civilization. My plan was to stay near the water source as long as possible, find a general direction that was passable, and keep us united and focused.

When Remy's GPSr was functioning and had located our position we zoomed out until the first cache appeared on the screen.

"What cache is that?" I asked.

"It is in French."

"I know, but tell what you can about the cache. Is it a remote one? Or will that direction take us back to civilization?"

"It is no good. It brags of the view from up on the mountain."

"Okay, zoom out until you get another one. One cache at a time so we retain as much detail as possible."

Three times we read the description, zoomed out, discarded the cache as a good destination and zoomed out again. Suddenly a group of three caches popped onto the screen.

"It is no good. Those caches are twenty one kilometers away."

"Twenty kilometers in the right direction are better than five in the wrong direction."

We zoomed in on the grouping and found out there were streets around the caches. We zoomed in closer and the river appeared.

"Okay," I said. "I need a map." I brushed away the weeds and forest litter until I had a dirt area to work on. I drew the little group of caches and followed the angle of the river tracing it as closely as I could on my little patch of dirt. I locked onto a cache in the group.

"Dude, what are you doing?" Darby asked.

"Figuring."

I took note of the bearing to reach the caches, then I followed the river and figured out the bearing to the section of the river that was closest to us.

"South," I mumbled to myself. "Al...most due south. If we head south we'll hit a river. The caches are north of there but if we head south we'll be okay."

"If we can reach it," Christophe said.

"Yes. But we can do it. All we have to do is decide we're going to do it."

"How far is it?" Christophe asked.

"To the river," I answered.

"The distance?" he asked again.

"Darby?"

"Make a way point on the river and it'll tell you."

I set a way point but I didn't like the number I saw so I didn't tell the guys how far it was.

"Okay," I said. "Ready to go?"

We were all rested so we found the correct bearing and headed south. I still had Remy's GPSr and after a while, like a proper geocacher, he felt better holding it so he held out his hand for it. I handed it to him reluctantly because he would see how far we had to hike. He glanced down at the screen and frowned. He stayed beside me and glanced to make sure we had a little distance before he asked, "Are you sure?"

"You can look at it yourself. That's the shortest route to the river."

"But we were five kilometers away and now we are seven."

"Just keep an eye on your brother. He feels the stress more than he should."

Remy nodded and clicked through screens on this GPS. He returned to the map and adjusted our path south.

That afternoon I began feeling shaky. Instinct told me we should be walking at an easy pace, but another day in the woods without food worried me. If I was shaky today, how much worse would it be tomorrow? I did not want to be a burden to my friends. I began watching for plants that looked appetizing but I knew to try eating them could invite disaster. We couldn't hunt. The only weapon we had was a knife and none of us were skilled enough to build a trap to catch an animal. Even if we caught one, we didn't know how to butcher it. Do animals need special preparation to make them edible? I had never even prepared meat from a butcher shop. I began to think I needed an education in life skills, that is, if I lived long enough to see my apartment again. Suddenly Jo came to mind and I dearly wished I could see her again. I had to stop myself from thinking about her circumstances and when I went over all the reasons why I shouldn't dwell on them I realized I was defeating my purpose and thinking about it anyway. I swore, if I reached LA again I would see Jo, even if it was for a last goodbye. Maybe I could learn something new, or convince her that living with a man who hurt her would be miserable.

My circumstances were dragging me down. My health was weighing on me. The forest seemed to mock us and send us in directions we didn't want to go. I was hot, hungry, bedraggled and just generally miserable, but I was not going to give up. I began telling myself that seven kilometers was not very far. People hiked that far in a day all the time. But they didn't do it cross country, through thick forest with no food and little water.

"Earl," Darby said but I continued on, waiting for him to continue on. "Earl, hold up dude."

I turned. Darby didn't want to draw attention to Christophe's condition and I was angry at myself for letting him fall behind. The man was limping and nearly stumbling through the woods. His focus was not sharp. His actions were almost drunken.

"All right," I said. "Time to stop."

Christophe didn't just sit when I called a stop. He flopped to the ground and gripped his leg.

"Take a look at it," I told Remy.

I thought Christophe would be more willing to let his brother examine his leg than he would me or Darby. When Remy moved the pants leg Christophe winced and I knew the news was not good. Even from a distance I could see the scrapes had scabbed over but the area around them was red and very tender to the touch. We couldn't afford to stop, but I could leave Remy and Christophe behind and send rescuers to a way point. I struggled with the decision, though. I thought we would cope better as a group even if one of us was slower than the rest. It was important to me that we conquer this forest together.

Remy spoke to his brother in French so Christophe would answer in his native language. This was a smart thing to do since Christophe could provide more details in his own language.

"His leg is very sore. He says he feels like he has a fever," Remy translated.

"Okay, maybe a slower pace and frequent rest stops?"

"Good luck. I think Christophe would like to get there as soon as possible. He will hurry, not slow down," Remy said.

He did indeed. He tried leading the group but bullied his way into brambles and walked straight into a bog. We had to pull him out shivering and cursing. I was glad I couldn't understand the words, but I understood his attitude just fine. He was mad at himself for allowing himself to be so unobservant that he nearly drowned himself in his haste. He could feel his health slipping and was fighting the urge to give in to it. I didn't know whether to grab him by the scruff of the neck and sit him down and risk revolt, or pat him on the back and tell him, "Way to go! Keep it up!" Remy was obviously torn between the two as well. His worry was blatant but he knew his brother and there was a little family pride showing as well.

"We'll make it," I assured him, though while we were knee deep in a bog, with the mud threatening to suck the shoes right off our feet, I didn't feel quite so sure. I'd never known reeds grew taller than a man, or that a waterway could be hidden completely by them. And we weren't even to the river yet! I didn't know where we were except that we were south of where we were half an hour ago. When the water was thigh deep I declared a stop.

"We don't know how deep it will get. We can't keep going like this. There's got to be a way around," I stated.

"You could'a decided that *before* we got soaked," Darby said.

Darkness descended upon us, catching us somewhat by surprise. We were in deep forest and the light was dim anyway, so it took a while for me to realize it had gradually become so dim that we should stop and make camp.

"But there's no place to set up tents," Remy said.

"Right. I guess we should locate a spot."

But there was no spot where we could set up two tents. There wasn't even a spot where we could set up one tent. The trees were too close together.

"Okay. What I say is we set up the two tents between the trees. Two sleep in the tents and two do not. We draw lots to see who gets to sleep in the tents. The next day we switch off."

"The next day?"

"Okay, if we make it out the two who got to sleep in the tents buy beer for those who didn't."

That seemed worth the sacrifice and I don't actually know who wished for a tent and who wished for a beer, but Christophe and Remy chose the longer twigs and Darby and I rolled out our sleeping bags out in the open. The tents looked like a tornado had gotten ahold of them. They were bent to fit in between the trees, so they barely stood at all and the material flapped about in the breeze because it was loose. Remy and Christophe even had trouble entering the tents. They half stepped, half slid their way in and we hoped they wouldn't have to make a quick exit.

"Dude, I never thought geocaching would come to this," Darby said as we attempted to find a comfortable spot and snuggle down into our sleeping bags.

"We'll make it out," I said, "And they'll buy the beers."

Chapter 27

My sleeping bag was damp. My attitude was dank. My body was filthy. But my mind was still attuned; of one thing I could be glad. I still had a handle on the situation, and I wondered where it came from. I was going to have a long talk with my dad when I got home. Where did this analytical thinking come from? When faced with a problem why was it I who did not fall apart? Remy and Christophe had much more experience in the outdoors. Darby had more experience making his way in the world. I was a spoiled rotten rich kid and yet it was I who seemed to be leading this whole operation. I only hoped I was doing the right thing.

We turned off the GPS during the night. I was sure it was running low on batteries. I only hoped when one GPSr died another would tell us where south was. Distances meant little. Even if we knew the numbers the terrain beat us to a pulp. All we could do was keep track of south and keep walking. Dang I was hungry. I now knew what the term "my stomach is gnawing on my backbone" referred to. At least my shakiness receded when my mind was busy planning. But I had to admit I was slipping. With each setback it slipped a little more. I prayed we would meet the river soon. Please God, if you're out there, lead us to the river. And if you have a boat handy that would be great. And... I fell asleep in mid prayer.

The GPS only lasted about ten minutes the next day. We grumbled about it and attempted to set up the next one, but we didn't have any caches in the memory to help us find the river so we just kept to a heading of due south as much as we could. That GPS lasted an hour.

We sat down to figure out if we were going to have the aid of a GPS all day and we decided we only had about three hours of GPS use left.

"I think we should turn them all off and try to keep the bearing ourselves. We can turn them on and check our position if we think we're too far off track."

Christophe was limping worse and sweat beaded his forehead. We were all beginning to get the shakes when we sped up. We all wore worried expressions. How far could ten kilometers be? A kilometer was less than a mile so it was less than ten miles from the mountain camp. We had to be close! How could it take us two days to travel ten kilometers?

"This is hopeless," Christophe said as we looked around and saw nothing but trees and brambles.

"It's not hopeless," I insisted. "We need to head south. If we could just see around us we'd know. We're getting close."

He swore in French and I got the idea I risked him running off on his own. He was in no condition to make logical decisions. He just wanted to be free of the forest and he was running on desperation. I'd heard of lost people panicking and doing random things. This was as close as I wanted to be to that state. I knew randomness shouldn't enter the situation any more than it had.

"Christophe," I said. "You know the geography of your country. The land is flat. What does that mean?"

"I means… we are fucking lost."

"No, it doesn't. We've left the mountains. The river is at the bottom of the mountains. It has to be close."

He punched the nearest tree, bloodying his knuckles. Remy stepped in to keep him from doing more damage to himself, but Christophe turned on his brother. Remy spoke in French. If I had to guess what he said it was something like, "Remember that time when you were going to jump your bike over the ditch and I tried to stop you from killing yourself? We fought until we both fell in? I'll do it again." There were words back and forth but the final statement, if I had to guess, was, "If we live, we live together. If we die, we die together. We will not give up." But I was really only guessing from intonations and attitudes. Christophe still took a swing at his brother but he didn't connect, just blew off steam.

"Dude, Christophe… mister nature expert…" Darby said. "What's that?"

We all turned as one and followed Darby's gaze.

"Whatever you do, don't run," I said. It was a dog of some kind. I didn't know much about wildlife, especially the wildlife of Europe, but it looked like a wolf to me. There was a motion beyond it and a younger one appeared. How many were there? I couldn't help but remember old wildlife documentaries that showed a pack of wolves bringing down a deer. If we were closer to civilization I might have guessed it was a domestic dog, but it was too wild looking, too independent and aloof. Darby made a move to find the camera and the wolf's ears pricked up and its focus narrowed to Darby. I didn't think it would attack a group of four men but I didn't want to take any chances either.

"Loop," Remy nearly whispered to Christophe, who nodded agreement. I wasn't sure what a loop was. Later I looked it up and found I had the spelling wrong. He had said *loup* and it was a wolf. Perhaps it was a little smaller than wolves I had seen pictures of in the United States, but I was captivated by the animal. The young one was skinnier and hungrier looking. I could identify with that young one. I wondered how long it had been since they had eaten. I had to stop wondering because it only made me feel hungrier. Darby's continued camera searching movements scared the wolf away and the two trotted off, vanishing into the woods and leaving me feeling a little vulnerable. If they could vanish that quickly while we were watching they could be anywhere and we'd never know it.

"How many of them are there likely to be?" I asked Remy.

"I don't know. I've never seen one before," he answered. "Why can't we find meat that won't attack?"

"You'd actually kill it if you could?" I asked.

"I'd eat that tree if I thought I could chew it," he said.

"Cows eat grass," Darby said. "I've chewed on a grass stem or two in my time. Can't hurt to try it."

That sounded safe, so we began watching for grass. The tender grass was manageable but the tougher grasses were stringy and hard to chew. It didn't taste very good, but it was green and I thought it was better than nothing at all. We found out that perhaps grass was not better than nothing at all because we all developed stomach cramps. We kept imagining movements and couldn't help but wonder if the wolves were following us. I thought the likelihood of that was rather slim, but I also couldn't figure out what movement I was seeing that seemed so elusive.

"You guys don't have a Bigfoot, do you?" Darby asked.

"Big... foot?" Christophe asked as he lifted his foot.

"It's a mythical creature that some Americans claim to have seen," I explained. "Like the Loch Ness Monster or Abominable Snowman."

"Ah... no," Remy said.

I was beginning to think we were hallucinating in the hopes of being found by hikers or coming across a house with pets around it. I dreamed of ice cream and steak. Why those two things I have no clue. I could see the piece of meat on a plate, could almost feel the resistance to a knife as I sliced it open to reveal the pink interior and juices running onto the plate. A mound of loaded mashed potatoes on the side. The ice cream was soft serve with some kind of topping and whipped cream. Images of these things would linger until I had to remind myself that we were lost in the woods and there would be no more steak and ice cream sundaes unless we found the river.

We almost fell into the river when we finally reached it. The tree line was right on the river bank and we pulled up short when we realized only three steps further and we'd be waist deep in water. We celebrated in the only way we could manage. We staggered to a little open spot, flopped down and stared at the water saying, "We made it." We didn't even have the strength to say it loudly. We just sat there nearly dumb with relief. I shook my water bottle. I had about an inch left so I unscrewed the top and drank it down, no longer needing to ration it.

It took a long wait before a boat appeared. I didn't even see it. Remy lurched to his feet and staggered to the river bank. He waved his arms frantically and yelled the French version of "Help! Help!"

The man in the boat squinted at Remy as if he was a lunatic so I got to my feet and waved too.

"Stop! Please stop!" I yelled across the water. "We've been lost for two days! A ride to town? Food? Water? Our friend is sick!"

Remy latched onto that and yelled the French version. The man made some adjustments to the rudder and the boat slowly changed course. The French flew back and forth across the water so fast I couldn't guess what was being said. The boat seemed to be transporting something, but the owner didn't seem to be in a hurry. If he had, he certainly wouldn't have chosen to go by boat. The boat was a little bigger than a row boat. Having very little to compare it to I'd have to say it was about the size of a comfortable bass boat, though it lacked seating. There was a little seat beside the rudder and the rest of it seemed to be used for cargo. We lined up on the river bank.

"Please," I said. "Can we ride to the next town?"

Remy translated.

"I'll pay!" I added feeling a bit guilty for flashing money about, but hey, people respond to that.

Remy glared at me, but we were so close I could *taste that steak*. He could have asked me for a thousand dollars and I would have eagerly said, "Yes! Yes! Just to the next town."

The river man frowned but he allowed us on board. Christophe stumbled into the boat and I caught him by the shoulders to keep him from going over the man's cargo and rolling off the other side. I didn't know how stable the boat was. I felt shaky on the shifting hull. My lunge toward Christophe was more an act of fear of the boat tipping than anything else, but the boat only rocked a little bit.

We found places to sit and the boat listed a little bit but the owner of the boat didn't seem concerned. He started up the outboard motor and maneuvered back into the center of the river. He talked to Remy as we floated away and Remy nodded and seemed pleased.

"An hour," Remy told me. "We will pass some villages but after two days I cannot complain about an hour. And the village will have a market center."

Remy returned to his conversation with the owner of the boat. I was too relieved to keep track of the flow of French coming from the two until the river man's eyebrows raised. He lifted a corner of tarp and pulled a bunch of grapes out of a crate. He handed us each a bunch of grapes.

I have never, ever had a grape that tasted that good. I don't know if it was just my hunger or if the grapes were really the best grapes ever, but they were sheer luxury after the misery we had just come through.

"Thank you. Thank you so much," Darby almost cried. He gripped his bunch of grapes like a life ring and plucked a handful off. He examined the first one before popping it into his mouth and chewing with his eyes closed.

Christophe had a hard time finding a comfortable place to sit. He tried not to bend his leg but there was no way to sit down and keep it straight so he winced on the way down and hoped he didn't have to move for a while.

Remy and the boatman chattered all the way to the village and when we arrived and helped the man unload his produce we parted ways. I wanted to do something for the man who helped us, but I worried that he would be insulted if I handed him money. There wasn't anything else I had on hand. I wasn't sure how much was too little and how much was too much, so I pulled two bills out of my pocket. They were still wet from getting dunked in the bog. I didn't look at them. They could have been hundred dollar bills and I wouldn't miss them at all. I clapped the man on the shoulder and told him thanks once again and pressed the bills into his hands.

"You helped us when we needed it most," I said. "Thank you."

He looked as if he didn't understand but I turned to catch up with Remy and the man fingered the bills and stuffed them into his pocket.

"It was a big story in all of west France," Remy said. "Guillaume didn't land. The basket hit electrical lines as he was trying to land in a field. There was a great fire."

"Is Guillaume okay?"

"He is in hospital."

"But will he be okay?"

"The news is still new. Adrienne didn't know."

I assumed the boatman's name was Adrienne.

"All was turmoil at the balloon company," Remy said. "There is a doctor at the next block. Maybe I can convince Christophe. Take Darby to the village square. They will have food carts there."

"Can I get you something?"

"I… go to the square. Christophe may want to eat before he visits the doctor."

I smiled. I bet Christophe would eat his hiking boot in the waiting room if he didn't go to the square first.

My head was swimming with possibilities as I entered the busyness that was the square. Apparently Mr. Boatman was just running back for more produce, because he had joined Mrs. Boatman at a tent and business was hopping.

I found Darby walking the square with a powdered sugar covered pastry in his hand gazing about as if he'd been woken up from a dream but couldn't quite place himself.

"What is that?" I asked when I caught up to him.

"I don't know, but it was only a dollar, so I bought it."

"I'm surprised it isn't gone by now."

"This is my third one, but I'm looking for real food. This is too rich."

"I agree, on the real food part. How's your stomach?"

"Lousy. Guess I'm not a cow."

"You know cows chew cud. Do you know what cud is?"

"Ick."

"It's the grass they couldn't digest the first time around."

"Double ick."

We found what would pass as a hotdog stand in New York City but this one sold different kinds of sausage. It smelled heavenly.

"Them dogs'll grease your inards so's the grass can pass," Darby suggested.

"Oh good," I answered sarcastically.

We walked up to the hotdog stand.

"Is there a café around here where we can get a full meal? Maybe a beer?"

The man looked me up and down as if I was dirtiest foreigner he had ever seen and I should go take a bath before I ruined his impression of Americans.

"Dis, the best!" he replied.

We kept walking but it seemed to be market day and it was hard to see the businesses behind the booths. When people began walking big circles to avoid us I thought the hotdog man might have a point. Maybe we didn't want to inflict ourselves on the customers of a café. While we were looking for a meal Remy and Christophe caught up to us and Remy grabbed me by the shoulders and pointed me down a side street.

"Where are we going?" I asked.

"I don't know. I have only directions."

He began reading street signs and then house numbers.

"Maybe that's the place?" I asked when a tiny patio area presented itself. The houses were all squished together so tightly that I thought of it more as apartments, though they were very skinny apartments. Flower boxes hung from windowsills and gauzy curtains fluttered in the breeze so when Remy reached for the door at the little patio I felt like we were going to walk right into somebody's home. I hung back waiting for a tirade, but it didn't come.

"Sit," he said as he went inside.

He came out with a bottle of wine and four plates.

"What's this?" I asked.

"A celebration! We found de cache! We got FTF!"

"Yeah, and we're still alive," mumbled Darby.

Leave it to a geocacher to celebrate an FTF and two days of misery but forget we could have died out there.

He went back inside and brought out four wine glasses. What was this place? A woman exited the building looking rather embarrassed. She took our wine bottle and began the wine bottle opening process. The bottle opened with a loud pop and she poured each glass half full before going into the building again.

Remy lifted his glass, "To life, love, and the pursuit of FTFs!"

We all toasted, though I thought my prospects for love at the moment were rather grim. The wine was good. Remy had chosen well. The woman came back with a bubbling pot. She set it down on our patio table, then she retreated and came back with a bread board. A large loaf of bread sat on it, browned and steaming, fresh from the oven, the aroma drifting over the patio. The meal was simple. Lamb stew. But it was unlike any stew I'd ever had. The lamb was in large chunks that flaked away with a fork. Potatoes, carrots, celery, turnips... I was guessing on the turnips, since I had never tasted them before. Chunks of tomato filled out the stew and the broth was excellent, especially if we dunked the bread in it. We ate the whole pot of stew and Remy ordered another bottle of wine. We sat relishing the feeling of being full again, the presence of people again, and the fact that we were back in civilization in one piece. After a while we were feeling just a bit drunk.

"Where are we and how are we going to get home?" Darby asked.

"Don't worry," I said. "We'll figure it out."

"Christophe's car is at the balloon airport," he pointed out.

"We'll get it. And we'll get back to Paris, too, but not today. Tomorrow."

"Don't you guys have to get back to work?" Darby asked. There was a silence as they remembered they were two days late for work.

The next stop was the local police station where Remy and Christophe sent word to their home towns that they were okay. The police questioned us at length about the balloon trip, the reason for our being left on the mountain and how we managed to walk out and from where. We found a tiny hotel. There were only two hotels in the village. We booked rooms in the larger one which just about filled it up.

"Wifi?" I asked.

"The laptop is in Christophe's car."

"Shoot," said Darby. "How are we going to claim our FTF? We're already two days late!"

"It'll just have to wait," I said. "It went two years without being found. I doubt if we need to worry about somebody beating their way up there before tomorrow evening. Okay, problem number two. Clothes. We're filthy."

"Yeah, that lady crinkled her nose at us," Darby said.

"Leave it to me," Remy said. "I will see to it while Christophe visits the doctor."

"Doctor?" Christophe said.

I gave Remy some money and trusted his judgment. We were all about the same size, wore casual pants and comfortable shirts. Christophe and Darby were a little taller. We only needed something to wear until we returned to Paris.

It didn't take Remy long to find four nearly identical outfits but his smile made me think he'd found something more important than khakis and camp shirts.

"Three blocks away, the village has an internet café!"

"All right!"

"Showers and new clothes, then the FTF and dinner."

"We just ate," Remy said.

"So? How is Christophe?"

"He will be fine. A little infection."

Even a rough day, a half bottle of wine, a visit to the doctor with orders to take it easy couldn't dim Christophe's determination to log his FTF. It turned into a bit of a race to see which one of us would truly be FTF but I didn't see a reason to rush. We claimed the find as a team so I wanted to tell my story to the geocaching world. For half an hour I typed. I told all about the balloon ride and the ancient village and spring. I don't know why but the whole thing spilled out including the ibex, the wolves, the bog and brambles, the fact that we went two days with hardly any food.

"Dude, you wrote a book!" Darby said when he had finished his log and I was still typing away. It was then that I thought that I could write a book, that this whole crazy geocaching hobby had led me through pain sorrow and tears and back. All I had to do was see how the ending turned out.

The ending of the story though was still in question especially when my cell phone came to life and announced that I had messages. I had plugged it in to charge while I used the computer and I heard the message tone right away, but the race had begun so I had logged my cache first. Afterwards I picked up my cell phone and listened to the recordings. One was from my dad, just checking to see if I was still alive. I had to laugh at that one. Another was from my accountant. I ignored that. The third brought me up short.

"I… I'm sorry Earl. I must be flustered. I pushed a wrong button. Forgive me. I was just… oh, shoot, I've gotta go. What's the number for…" and the recording went dead. It was Jo, clearly more than a little flustered. Why did she even have my number still in her phone? Who was she trying to call?

"What's wrong?" Darby asked.

"Nothing. Nothing's wrong," I said but I'm sure I wasn't very convincing. "Darby, is there anything else we need to do in France?"

"I think we done it all. We been to the top of the Eiffel Tower, gone underground, visited a nudie beach, and a mountain top. We found geocaches, not as many as I thought we would, but I can't complain. What do you think?"

"I think we should go home."

He sighed, "That means I gotta go up in the sky again."

We had to hire a taxi to take us to the car rental. The taxi had no sign on the side. The girl at the hotel called the taxi and when it pulled up and the driver got out it was local man who just drove people around. He was used to taking people to the next village to rent a car. Remy drove the rental car back to the balloon port where we got a detailed description of the accident and Remy got tickets for a free balloon ride and profuse apologies. Even though we'd been left on the mountain and basically forgotten I wasn't complaining. I got an adventure out of it that I would never forget.

Remy took the rental car to Paris and Christophe drove his own car to Bordeaux.

Chapter 28

The three of us stood outside the hotel in Paris in uncomfortable silence.

"Friend me on the geocaching site," I said.

"Okay."

"Thanks for the adventure."

"You are… most gracious."

"No, really, I do thank you. Now that I've lived through it I'm glad it happened that way. I hope Christophe will recover fully."

"He will be fine. The doctor gave him medicine."

"Antibiotics?"

"Yes, I think."

"We'll be going home as soon as I verify the plane tickets."

"Very well. I wish you bon voyage."

"Thank you."

It was rather stiff and uncomfortable. When Remy walked back to his car Darby said, "You don't think that boat guy will give us a ride home?" He did not want to get on another plane.

The hotel room was luxurious.

"You really are a rich guy to rent these rooms while we traipsed all over France!" Darby said.

"It was worth it. This bed is unbelievable. I am going to sleep like the dead."

The soonest I could get good airline tickets gave us one more day in Paris. On the bright side it was easier to get direct flights from Paris to LAX. Unfortunately that meant skipping another risky dash to a geocache in a foreign country. It also meant a less stressful return home for Darby and a quicker arrival. At this point I was willing to sacrifice the smiley.

We went back to that trail of caches that followed the Seine River, but it felt… tame.

"I think that balloon trip ruined it," I commented.

"Aw dude, you learned about geocaching, that's for sure. How come you consider the trip ruined?"

"Not the trip, my sense of adventure. We might as well be strolling through the Louvre."

"I bet there's some virtuals in there," he said. "How about we buy another helicopter and buzz the tourists?"

"That sounds fun, but we could get in trouble. I wonder if they have skydiving excursions here."

"Dang, dude, you have a death wish."

I sat down on the grassy river bank.

"I guess I just ought to get use to things being quiet and cultured."

"We could go for a five/five back in LA."

"I wonder how hard it would be."

"Don't know. It's easy to find out."

When we got back to the hotel that evening I did look up difficult caches in LA but I also looked up JoReilly James. I found an engagement announcement that her parents had published in the newspaper. I had to endure three weeks of misery before she would be lost to me forever. It didn't seem worth it to survive my time in the woods if I was going to live it without her.

Chapter 29

Darby called me early in the morning of our departure.

"We gotta find a cache before breakfast," he announced.

"Why?"

"See there's these things called stats. And eventually, if you stick with this geocaching you're going to want better stats and one of the stats is the distance between two cache finds in one day. So what you do is find a cache before you get on the plane, fly umpteen miles and then find another one. It looks good on the stats page to have two caches 5,000 miles apart on the same day."

"Oh, okay."

"It doesn't have to be a hard one. Nobody actually checks to see if you did a hard one. We can find one on the way to breakfast."

"We're landing at ten o'clock at night and you want to find a cache in LA?"

"I'll download an easy one."

"Okay, I'll shower and meet you downstairs in an hour. Pack your bags so we can find the cache, eat and go to the airport."

Darby did his research well. He downloaded a cache description only half a block from a restaurant that specialized in crepes, so we ate well before our full day in the air. The cache was a hide I had never seen before. It was a bison tube hidden in a knot hole on a sign post. Fortunately, Darby had found these caches several times in the past so it didn't take him long to find the cache, and he was able to show me how well it blended in with its surroundings. I had to admit that only a geocacher would ever find that one. Even after I knew it was there I had to stick my finger into the hole to feel the loop on top of the cache.

"The one in LA better be in a safe area," I said.

"I hope so. It ought to at least be easy. In LA parking is the problem. Maybe we can park right by it at night."

I didn't really care about the find in LA. Once the wheels hit tarmac all I wanted to do was jump in the car and drive directly to Jo's house. The cache in LA sounded like an easy one but it was hidden in a parking garage, so parking was not an issue, especially near midnight. Being questioned by security might be a bigger worry. We stopped on every level before we finally found the cache on the top deck. Then it was a matter of figuring out where

Darby was going to spend half a night. We decided it would be better just to sack out at my apartment until morning. It was a hard decision to make but I thought driving by Jo's house in the middle of the night wouldn't tell me much anyway.

We stumbled into the silent and overly still apartment, turned on the air conditioner and fell asleep before we could even get settled. We woke up the next morning with the sun blaring through the windows and the sound of a traffic jam below.

"I'm glad we flew first class again. I hate to think of flying for twelve hours straight in coach."

"And the food was better," I added.

"Yeah, they even had French wine, not that I was in a position to notice how it tasted."

"You did better on the return trip."

"That's 'cause I was only scared spitless on the take off. I was asleep for the landing."

I paid Darby for his time in Paris. At first I had paid him on a daily basis, but after he had enough pocket money he wanted to save it so I kept a tally and paid him when we got home.

"I feel guilty taking this," he said.

"Nonsense. You gave up over a week of your time to teach me how to geocache. It's what I hired you to do. I put you in fear of your life and..."

"I had the time of my life. What's life without a little risk?"

"Take it. Sock it away. If you want to keep working for me, find me a store front in a location geocachers would like to go."

"Dude, you're serious!"

"I am. I think we can fill a niche on the west coast. If it works out, we can even add a store in San Francisco. I want to check on Jo. You can use the Escort. Leave me a note if you plan to stay here."

"Aw, no man, I ain't going to intrude. You know where to find me."

"Still, you need the computer to do some research... that is... if you want to. I am offering you a job. I just expect some results. So what do you say?"

"Do you think taking the job will allow us to stay friends?"

"Of course."

"Then... okay. I'll check out the listings and see if I can take a look at some options."

"I want a property with a store front and a back room we can fix up for events. Location is important. It has to be someplace that a geocacher would like to visit. Maybe on the coast."

"I'll look around."

"Good. I am off to Jo's. I'll stop by my parents' house and tell them I am still alive."

"Okay, see ya later."

Chapter 30

"Oh my God! What happened to you?" my mother asked when she saw me at the door. It took me a moment to remember that I had a cast on my arm.

"Nothing. I took a fall while I was exploring a French fort."

She put her arms on her hips and pouted at me, the most disapproval she displayed since I left home.

"It was a very educational tour," I said.

"Come in, Earl, come in."

My father walked into the entryway adjusting his tie.

"Hey, Dad? Do you have an appointment?"

"No, why?" he asked.

"I'd like to ask you a question."

"Good," my mother said. "I promised a friend I would pick her up for lunch."

And so, like most of my youth, my parents switched off, but I was glad because I didn't want my mom to know about most of the trip. If I had told my mom about it I would have emphasized the sights of the city, while I could ask my father what I really wanted to know.

"What time will you be home?" my father asked.

"Ohh, three-ish? I'll text you if there's a change in plans."

"Okay."

I walked into the house and waited for my parents to finish their goodbyes.

"So… I see you saw a little action," my dad said after my mom had left.

"A little. Actually this," I said as I raised my arm, "was the easier part."

"Oh?"

"Dad, can we sit down?"

"Of course, of course."

We took seats in the living room, but it wasn't much more comfortable.

"When mom asks, just tell her I had a great time. The truth is it was tough in so many ways."

"What happened?"

"Well, first of all Jo broke off our relationship."

"I'm sorry to hear that. She seemed like a nice girl."

"Then I broke my arm and had to be belayed out of an oubliette. It knocked me out and scared the guys. I don't know if the balloon crash made the news here. We were not on board, but it was our ride off the mountain and nobody came to retrieve us the next day."

"What did you do?"

"We... well, we walked out. After spending a day and a half waiting for our ride. So we were out of food. We had water, and we found water, but it was a long walk with several difficulties involved. I had the broken arm. Christophe was banged up from a bicycle accident. We got lost. We lost all our resources one by one."

"But you made it."

"Yeah, we made it. Christophe developed an infection and ended up at the doctor's office when we finally found a village, but we made it."

"What's bothering you then?"

"We had four guys. Remy and Christophe were used to the outdoors, were familiar with the weather conditions in France. Darby was used to the outdoors, used to making do on very little, but not used to being in the mountains or forests of France. Then there was me. When problems came up we had guys reacting on emotions. They weren't seeing things right. Who had the calm head and thought through all the problems?"

He waited.

"Me! I want to know where that comes from."

"Well," he said as he thought. "I don't really know. What I do know is a calm, logical reaction to a tough problem is not limited to survival in the wilds of France. It comes into play in many other situations."

"I should have been the one to rely on the others. But when the going got tough it seemed logic vanished in the group."

"That's not unusual. Men naturally want things to go their way. They get hot under the collar when they think things are out of control."

"What about you?" I asked.

"Son, hotheadedness rarely pays off. If you are the calm amongst the storm people will listen. If it can get you out of a tough jam, so much the better. How rough was it?"

"I don't think our lives were in danger... but it was only because we were close to the river and the river had a lot of traffic on it. If we'd been more remote or didn't have the help of our GPSrs it might have been different."

"But you made it through, broken arm and all," he said.

"Yeah, we did."

"I'm proud of you, son."

"I didn't tell you about it so you'd be proud of me. I... I don't know why I did. I didn't understand how the least capable person ended up the leader of the group. It didn't make sense."

"A leader is not the man of rank. He is not the most important man in a group. He is not the richest or the one who commands. He is the man who, underneath it all, whether the group will even admit it amongst themselves, has quietly earned the respect of their peers."

"That's it?"

"I suspect so. How far was it to the river?"

"As the crow flies? We figured it was ten kilometers, but it's not that easy to walk ten kilometers cross country. The forest was thick. We couldn't see landmarks."

He cracked a smile and I was glad I had talked to my dad and not my mom.

"So tell me about this girl," he said. "What seems to be the problem there?"

"I didn't know she was engaged. I asked her out. We hit it off. But... I guess she decided to go through with it."

"I'm sorry to hear that. It was nice to run into you at Horatio's."

"She was in awe of Horatio's," I said laughing a little bit. "She works hard and she felt like she was asking a lot to go there."

"Did you tell her you eat lunch there twice a week?"

"No, though she now knows I go there frequently. Why is it that I can keep a straight head when it comes to finances, when I'm trapped in an oubliette in pitch blackness and can lead a group of men out of the wilderness, but one girl sets me in a tailspin?"

His eyes narrowed. "It's the emotions. None of those other situations touched your heart."

"It's not the break up that worries me. I'll go on. I'll find somebody else... eventually. But she's making a mistake. A mistake that will follow her until she realizes it's a mistake and then it'll be harder to escape from. If somebody was hurting mom. Physically hurting her. What would you do?"

"Well, we're kind of in different situations. Your mother is my wife which gives me every right to defend her. You're on the other side of the situation and it's risky to stick your nose where it doesn't belong."

"I know. That's what makes it insufferably frustrating."

"You could talk to the guy."

"No, I can't. If this is a typical abusive relationship it would only make things worse for Jo."

"Are you sure you want to get involved with a woman who lives with that kind of drama around her."

"I think she would like to be free of it. She isn't a drama queen. She's a transplanted Nebraska farm girl who thinks it's very stylish and exotic to sell women's lingerie in a department store."

"But she's too good looking for her own good," he said. "She attracts every guy within a mile of her."

"Even ones who don't deserve her."

"And it turns out she's engaged. Do you know when the wedding is?"

"Yeah, it was in the newspaper. Three weeks... well, almost three weeks from now."

"I wish I had a solution for you," he sighed. "But sometimes there isn't one. Sometimes you just have to let go."

That wasn't what I wanted to hear. But what *did* I want him to say? I ran through my options.

"If I talk to the guy he'll get mad and take it out on Jo. If I talk to Jo she will try to assure me everything will be fine, but it'll all be a lie. She knows what she's walking into. If I turn my back on her I'll be miserable."

"Have you checked in at the office?" he asked, presumably to change the subject.

"No, I guess I should. I'm trying something new."

"Oh?"

"I want to open a store."

"That sounds like a lot of work."

"It might be and it might be a flop, but I've got enough surplus to risk putting a few years into it. I've got a guy working on it. He needs a job. I want to fill a niche. If it takes off maybe I'll even work there. It's up to me, really. It's kind of nice to have that option. I know it sounds crazy but there's something appealing about being able to wear whatever I want to work, standing behind a counter and talking about geocaching to people just like me. I'm looking forward to it."

"So I see," he said.

"Only one thing would make it better."

And nobody needed to say what that one thing would be. Bummer.

I drove from my parents' house to Jo's house with no plans to stop. I just had to get a glimpse. My first pass revealed nothing, though the house lacked a certain cheerfulness that I had seen there before. Maybe it was my foul mood overshadowing the place. I drove around the block and drove slower, but this time I was surprised to catch Jo leaving the house. I knew she began her work day later than most people, but I didn't expect to see her. I pulled over and parked, feeling guilty for spying. She closed the front door and locked it behind her, then walked quickly to her car glancing behind her. Her actions were quick, quiet and calculated. She even closed her car door quietly. She didn't start her engine until traffic was clear and then she started it, put it in gear, and pulled out almost in one movement. I ducked as she drove past. I debated for two heartbeats before turning around and following her. However, it isn't easy following another car in LA traffic. I managed to keep her within sight until she reached a major street. Then I got tangled up in traffic. When she headed for the freeway I knew I didn't have a chance of catching up to her, even in the Jaguar, so I went back and drove by her house again. The yard needed mowing. The curtains were closed, the house brooding. There was an older model muscle car in the driveway. I went home sulking.

"Dude, what's wrong with you?" Darby said from my office.

"Nothing. What have you found?"

"Don't know until I go look. I like the looks of this one, though."

I looked over his shoulder as he found the webpage he wanted to show me. When it came up I didn't understand what I was seeing.

"I can't see a thing," I said.

"Lookee the map," he said as he scrolled down. "And picture it with a planter out front and maybe a giant ammo can."

The store was in the back corner of a strip mall, literally in the corner. The door was completely in shadow. I wasn't so sure but I trusted Darby to find a spot suitable for geocachers.

"Check it out," I told him. "Remember, location is more important than the cost of rent. If we get the right location it'll pay in the long run."

Darby seemed more chipper in LA with a real job to do. He seemed to relax into it. Maybe he enjoyed being free of the stigma of homelessness. I doubted he would stay at my apartment another night. He'd go back to Henry's camp. But perhaps he could work his way into a place of his own.

Chapter 31

Two weeks passed before I was able to get in to see my doctor. He sent me for X-rays. That was the one thing I was hoping to avoid. He asked me how long ago I broke it and I said, "six weeks," because that's what the doctor in France told me to wait. However, the X-rays didn't lie and I was told to come back in another week for removal of the cast. I made an appointment for two days before Jo's wedding. Maybe the doctor could be fooled into thinking a full week had passed.

During those two weeks Darby dragged me down to the little strip mall. It turned out to be nicer than it looked on the web page. It was on Highway 1, which meant it faced the beach. There was a Mexican restaurant next door. Palm trees sprang from the islands in the parking lot and colorful fake parrots swung from wires in front of the eatery. The door to the shop was in the shady back corner, bad news for any store wanting publicity but perhaps just hidden enough to feel like a find to a geocacher. The triangle of sidewalk in front of the door wouldn't be large enough for a giant ammo can, but I began picturing a statue that would fit with the Mexican theme next door, of an explorer. Hiding a cache on a statue appealed to me, too.

"There's actually two small pads next door to each other. We could put the store in one and the back room you were talking about in the other," Darby explained. "All we would need is a door between the two."

"How big is it?" I asked.

"Altogether? Fifteen hundred square feet. It used to be a boutique so some of the walls have hanger board. We can use it for shelving until we figure out something different."

"Are there others to look at?"

"Sure, it's just that... I don't know. This one just seems to be *the one* so far."

"What do you mean *the one*?"

"You know, the one! The one that says, 'I want to be a geocaching store when I grow up!'"

So we called the broker and took a look inside. As Darby animatedly gave me a tour of a place he had never seen before I realized he was right. Even if there were better locations, this was the one that had chosen him and I believed in going with the flow of things. If Darby believed in this location he'd be more inclined to put his all into making it work. So we took it. After a lot of paperwork, check writing, permit applications and contractor negotiations, Darby and I had a store in the works.

Chapter 32

The cast was removed just like I hoped, though I was advised to take it easy. I assumed that meant I wasn't to slug a certain boyfriend of Jo's. That might hurt me more than him. They gave me a sling but I had no intention of using it after I got to my car. Steering quickly convinced me the arm was not quite healed but I made it home without too much trouble. I stood before the big panorama window where my debates usually take place, with all of downtown LA below me. It seemed looking at the big picture helped focus my thoughts. I was just one piece of a very large puzzle. I was an ant. So why worry about my future? Why worry about Jo's? Because, I told myself, even ants have lives. Even if it was tiny and meaningless to some it meant something to her, to me. The big question begging to be answered was, what did Jo's life mean to Jarrod? And that I couldn't find a satisfactory answer for. Did he really love her? I tried to imagine trying to hurt Jo and even in an insane rage I don't think I could bring myself to strike her. I'd never been angry enough to strike anybody, so it was hard for me to imagine a man so full of rage that he would strike a woman. I could feel the anger building though. If there was a man I could build up enough anger for to strike them physically, it was Jarrod, and not out of jealousy, but just to show him what he was doing was wrong. And then I was mad at myself for thinking striking a violent man would teach him anything.

The day after tomorrow. Should I go? I hadn't been invited. Yet I knew when and where. Why put myself through the torture? To see it finally be finished? I didn't know and I did nothing but fight with myself over it for two days. And when I did go I loathed myself. I put on a suit, and a fake smile, and I drove to the church.

I watched the family and friends file in. They seemed happy. A car with tissue paper flowers was parked near the entrance, ready to go. I found a seat on the aisle so I wouldn't inconvenience any of the real guests. The organ music sounded funereal to me. Slow, stately, formal.

When the wedding march began I automatically looked toward the back of the church. Jo stood there, regal in a too formal gown. She looked like a model from a bridal magazine, but the winter edition. The church was stuffy and I thought she must be sweltering in that gown, gorgeous to be sure, but everything looked uncomfortable, stiff and forced. I remembered that I had not been invited and quickly turned around but that just made me stand out more. As she passed me Jo did a double-take and I looked her in the eye briefly. And then she was gone, followed by layers of white billows like the clouds I had seen from the plane. I swallowed hard and when the music stopped I sat with the rest of the guests.

I don't remember much about the ceremony. I suppose it was typical. I felt like a guy in a country western song watching the love of my life being taken by another man. And then something clicked.

Chapter 33

"If any man opposes this union speak now or forever hold your peace," the priest said.

Jo's eyes pled for help. Her parents nearly raised a hand. The groom looked afraid someone would say something. I sat there on the edge of my seat, shaking, afraid to step forward, afraid not to. I finally decided we were through anyway. All I could do was finalize that, but I couldn't let her marry that man. It was the only method I had to raise a final objection so I stepped quickly out into the aisle. I meant to raise a hand and shout, "I object!" But I stood there, sadness dripping off of me and said, my voice nearly breaking, "I do. I object. It's June. It's June in LA. And you're dressed like it's January in Minnesota. You're hiding something from all these people hoping, they will think you're a happy couple, but you're not. And these might be flower petals on the aisle, but they might as well be egg shells and building blocks, because that's what you'll be walking on for the rest of your life." My courage stepped in and my voice rose. "Every time you take a step you'll be breaking something. And it's going to hurt. I can't let you do that. So I do object, and not because I'm on some male ego trip. I object because…" and this is when the groom couldn't contain his rage any longer. He marched down the aisle and stood in front of me daring me to continue. I had witnesses. Close to a hundred of them. So I waited until he was standing about a foot away. "I object because somebody has to stop this man, before he kills someone. Marriage doesn't solve problems. If you marry this guy you become his. His own personal anger vent. And it'll be even harder to stop the rage." The groom was like a valve that was fixing to blow. His fists were clenched. He was doing everything in his power not to send my nose out my ear hole. If he did, it would be worth it. Everybody would see him for the man he was trying hide. "Jo, please. Don't let him hurt you again. He might be a nice guy. But kindness lives in the heart. It's not something that shows up when you're happy and goes away when you're mad. Kindness is love of your fellow man. If he really loved you, he *could not hurt you*. I know you said you couldn't see me again and I understand. Just know that I would never, ever strike you. I'll be on Main Street, if you ever want to talk." And I turned my back on the groom. I could hear him behind me and I didn't turn around to see what he was doing. I expected to be yanked off my feet and sucker punched into a pulp, but I reached the end of the aisle in one piece and I looked out the double doors. The ones the bride and groom would dash through to their honeymoon. The day was bright and hot and my temper was riled, and I really needed something to fend off the hopeless feeling that threatened to engulf me, but I'd made a statement and a promise and so I got in my car and drove to the happiest place on earth. I paid the admission again and found a bench with a view of the castle and I sat.

The park was busy that day, as it is all summer long. At first I had to share a bench with a family until the parents were rested enough to continue on. I sat, trying to let the crowd distract me and wring out the thoughts that were circling like vultures waiting for me to die.

Jo didn't show up that night. The fireworks show went on over the castle but I couldn't see it. Thousands of people stood in front of me and still I sat. The show ended, the crowds dispersed. The park emptied. The custodians swept up trash. I was going to get kicked out soon.

All the nearby hotels were booked solid. No surprise there. It would have been a convenience to be close by. I ended up driving home and then driving back the next day, but I was there when the park opened. I paid the admission and prepared to spend another day waiting. I had plenty of time to think of scenarios as to how this might end. I could give up and go home. I could sit on this bench every day until I was old and gray. I would look up and imagine Jo framed by the castle, brilliant in the summer sunshine and run to her and grasp her in a hug and kiss her like a princess.

What ended up happening was that one of the more dismal scenarios was dragging its way through my thoughts when someone sat down on the end of the bench. People had sat down with me frequently throughout the day just because they needed to get off their feet for a while. I glanced over at the person and this time it was Jo.

"Sorry I kept you waiting," she said. "Disasters take some time to work out."

"It's okay," I said. "What happened?"

"It wasn't pretty."

"Sorry."

"I had to quit my job," she said. "And I can't go home."

"Why?"

"Threats."

"Where did you go last night?"

"My mom and dad's hotel."

"What are you going to do next?"

"I don't know. I really don't. My neighbor is taking care of my dog. If she sees Jarrod she will call the police. It would be nice to find a place where I can keep Sparky."

"We'll find you a place."

"I might even need a new name."

"You can have mine."

She scooted closer to me.

"Most of what you said at the wedding I'd told myself every day for a year, that I was crazy, that I'd never have a day of peace. Then he'd be nice for a while and I thought I could love him. But what I'd never thought of before was that kindness and love are the same thing."

"I learned about kindness from a strange group of people. I hope you will meet them some day."

"I hope so too. Tell me about them."

"One of them we can go visit this evening. The other is busy setting up a store for me."

"A store?"

"A small business venture I'm stepping out into. Actually, it doesn't involve lingerie, but you are welcome to be a saleswoman there if you'll attend a brief educational training class. I'll teach it myself. I think these products will sell themselves, but you need to learn the lingo."

I parked the car nearer to camp. There was no reason to hide it. I opened the door for Jo and she stepped out.

"Is it safe here?" she asked.

"I've never met any ill fortune here," I said.

"Well, will you look who's here!" Henry exclaimed. "And he brought a guest! Long time no see! I thought once you took our Darby boy away we'd never see you again."

"Sorry, Henry, a friend is a friend. How are you?"

"Creaky, as always. I make more noise sitting down than a bag of popcorn makes in the microwave."

"Jo, this is Henry. Henry, this is JoReilly James."

"But this is…" Jo began.

"Yes, it is, but I told you I'd introduce you to the man who taught me kindness," I explained, then to Henry, "She's in a bit of culture shock right now."

"I understand. I understand completely. Have a seat. Did you bring a spoon?"

"No, Henry, we won't deplete your stew. How's it faring these days?"

"Good! Good! Darby brings us extra these days. Best stew we've had in years."

"I would have contributed some but I came directly from a place where stew ingredients are not sold."

"It's okay, son. And Miss JoReilly, I'm pleased to make your acquaintance."

"Thank you," Jo said.

"What have you been up to?" Henry asked me.

"Besides crashing weddings and starting up the new store?" I asked.

"Sounds like you've been busy!"

"Yeah."

"I can't imagine you crashin' a wedding," he said.

"Me neither, but it was for a good cause."

"And how's the store coming along. Is Darby doing good by you?"

"He is. He'll be a good manager. He had a good teacher."

Jo didn't understand the conversation. She didn't understand why we were sitting on the ground in a homeless camp exchanging pleasantries, but she was to have more surprises before the day was over.

"Now I don't want you to get the wrong impression," I said as I unlocked the door to my apartment. "This is home. My temporary home. You'll like it and you'll hate it, just like I do." I opened the door and all of LA sparkled below. She gasped with surprise.

"It's beautiful!"

"I know. It is. Sometimes."

"Why do you say it's temporary? It's fabulous!"

"Take a look around. It's my home, but you'll see that I don't have much of a life here. That's why I liked your house so much. This is fabulous. But fabulous is not a place to live, it's a place to take a wonderful woman on a date. It's a place to sip wine. I can't stand it here much longer. I know you're not ready for this, but eventually I'd like a house more like yours. One where everyday life happens. Where can I find a compromise?"

"Well, a little color might help," she admitted. "What do you like to do?"

"Work, geocache, really… what I like to do is hope for change."

She sat down on my couch. It faced the window.

"Are you thirsty? Can I get you something?"

"Have you got any wine? I guess you're right, this is just a wine sipping kind of a view."

"I do, but I don't know what kind. Most of it was gifts from clients. There's a bottle from my parents."

"Your parents give you wine?"

"It's a special bottle they bought on a trip. I'm supposed to save it for a special occasion. If you think it's an occasion worth opening it for, let me know."

There was a special cooler in the kitchen just for wine. It came with the apartment. I rarely opened it. This time, I opened it and took the bottles out and read the labels one by one.

"I wish I'd sent a bottle home from Paris," I said.

"Did you find a Christmas tree ornament?" she asked.

"Yes! I did! Hold on. Let me pour some wine and I'll get it for you. Actually, I got two."

I selected a bottle at random, simply because I never took much of an interest in wine. I opened it and took two wine glasses out of a cupboard, checked for dust, dusted them out and poured half a glass of wine for each of us. I took the two glasses to the living room and set them down on the coffee table, then went to my bedroom to retrieve the two bags I'd brought home from Paris. I brought them out to the living room where she was sipping her glass of wine, gazing at the city below.

"This one I bought because I thought it was exquisite. It's beautiful and delicate and it reminded me of how you make my heart sing." I handed her the bag, which was a gold and silver gift bag with a white shimmery cascade of ribbon on the side. She untied the ribbon on the handle and pulled out the tissue paper wrapped ornament. The tissue paper had little black silhouettes of the Eiffel Tower on it. She unwrapped the little stained glass sculpture.

"Oh my goodness," she said as she pulled it out. "I can just imagine it on my tree with the lights shimmering through it. Oh, it's beautiful! Thank you Earl! I don't know what to say! It's gorgeous!"

"Then wait. Here's the other one. Before I give it to you, though, I bought this from an artist. He was in a big park-like area facing the Eiffel Tower. And he was painting a picture. The Eiffel Tower dominated the park. I would expect any artist in that park to be painting the tower, but he wasn't painting a picture of the tower, or the park. He was painting a picture of a flower stand. I asked him, 'with all these grand buildings and the stunning view of the tower, why do you paint a flower stand?' He looked me up and down. Me, dressed in dirty jeans and hiking boots and he said, 'I paint what I see. I no see de tower. I no see de age, de grandeur. I see *life*.' And when I saw his painting he had put so much life into it that I asked him if he could paint me a picture, a little one, like the big one he was working on. I came back to buy it the next day. It was hard for me to believe he painted it in one day. And I bought it sight unseen. I told him I was buying it for a special lady and I wanted it to be a surprise for both of us. He took the painting behind his cart, did something to the back of it, then wrapped it up. I made sure to compliment him on the paintings he had on display. Most of them were of everyday subjects and they all had character to them. He handed me this bag. And so… here it is. A picture of life from the eyes and hands of a man I will never see again."

It was a plain brown bag, with plain white tissue wrapped around the painting. Jo unwrapped it carefully. The frame was carved, rough wood. The painting was the same scene of the flower cart, though I could tell it was done in a hastier fashion than the larger painting had been.

"The flowers are lovely," she said.

"The larger version was vibrant," I said.

"To think he could put that much detail onto a canvas this small. It's amazing." She turned the painting over. I had assumed the artist had been signing the back, or perhaps removing a price tag. What we saw on the back was a greeting, "To Life and Love! Gautier Claude"

"Did you buy this before or after our last phone call?" she asked.

"After. Even though things hadn't worked out, I had still made a promise. I was just waiting for a chance to fulfill it."

She sat there holding up the painting of the flower stand and then glancing out at the diamonds of the city. She held up the stained glass sculpture and let the twinkling lights shine through the etching on the glass.

"You would have liked the shop the stained glass ornament came from. The windows were framed in trellises full of flowers and the ornaments hung where the sunshine would stream through them. There were butterflies and tulips and Eiffel Towers, unicorns, fairies and angels."

"Why did you choose a star?"

"Because you light up my heart more than a million stars ever could. When I see you happy, it makes me happy. The worst thing I could think of happening would have been for you to marry that guy. I'm not a risk taker. This…" I said as a motioned toward the rest of the apartment, "is a cushy life, one I'd like to work my way out of. So to stand there and berate your boyfriend at his own wedding, I want you to know, was an act of desperation. If I didn't do that one thing, the only thing I could think of to stop you, I'd never be happy. Never. The light would no longer shine. All that beauty of the city shining at my fingertips would be nothing. I might as well move to the basement… I know. I'm not making much sense."

"Oh, but you are. I met Jerrod five years ago. He was charming. The first two years that I knew him he could do no wrong. If the wedding had happened two years ago I would have been trapped."

"What changed?"

"He asked me out. I was thrilled. I accepted. As long as life was good, he was good. Then one day his boss chewed him out at work. He came over to my place, very upset. I tried to make him see that one mistake at work was not the end of the world, but he blew it all of proportion. After that the paranoia became more evident. The more I tried to explain to him why things were not as bad as he thought the more he thought I was one of the problems. Life would ease up. He'd straighten out."

"Until something set off the chain again."

"Exactly. After you left the wedding I went to the bride's room to regroup. He stormed in there after me."

I wasn't sure I wanted to hear what happened next, but I decided I needed to know. I might have to deal with this guy one day and any information I had might be useful.

"He spun me around and got in my face. He said you were trying to ruin everything and turn me against him. He said he couldn't live with the humiliation."

"Making you feel guilty."

"Everything he worried about was him, while you... you would have let him hit you, wouldn't you?"

"Yes. I've never been truly struck by anyone. But I was willing to let him do anything he wanted just so he could show everyone in the church what kind of a man he really was."

"You're lucky he doesn't know who you are. You are a marked man, Earl O'Connor."

"Better to be marked for doing what I thought was right instead of my usual cruising through a boring life."

"I've never had a boring time when I'm with you."

"Nor I you. So, would you like to go back to Horatio's? Steal my dad's table again?"

"Doesn't your mom cook?"

"Occasionally. If she finds a recipe that will make her appear to be a stellar hostess, she does cook. But she follows the recipe exactly, to the letter, makes a big splash in her little group and then goes back to her normal routine of eating on the run, just like my dad."

"What were they like when you were a kid?"

"They tried to maintain a nine to five work schedule. Often my mom and I ended up eating by ourselves and my dad ate a reheated dinner later. So now, instead of going home and scrounging he stops anywhere he takes a liking to and eats on his own."

"It seems like a lonely existence."

"Maybe we can join him."

"I think... we should not go out tonight."

"I have nothing to cook."

"It's okay. We can call out."

We sat there quietly, the whole city dazzling before us and we talked for hours.

"I would like to know some more about you, about your plans. You... are a puzzle to me, one I'm not sure I want to solve."

"I'm not sure that is possible," I said. "I'm certainly having a tough time figuring myself out."

"Your apartment reflects the kind of person you are," she stated.

"I hope not."

"Why?"

"Because if I had my choice I wouldn't live here. I'd live in a neighborhood with kids riding bikes past my house. I'd have plants and trees. But I don't know how to take care of plants and trees. I don't know what to do to fix a plugged drain. I... I've been too sheltered. I've lived in a bubble my whole life and I want to pop it. I want to be part of society, not living above it. My parents raised me to *own* things. I don't want to *own* an art gallery. I want to meet artists on the street and find out where they came from and how they get the pictures in their mind onto a blank canvas. I don't want to own a company I want to immerse myself in the workings."

"So, do you have any plans?" she asked.

"Yes," I almost whined. "I am building a store, but I don't want to own a store either. I want to work in it, learn the hobby. That's what I went to Paris to do, to learn a hobby. In the process I learned there is no physical store that sells geocaching gear. There are two stores in the whole country. And the closest one is Seattle. So I am opening a store."

"Ah... so geocaching! What is it?"

"It's an odd hobby where you download the coordinates from a website and then go out and find hidden containers. It's like a cheap, gaudy treasure hunt. My theory is that even if the geocaching shop doesn't make it we can expand into sporting goods. It would just be really cool if the shop could make it. Geocachers are a friendly group of people and I know they would like a store where they can meet other geocachers, buy trackables and containers and..."

"I seem to have discovered a passion of yours," she said.

"A passion?"

"Yeah, you really like this hobby."

"I didn't think I would. I didn't while I was in LA but once I got away from the city and discovered all the little hidden places that exist around us, that's where I discovered... not the containers, but the journey to find them. It brought me to places I didn't know existed and caused me to search and see things differently than I had ever seen them before. Grass and trees looked greener. Brush was brushier. Skies were bluer. Spotting a mountain goat or a colorful bird made the whole search worthwhile. I never made so many discoveries in a single day than I did while I was geocaching."

"You'll have to show me sometime."

"I will. We can go while you're not working."

"But I need to look for a job."

"What kind?"

"One that will give me a paycheck."

"You don't have to look tomorrow. I've got tomorrow covered."

Actually I had the rest of her life covered but I didn't think she was ready to lose control over her future. She was still a headstrong lingerie saleswoman. And she was going to be cautious.

"My parents won't be leaving until the day after tomorrow. I should spend some time with them even though they expected to see the city alone."

"Thursday, then?"

"I'd like that, I think."

Actually it worked out perfectly. I had a chance to research and find a spot that I thought she would enjoy and in the process I found out I did indeed need a vehicle that would navigate some rougher roads than the surface streets of Los Angeles. I debated. I could go out and buy any vehicle on the market but my dealings with Henry and Darby had taught me to choose a car that suited my purposes, not the one that would impress, and I was in need of a car that could climb mountains and cross streams. It had to be dependable enough to get me out of situations resulting from my off road ignorance.

"What kind of car does a geocacher drive?" I asked Darby when I went to check on the progress at the store.

"Jeeps," he said. "Actually they drive all kinds of cars, but if you go to an event in the U.S. you will see Jeeps and a smattering of other cars. If you want a car that people expect to see a Travel Bug on, get a Jeep."

"There are lots of Jeeps," I said.

"Rubicon."

"Really? It's that easy to pinpoint a geocacher's car?"

"If you don't believe me go to the next event."

"I don't have time for that. I'm taking Jo geocaching tomorrow."

"You think they're going to let you drive it off the lot?"

"Yeah."

I stood in the lot debating again. Before me stood a bright yellow, a maroon, and a silver Rubicon. Brand, spanking new. One of them had all the bells and whistles. The maroon one.

"I want to take this thing off road."

"Then this is the car for you," the salesman said.

"No, I mean, I'm going to try to find a road it won't go down."

He just stood his ground.

"Do you have one that has been where I want to go?"

"A used one?"

"Yeah."

He was disappointed. A sale of a new Jeep was money in his pocket.

"You won't like it," he said.

"If I won't like the used one, I won't like the new one in a few years," I pointed out. "Show me."

The vehicle he had on the lot was white. It had been washed and polished but still had a few scratches.

"You'll want a hard top. The rag top is noisy."

"But the rag top I can remove on the road and stow it in the back. A hard top I would need a garage, right?"

"Uh, right."

"Then the rag top works."

"It's got eighty-five thousand miles on it," he pointed out.

The tires were a little worn. It looked comfortably broken in.

"I'd like to drive it," I said.

"Sure thing. Let me go get the keys."

I could imagine the talk at the key locker, the salesman asking how to steer me back to the new ones. He brought the keys back but when I inserted the key in the ignition I realized I had one problem. It wasn't automatic.

"Is there a problem?" the salesman asked.

"Uh, yeah. I haven't needed to learn how to drive a stick. I need to think about this."

"The maroon one is an automatic."

The one with all the bells and whistles.

"I need to phone a friend. I'll be back."

I startled Darby as I hurried through the door of the store.

"Do you know how to drive a Jeep?" I asked.

He smiled, knowing the bind I was in.

"No, but I'm sure Henry does."

Henry. Of course.

Once again I walked into camp asking advice of a homeless man.

"Henry, I'd like to hire you for the day."

"I don't know nothin' about construction," he said.

"I need a driving teacher. Darby says you can drive a car with a manual transmission. I need to learn how to drive a Jeep before tomorrow. You won't have to mow lawns for a week."

"You? You want to learn to drive a Jeep? Really?" his grin grew as he remembered what it was like to learn how to shift a car. "Hell, I'd do it just to do it! I taught my daughter and my son. You shoulda seen that car lurching cross the parking lot."

"You'll have to come with me," I said. "I can't drive it off the lot."

"You never cease to amaze me, Earl, you've been so entertaining. I'm glad to have you for a friend. I suppose I get to ride in that fine Jaguar."

"Yes, sir."

"Can I drive it?" he asked.

"Do you know where the dealership is?" I asked.

"No."

"How about while I'm practicing in the Jeep you can try out the Jaguar?"

"Yahoo! This is like Christmas day!" he bellowed as we headed for my car.

He sat in the passenger's seat like he was afraid to dirty it.

We pulled into the car dealership and the salesman was out the door before we stepped onto the curb.

"Zack, this is Henry. He's going to test drive my Jeep for me," I said.

Zack stood there eyeing Henry. He didn't extend his hand in greeting. I had to admit Henry was scruffy and hadn't had a bath in a few days, but to me it just seemed rude.

"I don't bite, son," Henry said.

When Zack still hesitated I turned on my heel.

"Let's go," I said to Henry. "There are other Jeeps. We don't need his."

"Earl, it's no big deal," Henry said.

"It might not be to you, but it is to me. We're going to keep looking until we find a salesman who will treat you with respect. I don't care if I pay fifty grand for hunk of junk. I will not give this man my money."

"You really got the money to just buy a Jeep outright?"

"Yeah, it's easier than making payments."

"Hey, can we have some fun then?"

"What kind of fun?"

"Go get enough cash to make their eyes bug out."

My bank knows me.

"Good afternoon, Mr. O'Connor, what can we do for you today?"

"I'd like to withdrawal twenty thousand dollars in cash."

The bank teller's eye brows went up.

"I'm buying a car," I explained.

She had to talk to her manager, but my reputation was good.

"How would you like it?" She asked.

"Hmm, give me a one thousand dollar bill and then eight five hundred dollar bills. The rest can be whatever you like, except I'd like a few small bills. We want to be counting for a little while," I explained.

"I'd like to see this deal. Remember to finance the rest through Connie."

"I doubt I need to but I'll remember."

"I'll have Myron walk you to your car."

"That won't be necessary."

She counted each bill out for me as she glanced around to make sure nobody was paying particular attention to my transaction. Then Myron did follow me out. Myron was a pleasant man, a tall very dark black man who always had a smile, but also looked like he could crush a man if need be.

"Have a good day," he told me as I opened my car door.

"You too," I said.

I ducked into my car and held the wad out to Henry. His eyes bugged out. I bet he had never seen a thousand dollar bill. I didn't like using them. Retailers were naturally leery of accepting large bills. I expected some flak from the car dealership.

"H... h... how much is this?" he asked.

"Enough to make their eyes bug out."

He leafed through the bills. "Holy smokes."

"I suggest not smoking it. Now remember, we're looking for a used Jeep Rubicon."

"Used."

"Yeah, it's got to look like it's seen some geocaching miles."

"You know I can count the number of people who would trust me with this much money on one hand."

"Me, Darby, Wanda..."

His eyes teared up. "My kids wouldn't even trust me with it. They'd think I was boozing and dealing drugs to have this much money."

"I've only seen you drink a beer once," I said.

"This is going to be fun. I just want to see the look on their faces."

We drove up to the next dealership.

"Let me work," he said. "You just watch."

Watch? Heck, I was going to make a video of this.

He got out of the car and walked onto the car lot. He glanced around at the cars, took a liking to a pricey one. He looked in the windows, checked the price, then looked about as if he was looking for something specific. Not one salesman made a move to help him. He spotted a Jeep and made his way across the parking lot. A Corvette caught his eye and he stopped to admire it. Still, no salesman made an appearance. I was getting irritated. If Henry had a haircut, wore slacks and a collared shirt they'd be flocking his direction, but he wore ragged shoes, baggy pants, and a soiled t-shirt. I thought the pants probably fit him five years ago but street life had stripped him of fifty or sixty pounds. He looked over a silver Jeep. Silver seemed to be a popular color for Jeeps in southern California.

A salesman finally appeared but he didn't approach Henry.

"Uh, sir? Could I get you to move on?"

"A po'r man can't shop for a car here?" Henry asked.

"Certainly, sir, but... I don't think you can afford one of these cars."

"Oh," Henry said disappointedly. "Could I test drive one?" he asked.

"You're interested in the Jeep?"

"Yes. I need me a Jeep. Not too many miles, but used. What's this one? A 2010?"

"I think so."

"How much would it take for me to get myself a Jeep?"

"Sir, that car is going for twenty-five thousand dollars. How much of a payment can you afford?"

"I wasn't planning on payments," Henry said.

The salesman crossed his arms and looked at Henry with condescension.

"If you'll show me the car, you just might make a sale," Henry said.

"All right sir, I'll humor you for a little while but only because business is slow and I've got to be doing something."

The salesman went back to the office to get the keys to the Jeep. While he was gone I closed in a little to hear better. A salesman spotted me and jogged out.

"I'm not interested," I told him. "You could say I'm doing a study on how homeless people are perceived in society."

"What do you mean?"

"That guy's trying to buy a car."

"You're kidding."

"No."

"There's no way..."

"Just watch."

We watched as Henry went through all the usual motions of sitting in the driver's seat and checking out the interior, then asking to see the engine. He asked for the history of the vehicle and looked over the tires.

"Can we take it for a test drive?" he asked.

"Look mister," the salesman said. "I think we're both wasting our time."

"I need a volunteer," Henry said. "I want an unbiased opinion on how this thing rides. You sir!" he said waving at me to come over.

The other salesman and I exchanged glances, "don't say a thing," I told him.

He shrugged and stayed behind while I walked toward the Jeep.

"I know you're a high falutin' businessman and you don't have much time to spare but I need somebody to ride in the back and tell me what they think of this here Jeep."

I walked around, checking the price, the year, the interior. I trusted Henry to find me a good vehicle. I doubted he would hand over my twenty thousand without a go-ahead of some kind.

"Well, I really…" I said as I pulled out my smart phone.

"Aw, come on, son. Humor an old man."

"Five minutes," I said acting as if I really had more important things to do.

"You've gotta be kidding," the salesman said to me.

"I think if the man wants to go for a test drive, he should go for a test drive," I stated. "Where in your advertisement does it say a man has to dress to impress in order to get a test drive?"

"It does say the price, payment options and what it takes to qualify," he said.

"Do I get a discount for being a veteran?" Henry asked.

The salesman rolled his eyes. It was almost like he was begging me to give him an escape but I wasn't going to do it.

"I've always been wondering about these," I said as I acted more interested in the Jeep.

"Oh, no you don't," Henry said. "I asked about it first!"

"You test drive it," I said. "See what you think."

The salesman was stuck. Even if the old man couldn't afford the Jeep he thought maybe I could, so he went to find a dealer plate to stick in the window. Just in case it would get him out of the test drive he asked Henry for his driver's license. He had to do some digging in his pockets but he finally produced a driver's license. I wondered how he kept it current. He didn't have an address or enough money to pay the fees.

The salesman gave Henry very specific instructions about where to turn and how far to go on each street, but Henry very cleverly had trouble getting his lane in time for the turns and we ended up very far afield.

"I need to feel the power in the engine," Henry announced. "How's a man supposed to judge an engine in this stop and go traffic of the city?"

When Henry ended up on a freeway exit I secretly laughed to myself and then when the freeway headed toward the hills I said, "I wonder how it would tackle that hill!"

"Mister Hofstadter, we have a designated route we are supposed to follow. I must ask you to return to the dealership at once."

"I thought you was in the business of selling cars," Henry said.

"I am, but…"

"Well, you aren't going to sell this car unless it'll do what we want it to do. If it will climb the hill, I'd be more interested," Henry said and he took the exit and pointed the Jeep toward the hill. It took some maneuvering to get to a road that wasn't paved but he finally found one. When he pointed the Jeep up the road the salesman held on tightly.

"If you damage this vehicle you will be charged…"

"Yeah! CHARGE!!!" Henry said as he hit the gas.

"Who…o…o…oa!" the salesman shrieked as the Jeep bumped up the hillside. "Down! Turn this thing around and drive it back to the dealership… right… now!"

"Turn it around?" Henry said. "Okay!" Then he whipped it into a U-turn despite the road being just two wheel ruts through the weeds. The Jeep hit a rock but managed to climb right over it and lurch back to the road. "And we weren't even in four wheel drive yet!" Henry whooped. "Hey! I didn't see this road on the way up!"

"You… are… crazy! A crazy man!" the salesman said as Henry turned down an ever shrinking road. I didn't even know roads like this existed in LA. We splashed down into a puddle and muddy water covered the windshield.

"Now we're going somewhere!" Henry said as he searched for the windshield wipers. As he searched, the Jeep sunk further and further into the muck, and when the windshield was clear again he hit the gas sending a plume of water spraying away behind us. The tires spun uselessly. "Easy does it," Henry said to himself, or maybe to me. "There is a time for power and a time for finesse. Easy, in four wheel drive. Traction is what we're lookin' for. Forward, back, forward, back. See how it's easing out? Forward, back now, forward, forward and there ya go up and out!"

The salesman was somewhat shaken when he stumbled out of the Jeep as soon as it stopped in the dealership parking lot.

"Well, what do you think?" Henry asked me. "Did she give you the ride you were looking for?"

"It certainly did," I said.

The salesman was stalking off to the office and Henry and I thought we would have to find another salesman but a young man in a dealership polo shirt jogged up and drove the Jeep away.

"Car wash time!" he said right before he sped off.

"So, what do you think?" Henry asked. "Do you want it?"

"It's got air conditioning?"

"Yup."

"Stereo?"

"Yeah, we shoulda tested it though."

"I think we put him through enough."

"We can get it for the twenty if we play our cards right," he said.

"Oh, here he comes."

Henry walked toward the salesman. "So... let me see... how much... I got..." he said. He managed to pull a very wrinkled hundred dollar bill out of his pocket. The salesman seemed to consider the bill to be a joke of some kind. His puzzled expression was funny. "Hold on, I got more," Henry said. He pulled and tugged another bill out of his pocket. A bill that was still in his pocket wriggled almost loose and threatened to blow away. He grabbed it and yanked it out, too.

"Maybe we should go to the office," the salesman said.

"I'll give you eighteen for it," I said.

"Naw, wait! I got more!" Henry said.

"Eighteen five," I said.

Henry glared at me.

"I tell you I got more. What are you going to use a Jeep for anyway, you who drove here in a fancy Jaguar! You can't drive a Jeep the way it should be driven."

"We'll see about that," I said.

"Gentlemen, gentlemen I'm sure we can settle this without any problems, but we should take our discussion inside."

"Yeah, so's my money doesn't blow away!" Henry said.

Henry and the salesman headed for the office and I gave them a head start. I really think Henry was crumpling each bill as he pretended to look for more money. Each bill that he pulled out of his pocket had to be smoothed out, added to the sum and stacked up.

"If I could give you twenty cash on the spot would you sell it to me for that?" he said.

"Cash out the door?" the salesman asked. "I'd have to talk to my manager."

"Ooo look, another hundred. Them rich homeowners got big yards to mow."

By the time we reached the office he'd managed to extricate two thousand one hundred dollars plus some small bills and he was still pulling money out of his pockets. He stacked them up in piles according to how much they were worth, then fished in his pockets for more.

I considered Henry to be one of the most honest people I'd met, but he told some doosies that I knew could not be true as he pulled more money from his pockets.

"I washed the whole fleet of busses for L.A. Transit for this!" he said of a five hundred dollar bill. "And the Rose Bowl! Dang! I thought I'd die of old age before I finished mowing the field and then the park around it." He pulled out a hundred dollar bill, "If anyone hires you to clean up elephant poop, don't do it. It ain't worth it." He pulled out a five dollar bill, "However, if Madonna didn't pay me one red cent, I'd still wash her car for her." Each bill was laid in its proper stack. I sat down and just enjoyed the show. I knew we'd have to tell the salesman the truth but if Henry could just get him to commit to selling the Jeep for $20,000 I'd be happy. All he had to do was say the Jeep was sold and it wouldn't matter whose money it was. I'd just make sure I signed the deal and we'd be set for Jeep driving lessons. That is if I could get out of the salesman's office in time to learn.

"There was this lady on Santa Monica Pier who caught three fish. She didn't know how to clean a fish! I told her I'd clean them if she'd give me a fish. I took them to the end of the pier and I'm a cleanin' fish, the seagulls are circling, waiting for a hand out and I'm a yackin' just like this. The lady was so grossed out about the whole procedure she paid me to take all three fish! Those were good fish. Fresh caught," Henry said as he laid another five dollar bill on a stack. "I walked somebody's dogs for this," he said of a twenty dollar bill. "One of them York esh shire mini dogs and a Great Dane. The little dog's running circles around the big dog, trippin' him up and he's trying not to step on his buddy. Took us an hour to walk around the block."

"Mr. Hofstadter, we don't need your life story. We just need to know you can pay for the car."

"I'll give you twenty for it," I said.

"Believe me, I'd love to be able to call your bank, arrange financing and sign the papers, but Mr. Hofstadter here test drove the car. He's first in line for the sale."

"All right Henry," I said. "Time to come clean. I still need to get some driving lessons in today."

"But I was having fun!" Henry complained.

"I know but you can tell me all those stories while you teach me to drive the Jeep. Just hand over the money," I said.

Henry reached into his pocket and pulled out the whole wad.

"That's a lot of stories," he said as he took note of exactly how many bills there were in the wad. "I don't think my brain could keep coming up with that many." He pulled the thousand dollar bill off the bundle of bills, smelled it and said, "And I painted all the lines down the 101 by hand, on my hands and knees one little brush stroke at a time. It don't smell like paint anymore."

"You mean you two were working together?"

"No," I said. "Henry was test driving the Jeep and as soon as it's mine he's going to teach me how to drive it. I have a date tomorrow and I need a vehicle that will take me up into the hills."

The salesman stood up and walked out of his cubicle. In a minute he came back with another man following. The manager stopped at the doorway. He looked at the stack of bills on the desk.

"Thank you John," the manager said. He stepped into the room and began a somewhat awkward and useless conversation in which the manager asked us to retell the whole story of coming in and asking for the test drive. When the cop appeared in the lobby it was obvious the manager had just been stalling for time. Three other police cars came screaming into the lot and took up position blocking all the exits from the building. I was irritated. They only jumped to conclusions because they had misjudged Henry.

"Look, you can call my bank. You can talk to Myron, Sylvia and Connie. All three will tell you Earl O'Connor came in about an hour and a half ago and withdrew twenty thousand dollars. It's all there, every dollar."

They glared at Henry.

"He don't know how to drive a standard!" Henry said.

It was rather embarrassing and funny at the same time. The cop went outside, talked to the officers stationed at the exits and they relaxed a bit but he came back inside and asked me for my ID. I handed over my driver's license and bank card so he would know which bank to call. The cop motioned for the salesman to follow and they went to the lobby where the cop could keep an eye on me and talk out of earshot at the same time, then he called my bank. As the officer waited to confirm my story I could see him through the glass wall as he spoke, listened, spoke, grinned. He came back shaking his head.

"That Myron is a real character," he said. "He thinks you must be nuts, but they backed up your story one hundred percent."

I breathed a sigh of relief. No matter how needless worry is, the relief is still real.

"Well, this is one sale that's going to be retold over the water cooler," the manager said.

The backup officers were cleared to leave. The responding officers completed their paperwork. I signed the documents to buy the Jeep, and counted out the cash. I handed over my card again for tax, registration and fees. I was quickly losing hours of driving practice.

"By the way," the officer said on his way out. "Next time you decide to buy a car with small bills, read the headlines first. We've had a string of bank robberies."

Chapter 34

"Now you gotta work your feet," Henry said. "Up with the gas down with the clutch. At the same time you go for the next gear."

"Different actions all at the same time in the middle of big city traffic?" I asked.

"We aren't in the traffic yet. We're in the only empty parking lot in the county! You need the clutch in to shift so... here we go..."

I wasn't mechanically inclined but I did have a sharp mind. However, I was beginning to realize that driving a car with a stick shift was a balance of knowing how it's done, having a feel for the workings of the car and just plain good luck. And I also had a feeling that the more I could practice the luckier I would be, but at first attempting to get a feel for the workings of the Jeep was getting in the way of knowing how the whole procedure worked.

Lurch, lurch, lurch die... went the Jeep. Henry had all the patience in the world. I think he rather enjoyed my failures. It was like watching a little baby walk down the mall taking four steps with adults rushing by all around him. You want to cheer on the little kid and at the same time you know they are going to fall and all those adults sure better be watching where they are going. Kids had it easy. They fall with a plop on a padded diaper, while if I had trouble in traffic it was more of a major mistake.

"I think you need to watch a little bit," Earl said. "Get in the back seat and position yourself where you can see what I'm doing and feel the car at the same time."

The sequence seemed to be much easier to do after the car was moving. I could feel the engine change and I could tell what Henry was waiting for before he shifted. However, from a standstill it was a little tougher. When I finally managed to get the Jeep to move forward in first gear I thought I was in business. I could shift roughly between gears, feel the vehicle and know when to shift. Over and over I practiced taking off from a standstill. I must have done it a dozen times trying to make sure I would still be able to do it with Jo in the car. While I struggled by myself Henry drove circles around me in the Jaguar. He turned up the satellite radio and sailed back and forth grinning ear to ear. I was happy to give him a little slice of his younger life. A life free of struggles and cold, hard streets. He pulled around the Jeep and yelled out the open window.

"Okay, stop! There's something else we need to work on," he said.

"Oh no, what?" I asked.

"Reverse! You don't think you're going to always be going forward, do you?"

"Shoot."

"It's just like taking off from a stop except you put it in reverse and watch behind you," he said.

"But taking off from a stop is the hardest part," I said.

"That's why we need to try it a few times," he said as he shut off the Jaguar and got out.

Reverse wasn't as hard as learning to take off from a stop had been. I knew where to shift to and I'd already practiced taking off forward.

"I want you to back a figure eight around those two light poles," he said.

"Okay."

After I did it with many starts and stops he made me attempt it again without stopping. Then after I'd completed the second figure eight he instructed me to pull the Jeep up beside a curb and back the Jeep in a perfectly straight line, not hitting the curb or jumping out of the gutter.

"There! You think you can handle that?" he asked when I'd backed the Jeep to his satisfaction.

"Yeah."

"Good. Then drive it to the dealership."

"What!"

"Or to my place or to your place. You need to get a feel for all the starts and stops of the city. You can't drive in parking lots to get from place to place."

You'd think I was back in driving school, I was so nervous. Give me a million dollars and tell me to make it grow and I'll make it grow. But give me a hundred unpredictable motorists and ask me to keep track of all them, plus the gas, clutch, shifter and route and I suddenly turned into a nervous wreck. What was it going to be like with Jo in the car? I decided I should drive home. I also had a parking garage to figure out. I only had two parking places assigned to me but Darby had my old Ford. He needed it to do errands for the store. After he got the store going I'd probably sell him the car cheap.

If I hit a red light I stopped and prayed for a smooth start, patient motorists, and for the next light to be green. I stalled the Jeep once but when I restarted it I got off to a smooth start. Turning into my parking garage was tricky. The street was busy and I had to make a left turn and then stop at the gate. The parking garage gave me a lesson in stopping and starting on a hill. The first time I tried to start from a stop going uphill the Jeep rolled back, startling me and forcing me to hit the brakes.

"There you go Earl. You're learning. You're learning good. Where are we?"

"My apartment building," I said. "I thought I better get a feel for the garage before I turn you loose again."

"But we have to go back for the Jaguar," he said.

"I know, but let's go upstairs and regroup. I owe you for the lessons."

"Aw no, Earl, it was my pleasure. You can't know how much fun I had with that Jaguar. It's been a long time since I took any real joy in driving."

"I promised you I'd pay for your lessons and if you won't accept it, well, then I guess I can't ask you for help anymore. You helped me. Why can't I help you?"

My parking spots were right next to each other, one was next to a pillar. One was not. But the parking spot without a pole frequently had a Cadillac parked in it. I figured I was better off with the Jeep next to the pole and the Jaguar next to the Caddy. Henry whistled low with surprise at all the expensive cars in the garage. You kind of had to have enough money to drive a fancy car just to live in the building. When we entered the glass doors and Henry saw the corridor to the elevators he acted like he shouldn't enter.

"Come on up," I said. "I have some figuring to do, then I'll pay you for your time and experience and we can get some dinner and the Jaguar."

"I can't believe you bought a car just to go on a date," he said as he stepped into the corridor.

"Can you think of a better reason?" I asked.

"Yeah, though I guess a car to get the girl would be right up there. I think she might like the Jaguar better."

"The Jaguar won't take me down dirt roads. I'm going to take Jo out geocaching and I want it to be off away from the muggles."

"You got a computer in that fancy apartment?"

"I do."

"Then let me show you a road you might consider. This being a date you're going on."

When we reached my apartment I showed him where the computer was, then I pulled out a piece of paper and listed his jobs for the day: Purchasing Agent, Driving Instructor, Travel Advisor.

I guessed at the incomes of the three jobs. A purchasing agent probably made $68,000 a year which worked out to $188 a day. Driving instructors made considerably less. And travel agents made a percentage of their sales, plus salary. Henry had spent most of the day with me. I would have liked to give him more than the couple hundred I figured he had earned but I had trouble tweaking the numbers to reflect a larger income. I rounded it to $300 and wrote it all out to make it look legitimate. I knew he wouldn't take more than he thought he had earned so he needed to see it in writing.

"Look at this road," he said when I brought the paper detailing his pay for the day into my office. "It runs along the mountains overlooking Santa Barbara. It's a dirt road, but the Jeep should have no problem with it. And look," he said as he moused over several icons. "This one here is one of the oldest geocaches in the state."

I wasn't sure I cared about the age of a cache but then considered the fact that you never know what other geocachers are going to think was important. If I was going to own a geocaching store I might want to have that cache on my finds list.

He continued, "You can look out over the city. There's probably great lookout spots you can stop at. And on a clear day you can see all the way to the Channel Islands."

"Is it a one day trip? I told her we could make a day of it."

"Sure it is. Just stop geocaching when you need to turn back. It's only a couple of hours, max."

"She's been roughed up by an abusive boyfriend for three years. Do you really think she's ready for lookout point?"

"She might be begging for a normal relationship. She's a woman. Women want to be wanted."

I wondered if I should add psychologist to the job list.

"Watch for little clues," he advised me. "Women don't shout from the rooftops that they want to get it on. Is she a touchy feely person?"

"No, not really."

"In a way that's good. It makes the invitation more obvious."

"Henry, I think I can take care of myself in the romance department."

On the way back to the parking lot we stopped for dinner. Henry took over an hour to savor the meal and I bought him a piece of apple pie a la mode to top it off.

"This has been a good day," he said. "A really good day. I got to drive a sports car like a kid again. I got to make a car salesman think I was nutso crazy. I helped a friend in need. And now I got apple pie. I ain't going to be hungry for a week after all this!"

"I feel guilty taking you home," I said.

"Aw, no, Earl, it is home. I could do better. I could do worse. Wanda and me, we're almost inseparable. I need to be there."

"Hopefully you'll do better for a few days with a little jingle in your pocket," I said. "And I do appreciate your knowledge and patience with me today."

"It was fun. Wasn't that fun? Heck it was like old times. You learned how to drive a stick a lot faster than my daughter did. Of course she didn't have the incentive you did. She wasn't trying to impress some hunk into marrying her."

"I'm not…"

"Oh, yes, you are," he said as he waggled a finger at me. "I saw them looks you were shooting her way. You love that girl and I don't blame you one bit. Don't let her get away."

It was late by the time we got both cars back to my apartment and Henry home to his camp. Wanda had heated the stew, and since Henry had already eaten there was more for the others.

"Since I got a good job today and I got to have a big dinner and dessert I think I'll treat the whole camp to dessert tomorrow," Henry announced as I was leaving. "You take good care of that girl tomorrow," he called out to me. "And if she marries you we all want to be invited to the wedding!"

I only stalled the Jeep once on the way home.

Chapter 35

When I picked up Jo from her parents' hotel the next day she met me in the lobby, but insisted that they wanted to meet me. The hotel had a pleasant and sunny café downstairs so we ended up eating breakfast there. Actually, I ended up eating a second breakfast there, but they didn't know that. Jo looked like an LL Bean model. Her polo shirt and jeans looked pressed and new. I hoped her shoes could get dirty.

We sat in the lobby exchanging small talk until her parents came down. She sprung to her feet and dragged me over for introductions as soon as they stepped out of the elevator. Her dad's reaction even before I shook his hand was mixed.

"Mark James," he said extending his hand. "And I'd like to thank you for what you did."

"It's good to meet you," I said. It didn't seem like you're welcome was quite the appropriate response, but I wasn't sure what was. "I'm Earl O'Connor."

"And this is my lovely wife, Andrea," he said.

"A pleasure to meet you. I hope the wedding didn't end in too much chaos," I said.

"Actually, it was just enough to be effective," Jo said. "Jarrod had to be restrained by his groomsmen. Father Stephen came down the aisle and prayed for peace to reign over the event. The bridesmaids scattered like school kids caught doing something wrong."

"The place came apart," Andrea said. "But I was so relieved. You can't imagine the worry a mother feels when her daughter is on the brink of a terrible, terrible mistake."

I thought I might be able to come pretty close, since I was imaging many of the same things at the time.

"That was a lot of careful planning," I pointed out.

"Yes," Jo's mother said. "And I don't think we can do it again. I don't see how. But… everything will be fine. Now it will be fine."

"I told Jo, when Jerrod was hauled off still in a rage, that she should chase you down and beg for forgiveness," Mark said. "But we had guests. We had a whole reception paid for and ready to go. We just pressed on accepting condolences from the guests. They were baffled by the day's happenings and left wondering what to do with their gifts. We had a rather somber catered dinner."

"Mom, Dad, you won't believe where Earl took me to dinner!" Jo said trying to brighten the mood. "Horatio's!"

"I read about that place in a magazine!" her mom said.

"It was gorgeous! The city was sparkling all around us. It was quiet and we had the best time!"

Breakfast was typical. I thought it was odd that Jo and I could live comfortably off half my investments, yet I didn't have the right answers to her dad's questions.

"So what do you do for a living?" Mark asked.

"Juggle investments."

"No, but what do you do?"

"Actually, I'm building a small business that fills a niche and nobody has opened a store for this hobby. Jo and I are going to Santa Barbara so I can show her what it involves. If the store doesn't make it on its own we can branch out into sporting goods."

"Seems a little risky considering all the big name sporting goods stores in the area," Mark said.

"I can afford a little risk," I said. "I think we can sink three years into the venture. With advertising and a good location we'll get business from people up and down the coast. Geocachers flying into LAX will want to stop by the shop. We'll have a geocache there guaranteeing every new customer a geocache find. You can't ask for cheaper advertising than a nice, big geocache when it comes to geocachers."

"Earl flew all the way to Paris just to go geocaching," Jo said.

And find myself, I thought. And turn my back on their daughter when she needed me the most.

"What do you do when you geocache?" Andrea asked.

"It's a lot like looking for a needle in a haystack," I said. "Except that if you search patiently and learn a few tricks for spotting needles you eventually begin finding them. Geocaches are larger than needles but they can be exceptionally hard to spot."

They nodded as if they understood, though they couldn't possibly.

"Earl is going to teach me how to do it," Jo said. "Is this okay?" she asked indicating her clothing.

"You'll get your shoes dusty," I warned her.

She shrugged, "Dust comes off."

I could feel the geocaching time ticking away as we leisurely ate omelets and coffee, then biscuits and jam. Jo hugged her parents goodbye and made them promise to call when they arrived home.

"They like you," she said as they drove away.

"That's good," I answered. "They might like anybody that isn't Jerrod, though."

"No, they really like you. They might not understand you but they're willing to give you some time and that means they like you."

"Are you ready to go?" I asked.

"What do I need?"

"Nothing. We'll be hiking around in the hills then we'll drop down into Santa Barbara for lunch, then go back and see if we can finish the caches on that road before dinner. There's no pressure though. We find the ones we find and we leave the ones behind for another trip if we run out of time."

I led her to the Jeep and opened the door for her. She took note of the backpack and GPS.

"Geocaching gear," I explained. "It's possible to geocache with just a GPS and a pen, but I've found a few other things come in handy."

She dropped her purse behind the seat and climbed in.

"I never would have taken you for a Jeep man," she said.

Hopefully I could still drive the Jeep like a Jeep man. Unfortunately the first thing we met was the traffic at a dead stop on the freeway. Stop, go stop, go, stop, stop, stop, go. I sure got a lot of practice pulling forward from a stop. I was beginning to feel the workings of the engine by the time the bottleneck cleared and traffic sped up. Like usual, there never seemed to be any logical reason for the traffic jam. The traffic just magically began speeding up and we went with the flow until we reached our Highway 101 exit.

"It's funny that I've lived in LA all this time and I hardly ever go to the beach," she said. "I love it, but it's so hard to get there at a good time. First I am getting ready for work, then I'm working. When I get off it is dark. I keep telling myself to just get out and go, but working retail means working weekends."

"I know what you mean. I hardly ever go the beach either. Maybe we can today."

When we caught sight of the ocean we both tried to steal glances at it as we drove along. Ahead we could see clouds over the highway. By the time we reached Santa Barbara the freeway was covered with fog. Traffic slowed but I was glad to have time to look for the right road. The shifting still took over a good portion of my brain. I was relieved that Highway 154 was well marked. I took the exit and drove up through town and then into the clouds and hills. I hadn't done much geocaching by car before.

"What are we looking for?" Jo asked as it became obvious I was looking for a street.

"I don't know if it will say Camino Cielo or Forest Route 5N12."

"Okay, I'll watch for it, too."

When I thought I'd gone too far I drove until I could turn around and came back down the hill. I pulled off in the general area of the street I needed and when I did I found myself on a narrow, shady residential street.

"Oh, how pretty!" Jo said. "Keep driving!"

I had to keep driving because there was no place wide enough to stop, so on and on we went, passing little cottages overlooking the city. The fog closed in and the cottages began looking like dwellings from an old movie. Little fingers of fog kept creeping in front of the Jeep. When the houses gave way to woods the scenery became even more eerie. Moss covered trees lined the road. We had only seen a few other cars since turning off the highway so I began to think it was safe to park, but then a tree would appear as if out of nowhere and I imagined we would appear just as quickly to oncoming traffic, so I kept driving until we finally spotted a ray of sunshine. We followed the road up a little rise and suddenly broke out into brilliant sunshine. When we looked out toward the ocean there was a thick blanket of clouds hiding our view of the city, but over the clouds we could see the ocean sparkling in the distance and the dark forms of islands. A cargo ship chugged up the channel while another sailed down. In my uncertainty I was sure I had passed many geocaches so I pulled to the side of the road and turned on the GPS.

"Show me how it works," Jo said as she leaned over to see the screen.

"It has to find us first. It's looking for satellites."

"How many are there?" she asked.

"I don't know. I guess I ought to take more of an interest in the technology if I am going to open a geocaching store."

"Technology is amazing. And weird. I use my computer, but really only to keep in touch with my family and check the news. When I was a kid news was on TV. Now, it's everywhere."

"At least we won't get lost. If we want to get to town we can just lock onto a cache that is in town and follow the map. Oh, hey, it found us. Now let's see how many caches we passed in the fog."

Amazingly there were no geocaches hidden in the neighborhood we had passed through. There were a few back on the highway but the ones I really wanted to look for were ahead of us.

"Wow, six hundred feet!" I said.

"What is?"

"A geocache."

"Six hundred feet?"

"Yeah!"

"We should be able to see it."

I didn't laugh at her. I had to remember she had never done this before. I reminded myself how skeptical I had been when I started looking for these nefarious boxes.

"We won't see it until we are very close to it," I explained. "You can be standing right on top of one and not know it. Remember that one at the microbrewery?"

"Yeah, or rather, no. Did you find it?"

"Darby and I went back and found it. You remember how we looked for it and couldn't spot it no matter what we did? All we had to do was get the right angle and it was in plain sight. Geocaches are frequently that way. I think we can get closer to this one before we start walking. Let's see if the road gets us closer."

"What's six hundred feet?" she asked.

"It's that direction. Do you really want to walk anywhere at all that direction?"

"Oh. No. How will we get there?"

"Let's drive a bit. Maybe there is a trail, or at least a better parking spot."

We located a sort of a trail. It looked very green and very much like it might disappear, but with only four hundred feet to go we thought we could walk it easily.

"One thing you have to keep in mind while geocaching is that distances are deceiving. Sometimes it is easier to walk a thousand feet than twenty feet. The GPS only tells you where the cache is. It doesn't tell you how to get there. So, with that in mind, we follow the trail, because that's what looks easiest right at the moment."

"It's pretty," she said as we gazed out the window and up the hillside.

"Let's hope it stays that way."

The trail was lush, green and shady. I handed her the GPS but she didn't really know what to look for as she squinted at the screen. When we got closer to the cache I helped her see how much information the screen contained and what it meant.

"The cache is that little icon right there and the arrow is us. The line shows you which way is the most direct route to the cache, but for right now we want to follow the trail. I don't feel like bushwhacking through all that," I said of the green vines that climbed the trees and covered the ground about knee deep. "This number right here tells how far it is to the cache along the line.

"The arrow is orange."

"That's because the GPS thinks we're pointed in the wrong direction. If you were to turn and walk directly away from the cache it would turn red. If you walk directly toward the cache it will turn green. Don't worry about the color for now. Just use the GPS for guidance. Use your eyes and your brain to find the cache."

"Is this what you were doing in Paris?"

"Partly. One thing you will find when you have been a geocacher for several hunts is that geocachers place caches in places that they want to share with other people. If they like a place enough to hide a cache there then perhaps I'd like to see that place, too. And people choose the oddest things to share with the world. It's usually something beautiful, tricky, quirky, funny, or just plain odd. I just like to see where the hunt takes me. Sometimes, even if I don't find the cache, the hunt for it makes the failure worth my time."

"This from a man who makes fortunes in minutes."

"And loses them just as quickly," I reminded her.

"How can you stand it?"

"Easy. I never risk more than I am willing to lose. If it pays off I just have more to risk next time. If I lose I have less but I learn something from it. When I learn from my investments it helps me lose less often, the investments grow, I have more to risk. Life is all just one big learning experience. The trick, I am beginning to find out, is to put your efforts into learning something worthwhile."

"So you geocache?" she asked as if she couldn't understand how hidden boxes were more important than investment portfolios. It was like comparing dew on a flower with diamonds on a watch. A diamond on a watch represents a number. Dew on a flower draws in the scenery around it. It requires you to sit quietly and calmly and drink in the weather, the color and the feeling of the day. So, fleeting as it is, dew can be more precious than diamonds.

"Yes, because a day out looking for geocaches is better than an office meeting anytime."

"I think the trail passed the cache," she said.

"Let me see."

"Okay, yeah, you're right but it's not far. Sixty-four feet back this way."

We turned around and walked the sixty-four feet off the trail and ended up in a tiny clearing, although clearing is a misnomer. The floor of the clearing was covered with knee high weeds but they were lush, green, tropical looking weeds that were much like the vines that climbed the trunks of the trees.

"Now you have to look around for anything that seems out of place. Think about where you would hide something if you were here and then check those places. One thing geocaching does is teach you new ways to think about things. Don't worry about not spotting them at first. You gradually develop what geocachers call geosenses. The hobby is a learning process. That's one of the things I like about it."

"You could drop anything here and it would be lost forever!" she said.

"Hmm, you're right."

The GPS pointed us to an old tree. The vines covered the trunk of the tree but it was one of the more sparsely covered trees surrounding the clearing. I wondered if that was because it was searched regularly by geocachers.

"Let's see how big this thing is," I said as I clicked through the screens to find the cache description. "It says it's a regular size. That means anything from soup can up to a large coffee can or a gallon of milk."

"How would anybody hide a package that big out here in the woods?"

"Surprisingly easily," I said. "Often when I see a cache it looks as if it belongs there."

She wasn't comfortable searching a glen for a container and I had to admit I was rather self-conscious at first, too. I wondered though if she was willing to sacrifice her penchant for neatness in order to find a geocache. So far she had been tentatively parting the vines and gazing underneath. I thought the cache was going to be tricky and a simple glance would skim right past the container. She hadn't learned yet how well geocachers could make something ordinary look like a vine or a tree branch. I tromped around the tree looking under the vines, probing to see if there were hollows in the tree behind the vines. Jo walked around mystified by the search and the sheer number of places something could be hidden. Then her focus changed and she began feeling her way quietly forward. I followed her gaze to a branch of a tree across the clearing where a little bird was perched, watching the goings on. I smiled, because this was just the thing I liked best about geocaching, little surprises that drew me away from the hunt. Little bright spots in a hunt for a trivial little box. I stopped my search so I wouldn't frighten the bird. She inched closer. The bird hopped to a higher branch. Jo stopped to watch it. The bird swiped its beak on the branch a few times revealing a bright white Mohawk stripe. It chirped cheerfully and bobbed up and down a couple of times. Joe stepped closer and the bird flitted away.

"Did you see him?" she asked.

"I did. What kind was it?"

"I don't know. I don't know anything about birds, but it was cute."

"I think I can narrow it down to a sparrow but Darby's told me there are lots of different sparrows and he didn't recognize any of the ones we saw in France. I'm not exactly your walking field guide to birds," I said. "There's a camera in the pack if you'd like to try your hand at that."

"Is it one of those high tech, take a picture of a bug on a mountain type cameras?"

"It's got some zoom on it. I haven't tried taking a picture of a bug."

"Can I see it? I've only tried taking pictures of my niece and nephew and Sparky, but you might like some pictures from our day. This place is awesome. Don't you want a picture of it?"

"Go for it," I said. "Just remember I want a picture of you, too."

The first cache turned into a photo shoot while I searched for the cache. It didn't help much when I found the cache by tripping over it and landing face first in the vines. Jo made sure to ask me if I was all right before she took my picture peeking over the knee high weeds.

"Yeah, I found it," I said. "And it sounded like a big one."

"Ooo! Let me see!"

I kicked my feet a bit and heard the rattle of geocaching swag in a large plastic container so I turned around and felt under the vines until I came up with a gallon sized pickle jar spray painted in mottled greens and browns to match the vines.

"See?" I showed her. "A little spray paint, drop it in the weeds, and it's hidden."

"Wow, it's amazing! It hardly shows up at all! What's in it?"

"Well, not much of anything, really," I said. "It isn't what's in the caches that makes me want to find them. It's seeing the places they are hidden. It's just cheap trinkets, kids toys. Here, we'll open it up and you can see. You need to choose a geocaching name to sign in the log books, too."

"I can't just sign my name?"

"You can, but it isn't generally done. Every real geocacher has a separate geocaching name."

"What's yours?" she asked.

"The Earl of Nothing."

"Aww, that sounds sad."

"I can change it. It just reflected my mental outlook at the time."

"Then I should be the Princess of Nothing," she said. "I can't even stay in my own home. I've got a deranged ex on my tail."

"We've got to get you another house. Do you own the one you're in now?"

"Sort of. I've had to borrow on it, but eventually my kids can own it."

"And it's home to you. I can tell. You've made it into a home. It's not just living quarters."

She sighed, "I know I shouldn't feel that way. I should let it go. It's not the greatest house. It's little and old."

"But it's friendly and welcoming and Sparky is there."

"Earl, you really need a home of your own. You appreciate the comfort of home so much. Why don't you make your apartment a home?"

"Because I don't know how. My apartment is much like my parents' house. My mom has had a professional decorator come in and tell her how to create a professional looking home. It's always been that way. It's not that my parents' house is uncomfortable. It's just… they have learned to live with professionalism. But I like your house a lot better than I like mine, or theirs."

"Well, tomorrow I need to begin job hunting in earnest or I will lose that wonderful house. I'd like to think I have enough cushion to last until your store opens up, but I can't. And I can't swing a hammer enough to help. I should find a job at something I am good at."

"I'm sure you were a great lingerie saleswoman," I told her. "I'd probably buy anything you recommended."

"That's sweet of you, Earl. It isn't going to make it easy to find a job when I have to admit I left my last job to avoid being found out by a crazy ex. And I should get a job doing something a little different. He knows where I'd like to work. So I can't go there."

"We found the cache," I reminded her. "Do you want to see what's in it?"

"Oh yes!"

I unscrewed the lid and looked down inside. It was the usual junk.

"Have you ever seen something that was alike all the time but you liked to see it anyway, because it's also different every time?" I asked.

"Yes! It was like that at the store. There's only a few basic styles but they make them look pretty in different ways. And each person looks different in it, too."

"Well, this is geocaching swag. There's nothing glamorous about it. But it's kind of like that. I like sorting through the junk. And most of it is just junk. So what have we here?" I reached in and pulled out a three inch long plastic snake, then a Match Box car. An eraser was next followed by a very creased and worn three of clubs playing card. I glanced inside again and spotted the log book. I pulled it out and handed it to Jo.

"This is what we need to sign."

She opened the notepad and her expression changed to curiosity.

"DeRanger? Quartet of Drums? Captain Jack and Melady. Silver Shadow. This is like reading a comic book."

"DeRanger is probably a forest ranger and his name is a job description. Quartet of Drums is probably just a family of four named Drum. Captain Jack and Melady are probably just pirate themed names. There are a lot of odd reasons for choosing a certain name. I doubt if DeRanger is really deranged."

"I wish you had told me to choose a name earlier. I could have been thinking about it."

"Sorry."

I signed the log while she thought of a name. Then we sorted through the rest of the swag. She picked up the notebook again and asked, "I can change it later, right?"

"Probably."

"So it doesn't matter what I write?"

"No, not really."

"Okay."

She scribbled something in the notebook and handed it back.

"Is it okay if I look?" I asked.

"If you want. I doubt if I keep it."

I flipped open the book and she had signed it C#.

"I've always liked music," she said. "Now I guess I better live up to it and find the next one, or I could make it longer and make it a word of advice to you. See sharp or be flat."

I'd taken enough violin lessons to understand her pun, but my parents hadn't seen any future in it so they discontinued the lessons. The same was true of little league. I was never going to grow up to be a star so why pursue it? The truth was I was never going to be a star at anything, so the least my parents could do was see to it that I learned how to manage my money. And so I was given money as a play toy. We played fantasy stock market just like fathers and sons played fantasy football, except we had real stocks.

"A little embarrassment is worth a smiley," I said.

She smiled.

"That kind, too," I added. "When you log your find online it puts a smiley face on the map where the cache icon used to be."

"How many caches have you found?"

"Compared to most? Very few. But you can only find them one cache at a time, so everybody has to start out with a low cache count."

"So how many have you found?"

"A little over a hundred," I confessed.

"A hundred!"

"Yeah, but I've met people with thousands of finds, so I have a long way to go. Do you want a souvenir from your first cache find?"

"Oh, I guess I should. Let's see…" She chose a little penguin made out of melted beads. "I can hang it on my tree with the ornaments you gave me."

I thought the penguin was tacky, especially next to a hundred dollar stained glass sculpture but I wasn't going to pass judgment. It was her Christmas tree. She changed my opinion of it considerably by asking, "Do you think parents involve their kids in geocaching?"

Sure, why not? I thought. Maybe this was made by a kid and it was their contribution to the sport. In that case I thought they did a darn good job.

"I haven't run into any kids on the trail, but I'm sure they do," I answered.

We put the cache back together and I hid it again approximately where I thought I had tripped over it.

"Can you see it?" I asked.

"Nope. That's weird. It's not even painted a leafy pattern but it vanishes under the vines."

"That's one of the signs of a good geocache. They should be hidden well enough that anybody not looking for a cache would never notice it. And sometimes the oddest colors make them disappear. So, high fives on your first geocache find!"

We stood up, exchanged high fives and found the trail. The trail was even prettier on the way back down with sunlight streaming through the canopy of trees and dappling the trail ahead of us.

By the time we reached the Jeep again I was trying not to scratch. We climbed into the Jeep and motored to the next cache. So far the road seemed passable even for my Jaguar, but the road was also just beginning to test us. The further from civilization we went the more likely we were to find rough spots.

"Isn't a bison like a buffalo?" Jo asked at the next cache where we were supposed to find a bison on a fence.

"Yes, but in geocaching it's one of the things we will sell in the store. It's a type of container. When you see it, the name will not make more sense, but you'll recognize a bison tube when you see one next time and you'll know why you should watch for them."

"Why name it after an animal?"

"Because they are indestructible, I guess."

"So, how big is this bison?"

"Very small. The size of my thumb."

"What's in it?"

"A log to sign."

"I don't see why you do this. Why spend half an hour examining a fence minutely just to be able to sign a piece of paper?"

"Because it takes a sharp-eyed, intelligent individual to be able to spot it. Signing the log means I at least choose sharp eyed friends," I smiled her way.

"You expect me to find it?" she asked.

"I don't know. You've got as good a chance as I do. You won't understand the satisfaction of finding a cache until you find a few."

"Why can't I just follow along and shake my head incredulously at you and take pictures?"

"That works, too, I suppose," I said, though I really wished she would search a little harder. You have to invest a little bit of yourself into the hunt before the realization dawns on you that you've been staring an inanimate object in the eye for half an hour and it's been mocking you all along. That is the moment you claim the victory. You see it and it cannot get away. The cache is in hand! Except that this one wasn't yet.

I tried putting on an animated, energetic face on the search but it didn't take long for the elusive little bison tube to knock that flat. I had to admit it was beginning to frustrate me, too, although part of the game was the frustration. I had been looking forward to making this a fun little jaunt into the hills to get to know Jo better. It was infuriating to have that stolen from me by a tiny aluminum tube that should have been easily spotted. All I could do was keep smiling and keep looking. Every once in a while I heard the click of the camera as Jo took yet another picture of my growing frustration.

The cache wasn't clipped to the barbed wire. It was not laying next to the post inconspicuously out of view. There were no piles of rocks, sticks, bark or any unnatural piles of anything that would hide a bison tube. The title and hint indicated the tube was on the fence, not hanging in a bush or tree.

"Are you ready to give up?" I finally asked Jo.

"What color is it?" she asked.

"I don't know. Bison tubes are usually bright colors but they also are usually chosen to blend in with their surroundings. They can even be painted and have camouflage glued onto them."

"You keep going around and around this post and I keep meaning to look at this weird green spot, and then you come back around again just as I think I have a chance. It's green like the post but it's got a silver line that a post might not."

She squatted down and squinted at the post.

"See?" she asked. "How do you get it out?"

I squatted beside her and tried to see what she had spotted. Dang. How did she do that? Beginner's luck? The bison tube was the same color as the post and it was slipped inside a knot hole so that only the base of it was showing. The cache owner had even drawn rough circles on the base to imitate the rings on a sawed off branch. A little dust and a few scratches made it blend in even more. The worn silver line was the only thing giving it away and that appeared to have been added by geocachers trying to pry the tube out of the hole.

"Maybe I can hook my nails around it," she said.

I had never noticed her fingernails before. They were tastefully manicured in colorful patterns that probably matched most of her work clothes.

"Don't tear up your nails for this," I said. "We have a tool of the trade for everything in the Jeep. I don't get to use them very often. Let's see what we can do."

We went to the Jeep and opened up my little tool kit.

"Oh! Here we go! Just the thing!" Jo said. She plucked the roll of duct tape from the box and ripped off a small piece. She stuck the tape to the bison tube and it slid right out of its hiding place. She held it up for me to see, then she blushed. "I guess my redneck roots are showing," she admitted. "Duct tape holds the world together, right?"

"Right," I said though I had never owned anything long enough for it to need duct tape repairs. "You had to see sharp to spot that one, too, so you lived up to your name."

We signed the log and I took her picture as she put it back in its hiding spot. It seemed for every picture I took of her she took five or six of me and I was a little embarrassed to be photographed so much, but once again I found a little embarrassment paid off. She hesitated when I held the door open for her.

"Earl, can I keep the pictures?" She asked.

"Sure. When we get back just copy them onto your computer."

"Can I have all of them?"

I'd just told her she could have any she wanted so I wasn't sure what she was thinking. She held the camera like it contained top secret information.

"You can even have the camera if it means that much to you," I said.

"I see something when I take your picture," she said. "It's an even temperedness that I've seldom seen in people and certainly haven't seen in my life in a long, long time. You get frustrated but it doesn't show. You don't lash out. You don't cuss."

"Why would I do that? It's just a container on a fence."

"That's just it. Jarrod would be stomping around cussing and he would have given up after five minutes. A couple of tough searches and I'd become the problem. And if I found the container first he would think I was trying to show him up. You can't know how good it feels to be able do something without ridicule."

I was taken aback even though I knew Jarrod was likely overbearing in that way. She flipped back through the pictures of me hunting for the cache. Her expression changed with mine as she looked at each picture. Apparently my only sign of frustration had been a slightly furrowed brow.

"This is just a hobby," I told her. "If you find a cache first it just means you're developing geosenses and you have sharp eyes. I would hope if there is any rivalry at all that it is friendly. I don't care if you find every cache on this road as long as we have fun."

"When's lunch?" she asked as she hopped into the passenger's seat.

I glanced at my GPS and realized it was already past noon.

"There is one specific cache I want on my finds list," I said. "Let's go for that one and then drive into town for lunch."

"Okay, which one is it?"

"It's one of the oldest caches in California. It's been sitting up on a hill overlooking the city since 2001."

"Wow, do you think it's still there?"

"It's still there, because there are very recent logs for it. It's the most popular cache on the road, probably just because people like to find these vintage hides. It's there and if it went missing I'm sure somebody would repair or replace it. Geocachers tend to watch out for other people's caches."

"So how old is the oldest cache?" she asked.

"Darby said the very first geocache was placed in the year 2000 and the owner of it never expected to start a new hobby worldwide. They only wondered if anybody would find a cache if they hid one."

"I guess somebody did," she pointed out.

"Yeah, and then somebody else hid one. It would have been very different to go looking for a cache in the very early days of geocaching. Nobody would understand what you were doing or why."

"Well, maybe that part hasn't changed much."

"No, but it kind of helps that there are millions of people geocaching now, not just a few random crazies."

We had to pass up several geocaches in order to reach Santa Barbara One. The road became rougher but as long as I took the bumps slowly and gave Jo enough time to brace herself we made our way over them with little difficulty. It was on this leg of our trip that I made a couple of errors. First I rubbed my eyes. I didn't consider the fact that the nearly constant itch on my hands and arms might rub off on onto other parts of me. I was doing my best to ignore the itching, but when I rubbed my eyes it gradually spread. I found a wide spot in the road to park in and looked at the reading on the GPS. The distance read six hundred thirty-four feet. A short hike up a gradual hill. The view from the top should be spectacular. The fog had been gradually burning away and Santa Barbara beckoned below with its pleasant, shady shopping and dazzling beach. I was looking forward to eating lunch with Jo at an ocean view table. I got a slight hint that it wasn't going to be quite as romantic as I hoped when she hopped out of the Jeep, took one look at me and said, "My God, Earl, are you okay?"

"Yeah, why?" I asked.

"Look at yourself! What happened?"

I bent down and glanced at my reflection in the Jeep mirror and a stranger looked back. My face was red and swollen. The backs of my hands were covered with welts and when I had rubbed my eyes the rash had spread from my hands and arms to my face and neck.

"I came all this way to find this cache. A little rash is not going to stop me," I declared.

"But aren't you totally miserable?" she asked.

"A little itchy, but perfectly capable of hiking up this hill," I said.

I pulled out the geocaching pack and slung it on my back.

"I have a bad feeling about this," Jo said. "A bad, bad feeling."

"Did you get a rash, too?" I asked.

"I hope not."

"Here, you take the GPS so you learn how to follow the map."

I also wanted her to watch the GPS so she wouldn't watch me.

"But there's no trail," she pointed out.

"I guess we get to make our own," I said.

"But isn't that how people get lost?" she said.

"Let me see the GPS."

I walked around with the GPS until it gave me a direction and then I looked around, got our bearings and found a first target that was a likely hiding spot up on the hill.

"See those rocks? Head that direction and watch the screen."

I followed Jo up the hillside where she proved she wasn't used to hiking off trail at all. It was difficult for her to pick a route around the brush and follow the GPS, too. We were both city slickers but it became even more obvious the more I followed her. It took us half an hour, a lot of huffing and puffing and several stops to catch our breath before we reached the rocks I thought the cache was hidden at. My geosenses proved to be true, but we walked around and around the rocks, watching the GPS and looking in the shadows hoping to catch a glimpse of a container. All the while I was itching and scratching and thinking more and more about getting some calamine lotion in town right before lunch.

"Earl, you're getting worse," Jo said. "Don't you think we could come back another time?"

"But we're already here," I said. "Let's find it."

The hide was not difficult. I spotted the container and realized it was going to take a trip into the rocks to retrieve it.

"I found it," I reported. "I'll climb in and hand it up to you."

"Aren't you afraid of snakes?"

"No. I hadn't even thought of it," I said as I glanced into the rocky, shady space I needed to crawl into. I didn't see any snakes but I didn't know how rock-like a snake could appear. Probably I wouldn't see one until it was too late. I tried not to think about snakes as I climbed over a round boulder and slid into a crevasse between two other rocks. I squeezed down, reaching in and I closed my hand over the lid of the container. It took a little squirming to get it back up.

"Wow, another big one!" Jo said.

I handed it over and frantically rubbed at my eyes. The welts on my hands were looking worse.

"I need to trade for something," I said. "I'd like to make a display in the store of landmark finds so I need a piece of swag from this cache."

"What if there isn't anything?" she asked.

"That's part of the quirkiness of the sport," I pointed out. "You might hike for ten miles only to find a bottle cap identical to one to you stepped on getting out of your car. The randomness of it all is part of what makes it fun."

She unscrewed the lid and began taking out the contents one by one.

"Let's see… here's a lanyard with purple cupcakes printed on it. Cute. You could use it for your GPS."

"No thanks, though I'll buy you a GPS if you want to use it."

"I don't think I'm quite ready for that yet. Here's a pocket schedule for the 2010 Visalia Oaks, a pickle fork, a poker chip, a wooden coin sort of thing with a geocacher's name on it, a Hot Wheel car with a tag attached to it…"

"Hold it! Let me see the car."

"There's other things in here with tags on them."

"Really? Do any of them look interesting?"

"Here's the car. There's a gorilla, a pink doughnut with sprinkles, and a half a Weiner dude antennae topper, all with some kind of tag attached to them. Why do they have a metal tag? Oh wait, there might be another one." She dug down into the cache and pulled out a clear plastic high healed shoe with a plain Travel Bug attached. A princess slipper. When I saw that shoe, and Jo standing there holding it, my worlds suddenly snapped into place. It was like everything had come full circle and I knew what I had to do, but not right away, so my focus snapped back to the present.

"It's got a number engraved on it and it's trackable, like a UPS package," I said.

"How odd. There's more little toys, too. There's a plastic cow, a fishing lure, a deck of cards, and…" she dumped the rest of the contents into her hand and it looked like it consisted of several dirty erasers and shaped rubber bands.

"What do you think would make a good addition to the map on the wall?" I asked.

"Well, considering you will have to keep it clean? The poker chip, though I think the wooden coin is more geocacher themed."

"No plastic cows on the wall?"

"Only if you want to dust a plastic cow. Plus, the... DaringDelgadoDuo might appreciate being on the wall of the geocaching store. It's not every day your personal coin ends up on a wall."

"Okay, we'll keep the wooden nickel. We should have some with the name of the store made up. They'd be good advertising and give me something to drop in the caches."

It took me a while to come up with appropriate swag to put into caches. When I started buying swag I set my standards way too high. I used items nobody could trade for. I had to tone down my idea of what a trinket was. Even before I went to Paris I had to learn to think like a five year old at a birthday party. After I got past the expensive swag I began to think of useful swag, so I had toned down my leavings to things that looked handy: stubby screwdrivers, souvenir bottle openers, key chains. In fact, I had fun watching for the quirkiest things I could find. It seemed I went from one extreme to the other. Where once I had bought a diamond studded key chain now I was drawn to plastic Superman glasses and painted surfboard key chains. Anything tacky, random and quirky made it into my swag bag. I debated about what to leave in trade for the wooden nickel. A lot of my tacky swag I had picked up near the beach so it wasn't as tacky to local geocachers. I dug down to look for something a little less expected to southern California geocachers. I came up with a tiny beaded rooster that I had bought in France.

"Ooo, what is that?" Jo asked.

"A tacky beaded rooster."

"Where on earth did you get that?"

"Paris."

"Are you going to put it into the cache?"

"Yes. That's what I bought it for."

"But it's intricate! How many beads and knots does it take to make one of those?"

"I don't know."

"What else is in that bag of yours?"

"Anything weird and unusual that I thought would fit into a geocache."

"Can I look?"

"I...uh... sure."

It didn't take her long to look at me with raised eyebrows.

"You went to Montalivet?" she asked.

"I… how do you know what Montalivet is?"

"I'm a lingerie saleswoman. My customers are looking for something special to wear on a European cruise. The ones that are really interested in lingerie are more interested in how easily it comes off. I happen to know where most of the nude beaches are and you don't have to go to France."

"I figured American geocachers would just see a little bottle of beach sand. Kids wouldn't know it came from a nude beach and the few adults who knew would be amused by it."

"So, did you have fun?"

"Yes, I did. I found three geocaches there."

"Were they covered up?"

"More than the people."

"So, what was your impression of Montalivet?"

"It was interesting. And disappointing. It was easy to spot the Americans."

"So I've heard."

"The food was good."

"Earl, are you embarrassed to admit you're a normal red blooded American male?" She asked. "Because I've been wondering."

"No, of course not."

"So, you're walking down the beach and you notice you strayed into a clothing optional zone. What do you do?"

"Nothing. You don't gawk, you don't suddenly disrobe. So clothing is optional? It also means you can wear clothes if you want to. The only difference between a nude beach and a normal beach that I noticed was a calmness. You give people the same space and same consideration as you normally would."

"But…"

"But maybe you enjoy the view a little more."

"I think we should go to one," she said.

"You… what! I mean, I know what you said. You really want to go to a nude beach?"

"Not at this moment. You need a doctor first. But sometime we should do that."

Stupid rash, I thought.

We added the rooster to the cache, and took the glass slipper Travel Bug, closed up the cache, snapped a very red, splotchy picture of me with the cache and then a beautiful view from ground zero. I rehid the cache and we hiked back down. The further I hiked the more my rash swelled until, by the time we reached the Jeep, I could barely see. My eyes were swelling shut! I stuffed the pack into the back of the Jeep knowing the day was over. I was not going to geocache the rest of this road. The views were lost to me. And I wasn't going to see a nude beach with JoReilly James any time soon. I slammed the door shut with a frustrated shove and walked away wondering what to do next. The slam started the Jeep rolling slowly forward, but my eyes were so swollen I didn't see it until Jo began yelling, "Oh! Oh stop! Earl! It's moving!"

I pried my eyes open enough to see Jo grasping the back bumper and pulling back with all her might.

"Let go! Jo, don't try to stop it! It's too heavy for you!" I yelled.

The Jeep began picking up speed when the hill became steeper. I jogged after my Jeep.

Jo stood there helplessly in the middle of the road as the Jeep bumped on down the hill. I thought I might be able to catch it, jump into the front seat and pull the emergency brake. I ran after it, stumbling over rocks I could not see in the road. I had just yanked open the driver's side door and took a firm hold of the steering wheel, when the Jeep hit the low berm separating the road from the drop off. The Jeep leapt, yanking the door from my grasp, then tilted and rolled slowly down the incline. The door slammed into my back knocking the wind out of me, as the Jeep lurched down the hill. I pulled myself inside even though the brake was useless at this point. I had to give it credit. The Jeep did not overturn. All four wheels remained on the ground until it came to a rest in a large bush. When the vehicle had stopped I stumbled out and nearly slipped further down the hill. I could hear Jo above on the road. She was frantic.

"Earl! Oh Earl, where are you? Please say something!"

My eyes were so swollen. I had to pry them open to see Jo up above on the road, pacing back and forth, and wringing her hands.

"I'm okay!" I called up. I took one step to climb the hill and my leg went out from under me.

What else could go wrong on this trip?

So there I was, a hundred feet down a hill, my only means of transportation lodged in a Manzanita tree, my eyes swollen shut, my leg battered by a swinging car door, and my girlfriend up on the road wondering if I was still alive. All I had to do was climb the hill without benefit of sight and call for help. I guess the one bright spot to this whole mess was that I could afford any kind of help I might need.

"Earl! Where are we?" Jo called out. "They want to know where we are!"

"Who does?"

"911!"

"Why did you call 911?"

"Because! We're stuck! And you're hurt! And I didn't know what else to do!"

"Tell them we'll be fine, or to send a tow truck," I yelled back.

"But we're not fine!"

"This is not an emergency. Let them go handle a real emergency," I yelled. I tried not to sound irritated. She'd only done what she thought was right, but I did not want a fire truck and rescue squad to come looking for us. I knew where we were and all we needed was to get the Jeep back.

"They can't send a tow truck unless they know where we are!" Jo called down to me.

"Do you still have the GPS?" I called back.

"Yeah!"

"Read the coordinates off the description for Santa Barbara One!"

Every time I attempted to climb the hill back up to the road my leg stopped me, either by buckling completely or just paining me too much to take more than a couple of steps. The itching was driving me to distraction and I couldn't even open my eyes to find a way past the brush and weeds. When our rescuers appeared on the road above I was still attempting the climb. Two firemen came down the hill on a cable. One carried a bright orange box.

"Mr. O'Connor?"

"You can call me Earl," I told him.

"What happened to your face?"

"I don't know. I think I am reacting to some weeds I hiked through earlier today."

"Weeds? These hills are covered in poison ivy. Did you know that?"

"No."

"What's up with your leg?"

"I was trying to stop the Jeep and the door slammed on my leg as it went down the hill."

"All right, have a seat."

"All I really need is the Jeep on the road and I think we can get back on our own just fine."

"I'm afraid not, sir."

I learned that once the fire department shows up they go by the book and you really cannot hope to escape until they close it. Unfortunately that meant that I had to prove that I was uninjured, which was a little difficult to do considering I couldn't see or walk. They determined that I needed transport to the local hospital to have my leg x-rayed and they could not permit me to drive because of the state of my eyes. I was given a ride to town via the local ambulance service. The best part of the whole ordeal was imagining the jealous looks from the firemen when Jo clasped me in a very relieved hug when I finally was hauled back up onto the road.

Instead of a romantic lunch over the bay we had a hospital lunch in ER. We did have dinner with a view but it was back at my apartment with Chinese takeout. My leg was in a cast and Jo decided that her financial status and my crippled state made it necessary for her to stay with me so I wouldn't starve. Though I disagreed, I didn't put up much of a fuss. She was welcome to stay at my apartment. She could even attempt to cook in it, though I couldn't for the life of me remember if I had any cooking utensils.

"How do you live without cooking?" she asked.

"This is LA. There's food everywhere. When I get hungry I stop and eat."

"Breakfast?"

"Coffee."

"You sir, are in serious need of some real home cooked meals."

"I won't argue with that. Just tell me what you need and we'll get it."

"I need my pots and pans, a spatula and spoon. You don't even have dishes."

"I have forks."

"I'll stop by my house tomorrow and pick up a few things."

"Don't go alone."

Except for the barking of Sparky, Jo's house felt abandoned. Without her there it was just a house. All the decorations and homey throw pillows and quilts meant nothing unless they were connected to an individual. When we stepped into the house it felt impersonal, but as Jo moved around and fell into her normal activities the house seemed to morph around her and the warmth and color came back to it. I sat on the couch and put my leg up on the coffee table as she rattled around.

"It's amazing the amount of kitchen things a person accumulates over time. I don't need all this. Just the basics will be fine. Why do I have a double boiler? I've never used it as a double boiler. I use the big pot for soups and stews. This old orange spatula I got when I first left home. It's always been my favorite. I've bought half a dozen other ones but the orange one has lasted all these years..."

Sparky followed Jo around the kitchen and came to check on me every once in a while.

"I hate to bring it to your house. It's like it lives here," she said of the spatula.

I got up and crutched my way into the kitchen. She looked so at home here.

"We've got to find a way for you to stay home," I said. "Whenever I see you here it's… perfection. I can't dream of taking you away from all this."

"If I stayed here it wouldn't last. The dishes would be smashed. The nick knacks would be broken, just out of spite. I can't keep him out. If I change the locks he'd smash a window. I have three sets of dishes, all mismatched because a dish is a nice solid object to threaten with. It's not perfection you see. It's a struggle for normality."

"If you could start over, get a fresh start, would you do it?"

"I can't!"

"If you were handed a check for this house and it was enough to buy another would you do it?"

"I owe too much."

"Jo, if money were no object, where would you choose to live?"

She stopped putting pots and pans into the box. "I… Earl, I can't answer that right now. If could live anywhere I'd live wherever you are. But I can't stay with you forever. You have your own life."

Well, slap me on the head with a cold fish. I never imagined she felt that way. Talk about awkward moments.

"Our lives are so different," she went on. "I don't know how you feel. I… I just know I can't stay here."

I set my crutches down and clumped over.

"Earl, don't. You're not supposed to…"

"To what? Tell you that I love you?"

"You… you do?"

"Or that you really could stay with me forever?"

"I could?"

"We both need a new life. Could we do that together? Buy a whole new place? Make it as much of a home as this one is to you? Where?"

"Earl… you're serious!"

"A man does not crash a wedding unless he's serious."

"And this house?" she asked.

"I know somebody who desperately needs a home if his family is going to be reunited again. I'll buy it from you and sell it to Darby. He's a got a wife and a daughter. When his daughter heard he found a job her first question was if they could live in a real house. Darby doesn't see how that could ever happen, but he didn't have it in his heart to tell her no."

"A little girl?"

"Her name is Adele. Think about it. And think about where you might like to settle. I don't want to think about life in that apartment for the rest of my life. It's a place to call my own but it is not *home*."

"Earl, if you really want to make a new life together it's going to take a commitment. When you're ready. Really, truly, ready. Ask me."

My heart skipped a beat. It sounded like there was every hope that if I proposed she would say yes. It sounded that way to me, but she wanted to be asked. She wanted that final step, a proposal that said "I love you. Would you marry me?"

Chapter 36

Jo went out job hunting the next day. I had to respect the fact that she was willing to stick to her plan and get back on her feet, no matter what I might be doing or planning. Many people would see an easy out and take it. Jo was determined to stand up to her situation.

I sat at my desk fingering the little glass slipper. I remembered that I needed to log that I retrieved it from the cache, so I checked the code: 2W7FGE and made sure it was correct in the search field. I brought up the Travel Bug's web page and was amused by the mission: "I am a little glass slipper looking for a princess. Please log me in and out of caches until I find her. I don't care where I go as long as I know I will find my princess."

I called a business associate of mine and told him my dilemma.

"I need to find a house. One that will impress a lady. I don't think I want to buy it, but if by chance she likes it I wouldn't be opposed to making an offer."

"What range are you looking at?"

"It's more a matter of the atmosphere, ease of care, and the view. I want this house to ooze possibilities. What can you find for me?"

"I'll call you back."

While William looked through his listings I called a limo to take me to a jewelry store and I chose a rock that left no question that I was serious. I didn't know what Jo liked as far as jewelry went but I chose the kind of ring that any girl would show off.

William called me back and sent me to a list of houses on the internet and I arranged to meet him that evening at a beach house in Malibu. It had a wonderful view of the coast and large, relaxing decks. The floor plan was open and looked as if it could be dressed up or down depending on the mood of the homemaker. The bedroom had large windows that let in the sea breezes and there was a loft above that looked like it would make a wonderful reading nook. The back yard was nearly nonexistent, but Sparky could have daily walks on the beach. The little patch of grass next to the back door was home to three white barked trees whose tops fluttered in the breeze and made the reading nook seem whimsical and airy. At first glance I thought it looked too grand, and I really didn't count on Jo liking it, but I really only wanted a place to pop the question.

Jo hurried into the apartment in the late afternoon and placed three grocery sacks on the counter.

"You don't need to cook tonight. I have a surprise. We can eat out afterwards," I told her.

"What kind of surprise?"

I called another limo wishing I didn't have the crutches and cast to worry about. Ordinarily I'd love a drive to Malibu but I couldn't move my foot.

"Why call a limo?" Jo asked. "I could drive."

"Then it wouldn't be a surprise."

"A taxi would be fine."

"Too dirty and impersonal."

"You're spoiled, admit it."

"Okay, I admit it," I said. "And I'd like to spoil you, too."

When the limo pulled up outside the beach house Jo wasn't sure what to think. She noticed the real estate sign by the sidewalk. William got out of his car and walked up hand extended.

"JoReilly James, this is a friend of mine, William Darington. He's going to show us some houses."

"Some... but this is Malibu. I know what houses cost in Malibu. Or at least sort of, kind of."

"Just forget about where you are. Picture yourself in the house. Think of what you'd like to do to make it home. This is not the surprise." This is giving me time to spot my chance, I thought.

The beach house was even nicer than the website led me to believe. Jo looked like the perfect hostess as she walked through the rooms. She was hesitant to open doors, so William began a tour but he knew the sale was unlikely and so eventually he disappeared.

"Earl, why are we here?"

Damn, I was too chicken to just do it.

"I want you to think about what kind of a new life you'd like. What do you think of a beach house? We could see the weather every morning, have breakfast on the deck, take long walks on the beach..."

"Four bedrooms?"

"Sure, a hobby room for you, an office for me, a guestroom."

"It's huge."

"Then we'll look for something smaller. This is a process," I said though I was a little disappointed in losing the beach house. Except for the lack of a yard it seemed perfect. Put Jo's comfortable furniture and artwork in the house and it would take on a homey feel. Take the furniture from my apartment and put it in the beach house and it would take on a whole new personality, one I preferred not to think about. I had really envisioned bringing Jo out onto the deck with a view up the coast and proposing there but when the time came it didn't seem quite right and then William appeared.

"What's up?" he asked me while Jo was looking at another part of the house.

"I'm trying to propose," I said, a little discouraged. "If I can get her to say yes, I can guarantee a sale eventually."

"Really?"

"I sure am hoping."

His grin spread but I don't think it was because of the commission he'd receive. He wanted Jo to say yes because he knew how hopelessly I was in love with her. Any guy who has my paycheck and still has cold feet is hopeless. I'd had my share of girls who approached me just because they'd never dated a guy who drove a Jaguar. They were shallow. I'd never had a woman approach me just because I sat alone on a park bench with a little goofy Mickey Mouse toy until Jo came along. Just the fact that she was willing to go along and help with the pictures made me love her. She wasn't after me for my money, that's for sure.

"What happened to your leg?" he asked as Jo wandered into the kitchen.

"Small parking accident," I said.

"Not a traffic accident?"

"No."

"Was she there?"

"Yeah."

"And she's still with you?"

"Yeah."

"Then there's still hope."

"It's worse than that," I admitted.

"Oh? How's that?"

"I ruined her wedding. He was a jerk. Proved it in fine fashion in front of the whole crowd."

"Ooo, you sure know how to pick 'em."

"Thanks, I guess."

"And this isn't the right house."

"No, I guess not, though if it was just me I'd take it. I don't think she will be content in a smaller house. Maybe one that *feels* smaller."

"And you?"

"I want out of the apartment."

"You got it."

"Two ovens?" Jo said when we caught up.

"You don't have to use both of them. Dirty up one and save the clean one for company."

"I like your thinking," she said. "Do you like it?"

"I do, but I have romantic notions of reading in the treetops and making love with the fog creeping in and the waves crashing on the shore. I'll be the first to admit my fantasies are unrealistic."

She climbed the stairs to the master suite and looked at it again, then climbed to the loft. I wished I could follow but the clumping of the cast on the stairs would ruin any images she was conjuring up. Maybe I should wait for the cast to be removed to try the proposal.

"I think you've got it backwards," she said.

"See?" William said. "She'll say yes. All you have to do is ask."

Jo descended the stairs looking like a starlet in a movie.

"If it were just me," she said, "I'd love it. But Sparky is getting old. I don't want to think about carrying a dog up and down the stairs."

"Ah, you didn't tell me a dog factored into this," William said.

"It's okay. It's a nice dog," I said.

"What kind is it?" William asked.

"I don't know," Jo said. "I've heard different theories ranging from cockapoo to maltiapso."

"What's a maltiapso?"

"Maltese Lhasa Apso. Let's see, one person said maybe a Chihuahua Pekinese. What would that be a Pekahuhua? A Chihuahuanese? It doesn't matter what she is. She adopted me and we've been friends ever since."

"A fenced yard might be preferable," I said. "Though I don't mind hiring a landscaper to solve that problem."

Armed with this new found information William was able to take us to a house better suited to our needs.

I knew we were getting closer to the ideal house when we pulled up to a rock fronted bungalow, the walks lined with flowers, and we opened the front door to a woodsy, rocky, almost lodge type living room. It wasn't large but it had the feel of being in the woods. On the wall facing the front door was a fireplace made of the same river rock as the house, but beyond the living room we could see through a dining area into the back yard. I couldn't see a fence back there but it was obvious the plantings hid a barrier of some kind. A flagstone patio surrounded a swimming pool and a gazebo with a wet bar.

"Oh my word," Jo said. "It's beautiful! I don't care what the rest of the house looks like. I could stand in this one spot forever!"

The kitchen was small, but the décor blended in with the rest of the quaintness of the house. A window opened between the kitchen and the patio allowing the cook to serve people seated at a bar outside. The view from the master suite was like a jungle. A hired gardener would definitely be needed.

"I heard the former owners actually had an aviary back there," William said.

"I can believe it," Jo said. "I almost can't look. I'm afraid to like it."

"Why?"

"Because I know it's impossible to buy a house like this. It's unheard of!"

William gave me a wink and left to wait in the car.

"Come sit with me," I said. I led her into the back yard where there were wrought iron chairs sitting around a breakfast bar area. We sat down and I took her hands. "So you like it."

"No, I don't like it. I love it! I never imagined a house like this in the city. It's like living far away, like being on vacation at home."

I decided I would never find the perfect time. I would chicken out every time. I convinced myself that I had to just do it. Like Darby getting in that balloon basket.

"William wouldn't have shown me the house if he thought I couldn't buy it. I am going to make an offer. It's a house that will become the home I never had. Only one thing would make it better and that would be you. Jo, would you marry me?" I took the ring box out of my pocket and put it on the bar in front of her. Her hands were shaking as she took the box. Tears were running down her face and she couldn't open the box. She looked around at the lush landscaping as she tried to get the box open. I pulled the lid open as she wiped some tears away.

"Oh my god," she said. She looked around the yard. "I can't believe this is happening."

I waited.

"Nobody has ever proposed to me before."

"But your wedding... surely..."

She shook her head. "Everybody just assumed and then the planning started and I just went with the flow. Nobody has cared for me like you have."

I was a little amused and a little saddened by her response and I still didn't have an answer, yet I didn't feel as if I should insist on one.

"I care for you because I love you like crazy," I said. "And I'd like to be able to do it every day for the rest of our lives."

"When?" she sniffed.

"Well, a honeymoon would be a lot more romantic without the cast," I said. "But if you wanted to do it today that would be fine, too."

"Oh! What are we doing just sitting here?" She cried. She leaped off her chair and wrapped me in a hug and planted the first real kiss I'd received from her. The tears never stopped as she walked the house, pausing every once in a while and adding little comments like, "Walk in closets!"... "Oh it's so beautiful!"... "his and hers sinks"... "a dip in the pool." She looked to see if the neighbors would be able to see into the yard then added "skinny dipping in the pool."

"Jo, I'm a guy. Is that a yes? A no? A maybe someday?"

"I don't know how. I just wish it could be."

"We'll make it happen!" I added quickly.

"He'll ruin everything."

"We'll elope!"

"But my parents..."

"We can get married anywhere you want to. Hawaii? Paris? Venice? Tahiti? It can be done. Parents included."

"Yes! Yes, yes, yes, yes, yes!"

So it appeared I was finally discovering what life really consisted of: exploring new places with someone to share it with. Giving my time and my money to something and someone that mattered more to me than myself. To be able to help Jo move into that house and watch it change before my eyes into a place full of warmth and welcome made me feel lucky every day to be able to come home to that.

The cruise was a normal getaway for my parents but Jo's mom and dad basked in the luxury of it. They spent hours lounging around the pool, and taking advantage of the onboard gym. Her mom had her nails and hair done at the salon.

Henry walked around with a permanent grin plastered on his face. He had a bed, free meals and he was enough of a people person that he talked for hours with people from all over the world. Darby was my best man. He teared up during his speech and it got a little embarrassing for me. I didn't see much of Wanda. Reggie stayed in LA. We never got to know each other well. He held down the fort for Henry. Jo and I were wed in a little chapel on board the ship but you'd never guess it was just a room on a cruise ship. With all the flowers and stained glass windows it might have been a cathedral.

The geocaching store opened a few months after our honeymoon. Darby manages it. We built a large meeting room in the back of the shop. If there is no event planned for the month we schedule one at the shop. There's no pressure to buy. We just like the people who show up and we think it's important for geocachers to meet occasionally. New geocachers get advice from the more experienced. Everybody gets a little recognition and in turn their caches get visited more often. We have door prizes and contests. I never thought having a business would be this much fun. Darby definitely earns every penny of his paycheck ordering, stocking, and paying the bills. His wife hasn't moved into the house yet, but Adele visits often. We're still hoping the family will reunite.

Sparky must be part water spaniel. I'm not sure a swimming pool is good for dogs, but we have to be careful to close the gate or she jumps in. She is only allowed to take short swims if we are in the yard to help her climb out.

And instead of going to meetings, I go stand behind a counter.

"Hey, I'm looking for a geocoin for my wife. Her three thousandth find is coming up and I want to surprise her."

"Cool! What cache are you going for?" I asked as I led the way to the achievement coins.

"We're hoping to be FTF on a new one but there's no guarantees on that."

Jo can now talk shop with the best of them and if she knows a special occasion is coming up she has been known to run out and hide a cache just to help the situation along. The cache at the store is really my only hide. I can say it has a lot of favorite points but people will generally like any novel cache and this one is hidden within a statue of a prospector. It looks like he is holding a gold pan but the bottom of the pan opens into the base of the statue and a large bin can be pulled out. We have several pictures up on the map of geocachers who had their picture taken with the statue. People from as far away as Europe and Australia have come by the shop just because there are so few physical geocaching stores. I've thought of expanding into general sporting goods but I worry about losing that geocaching connection. I can't count on bikers or joggers being able to tell me a good geocaching story but geocachers treat a stop at the store like an event and I often end up talking to them for a good long while, learning what the favorite caches are in whatever city they are from. I'm developing a bucket list of geocaches to go find some day.

Jo and I go on four trips a year. Two are road trips and we carefully plan what geocaches we are going to find along the way. The other two trips we plan to not geocache, but at the same time we have to find one or two just to log the country. We have finds in Europe, on several islands in the Pacific, the geocache at the Arctic Circle sign and one at the tip of Chile. Even though we say we will not geocache we find the temptation to add to our map is too strong and usually our geocache find ends up being the highlight of the whole trip. Our visits with our parents sound like this:

"Yes, the Alps were wonderful. We went skiing and we took a tour of Bern, but there was this cute little chapel way up on the mountain and it had a geocache hidden in the corner of a stairwell. The views were magnificent. We could see miles of mountain ranges as we searched for the cache and it was only a micro! I wish we could have traded." Europe has a lot of micros. We're thinking of having a path tag made so we have micro-sized swag to leave behind.

My parents are still muggles, though they are beginning to understand us when we talk about our travels. My mom sits there with a furrowed brow thinking of how I used to be cultured and stable. My dad seems to be glad I can relax and explore.

Geocaching and marriage have worked together to complete a life that felt empty. I still visit Henry and he still apologizes for my broken leg. But it's far in the past now. I know how to park the Jeep now and, though it has a few experience marks from its tumble down the hill, it still takes us out into the barren desert over the hills from LA and into the mountains that separate the city from the desert communities on the other side. There are little pockets of beauty in those mountains and we are determined to find them all, one geocache at a time. It might take a while. Maybe a lifetime. But a lifetime is all we have to spend.